THE HEROD MOSAIC

By
Sander A. Diamond

To my devoted and loving wife of a half century,
Susan, who helped plan the historical tours and stood by me
with patience as I pecked away on my venerable IBM Selectric
for decades, quietly writing night after night in my study.

And to my mother, Bess,
who passed away in 2014 at age 101.

STORMS

1

CHAPTER ONE

Wednesday, November 28, 2012.
The year 5773 on the Hebrew calendar.

"Assalamu aleikum," the Arab worker said, smiling, looking up over his bare shoulder as he leaned on his shovel, breathing heavily from the exertion of the past two hours.

"Wa aleikum salam," Dr. Dov Rosenberg replied reflexively, unsmiling, running his thick fingers through what was left of his unruly snow white hair. "Keep digging. You, too." He pointed individually at the digger's three co-workers.

Peering into the deepening hole, part of the flat surface of what appeared to be a sandstone or limestone chamber was visible. Whether it was actually a chamber, he couldn't be sure. What he could tell even at a distance of three meters was that the quality of the stone from which it was formed was superior, the masonry that went into crafting it expert. Whatever the structure was, situated prominently on the Mount of Olives lower slope and facing the Temple Mount, it must have belonged to one ancient Jerusalem's wealthier families.

Rosenberg gingerly slid and half-tumbled into the shallow excavation for a closer look. He grabbed a shovel from one of the workers, and gently tapped the stone surface. The light strike echoed hollow against the shovel's steel blade. Pulling the red bandana from around his neck, he mopped his brow, ignoring the grasp of wet dirt that further soiled his shirt as he leaned back against the hole's side.

"Okay, keep digging," he repeated, handing the shovel back to the digger before he clambered and crawled out of the hole, up and over the excavation's lip.

Rosenberg's eyeglasses were smudged and misted over, his shirt sweat-saturated and filthy, his pants encrusted with swatches of mud. As he stood upright, his Wellingtons sank into the muck above his ankles. The world-renowned Israel Museum director was, despite his inevitable protestations, in his preferred element. A dig. An unforeseen, unplanned dig but a dig nevertheless.

"Jesus, this is worse than I thought, worse than I thought," he said for a third time. Shielding his eyes from the rising sun, he surveyed the devastation that was once the Kidron Valley. Whatever sparse grass that once grew within the City of David had been swept away. The Kidron had been reduced and redesigned by the storms and floods and the wadi's overflow to a spongy, waterlogged, barely recognizable nutbrown moonscape, its perimeter now staked and roped off with strands of IDF-issue orange plastic tape. Nothing was where it had been weeks before.

Two soldiers, part of the battalion rushed to the Kidron to control the chaos and prevent tomb looting, stood at an opening in the tape, desultorily checking ID cards and waving through the scores of Palestinians lining up, seeking an unexpected day's work righting the upended tombs and gravestones. Elsewhere and everywhere within the closed-off area, several groups of archaeological students from the Hebrew University were collecting the artifacts, sarcophagi shards, and bone fragments that had spilled from the Kidron graves themselves, wheel-barrowing them over and arranging their finds on tables hastily slapped together from plywood and sawhorses taken from a nearby, half-inundated construction site.

The small detachment of IDF soldiers assigned to Rosenberg's site, near the reputed tomb of Absolom with its conical roof now shattered and strewn, the tomb itself lifted by the floodwaters and shifted from its original location, stared at the museum director.

"What's the plan, Dov? How much longer? We've been here for hours. The guys need a break. I'm facing a mutiny..." their commanding officer said, half-jokingly.

Dov Rosenberg lifted one leg, then the other, duck-like, the ooze quickly filling the sucking gaps in the mud where his boots had been. When he found purchase on slightly firmer ground, he wiped his palms on his pants and turned to face the IDF officer.

"They'll get a break when I say it's break time," he snapped, eyes narrowing, hands gesticulating. "You don't see these guys rushing to answer the *muzzein's* call, do you?" He swept his hand in the general direction of the diggers. "I've only got two eyes, Jonah, I can't be everywhere and I can't watch everyone, can I? Whatever we've got here," he thumbed towards the hole, "I want it to stay here, not disappearing in one of these guys' underwear and finding it for sale next week in some Bethlehem shithole-in-the wall."

One of the older diggers looked up and frowned, shaking his head slowly, a reflex reaction to a slight so frequent and familiar.

"Yeah, yeah," the officer said, raising both hands in mock surrender as he turned and walked back to his men, shrugging as he did so. Immediate, unintelligible grumbling and sighs came from the small rank and they dispersed and re-formed around the hole again.

Eight hours later with the heat of the sun easing slightly, the workmen had managed to expose three sides of the chamber. Three stood back, as if admiring what they'd uncovered, laying their shovels down while a fourth busied himself sweeping the remaining dirt from the surfaces. Centered on the side facing the Temple Mount, there appeared to be an access point, an entryway to the chamber, a blackened rectangle of wood, hinged and set inside an arched stone door frame.

Dov Rosenberg's heart began to race, his face flushed, and his breathing sounded irregular.

"Get me down there!" he demanded. "Where's that goddamned ladder?"

Even before the ladder was positioned and secured, Dov's boot was on the top rung. Halfway down, he jumped, an ungainly leap that sent him stumbling into one of the workers, almost knocking the smaller man to the ground. Two of the Arab's co-workers looked away, covering their mouths, trying with limited success to stifle their laughter. The remaining worker, meanwhile, was already having at the door with a crowbar, trying to pry it away from its tarnished hinges.

Rosenberg virtually leaped at the worker, grabbed the crowbar and wrested it from his hands.

"What are you doing?" Rosenberg shouted into the startled man's face. The digger recoiled as if he was about to be struck, chastened but for reasons that escaped him.

"Don't you want to know what's in there?" he asked softly.

"Of course I do, boychick! *Haver* ... you understand Hebrew, don't you? Patience! We don't know what's in there, haven't the slightest idea. Maybe it's treasure, maybe it's dreck or maybe just dead air. But let's try to find out before we go smashing everything to pieces like some firefighter running into a burning building..."

Dov Rosenberg knew he was overreacting. The heat, the incomprehensible devastation as far as the eye could see, almost too profound for the mind to grasp, the fraught circumstances had tolled up. Dov understood why he was behaving as if he was half-mad but he couldn't help himself. Now he was beginning to feel badly. Worse. Foolish. Losing his temper like that. What the hell's happening to me? He chided himself. How would this guy know any better? By way of apology, he drew a deep breath, patted the worker's shoulder, forced a smile, and rasped "Sorry."

Then, pulling his cell from his pants, he speed-dialed the museum.

"Yeah, it's Dov," he said, speaking loudly and rapidly, as if his life depended on what he was saying. "I need you to send Yossi over with that sonar device or whatever the hell it's called." He wiped his brow again, this time with his sleeve, leaving a trace of dirt on his forehead. "Yeah, the unit they sent up from Dimona last week, the one in the aluminum case next to the cabinet. Why? What, now you're asking me questions, too?" He held the phone at arm's length, looking at it with distaste before responding sharply. "Because! That's why! Why is because we may have something interesting, very interesting here ..."

Christ, Rosenberg thought, clapping the cell closed, I need a smoke!

CHAPTER TWO

Michelangelo Urban Lorenzo's parents lived quietly as they had for decades in an exclusive section of Rome. The Lorenzos, Silvio and Romana, lived in the heart of a vast and grand outdoor museum where the graceful three-arched Ponte Sant'Angelo, like its sister Crossing, spanned the murky Tiber. Their spacious apartment sat virtually opposite Vatican City. The apartment's monetary value was almost incalculable. High ceilings, polished parquet floors, sedate marble statuary, walls hung with muted nineteenth- century oils- all marking it as the home of a family with the deepest roots in the Eternal City. French doors opened off the living room onto a broad terrace; on the left, the imposing and ornate Dome of St. Peter's. If one turned right, the eyes were treated to a clear view of the imposing and massive Castel Sant' Angelo, the fortress that had guarded the Vatican and held the remains of the Emperor Hadrian. At its core, the Castel's huge subterranean vault served as the final resting place of the Antonine Dynasty that ruled Rome during the height of the Roman Empire. The Lorenzos' neighborhood was far more than one of many upscale Rome neighborhoods. It was the wellspring from whence Christianity was spread across the ancient world.

From their perch above the Tiber, the Lorenzos were living witnesses to the century past. They could easily recall the jaw-jutting presence of Benito Mussolini sitting in the back seat of his gleaming Hispano Suiza, gliding along the Tiber's embankment, waving to his adoring minions. They remembered the dark days of 1943 when Italy surrendered, threw in its lot with the Allies, a decision that brought SS divisions streaming into the city. The murderous events that followed still pursued the Lorenzos in their dreams, particularly the mockingly pleasant, mid-October day when black-clad SS cadres carted away those they had known from childhood. The images were graven into their memories. Many of their friends were taken in trucks from Rome's ancient ghetto, past the temple that marks the entrance to the Jewish community, to the central train station and then north to a certain fate. As devout as they were, the Lorenzos still could not find it in their hearts to forgive the then-reigning pope, Pius XII, for his passivity in the face of the atrocity.

In 1944, the victorious armies of America and Britain marched through Rome's gates, occupied it for a time, and marched on, replaced in turn by Italy's postwar revolving governments, many with a mayfly's lifespan, all the comings and goings watched with something less than amusement by its European neighbors and Western allies. On the cusp of the 21st century, the advent of the European Union and Italy's membership within it marked the beginning of a new era in much the same way the Crucifixion marked a similarly new beginning two millenia before. All the events that they had lived and suffered through in their lifetime only reminded the Lorenzos of how old they really were.

Four of their five children had given the Lorenzos fifteen grandchildren, and two of their grandchildren had already blessed them with great-grandchildren, all confirmed by the several photos that decorated their grandparents' home. Their fifth and last child chose the priesthood as his life's path. While there would be no grandchildren from Michaelangelo for the Lorenzos to dote over, he had provided his family with a deeply-felt sense of satisfaction, of pride. In many circles, the mere mention of his name brought approving nods. For Michelangelo Urban Lorenzo was widely known, a man with an international reputation. As the renowned Father Angelo, he was among the world's leading authorities on the art and relics of Christianity's first hundred years, the critical period when the breakaway Jewish sect was transformed into a religion.

The Lorenzos were convinced they had named their last child wisely and well— for the great master Michelangelo, and for Pope Urban IV, the French-born Patriarch of Jerusalem, the 13th-century pope responsible for the celebration of the Feast of Corpus Christi. Now, sixty-three years after the birth of their second son, the Lorenzos were convinced that Father Angelo had been picked by God for a special mission in life.

14

Dr. Paolo Pisa's parents lived five bridges distant from the Lorenzos on the Tiber's opposite bank. The Pisas traced their lineage to the seventh decade of the first century. They often intimated that their ancestors were among the first Jewish slaves brought to Rome by Titus as punishment for the Jewish uprising against their Roman rulers. It made for an interesting family narrative but the Pisas' true roots were more than likely Spanish, among the thousands exiled from Spain during the 15th century Inquisition. Wherever the truth lay, the Pisas and their forebears, like the Lorenzos, had lived in Rome for centuries, the Pisas trading their Hebrew names for Italian names following Italy's unification in the mid-19th century. And heeding a long-standing tradition, they assumed the name of an Italian town or city.

Guido Pisa and his younger brother Sandro had made a small fortune in the olive wood business, fashioning music boxes and Christian symbols and hawking them to tourists before and after World War II. The brothers Pisa saw no contradiction in carving and selling Christian artifacts. Guido had a sixth sense when it came to business, along with a sensitive finger on history's pulse. Once Rommel's *Afrika Korps* was routed in North Africa, once von Paulus' vaunted army collapsed at Stalingrad's gates, Guido and Sandro knew the tide of war had turned irrevocably in the Allies' favor.

Hitler would be soundly defeated but Guido also knew that Europe's Jews shared the Fuehrer's doom.

The Pisas had gone into hiding during the first days of the Nazi occupation of Rome. Sheltered by neighbors in a dank coal cellar in a decrepit, abandoned warehouse nearby, they were all too aware of the roundup of their brethren. What they could not see they could hear. When the Allies landed in force on the beaches of Salerno and then Anzio to begin their inexorable push north towards Rome, the Pisas seized upon the chaos that war brings and managed to escape south on foot to Reggio, safe at last three days later behind the Allies lines.

Soon after the Germans abandoned Rome and it was declared an open city, the Pisas returned, amazed at finding their apartment undamaged, untouched, their possessions intact. If Guido believed in miracles, this would certainly have provided him proof of such. But Guido was more inclined to thank circumstance and luck, such luck that had eluded his and Sandro's friends. They had not long before been converted en masse into pale columns of smoke in Poland's death factories.

Guido often wondered how he, a loyal member not only of the temple but of Mussolini's Fascist Party as loyal as his father had been, the father who served valiantly on the French Front during the Great War, could have become such a pariah in his own land. Even if Mussolini only half-heartedly promulgated the Nazi race laws, the laws eased the way to the endgame for Italy's Jews. And the endgame was the endgame. Rome's Jewish community was nearly erased. Even in his nineties with the war years a distant and fading memory, like Silvio Lorenzo he could not forgive the pope his wartime fecklessness nor Rome's chief rabbi his conversion to Catholicism. Nor could he, Guido Pisa, ever again feel quite comfortable in the land of his birth.

Months before the outbreak of war, a department deep within the Italian bureaucracy ruled that the brothers Pisa could no longer stamp their music boxes *S&G Boxes, Olivewood from the Holy Land* for no other reason than the wood, brought from the British Mandate of Palestine, was no longer available. A friend laughingly suggested changing the stamp to read *Sodom & Gomorrah Music Boxes* but the Pisas were not amused. Instead, they adapted quickly and made do with olivewood from the south and Sicily. Before they went underground, Guido and Sandro hasted to fill the increasing demand by soldiers in the *Wehrmacht* for the boxes and relics, a bitter irony that nevertheless amused the brothers.

The war over, the brothers' struggle for business survival eased in 1948 with the creation of the State of Israel. Importing olivewood from the Holy Land was no longer under quarantine. The new nation, hanging by a thread from its inception, its very existence dependent in its early years on the largesse of the West and reparations from Germany, exported whatever, whenever, and to whomever it could. Desert blooms to Western Europe, fruit from its citrus farms, olives and olivewood, and minerals from the Dead Sea. But Guido Pisa had an uncharacteristically optimistic vision of what Israel would become in the post-Holocaust world. He knew Washington, even in the face of opposition by influential Arabists in the State Department and members of President Truman's own cabinet, Soviet hostility, Cold War politics, and

16

Israel's own internal dissension, wouldn't let the Jewish state go under. For reasons moral and political, the future of both nations would forever be intertwined. Guido also recognized the obvious, that while Israel would become a haven for the world's Jews, it would also remain the Holy Land for all of Christendom. In time, the tourists would come, first a trickle and then in droves, cash-rich Americans and Europeans with pockets dripping dollars.

In 1956, the brothers Pisa decided to expand, to move their operations to their supply source. Shortly before Israel, France, and Great Britain launched their attack on the Suez Canal, the Pisas opened a factory in Jerusalem. They hired several Palestinian craftsmen to harvest and cure the olivewood, and later fabricate it into the music boxes and crucifixes by which S&G originally gained its fame and fortune. All who knew the brothers considered their decision a stroke of genius. In spite of the Suez crisis, S&G saw its business increase threefold in its first year, its products finding their greatest favor in Italy, particularly within the confines of the Vatican City itself. It seemed as if Guido and Sandro, favored by timing and circumstance, could put no foot wrong.

By 1957 Guido Pisa had become an Israeli citizen, a Jew from the Diaspora returned at last to the bosom of his people and the land from which they all had sprung. Whether Guido viewed himself in such exalted terms was questionable but he knew that to succeed and prosper in Israel, he would have to immerse himself over completely.

Inasmuch as he was well-versed in both Jewish and Italian history, so choosing a Hebrew name to replace Guido Pisa was not a difficult choice. He chose to follow the path of the Jewish general, born as Yosef Ben Matityahu into the Tribe of Levi, who befriended the Roman general Titus during the Jewish War and, as the Italians did in 1943, in the end changed sides. It was Yosef Ben Matityahu who pled with Titus not to destroy Jerusalem and the Second Temple. But Titus' father, Vespasian, ignored his son's request, dismissing it outright. Like Carthage at the end of the Punic Wars, the Jews would have to be made an example of, a warning to all who thought to question Rome's hegemony. Jerusalem was leveled and the Second Temple looted. Only the Western Wall remained standing. Ancient Israel had thus by the Roman sword come to a bitter end. Yosef Ben Matityahu returned with Titus to Rome where he shed his Hebrew name and assumed the name

Flavius Josephus, immortalizing himself with his vivid account of the Hebrews' uprising against their Roman overlords, *The Jewish War*.

On November I, 1958, in Tel-Aviv's registration office, Roman-born Guido Pisa became Baruch Josephus with the stroke of a pen— his wife remained Sarah. And his four-year old son Paolo became Moshe. When in Italy, they would use their Italian names-for if nothing else Guido Pisa was in most respects, like his hero Josephus, flexible. But in Israel they would be known as Baruch, Sarah, and Moshe. Paolo's older brother Giacomo became Jacob, Paolo's younger sister Sophia was now Deborah, the quintet the family Josephus.

Moshe, nee Paolo, was an exceptional student. His teen years were spent in Jerusalem, speaking Hebrew. He mastered Greek, learned first-hand from local merchants, and Arabic from the woodcarvers in his father's and uncle's factory. And when Paolo returned to Rome and entered the university. His fluency in these tongues and English never failed to impress his professors. His mentor, a German-born expert in the art of the early Christian Era, insisted Paolo pursue his doctoral studies in the subject.

"Get your hands dirty, Paolo. Dirty your hands in the soil of the Holy Land," the aging professor advised him. "You have too much talent to walk away from it."

Paolo initially bridled against the idea of closeting himself away, pursuing a doctorate to the exclusion of beginning life in a less restricting pursuit. A lawyer, perhaps, or an architect. Guido to his credit never demanded that either son join the olivewood business. Nor was it necessary to follow in their father's footsteps. Sandro's two boys had already entered the firm.

"We have more than enough Pisas in the office," Guido often remarked. "Who needs another one? "

Fortunately, Guido and Sandro's world overlapped what would become Paolo's. Before they limited themselves to producing their replicas and music boxes, their earlier trade in relics brought the brothers Pisa into constant contact with several dealers of antiquities. Many were legitimate and licensed by the Israeli government. Their official stamp of approval permitted them to hawk their suppliers' wares as genuine. Others, Bedouins, Palestinians, Israeli Jews, anyone with a pick and shovel, fed the distant black markets with their artifacts. Some were real, some phony but rendered so precisely that only a Pisa could tell the difference. For the Pisas, if the artifacts didn't pass muster, they were rejected, discarded, the supplier blacklisted. With their jeweler's loupe eyes, the Pisas could distinguish the real from the *ersatz* and they were respected and sought after for their expertise. And the brothers guarded their integrity closely.

It was a rare week when an artifacts scandal failed to appear in the Israeli press, the most outrageous example being the antiquities dealer who announced he'd found the ossuary box containing the bones of Jesus. In a world where faith often trumped reality, people were quick to accept and believe. Paolo/Moshe knew this world and its practitioners well and they repelled him. He knew from his studies and work that under God's chosen land there were true treasures waiting to be unearthed. He knew too that if one was to dig, one would need the proper authority of a doctorate. But while he decided to accept his mentor's charge, he would not permit himself to be trapped in the world of academia. Moshe Josephus/Paolo Pisa's life would be all hands-on, no armchairs, his hands dirtied in Israel's earth.

By 1978, his studies completed, only his dissertation lay before Paolo. His doctoral work furthered the research of noted German scholars who had focused on the nineteenth- and early twentieth-century reign of the Ottomans. Paolo refined his research to the evolution of early Christian art following Paul's departure from the Holy Land to seek recruits for the growing cult of Christianity.

Paolo's Italian passport permitted him access to many sites that his Israeli passport would have denied him: Pergamum, Smyrna, Assos, Olba, and Tarsus. On Cyprus, the ruins of Cyruss, Soli, Salamis, and Cilium. His archaeological digs and observations produced little new but it did offer a more comprehensive understanding of the era and its art. His was, unlike most scholarly efforts, easily accessible to the lay reader. His mentor, barely concealing his pride, applauded his student's impeccable scholarship and urged Paolo to publish his work. The dissertation, titled *The Art of the Early Christian Era,* easily found a publisher and, in spite of its pedestrian title, became an international bestseller, appearing in no less than fourteen translations including English, German, French, Spanish (and Catalan), Japanese, and Mandarin Chinese. *The New York Times* reviewer, taking note of Paolo's Hebrew name, commented that "We now have another, more scholarly Josephus." Paolo Pisa/Moshe Josephus was a prodigy, twenty-four years old and already a major academic celebrity.

The success of *The Art of the Early Christian Era* was repeated two years later with the publication of *Art in the History of the Jews of Italy*. His research carried him to Capus where a Jew had run the royal mint in the year 1000; then on to Amalfi and Salerno where family myth had his people living until their deportation in 1290. And to Sicily where forty thousand Jews lived before the Spanish throne ordered their expulsion in 1492. To Ostia, at the mouth of the Tiber, where the temple prayed in by the Jewish grain dealers during the reign of Augustus Caeser still stood. And then, naturally, to Rome, where all roads led, to the ghetto, a stone's throw from where his parents lived. For Paolo Pisa, it was a homecoming.

With the royalties earned from his writings and the occasional lecture fee, Paolo Pisa was in a position to pursue his true dream, discovering that which would change the way the world viewed the period when Judaism birthed its successor, Christianity. It had happened once before, in 1947, a discovery of such magnitude, when a Bedouin goatherd discovered the first of the Dead Sea Scrolls in a cave near Qu'ram, a ramshackle settlement just north of the Dead Sea. In a land so arid that the past is often preserved just below the land's surface, particularly in the narrow Negev or below the cobbled streets of Jerusalem, such a discovery, Paolo hoped, could well happen once more.

* * *

Dr. Paolo Pisa and Michelangelo Urban Lorenzo or Father Angelo's careers paralleled each others, separated as they were in age by less than five years. They even shared the same mentor and researched the same Biblical era. In public, Paolo and Father Angelo tended to avoid each other in a profession where one was more inclined to seek affirmation from those on top than their peers. When Paolo's first book appeared, Father Angelo regarded it as "too popular" and "basically coffee table fare." Father Angelo was, in his heart and in his work, a purist. His work and the conclusions the cleric drew from it made him the darling of most of the Vatican's scholarly hierarchy. His books were far more scholarly, more densely written than Paolo's, intended for a limited circle of scholars. Father Angelo was also bothered by Dr. Paolo Pisa's dual nationality. While he viewed, as did all Roman Catholics, the Church of Rome as universal, his allegiance to Italy was absolute. Although Israel had been resurrected as a nation-state, for Father Angelo it was less a nation-state but more the Holy Land. He, like many of his colleagues, was a man of certain biases. As a Jesuit, he counted himself among the Church's elite. In so doing he shared the order's contempt for those who deviated from the faith's true path, regardless of whether their endeavor be secular or religious.

For Father Angelo, a man sporting dual names— Paolo and Moshe— was suspect, but this was a cultural bias, a matter of class, not a product of anti-Semitism. In point of fact, he was philo-Semitic, one of a small group of younger priests who helped Pope John Paul II prepare the statement lifting the millennial curse on the Jews, proclaiming to the world that they were in fact "the elder brothers of the Church." Father Angelo Lorenzo personally observed the pope placing a note of forgiveness in the Western Wall, the pontiff's act recalling his own father's own eyewitness report of what happened down the street in October, 1943. His father's story had burned itself into his soul, a flesh-and-blood remembrance of intolerance and where it ultimately leads. No, Father Angelo was not even remotely anti-Semitic but he truly felt that Dr. Paolo Pisa/Moshe Josephus had been derailed from pure scholarship, the two names he'd chosen merely flags of convenience.

This would all change when the two men found themselves together as guests at a hotel in Tiberias on the shores of the Sea of Galilee. The rivals had by apparent coincidence been invited by the Israeli government to examine artifacts recently found in the area where many Christians believed the apostle Peter had lived.

CHAPTER THREE

Not much remains of Biblical Capernaum, the town known as the "town of Jesus" that sits on Galilee's shore. In the summer months, herds of buses arrive filled with tourists from the world over. Capernaum is part of the Grand Tour of Israel for Jews and the Grand Tour of the Holy Land for Christians. Cargoes of Jews and Gentiles from America spill from the buses, their passports and Bibles in hand, many of the Christians fresh from a stopover baptism in the nearby river Jordan. Adding to the mix of Eastern Europeans and Germans in sandals, groups of Orthodox Jewish boys wearing skullcaps with cell phones pressed to their ears, assuring their parents from afar that, no, stop worrying, they're safe. And the Japanese, of course, their cameras feverishly clicking away at the sights and at each other.

Christians know the region well from their New Testament studies. It was not far from Capernaum that Jesus delivered his Sermon on the Mount. Much of his youth was passed here. The Romans knew the area well, its vineyards, fruit trees, and its rich fishing grounds, the world of Peter the Apostle. The descendants of the original inhabitants and their conquerors still people the Galilee. Pre-Zionist Jews, the descendants of ancient Romans, the Crusaders charged with rescuing the True Cross, fierce Ottoman Turks, Greek merchants who plied their trade anywhere and everywhere, nineteenth-century Zionists, and a people forged by the struggles of modern times, the Palestinians. Traces of them all can be found in the faces of the people of Galilee, each claiming the land as theirs.

The tourists come not to visit the decaying black basalt buildings, a remnant of the Ottoman Empire, nor the kibbutz hugging the shoreline, once the target of Syrian guns from the heights of Golan. They come to see the ancient limestone synagogue where in Roman times wealthy Jews recited their prayers during Herod's rule before the fall of Jerusalem to the Roman legions. Its importance was such that the synagogue is even mentioned in the Book of Matthew 4:12. The intricately carved floral designs on its ashlars and its floor attest to the congregation's wealth. It is at the same time a rationale for the return of the Jewish people to their land. To many, modern Israel is viewed as part of a continuum, a linear progression that includes the Israel of ancient Judea and Samaria and its religious beliefs begun more than five millennia before. It was here in the Galilee where the Jews fought with their brethren who believed Jesus the Messiah, the prophecy of his return for these believers fulfilled. And it was here that Jesus as Messiah was rejected by most of the Jews. These struggles are recorded in the Book of Luke 10:13-15 and it is in the Galilee town of Korazim, according to Matthew's Gospel, that Jesus performed miracles yet found himself scorned by its citizens. The conflicts of Biblical times are no longer ever-present in a place where all cultures and religions mingle in peace. Christians visit the reputed tomb of Magdala, Mary Magdalen, and the Mount of Beatitudes, which the more religious Jews still consider the seedbed of the Talmudic heresy of Christianity. It was also here that Father Angelo Lorenzo and Dr. Paolo Pisa came to know each other after decades of maintaining a respectful, if chilly academic distance.

The two scholars had crossed paths infrequently but had encountered one another at conferences and congresses from Berlin to Tokyo, from Oxford to Austin and several places in between. On occasion they could be found sitting next to each other on Italian television, in German documentaries, and on American public television. In the winter of 2010, they were invited onto the *Larry King Show* to share their assessment of the site where it was claimed the family of Jesus was buried.

"How do you like to be called, Father or Doctor?" the host asked of Father Angelo.

"As one who believes in the Trinity, Larry," he responded, "not to worry, the doctor is always father to the priest."

"Point taken," Larry chuckled.

"My Jewish mother in Rome considers neither of us real doctors, Larry," Dr. Pisa chimed in.

"So neither of you guys can talk about my heart. You're better at assessing the past than my heart condition, right?" Both guests smiled.

King turned to Dr. Pisa.

"You go by two names, Dr. Pisa. So which is it, Moshe Josephus or Paola Pisa when you leave my studio?"

It's a long, long story, Larry. It has more to do with olivewood than my life's work. You probably know my family's involved in making and exporting relics in Israel where we're known by the name of Josephus." Then he added, "Even though we were born Pisas in Rome."

Larry chose not to pursue the name issue, switching instead to the question of a potentially real relic, and the disposition of the recent discovery, one that had already captured the attention of millions.

"So whaddya think," King continued, "another hoax or what?" Both archaeologists demurred.

"Michelangelo, the floor's yours," King said, in his familiar, gravelly voice, resting his chin on his fist. "Whaddya think?" he repeated.

"The site and the ossuaries are real, the script authentic," Father Angelo responded, "but there's no hard evidence to suggest that they're the Biblical burial boxes from what was called a 'double burial.' Or that other families from that period didn't share the same names. After all, Jesus, Mary, Joseph, and James are all Latinized Hebrew names. They're as common as, say, Sarah, Chaim, Judith, and Samuel might be in some modern Jewish families. Even if, for sake of argument, they're the real thing, it's questionable whether the Church would declare them sacred as they did when bones were discovered in the location where Peter was buried. The evidence that these were Peter's was compelling. They were declared authentic relics and in fact lie in a vault below the Vatican today."

"But if they're real, the real deal," King pressed, "why not declare them sacred?"

"Until there's unassailable, substantiated evidence, Larry, it just won't happen, and that evidence has yet to be presented."

As the program wound down, King asked each scholar what they dream of finding, what discovery would be the most significant in their life's work.

"We've both dug beneath the soil of Israel for more decades than we wish to count." Paolo replied. "And our names are affixed to many major findings from the Church's early years and the last days of the Hebrew people before the Diaspora. For me, as a Jew, if l could lay my hands on the contents of the Second Temple that Titus carted away in 70 A.D., I'd die a happy man, a life's work fulfilled. You may have heard, Larry, about the recent exploration efforts in Rome that used advanced sonar and radar developments searching under the Tiber. Some scholars believe the stolen temple pieces were secreted there during the Barbarian Invasions in the 5th century. You can't imagine what's been dredged up, from shipwrecks to ancient coins, even an intact German Panzer from the war. But sadly, nothing from the Temple of Herod. Anyway, Larry, in capsule form, that's my dream."

"And you, Father?"

"That's a difficult question, Larry. Look, there's still a great deal out there undiscovered but you've got to know where to look. Or else get lucky. Or both. It was sheer luck that revealed the Dead Sea Scrolls. If that goat hadn't wandered off or if the Bedouin had tossed away what he'd found ... well, you see what I'm getting at here. I suspect that something from the Christian era's dawning lies under the Middle East's sands, and that something may very well change how we view our common roots. Exactly what it is or what form it may take, I certainly can't even begin to say. But if I was fortunate enough to discover it, or to be a part of the discovery team, I'd want to make sure beyond a reasonable doubt that it was authentic."

Father Angelo paused, conscious that he was rambling, going off track.

"Go on," King urged.

"As I said, whatever it is, it's got to be authenticated. We've a variety of virtually foolproof lab tests that separate gold from fool's gold, so to say. As they say in Brooklyn, Larry, there're too many guys looking to make a quick buck. If they're caught, they end up in prison, but in a world where so many people willingly suspend disbelief in favor of faith, well, there're enough people out to take a chance."

Father Angelo glanced at Paolo Pisa, adding: "And I know Dr. Pisa would agree when I say that if we turn up anything of earthshaking importance, we'll return to your show."

"Promise?"

"Promise," Father Angelo smiled modestly.

"Done deal," Larry said. "By the way, I've been told that

relics from the Second Temple are under the Dome of the Rock, behind the Western Wall. What about digging there?"

"Larry, you can be the first to start that excavation," Dr. Pisa laughed. "Meanwhile Father Angelo and I will be tucked into our bomb shelters when WWIII breaks out after your shovel cuts into the dirt."

"Uh, noted," King replied dryly, looking down at his notes as the show ended.

* * *

No, Father Angelo and Dr. Pisa weren't strangers to one another, but neither were they friends. Father Angelo always believed his being rooted in the Church and its teachings also worked to keep them apart. He considered that perhaps Paolo Pisa believed his Catholicism unduly influenced his interpretations of the past. On the other hand, Paolo Pisa felt that his Judaism made his own interpretations suspect for similar reasons. The men were in many respects mirror images of one another but on this cloudless late November day in 2012, on the hotel patio overlooking the Sea of Galilee, their differences, if not entirely melted away, seemed for the moment suspended. One man was married to the Church and his work, the other married almost to the exclusion of all else to his work. Their hair, once dark and lush, was now streaked with gray, their hairlines receding, their faces lined. Both men's skin now leathery from countless days under broiling desert suns. To the untutored eye they could even be mistaken for cousins— the elder Angelo, his profile an ascetic cast, his clerical collar loosened in the heat, the younger, taller Paolo, his flowered shirt unbuttoned. Men eerily similar in aspect, they engaged in animated conversation about their work in Tiberias.

As they drank Israeli beer in the region where Peter fished in Jesus' time, near the Franciscan church built over the rooms alleged to have been the Apostle's, they discussed the fishhooks found buried beneath the dirt floor and the sayings found scratched into the walls of the rooms. Both hewed to the scholar's creed. Neither accepted the discovery on faith; both agreed the jury was still out on whether either the fishhooks or the barely legible scribblings constituted true relics.

"Where's the evidence?" Father Angelo shook his head as

Paolo Pisa nodded his in agreement. "If we accepted every splinter presented as a piece of the true Cross, we could build a footbridge from Jerusalem to Tokyo and halfway back."

"And imagine the tolls we could charge, Angelo." The priest laughed at the absurd notion.

Over the cold beer, competing with the unintelligible lyrics of a rock tune blaring from the restaurant's four loudspeakers, they discussed why they were sitting in Tiberias instead of Jerusalem just as their St. Peter's fish arrived. Two weeks earlier, Father Angelo had dined with the pope and a month before that he'd been a guest at Gracie Mansion, lecturing New York's mayor and his coterie of pols and high rollers on ancient art.

"At least no one nodded off," he recalled, adding, "I think but I wouldn't swear to it. Uh, even if I did swear."

Paolo grinned, recalling a similar conversation the year before over the same dish with Israel's prime minister. Well, at least the fish was fresh, not the canned fare both men endured on their respective digs in the Negev and elsewhere.

"No one ever died from this," Father Angelo noted, removing a small bone from between his teeth.

"Perhaps only Peter, Angelo," Paolo said. "But who knows for sure? Who knows anything for sure these days?"

* * *

They had come to Tiberias to pass judgment on a recent find made in the Roman theatre at Beit She'an. It might not change history's course but it might add to the fund of knowledge about the early years of the Nazarean cult. The two scholars would know only after they'd examined it. After all, it wasn't another coin like those the earth belches up daily, talents, mina, shekels, beka, and gerah, coins of the ancient Hebrews, or the Roman coins inscribed in Greek for use in the empire's eastern reaches. What made this discovery interesting was a dated manuscript, more precisely a script written on stained, parchment pages tucked within a lead box in a larger, ancient olivewood box. The box had a number— 60— perhaps a date?— carved into it. Although the Christian calendar was not in use in the first century following Christ's birth, finding an ancient object with an inscribed number certainly demanded attention and, at the very least, an expert opinion. The head of the archaelogical team that found the box had phoned Rome and requested the assistance of Father Angelo and Paolo Pisa/Moshe Josephus. The following week, they were on an early morning Alitalia flight to Tel Aviv.

Both men were intimately conversant with ancient Judea's history and its conflicts. Of the lands and cultures living under Roman law, the most troublesome was Judea. During Nero's reign, the sporadic violence visited upon Judea's Roman occupiers began to spread. The Roman empire in the first century A.D. stretched from the Iberian peninsula to the gates of Parthia, from Britannia in the north to Mauretania on Africa's western coast, through the whole of North Africa, and from the Mediterranean Sea deep inland, absorbing into its world nearly eighty million souls.

The mad emperor assumed power in 66 A.D., two years after the Great Fire and following the increasingly disastrous wars with Parthia. Few mourned Nero's forced suicide in 68 A.D., but his immediate legacy to Rome was further instability and confusion. Emperor followed emperor in short order; Galba ruled from June 68 to January 69, replaced by his murderer Otho, who lasted until March 69. The forgettable Vitellius deposed Otho, his rule lasting until the last week of December. Displeased with the chaos that had gripped Rome, the Roman legions were prepared to march on Rome and assume control of the empire. The panicky Senate prodded Vitellius to abdicate but the legions' commander, Vespasian, had already written another ending for Vitellius. The game of revolving emperors ended with the execution of Vitellius and Vespasian's enthroning in late December 69. Vespasian saw as his urgent mandate the revival of Caesar Augustus's tottering *Pax Romana*. His first order of business was inevitable— crushing the insurrections in Judea.

When the Roman general, Pompei, arrived with his legions in 63 B.C., he asked the priests at the temple in Jerusalem to show him their gods. In turn, they presented Pompei their scrolls containing the word of their god. Jews comprised barely five percent of the empire's population. Since they lived in all Rome's provinces, Pompei was familiar with them. What he was forever unable to comprehend was a world, the world of the Jews, where a people's god was reduced to words on parchment. In Pompei's world, gods were on display, in statuary, in graven images. Gods must be visible, cast in marble, everpresent reminders for the populace.

Even in Rome, at the mouth of the Tiber, in the port of Ostia where they supplied the Romans with grain, or in the far-flung areas where as slave traders they brought slaves to serve the wealthy in Rome's villas, these Jews remained untouched by the Roman's pagan religion, adhering fiercely to their own beliefs, praying in their own temples. These odd beliefs meant little to Rome's rulers who, to maintain peace among a people whose religious tenets they could not grasp, relaxed the rules, exempting the Jews from the cult of emperor worship. For Pompei and the others, the Jews would remain an enigma, a puzzle they would never solve.

Shortly before Christ's birth, Judea was ruled by the Roman client king, Herod. His affinity for all things Roman and Rome's leaders rendered him suspect in the eyes and hearts of those living under his sway. Even his Judaism was questioned, his tribal roots mysteriously obscure. Paolo Pisa was himself of two minds, still undecided after decades of inquiry regarding Herod's Judaism, while Father Angelo Lorenzo proffered no opinion on the matter. The king's Judaism may continue to invite debate but his canniness as a politician was never in question. Herod was a monarch intimately aware of the tenuousness of his power. He recognized that his survival depended on the beneficence of Rome.

As an appointed ruler, whatever the true nature of his religious affiliation, it was essential that he did his masters' bidding. After the murder of his protector, Julius Caesar, he hasted to curry the favor of Marc Antony and Octavian. And finally, when driven temporarily from power, Herod sailed to Rome and successfully pled his case for restoration as King of the Jews before the Senate. He honored Caesar with grand building projects, the grandest being the deep-water port of Caesarea on the Mediterranean near modern Haifa, an ancient engineering marvel of its day. After Caesar's assassination on the floor of the Forum, to please his subjects Herod ordered the construction of the Second Temple in the heart of Jerusalem. Like Caesarea, this Herodian masterpiece was equally impressive, a gift to the Jews. Herod's legacy outlasted the legacy of his political duplicity, his gestures grand, as enduring as the empire that he served was not.

The Sanhedrin, the Second Temple's governing body, rendered decisions and interpretations of Judaic law and, like

Herod, worked in concert with the Roman hierarchy, relieving their Roman overlords of at least part of their burden in governing such a restive people. As the theocratic power in Jerusalem, members of the Sanhedrin were in perpetual debate over how to remain true to the Torah in a world governed by Rome. In the eastern part of the empire, Greek had become the language of commerce; Hebrew was relegated as a sacred language, while the common man spoke Aramaic in the markets of Jerusalem and Judea. Added to the cares of the Romans were the nagging disputes over a crucified upstart called Jesus, a carpenter from Nazareth whose followers believed him to be the Son of God.

For most Jews, to claim divinity or for one's followers to do so constituted heresy and was declared as such. For the Romans, there could be only one god on earth, the living god embodied in the emperor in Rome who, at the time of Jesus' crucifixion, was Tiberius. Whether Tiberius was aware of this incident, the most recent in a seemingly endless string of disturbances originating in Judea, is unknown. Whatever the case, it was of no immediate importance to Rome. This latest thorn in the side of the Romans, this soldier in the small army of renegades that plagued the occupiers, was soon dispatched. Jesus, the Nazarene, was condemned by both the Sanhedrin and the Roman governor, Pontius Pilate, nailed to a wooden Cross and hoisted aloft in Golgotha, in Jerusalem, in the third decade A.D. While the Romans were careful record keepers, to the world's dismay no records of the crucifixion survived and those documents kept by the Sanhedrin were reduced to ashes in the conflagration that destroyed the Second Temple in August, 70 A.D. at the tail end of the Great Jewish Revolt.

By 66 A.D., a radical Jewish sect known as the Zealots had already called upon all Jews to rise up and drive the Romans from Judea and from the holy city of Jerusalem. The decision to take up arms in revolt against the Romans was ill conceived and disastrous for the Jews and, as history shows, a misjudgment so monumental that it sealed a people's fate. Tragically underestimating Roman power and determination, the Zealots believed wrongly that an empire with its epicenter so far distant and its ruling circle weakened and in chaos would never seek to recover its lost territory.

But the Roman Senate's decision was in keeping with its philosophy that to maintain order throughout the empire, it must maintain and restore order to all its component parts. Just as Rome had destroyed Carthage, it would destroy Judea. It mattered little that ascending the emperor's throne had become a lethal merry-go-round. In 67 A.D. Rome was still unchallenged as the world's greatest power.

The Roman legions set sail amid great fanfare, commanded by the soon-to-be Roman emperor, Vespasian. Landing at Antioch with several squadrons, Vespasian's legions made short work of the poorly-trained and ill-equipped Jewish rebels. The Romans' siege machines shredded the rebel forces in their path, taking no prisoners along the way. By the time Vespasian's army rumbled to the gates of Jerusalem, the revolt was buckling, nearing collapse. The Second Temple, the repository of all the Sanhedrins' records, was set aflame and crumbled, only its scorched western wall left standing.

The savagery of the assault was recorded by the historian Josephus, who noted that, "the Romans' horses were up to their knees in blood," that at the end of the week nearly six hundred thousand had lost their lives during the Roman onslaught. The survivors were shipped as slaves to Ostia, where many died enroute, or to Hispania, where a certain death sentence awaited them as they labored in the Roman province's silver mines. Others found themselves transported to the far reaches of the empire.

The revolt's last gasp occurred at the fortress of Masada, overlooking the Dead Sea on the eastern edge of the Judean desert in April, 73 A.D. After a three-month siege, the Romans breached its battlements, overrunning the mountaintop stronghold. What the Romans found when they conquered Masada stunned even the most battle-hardened legionnaire. Masada's defenders, numbering more than nine hundred, had taken their own lives, determined not to endure capture, enslavement, or execution by the Roman invaders. With the fall of Masada, the defeat of the Jews was complete. The Jewish Diaspora, resulting directly from the Zealots mad misadventure, had begun.

* * *

It was the possible date on the as yet unexamined olivewood box that kindled fires in both scholars' imaginations. Both Father Angelo and Paolo Pisa were in accord. If the finding could be verified, it was undoubtedly hidden under the stone in the Roman amphitheatre in Bet She'an during the Jewish Revolt. Logic dictated such a conclusion.

"What's interesting, Angelo, is that they say the box's lid contains both the Roman and Hebrew time calculation."

"The dates are definitely the key," the priest agreed. "Sixty would've been three years after the ministry of St. Paul, and half a decade before the outbreak of the revolt."

The men were speaking in half-sentences, thinking their disparate thoughts aloud. "And the date in Hebrew, 3820, corresponds to 60 in the beginning of the Christian era ..."

Father Angelo nodded. He could feel the second beer's dulling effect as he pressed forward to expound slowly on one of his favorite themes.

"Yes, and the Roman date under it, DCCCXIV or 814, reminds us of how far along the use of Roman dating had come by 60 A.D. At the behest of Julius Caesar in 46 B.C., an Alexandrian Greek astronomer named Sosigenes devised a method of measuring time. Caesar approved and abolished the old lunar calendar, replacing it with the solar calendar, the Julian Calendar. Added time caused some initial confusion but, for all intents and purposes, Sosigenes' calendar worked well enough. In the late 16th century, our very own Pope Gregory XIII had the Julian Calendar revised and replaced. Eventually even the Protestants accepted the change." He smiled approvingly. "The time differentials, the rough edges of both calendars were smoothed out and cleaned up, a symmetry established. "And voila! Paolo," he said, a wisp more pompously than he'd intended, "we have Pope Gregory's efforts to thank for the modern calendar that hangs on our kitchen walls."

"Or our ancient ones," Paolo, who knew the calendar history well, joked. "Take your pick. But not if you've got a flight to catch."

The wind over Galilee had picked up suddenly and swirled, white-capping the lake's surface, the air, heavy and pregnant with rain. In moments, the first raindrops of a storm approaching from the west bounced fat, stinging drops off their table.

"Hey, we'd better move inside," Paolo said.

Father Angelo began to rise, a little unsteadily at first, and turned towards the hotel. Paolo glanced up at the sky, quickly turning a heavy leaden gray, and followed the priest into the restaurant.

CHAPTER 4

The waterside restaurant was crowded and smoky, Israelis and tourists, staff and guests, all eyes turned upward at the massive television screen that sat like a raptor, bolted to the wall above and running half the length of the bar. Even the bartender craned his neck for a better view. Someone ordered a beer but the request was ignored. The channel was turned to CNN, where a familiar commentator in a bright yellow Sou'easter struggled to remain upright under the whipping wind and pelting rain in Dacca. He resembled a marionette tangled in his strings, his movements comic and jerky, less a grown man reporting from the world's latest disaster zone than a rag doll steadying a slippery mike in a clenched fist, vainly seeking purchase for his booted feet.

Paolo and Father Angelo stood off to the side, near the patio doors. That overused term— a perfect storm— popped into Paolo's head, and repeated itself like a mantra. Images of drowned New Orleans more than seven years earlier, courtesy of the news channels' blanket coverage, bloated bodies bobbing in oil-slicked waters, and half-naked men and women clinging desperately to the rooftops of their sinking houses. Or upended lawn chairs shattering windows in collapsing five-star Indonesian hotels, crumbling under the Asian tsunami's lethal course inland, all the horrifying memories of recent catastrophes merging together, flitted through his mind before evaporating.

"Look at this, Angelo," Paolo exclaimed, pointing at the screen. "History seems to be repeating itself."

"Jesus! What the hell?' a too-loud voice barked, as its owner lifted his head from the bar. It was unclear whether he was complaining of being awakened or expressing shock at what he saw on the screen above him.

The horrifying images from the Indian subcontinent, from Bangladesh, from much of Southeast Asia, were reminiscent of the Biblical tale of the flood. The storm was massive, truly the storm of any century, and uncharacteristically it was moving westward. Two fronts, their size startling even the most seasoned storm forecasters, had collided over Sri Lanka. First Tehran, then Baghdad were flooded, both cities' streets awash within an hour of the storm's hitting. The small settlements and towns and cities in between the two Middle East capitals were already under water.

In Bagdhad, the Tigris and Euphrates banks had overflowed, creating an instant raging river of clutter that gathered and raced through the sprawling city, upending market stalls, strewing fresh fruit and vegetables, Humvees, buses, and all forms of military vehicles and equipment in its path as if they were but toys. The buzz from many of the television watchers in Galilee, their eyes occasionally and nervously glancing at one another, seemed to mouth another catchall phrase: "global warming."

"Must be," one said in Hebrew.

"Yes, must be," his friend echoed, clutching his beer glass tightly, eyes riveted to the television screen.

Paolo shook his head sadly. Father Angelo grimaced and sighed.

The television commentator announced that in some regions it was reported that nearly a foot of rain an hour was falling. In Naples, as a precaution, the bulk of the US Sixth Fleet left port, preferring to take its chances at sea rather than docked and anchored, in constant danger of a falling cargo crane or ramming into a bulkhead or an accidental scuttling. The fleet's cohort at the mouth of the Straits of Honnuz now rode at anchor, capsized dhows and an occasional pleasure craft drifting nearby, its orders to monitor the stalled Iranian seaborne movements rescinded. The IDF's navy had left Haifa earlier under orders from headquarters in Jerusalem, sailing westward towards Cyprus and open water, its reasoning the same as its American ally.

Widespread flooding was reported as far north as Dresden where the Elbe had breached its banks. There were no wartime scenes of ragged refugees pushing carriages, or horses pulling carts stacked high with furniture, clothing, and the aged. Dresden was a beautiful, restored city, not the devastated city of memory. It had suffered badly in the floods of 2002 and was, for the second time in sixty years, repaired and rebuilt. But this monster storm caught the German city, all cities in its way— east and west— unawares. The 2002 storm with all its destructive power seemed like a summer squall in comparison. How could one heed the alarms, the warnings, the calls, the orders that came from television channels and radios still transmitting? The size of the storm had not been, could not have been, predicted, hence catching everyone unprepared for what they now faced or for the life-and-death decisions they now had to make. There was no time and no place to run, only the lucky could rush to higher ground. If there was higher ground to be reached.

To the south, the Danube had crested in Vienna, too. A loaded fuel barge slipped its hawsers upstream and slammed into the embankment under the Reichsbruecke, the mile-long Danube span. The spill was being contained but the barge had caught fire. The city's fireboats were working gamely to douse the spreading flames. A radio bulletin blared that the Reichsbrucke was closed to all traffic. Of which there was none, other than the once-parked smaller cars that were strewn across the broad Lasallestrasse, turning the eastern end of the boulevard into a sludge-covered, watery parking lot. The storm's wake had equaled the losses seen in Vienna, in Bratislava, Budapest and Bucharest along the length of the Danube. As the river emptied through Bulgaria into the Black Sea, it brought with it shattered souvenirs of each city it had passed through.

In Holland, emergency radio ordered all who could to move inland for there was no guarantee the dikes would hold back the storm surge. And in the Netherlands there was no higher ground. The nearest higher ground lay further to the east, in Germany. What had happened in 1953, when the North Sea flood inundated the lowlands, overwhelming the dikes in Zeeland, could very well and would happen again. No design, no structure no matter how extensively tested on paper or in the laboratory, could withstand the winds and rush of water from a storm of this magnitude.

In Paris, the Seine, like its sister European waterways, was no longer navigable, the boites from the riverside bookstalls sailed away, adrift in its filthy waters. The Ile St.-Louis resembled a half-visible Atlantis, the water now a roaring stream that soaked the ground floors of the islet's ancient townhouses. Quick action by the authorities had evacuated the lower floor collections of the Louvre and the Musee D'Orsay and the other central city museums within three days. Shelters were hastily arranged in the higher elevations of the Montparnasse and Montmarte *arrondissements* for those who needed them.

By Day Two of the storm, Notre-Dame's marble floor was a murky pond, with the cathedral's wooden pews afloat, many bunching up against the nave. Paris' sewers had backed up, emptying torrents into the Metro's underground stations, short-circuiting the entire rail system. The extensive ossuary of the Catacombs was filled ground to ceiling with waters rushing, not from the storm itself, but from a burst medieval aqueduct, its caramel-colored bone fragments mixing with the stones unearthed by the uncharted aqueduct's breaking apart.

* * *

The Arno had reached flood stage but the government had, against all expectations, acted swiftly and secured the portable treasures of both Florence and Pisa. With the assistance of the Italian army, the treasures— paintings, sculptures, other works of art— were emptied from the cities' museums and secured near Fiesole, in waterproof vaults built during the war, the government noted, especially for "unforseen circumstances." Michelangelo's David, unfortunately, would have to remain at his post, fronting the Palazzo Vecchio, knee deep in water, the massive sculpture too large to move on such short notice.

Similar precautions were taken in Rome as the Tiber rose, providentially more slowly than the Rhine, the Po, and the Danube, but rapidly enough to drive the government into frenzied efforts to avoid further devastation. The sea had come for Venice. The Piazza San Marco, inevitably awash by mid-November, was a stagnant lake; the turbid waters running from the Grand Canal to the piazza had short-circuited the elevator that hauled tourists to the top of the Campanile. There would be no breathtaking, panoramic views of Venice today or for several tomorrows. The water level rose slowly up the columned walls of the Doges' Palace. Emergency workers and tourists alike moved around aimlessly, sloshing through the opaque waters, looking for any escape route as the canal waters inched up the stately quayside monuments next to the palace, their columns topped by the lions that gazed blindly seawards.

With frantic speed, vaporettos, motorboats, even gondolas, all riding low in the water, moved panicky tourists and locals to Mestre. Idling buses gathered at the western entry of the Liberta causeway that connects Venice and the mainland, the waters kissing their hubcaps, and picked up the overflow of passengers and the occasional straggler, carrying them away from Venice. The Peggy Guggenheim Museum, located virtually at water level, lost its courtyard sculptures. All but a few of its treasures and most of the invaluable artworks from the lower floors of Venice's churches and its other museums were saved, spirited off to secure locations inland.

Always on the verge of harm, Venice was better prepared for disaster than its sister cities. Rapid organization of the rescue operations kept fatalities by drowning to a minimum, although the true number of lives lost in Venice, Florence, and Rome, as in the other European cities along the storm's march, would never be accurately accounted for.

"Thank God my parents live on a high floor, Paolo. I spoke to them yesterday and they told me it was already raining in buckets. They'd never seen anything like it. They could barely see the street from their window the sheets of rain were so heavy.

"Yes, thank God," Paolo responded automatically.

Paolo excused himself, found a corner in an adjoining room, and phoned Rome. His father answered, immediately assuring his son they were safe and dry, and not to worry. In spite of his son's protestations, Guido Pisa told him in no uncertain terms that, no, they wouldn't evacuate.

"I don't mean to sound melodramatic, Paolo," the elder Pisa said, his voice gruff and hoarse from years of smoking, "but where would we go? Back to Israel? I was born here and I plan to die here. I was gone from here long enough. And if you recall, I was the one who taught you to swim. By the way, when are you coming home? Your mother misses you."

Paolo almost laughed at his father's intransigence. His insouciant dismissal, his shrugging off the obvious and imminent danger he and for that matter all in the city faced, was in keeping with his character. Guido Pisa was nothing if not a tough, stubborn old survivor of wars, deprivation, and worse and Paolo knew once his father planted his feet, they remained planted unless Guido and only Guido himself decided to unplant them. It would be of no benefit for Paolo to argue. "Don't do anything foolish, Papa," Paolo said.

"I wouldn't, Paolo, I leave that to you, my dear son," Guido replied, laughing, "and take care."

Paolo heard his mother chuckling in the background as he rang off and rejoined Father Angelo in the dining room.

All eyes were still fixed on the enormous television screen where the weather reporter had been replaced by Israel's defense minister, backgrounded as was custom by Israel's blue-and-white flag with the symbol of the state, Star of David, in its center.

"Today," he began, "we're all faced with a complex and dangerous situation. The people of Israel and the entire region must prepare for a national emergency, one not arising out of our political problems and differences for once, but related to two massive storms converging on the Middle East from separate directions. From northern Turkey south to the Sudan, they will collide. These are not separate storms. They are part of several storm systems that we've been monitoring over the past week. Our computer models indicate, and the government agrees, that low lying areas could be inundated as many of Europe's cities already have been by as much as four or more feet of water. Both banks of the Jordan River and the Negev ..."

"How could this happen?" a lone voice murmured, an elderly man standing behind Father Angelo. "It never rains in Israel like this in November."

"It never rains anywhere like this, Morris. Shhh, listen, don't talk," a woman's voice remonstrated.

"Don't shush me!" the first voice complained.

Americans, Paolo concluded reflexively, bickering as if they were ensconced in their own living room. Or perhaps English? Or Australians? Or maybe Israelis? Or? He was a scholar, a scientist, he scolded himself, mindful of the trap that lay in jumping to conclusions. Whichever, he was glad he'd never remarried after his own very personal tragedy. Listening to the couple snapping at each other confirmed for him that he'd made the correct decision.

Paolo was tall, slim, and by any measure still handsome, his blue eyes piercing. He'd had his opportunities, his lovers over the years, but none seemed suited or as willing as Leah had once been, however briefly, to share the life's work he had chosen. His Roman parents were deeply disappointed that he hadn't gifted them with another grandchild, as had his younger brothers and sister.

"You might as well have become a priest," his father had years ago nattered at him incessantly. "What's a Jewish man without a wife, without a family?" His mother only sighed deeply, the memory of her son's and indeed all their profound loss a fresh, unhealed wound. One evening after dinner, Paolo Pisa had heard enough too often. He drew the line with such a harsh finality that Guido was rendered speechless.

"Pop, have you forgotten? I was a Jewish man with a family. Once," he said forcefully, his voice cold, lacking affect. "The circle's been broken, it can't be repaired. This is the last time, the very last time I want to hear this speech, this marriage and family fantasy of yours. The last time, understood? I won't discuss this with you. Ever again."

But Guido's shock and Sarah's sorrow and disappointment had long since been repressed. They had no choice but to heed their son's wishes. Paolo followed his own star, did as he wished, just as, his father came to realize and accept, he had done before him.

"...are in harm's way," the minister was saying. "Anyone and everyone living within four miles of the Jordan or its feeders must leave for higher ground immediately. People living in high rises along the coastal plain, those below the sixth floor, are instructed to also leave for higher ground. Use common sense. Under no circumstances should basements or bomb shelters be used for protection. If our models predict correctly, and we believe they do, all those living along coastal highways 2 and 4, along 85 near Safed, 90 in the West Bank, and the main artery from Jenin to Nablus to Jericho and Hebron must, I repeat, must leave for higher ground.

"I want to assure all, Israelis and our Palestinian neighbors in the West Bank and in Gaza, of the critical nature of this situation. As I speak, government representatives and members of the Palestinian Authority are meeting to coordinate all evacuation efforts to ensure a minimum of disruption and the protection of life and property. The Red Crescent and the Mogen David, all rescue services and military personnel will be working in a collective effort in their respective areas for what portends to be a situation far different than anything we have ever experienced in the region."

"It was not caused by what daily separates us; this is an act of God. The storms that we've witnessed in reports coming from

Europe and Asia are headed this way. Again, those of you in the low-lying areas," he repeated, "from the Golan to the rift areas, from the Galilee to Yotvata in the Negev are vulnerable. Move to higher ground. All airports have been closed," he added unnecessarily, "as well as all port facilities which are shut down. In closing," he cleared his throat, "I offer this prayer in Hebrew and Arabic ..."

The bar's viewers stood in the glare of the television screen, stunned into silence, some paralyzed with fear, an incipient panic rising in the chest of others, most planning an escape route out of the Galilee to somewhere, anywhere higher ground could be reached.

Paolo turned to Father Angelo.

"Act of God? More like acts of man. Guess we'd better go to the room and pack," Paolo said, trying to tamp down his own growing anxiety.

"Yes," Angelo agreed, already rising, "we'd better."

CHAPTER 5

When not in the field on their respective digs, both Paolo Pisa and Father Angelo Lorenzo favored the comfort of four- or five-star hotels. Or hotels that claimed that singular honor among the traveling *cognoscenti*. Both men were soaked through when they entered the lobby of the Radisson Moriah Plaza Tiberias, a stone's throw from the restaurant, on Tiberias' Waterfront Promenade. The numerous man-made beaches- the Blue, the Quiet, the Shell, the Nelson, and the pretentiously-named Lido- where the religious and the holy swam in waters fed by the River Jordan, lay a short stroll from the fourteen-story hotel. Tiberias was, as were all the towns circling the Galilee, a thriving tourist center, once sleepy but now bustling, a required stopover for the millions who visit the Holy Land annually.

Tourism is Israel's lifeblood, a tenuous multi-billion dollar industry dependent on peace and security. Tourism in Israel has always been at the mercy of external forces. A hint of strife along the Lebanese or Syrian borders, or in Gaza, armed conflict in Jenin or other Palestinian refugee camps, or a suicide bomber eluding a Tel Aviv bus's metal detector can, with the press of a button, bring the entire industry to its knees. Flights from America, Europe, and Asia suddenly cancelled, hotels standing half-empty, restaurants closed till the latest crisis passes, tour buses without tourists, and taxis sitting idle at curbside outside Ben Gurion Airport, awaiting passengers that never arrive.

These are the fears of the industry, fears that have been realized periodically and all too often in Israel's six decade history.

As a Galilean town, Tiberias sits atop the Great Rift, the active earthquake zone that begins in Africa and ends in Turkey. The area, especially at its northern edge, has suffered several earthquakes in recent years. In its formative days, Tiberias was predominantly a Greek city, the home of Greek traders who competed with their Jewish counterparts in the marketplace where Greek became the official language as their merchants spread trade outwards and south along the Mediterranean shoreline.

When Vespasian's army landed to restore order in restive Judea, the elders of Tiberias, seeking to secure what great wealth they'd already accumulated, surrendered immediately. At one time, before the creation of the Babylonian Talmud, Rabbi Judah, who inscribed Jewish oral traditions into written form in the *Mishna,* had also been a resident. And as Constantine the Great accepted and propagated Christianity throughout the empire in the 4th century, one among the religion's first churches was built in Tiberias. Tiberias's early connection to Christianity harked back to the religion's beginnings.

When Rome fell in 404 A.D. at the dawn of the 5th century, the area began to fall into decay, too. Power was increasingly centralized in the East, in Byzantium, the future Constantinople, astride the Bosphorus, today's Istanbul. Islam and its Arab practitioners arrived in force in the 7th century and, although they were in turn briefly conquered and driven out of Jerusalem by the crusader prince Tancred at the beginning of the 12th century, by the century's end the sword of Saladin had restored Islam's supremacy. Several later Christian challenges had the crusaders slaughtering the inhabitants of Palestine as they marched inland, intent on regaining the Holy Land for Mother Church and profiting in the process, but ultimately ending in the invaders' defeat. The fifth and last crusade in 1290 marked the end of Christian rule as the Sultan Qulawun's armies mercilessly assaulted and regained the Crusader stronghold of Acre, bringing down the fortress and enslaving thousands of its fighters. As a religious and political force in Palestine, Christianity had seen its day.

Under the succeeding Ottoman Empire, Palestine remained a sleepy backwater. Upon the collapse of the empire following World War I, a British Mandate was sanctioned and, in 1948, the mandate by a United Nations vote came to an end. In May of that year, the state of Israel was born.

Tiberias remained Tiberias. Little had changed for the

better by 1948. It was still squalid, dirty, and infested with insects, so much so that a local Arab saying held that "The King of the Fleas holds his court in Tiberias." The king and his court were ultimately dethroned by DDT but Tiberias remained undeniably poor for decades until it was revived by recreating itself as a must-see destination for the devout and the curious of all faiths. The destruction brought down upon the town by the monster storm had returned Tiberias within two days to what it had painfully evolved from, a wretched backwater.

* * *

After a quick change of clothing, Paolo and Father Angelo sat together, gazing intently at the suite's television screen, as the staccato of weather reports continued unceasingly. The storms to the north in Europe had abated, the floodwaters were receding; the Asian storms had run their course, the enormous and incalculable damage done, the massive cleanup in progress. But over Israel and its neighbors, north and east, new storm fronts gained force, the rainfall intensified, the crashing thunder and blinding lightning constant and seemingly endless.

"It reminds me of Camus, Angelo, we're trapped. Like the people in Oran in *The Plague.*"

"That was metaphorical, Paolo, this is real. When these storms pass, my friend, prepare yourself for the cacophony, the grand debate, the talking heads arguing over whether all this was caused by global warming or divine punishment for our sins, our mismanagement of the earth."

"No doubt, no doubt," Paolo agreed. "Remember what we used to say as kids, Angelo? We're screwed."

"Royally," Father Angelo added, laughing mirthlessly, his face grim.

"This, I'm afraid, isn't up to the Almighty. We've got to count on the rescue services doing their job," Paolo said, stating what was obvious to both. "We're naked, our fate's in the hands of others so let's hope and pray they're equal to the task. Or maybe history'll repeat itself. We'll be swallowed by a whale and coughed up three days later onto dry land. From the looks of it, more likely we'll be backstroking in the Persian Gulf by *Shabbos.*"

"If we're praying for miracles, I'm more inclined to put my faith in an encore from Noah. But this isn't a land of seafarers …" Angelo ran his finger around his clerical collar. "I never learned to swim," he said absently, more to himself than to Paolo.

The two men sat, both aware of their helplessness. As in most crises, people spoke of their pasts. It was no different for Father Angelo and Paolo Pisa, for theirs was a past of many parallels. Closely knit families, large gatherings, black shirts mothballed, the guilt of Nazi occupation, fathers separated by their different faiths yet both still harboring the belief that Mussolini had fumbled away their homeland's greatness through his avarice and stupidity. These were burdens shared and carried to the grave by countless Italian families from the Alps to Palermo.

"You know, Angelo, it's strange, isn't it?" Paolo sensed an opening and took a stab at lessening the formal distance between the two of them. "We're both in the same field, have been for decades, sort of but not really competitors. What's there to compete for? At least that's how I see it. A discovery's a discovery, something to be celebrated by all. We've had our scholarly differences but there's little in our interpretations that's open to question from one another. We're called upon before any other so-called experts to verify the work of others. Equally. Yet after all this time, although we should have been, we've never been close, never shared a friendship. It's odd, Angelo, odd."

The normally imperturbable Father Angelo was caught off guard and found himself unable to craft a response. The query unsettled him and he averted Paolo's eyes. After an uncomfortable pause, he shrugged, for he had no answer to offer. Paolo let the question lay there, pressing no further. Perhaps another time in another place, Paolo thought to himself.

Both men distracted themselves watching the rain hammer against the suite's windows, obscuring even the flickering streetlights below. The rolling thunder, the sharp bolts of lightning seemed to come from all directions, Syria and Jordan to the east, the Mediterranean to the west.

Angelo's mind filled with the image of one of Michelangelo's many masterpieces. This many-paneled work hung in his patron Pope Julius II's private chapel near the Vatican.

Below its central panel is the scene called *The Drunkeness of Noah* and below that one of *The Flood*. In it, people are seated half naked on a rock outcropping, not daring to gaze upon those trapped in the sea of oncoming water that will soon drown them, God's punishment for their earthly transgressions. How fitting, the priest thought.

Half a millenium later, visitors to the Holy Land, they themselves were trapped in a figurative outcropping made of brick and glass, peering from the lobby, recording digitally another flood in the making. The rain rendered the Sea of Galilee invisible but the guests keep clicking away, gamely working to quell their fear. Some must have concluded the Galilee was rising rapidly— Paolo surely had— brimming with waters from the Jordan while cloud bursts dropped metric tons of water from the skies at a rate no one could calculate.

"Never in recorded memory," the TV weatherman droned, "has so much water fallen in so short a time ... and it's expected to continue. Preparations are underway for mass evacuations by sea once the fleets can move into position ..."

The claps of thunder reminded the Israelis among them of the artillery duels between the IDF and Syria in the Golan Heights, others of the Hezbollah rocket assaults in 2006. No different than the men in the trenches of WWI and WWII as the bombs burst in air overhead or the characters portrayed in Camus' plague-ridden Oran. Each was lost to his or her own thoughts and terrors. No matter what the television said, escape was now impossible. They knew they would have to ride the storm out, the storm itself robbing them of any choice.

Father Angelo's thoughts raced between the odds for all their survival and Paolo's unanswered question. In his mid-sixties, he was still able but the drenching he'd taken on the short walk to the hotel had weakened his reserves. There was a time when such discomfort would be ignored but he was no longer the man who wielded the shovel in the Negev's sands, or in the broiling heat of Sinai, or in the desert wastes of Syria. He now supervised others on these digs and wrote of them in the comfort of his study. But he was still the man with the middleweight's build and muscles, a shade shorter than Paolo, with a profile made for a Roman coin. Seated there in his priestly uniform, his black habit, his silver Cross resting against his broad chest, he was at his duty station in the event he was needed for spiritual succor in this perilous time. Father Angelo wore the guarded and weary look of a man soon to be confronted with the ultimate test of faith.

His inner self and, by extension, the religious community he was a part of, did not for a moment question the Trinity nor the promise of resurrection. These were articles of faith, accepted on faith. He was from the beginning, in the secular phrase, a party man, a man who dined with popes, cardinals, archbishops, and bishops, the heirarchy that ruled over a flock of believers numbering nearly a billion souls. Faith was the essence, the underpinning of his and his religion's world, the Nicean Creed more than merely dogma. One's life on earth was transitory, a stage from which one would enter eternal life if one was just and had adhered to the sacraments along the way.

As an archaeologist, though, Father Angelo held to another dogma, refusing to permit his faith to interfere with his work in a world in which belief was based on evidence. But tonight, his faith overrode all other aspects of that life. In the unlikely event the Sea of Galilee rose above his window level and he ultimately succumbed, he would die believing the environmentalists were right. But for the wrong reasons. Yes, the carbon emissions from the world's automobiles and factories had in part brought on this catastrophe, on this he wholeheartedly agreed. But this catastrophe was the vehicle for God's punishment of humankind, for their misuse as stewards of the sacred trust that God had granted them. He recalled the late John Paul II's comment on global warming during a dinner they'd shared years before. The pope had said that "all of us have been miserable stewards and in time we will pay a very high price. I intend to issue a papal encyclical not much different than that of Leo XIII's 'On Modern Things.' You'll remember, Father Angelo, that the Holy Father condemned both capitalism and socialism as un-Christian." Sadly, John Paul II died not long after, before he could fulfill his intention.

The half-forgotten question posed by Paolo returned and troubled him, a discomfort made acute by his own inability or unwillingness to answer it. He pondered a confession, then rejected it. To whom should he now confess and where? Himself? Here? The situation in which both men found themselves was bizarre. Two professionals, rivals really, sharing drinks in a luxury hotel atop a sliver of disputed land over which people had fought and died since time immemoriam. Melodramatic yet real, true prisoners of the storm and in mortal danger? Why and for what? To examine and pass judgment on a box containing a manuscript maybe or maybe not from the year 60 A.D. The absurdity of the moment was clear to Father Angelo. He wondered if Paolo viewed their plight as he did.

Father Angelo recognized that Paolo was reaching out though the nagging uncertainty that he disliked him lingered. Perhaps he shared his people's deep suspicion of the Vatican. And not, he had to admit to himself, without good reason.

As Eugenio Pacelli, the papal nuncio, the Vatican's primary representative in Germany, the future pope was instrumental in negotiating the agreement, the so-called Concordat in the summer of 1933, that eased Adolf Hitler's assumption of absolute power. Pacelli was and remained throughout the war more than a *sotto voce* anti-Semite. In a letter later discovered in the Vatican's archives, while papal nuncio in Germany he wrote that "the Jews were responsible for the Bolshevik Revolution and are in control of the Soviet Union." Doubling down, he blamed the Jews for the creation of the capitalist system as well, describing them as "troublemakers."

As the wartime pope when the Jews of Europe were in their greatest peril, he assisted those who were of "the same stock as us," namely Italians, but like the French, the rest were expendable. The colleague's book not unsurprisingly failed to find an Italian publisher but the information he had rooted out reached historians beyond the Vatican's confines. Many of the stories saw print; all were predictably dismissed as anti-Catholic, as "faulty revisionism" and, in the words of one critic, "blasphemous." Once the accusations were made, however strident the Church's criticism of them became, in the world of serious scholarship they had found traction.

Father Angelo was profoundly disturbed by the Church's wartime acquiescence to the forces of evil. He had great difficulty reconciling himself to its record of accommodation with the murderous secular regimes that brought destruction and ruin to the nations of Europe and visited genocide on the Jewish people. He viewed the Jews as the elder brothers of the one Church. As a child, he had many Jewish playmates and neighbors. Yes, he'd heard an occasional anti-Semitic remark uttered by some friends. He'd even laughed at some of the more clever offerings. But Michaelangelo Lorenzo knew well that if he repeated them, his mother would wash his mouth with soap. At seminary, he took singular pleasure in debating the anti-Semites, his virtuosity, his record of verbal victories the pride of his teachers who admired his skills but, nonetheless, rarely shared his views.

As he rose rapidly within the Vatican's vast bureaucracy, he began to gain a reputation as a philo-Semite. This reputation proved to be not a black mark but a mark in his favor as he was chosen by Pope John Paul II to assist in preparing his statement on the Jews, read aloud during John Paul's famous journey to Jerusalem in 2000, five years before his death, during which he asked forgiveness for Christianity's transgressions. For Father Angelo Lorenzo, the Jews were just Jews, an ancient people who survived in part because Rome always harbored the hope that they would one day see the light and accept Jesus as their one and true savior.

In his heart, Father Angelo knew the Church's dream was a pipe dream, one never to be realized. These were an obdurate people, obstinate and resistant to conversion, arguing religious meaning and belief among themselves more fiercely than with outsiders. If all belief in the Almighty and the precepts of Judaism were lost or forgotten, it was more than likely the doubter would fall away rather than join another faith. The prevailing view, expressed succinctly by a Jewish friend of Father Angelo's who, upon learning his first cousin had converted to Catholicism, remarked, "our loss is your loss, Angelo." The native intelligence and industry of many and their accomplishments were legion, an indisputable fact. His own father, Silvio, never sought medical advice from a Christian doctor if a Jewish doctor was available. Nor did his priest son, taking a page from the medieval popes themselves.

But despite his efforts as the head of the Vatican's Committee on Jewish-Christian Reconciliation, he was to this day constitutionally unable to fathom why the Jews failed to see the ultimate truth in Christ who, after all, was one of their own.

It was not their dogged adherence to their religion, or their questioning, or their endless interpretations of their scriptures that in any way altered Father Angelo's respect for those he considered his Jewish brethren. After all, religion was barely a major consideration in this age of secularism for Rome's own Jews. The differences between the two cultures were minimized even further by the daily onslaught of modern life. No, there was something entirely separate from religious differences that irritated him about his colleague, Dr. Paolo Pisa, aka Moshe Josephus, an affectation that grated like a burr in a shoe.

The evening prior to his departure for Israel, Father Angelo dined with his parents, his two younger brothers, and their families. Alfredo, his brother Giancarlo's youngest son, he of the spiked hair of indeterminate color, the earring, and a smart, whipping sarcasm sharpened by his addiction to American television programs, took pleasure in goading his uncle.

"Israel again, Uncle Angelo?" he said, feigning exasperation. "What is it now, your umpteenth visit? And they haven't made you an honorary citizen? Shame, shame! When're you gonna convert, give up the Church?"

Silvio reached over and gently but firmly yanked his grandson's ear.

"Hey, you watch your mouth! You're talking to a priest! Even if he is your uncle!" he snapped.

"Yeah, Papa, yeah, yeah, I was only kidding," Alfredo said, rubbing his ear, feigning hurt, winking at his uncle.

"It's okay, Papa," Angelo said, laughing, affectionately squeezing his nephew's shoulder. "It's a valid question. Almost."

"So what is it, Angelo, why're you going this time, a mission for Rome or the university?" Silvio asked, glaring at a smirking Alfredo.

"A little of both. I'll be in Tiberias for maybe a week. The antiquities people found something they think is significant and they want me to have a look at it ..."

Silvio interrupted his son's explanation, as was his wont, a Lorenzo family tradition. If a question popped into his father's head, a *non sequitur* maybe, irrelevant or not it was posed a millisecond later. It could be about the Euro's value, or the insoluble trash situation in Naples, or the parking, or how every other driver in Rome was an imbecile even though Silvio no longer drove, the subject hardly mattered. It was a question and to Silvio all questions were pressing so it had to be asked immediately.

"The Israelis know Jesus was Jewish, yes?"

His father's questions were growing more absurd, his rapid aging more apparent lately.

"Of course they do, Papa," he replied gently.

"And will your ..." Silvio paused, searching for the appropriate term, "your nemesis be there, this Pisa?"

"I assume you mean Professor Paolo Pisa?"

"You know exactly who I mean," Silvio replied. "Forgive me for saying this, but Christ, I saw him on television a couple of nights ago. He seems like a nice man. Smooth, quick. He was on, what's the name of that show? Something about ..." Silvio stopped, frustrated. "I can't remember what I was going to say ..."

"He's not my nemesis, Papa. We're, uh, friendly rivals, different birds often landing in the same nest. Sometimes we agree, other times not. He's very direct, never minces a word. Very self-assured is Dr. Pisa."

"He's a Roman, Angelo, he's from here, no different than you before you entered the seminary. Is he married, has he a family? He's Jewish so he probably does, eh?"

Angelo considered whether Silvio meant this as a veiled recrimination, a slight for his having taken the priest's vows. But he thought not. Those sorts of barbs were never hurled at him. He had in his early years coveted women, even lusted after them but his religious calling was such that he overcame the powerful pull of what he knew were natural desires. It surprised his parents when he turned to the Church, perhaps even disappointed them but they managed to keep whatever disappointments they harbored to themselves. Both parents accepted his life's choice the moment he announced his intention. No, Silvio's queries were just an old man's disparate, tenuously connected thoughts; he was sure that's all it was.

"Not that I know of, Papa, but I'll make it my business to find out when I meet up with him in Tiberias," he said, trying to shift the conversation in another direction.

Not dissuaded, Silvio launched into an all too familiar tale, the October, 1943 roundup by the SS of Rome's Jews, the waiting trucks, engines running, a few courageous neighbors, their faces tear-stained, standing on their balconies waving goodbye. Silvio repeated the story more often lately, increasingly tormented more than he realized by the memory, repeating it so frequently that it had become a litany, the end of which tonight left him alone at the dinner table but for Angelo, his son's hand holding his, comforting.

"Very direct," Angelo thought to himself, turning the words over and over, a euphemism that held several meanings. Paolo Pisa was, as his father remarked, a Roman kid, a Jewish kid, his personality not dissimilar from others in the city and certainly an easy, comfortable fit with the brash, even more direct Israelis. Where Angelo was often a dour, respected presence at professional convocations, Paolo Pisa was animated, viewed by many of his more staid and far less successful academic colleagues as a showman, a purveyor of oversized coffee table books rather than a serious scholar. Not a few were dismayed that Paolo Pisa's scholarship always proved unassailable.

Angelo was not among Paolo's carping academic detractors. His complaint was personal. It was Paolo Pisa's personality that so abraded Angelo's nerves. He, Angelo, was a party man whether inside or outside the Church. He'd followed the traditional path to erudition and acclaim, to a professorship at the university. He had given up family for Mother Church. Perhaps he wasn't, like those carping colleagues of his, free from jealousy. Perhaps at a deeper level he too resented Pisa's fame, his lifestyle, the generosity of a supportive father who'd made his fortune selling olivewood boxes and relics from the Holy Land. Perhaps it was the irony of it all that occasionally took his breath away. He was used to dealing with princes of the Church, many of whom had clay feet.

But for Father Angelo Lorenzo it was far more difficult, painfully difficult having to deal with the likes of Dr. Paolo Pisa, whose mannerisms reminded him of a Florentine nobleman from the era of the Medicis. But Pisa was somehow different, almost unique. His urbanity was evident whether he spoke Italian, Hebrew, Greek, or charmingly accented English. He navigated through life as a skilled mariner might an unfriendly sea. His television and convention audiences were seduced by his words and phrases, his rivals left squirming in their chairs, feeling somehow inferior, their eyes burning with envy, consoling each other in the hope that each would live to witness the celebrated Dr. Pisa stumble and fall. Paolo Pisa, for his part, was hardly free of antipathy towards his critics. He harbored the unshakeable notion that the professional jealousy, the backbiting had its origins in his origins but he was mistaken. The resentment was born of his unrivaled success in the field in which they all labored, where the recognition he garnered was almost a lion's share. Surely he knew that in the world in which he lived and worked, he would never be given a free pass or forgiven. It was an article of faith in academia that it was never enough for one to succeed. One's enemies must also fail.

CHAPTER SIX

Angelo remained seated, in place, attentive to the weather reports that were being updated every couple of minutes. More peals of thunder exploded overhead, rattling the hotel's windows, followed by sheet lightning, momentarily turning night to day, illuminating Tiberias' waterfront. Paolo stood, staring out of the misted window.

"Whew," he exclaimed, "the docks're under water, the rowboats've been tossed onto that restaurant's terrace. I couldn't see the tables or chairs, though. Gone to sea, I guess. Looks like a couple of palms have been uprooted, too. What an unholy mess, if you'll excuse the expression!"

Angelo grimaced, wondering "if we drown tonight, will it be Pisa's work that is remembered?" He chastened himself silently. For a priest, jealousy was an impermissable sin. No, he decided, he was unable to answer Paolo's earlier question as he might have done if Paolo was a fellow priest. How to phrase a truthful response, a response that wouldn't sound hurtful - this eluded him. His priestly training, his share of confessions taken in the confessional had taught him to carpenter his words carefully.

He knew he'd have to be evasive and that discomfited him. He owed Paolo an answer, as truthful a one as he was able to deliver. He stood and placed a hand on Paolo's shoulder.

"You asked me a question before that I failed to answer. That was rude of me. My apologies."

"Forget it, Angelo, it was nothing," Paolo said, waving off the apology.

"Unimportant. Just one of my all too many ruminations. It requires no further comment."

"But it does for me, Paolo. It was an honest question and it deserves as close to an honest response as I'm capable of giving."

"Well, ..."

"I've noticed over the years," Angelo began, "that you extend yourself and your work to a public far beyond academia, and through your work you've popularized the work of many of us. For which, with a few exceptions, we are, or certainly should be, grateful. You're a very popular guy, colorful, while the rest of us are - gray, backgrounders. By all measure, you should but you appear to be close to no one, almost friendless or at the very least, you've no close friends, certainly none in our field." Angelo realized that he was speaking rapidly, sounding much like a lecturer, more like a scold. He paused, took a breath, continuing, more slowly and evenly. "I've observed this for myself at conferences, on digs, even when we were at university. You seem unreachable, above and away from the rest. It's almost as if you've imposed upon yourself a ... an isolation, a distinct, conscious distancing of yourself from any of us." From everyone, he thought.

After a moment's consideration, Paolo spoke.

"I've got to admit there's more than a grain of truth in what you're saying, Angelo," he admitted equably, more than Angelo expected he would. Angelo had feared Paolo would take offense and when he hadn't, he was relieved. "While we're at it, in the interests of truth-telling, I always thought— and correct me if what I say here is baseless— that you occasionally dismissed my research out of envy for my success, my popularizing. Whether I'm right or wrong in thinking that that's the primary reason, it bruised me. Deeply. Maybe my ego got the best of me, whatever, it's been known to happen." He laughed. "More often than not. I'm sometimes not as thick-skinned as I'd like to be. Who knows? I'm only going by what I've read in the journals, mind you ..."

Paolo was interrupted by another clap of thunder, a piercing lightning flash lit up the suite. Angelo blinked and flinched, momentarily blinded by the light, focusing intently on Paolo's words. "But," Paolo went on, smiling, "there's always a *but* with me, Angelo. If we don't survive this hellish night, I want you to know that however you think of me, I'll always believe, have always believed, that you're the greatest scholar of our generation. When you're sitting in Heaven and my books are being used to keep people afloat in this mess, yours will still be read . . . This isn't flattery, not in the least. I mean it, sincerely. Okay, enough." He raised both arms in mock surrender. "I've got a big mouth and ..." Paolo hesitated, momentarily unsure whether or not to proceed, then almost inaudibly, "You're right about the isolation,

56

Angelo, it's true, it destroyed my marriage."

"I didn't realize you were married," Angelo said, surprise in his voice. "We all thought you were only wedded to your work."

"It was when we lived in Jerusalem, commuting between Israel and Rome, selling the wares, 'internationalizing' was my father's pet term for it. I'd just gotten my professorship. She was quite beautiful but ...her name was Leah. Is Leah," he repeated, as if confirming her existence. "She was born here in Israel, in a displaced persons camp in 1950. Her parents were classic *yekkes*, Berliners who survived the war. Like my parents, they were hidden by neighbors, a real life drama. And like mine they managed to beat the odds. Never recovered, though, never adapted, tried to recreate their German past in Tel Aviv of all places. Her father tried his hand at importing furniture, mostly heavy, pre-war stuff from Gennany. He succeeded for a while but ultimately the business failed.

"The post-1956 immigrants wanted something different, something lighter, something that didn't remind them of where they'd been, where they'd run from. Not Leah's family, though. They lived in a dark apartment, too, made even darker by that cherished furniture, the heavy, maroon velvet drapes, like shrouds that shut out all light, and the Persian rugs that smothered every surface. You'd never have thought you were in Tel Aviv. Looked and felt like a movie set from the Thirties. It was a tomb, a cheerless, living tomb. They just never let go of the past. Imagine. Anyway, her father passed the rest of his life as the head bookkeeper in some department store on Dizengoff where his wife worked as a saleslady. Keeled over at his desk, aged 52. He was working late as usual, proofing the books, so he wasn't found till the next morning."

Angelo nodded sympathetically.

"They hated me, of course. A Jew, yes, but an Italian, certainly not what they'd envisioned for their precious daughter although German beaus were, shall we say, in short supply in Israel." Paolo pinched the bridge of his nose, shaking his head as if to dispel an unwanted thought. "And my parents hated them with their Teutonic pomposity, their clinging to the old ways-the best ways, they would insist-the ways that but for the courage of their neighbors would almost certainly have assured them an inscription at Yad Vashem. Whenever we were all together, which thankfully was rare, my father seethed to the point where I feared he'd have a stroke but he managed to hold his tongue, though how he did so remains for me a mystery to this day. We were young, so in the face of all this familial opposition and hostility, we ignored the pitfalls, married, had one child and not long after, a messy divorce."

"Where does the child live, Paolo? "

"She doesn't. Shana was killed in 1994. On patrol along the Lebanese border. A sniper's shot. Her unit's only casualty."

Angelo instinctively reached out, clasping Paolo's hand in his.

"Leah never recovered, slipped into a deep depression. In and out of hospitals to this day. She lives, if you can call it living, in Tel Aviv, in her parents' old, airless apartment, surrounded by photos, memories, whatever. Being in that flat only makes it worse, but for her it's a link to what was for a while a better time. But who am I to judge, eh?" Paolo, his eyes glassed over, wanted no answer. "Something died in me when Shana was killed. So if I die tonight, if this storm washes me down to the Persian Gulf, well, so what?"

"Paolo, I'm so very sorry," Angelo said, gently adding, "May she have eternal life."

The hotel's PA system cut in, announcing, first in Hebrew, then in English, that everyone below the fifth floor must seek shelter above the ninth floor.

"We have rooms to spare," the announcement continued. "You will be assigned new rooms. Use the stairs in case we lose electrical power. If you need help with your luggage, call down, we'll send someone to assist you. We apologize for the inconvenience. Breakfast will be served at 8 A.M. in the ninth floor's conference room."

Paolo snorted a laugh.

"God forbid anyone misses breakfast."

It was 3 A. M. With the streets of Tiberias already flooded, the exits to the underground garage, with its cargo of drowned cars within, were impassable.

"I'm spent," Angelo said, heading for the door. "I have to

lie down, get some rest. All this has taken a lot out of me. Not as young as I think I am … or want to be."

Four hours later, a weak sun peeked over Jordan's hills before disappearing again behind a widening curtain of rain. Paolo heard a loud, disembodied voice in the hallway outside the suite, braying, "This is Israel. We can handle anything."

"Bullshit!" Paolo said, half to himself, shaking his head at the false bravado, unawares for a moment that Angelo had awakened and rejoined him.

"I don't think you'll find that reference in the Torah, Paolo," Angelo smiled. Paolo slid open the terrace door, surveying the damage done below, before retreating to the room as the rain moved westward once more. The shrubbery was torn up, power lines knocked down, crisscrossed with countless uprooted palms lying haphazardly across the street fronting the hotel. Glass in sheets and shards from broken windows and shop doors carpeted every surface, glittering briefly in the quickly dimming daylight. Angelo picked up the remote and turned on the television. The news wasn't good; the live pictures transmitted from strategically located security cameras were chilling.

The ancient Crusader port of Akko was under three feet of water and enormous waves were still breaking on the city's seawall. The hilltop section of Haifa was safe. Along the Golden Coast, the towns and cities of Caesarea, Bel Yanal, and Netanya were inundated. Further south, Jaffa, situated on high ground overlooking the Mediterranean, was spared the brunt of the storm but Tel-Aviv, with its beachfront hotels, looked as if it had suffered a series of bombings. All hotels had their windows smashed, their curtains fluttering through their frames like so many flags whipping in the high winds. The sea had generated waves of tidal proportions; a small river flowed down Ben Yehuda Street, cars spinning without direction, at the mercy of the currents created by the onrush of rising Mediterranean waters and the hurricane force winds that accompanied them.

Whenever and wherever a camera could focus in and provide a close up, the common facial expression caught was one of shock, utter disbelief. Thousands, perhaps tens of thousands struggled towards higher ground in what could only be described as a mass exodus on foot, the roads and highways washed out, the mobile rescue services long since overwhelmed by the enormity of the monster storm.

In Gaza, the images were heart-wrenching. Over a million Palestinians, penned into an area twenty miles long and four miles wide, flat as a pancake and living for the most part in jerrybuilt housing, saw many of their poorly-constructed sandstone-and-brick homes collapse, unable to withstand the pressure visited upon them by the Med's raging waters.

The IDF acted immediately, opening the security checkpoints to free up access to Israel and, at Rafah on Gaza's southern border, the Egyptians removed their border barriers. Many who fled only found what they had left, rising and entrapping seawaters. Some made it to their small, foundering boats at Gaza City's port while others clung to homemade rafts, anything that might float and offer salvation should the storm weaken or change course. The catastrophic horror of the storm was accentuated when news spread that hundreds trying to escape through tunnels dug to smuggle weapons and suicide bombers into Israel proper had drowned. Either the tunnels collapsed, crushing them under the weight of the support beams or the water rose so quickly within them, as if a sluice had been opened, had been trapped and dragged under. An exact death count would never be posted.

As a macabre coda to what occurred in Gaza, the strip's coal-fired power plant, the main supplier of electricity to the beleaguered tenitory, exploded as seawater seeped into its transformers. The cataclysmic blast sounded as if a torpedo had struck a supertanker, the explosion was so profound and deafening. Several days later, the Israeli government, the Palestinian Authority, and Hamas roughly estimated that 190,000 Gazans had perished in the first two days of the storm.

Paolo and Angelo stared speechless, dumbstruck by the realization of how extensive the totality of the catastrophe they were witnessing was. Paolo thought of the late Itzhak Rabin's perhaps apocryphal comment, made in the midst of one of Yasser Arafat's *intifadas,* that he dreamed he'd awake one morning and Gaza would be gone, sunk into the sea. His wish, seventeen years after his assassination, was apparently coming true.

Angelo picked up the remote and switched to another station, catching the end of a report from the United States about four cruise ships plying the Arabian Sea. All had foundered and capsized, their lifeboats useless, victims of rogue waves. Three thousand or more passengers were added to the storm's growing casualty count.

"Tragically," the reporter intoned, "no rescue was possible."

CHAPTER SEVEN

At 8 A. M., the suite's intercom instructed all those in rooms facing eastward and the Galilee to cross the hallway and move themselves and their possessions into any empty room on the hotel's west side.

On his way back to his room, Angelo heard a guest complain bitterly about breakfast being cancelled. He laughed quietly to himself as he let himself into his room. "Ah, perspective," he thought, "a rarity in our times." He made a mental note to report what he'd heard to Paolo.

An hour later, Paolo knocked on his door. He found Angelo genuflecting in prayer, saying the rosary, passing the small, blue stones through his fingers. Paolo seated himself, waiting for Angelo to complete his prayers, impatient and anxious to follow the storm's course. As Angelo completed his devotion and stood stiffly, Paolo turned on the television.

Somehow a local TV crew managed to boat into the Negev where most of its residents were now high above sea level. The Negev's configuration was a huge, natural conduit, greeting the waters that rushed seawards through the West Bank, swamping Ramallah, Jericho, and Hebron, through the Judean Desert, raising the level of the Dead Sea on its eastern side, and running rapidly under and around the plateau upon which Masada stood to its west. Several *kibbutzim* and the small towns of Sodom, Ein Hatzeva, Sapir, and Samar disappeared as the waters spilled into the Gulf of Eilat.

"A wall of water ..." the reporter in the boat said, the phrase already made trite by constant repetition. Occasionally a hand-held videocam captured the fleeing, their faces contorted in blind terror.

The military coordinated their reports with the newsmen in the powerboat. Their camera spoke through live coverage where words inevitably failed. As the waters slashed through the Judean Desert and the Negev, the bobbing, endless stream of cars, buses, military vehicles, trailers, broken-apart housing, dead livestock, light poles, Palestinian and Israeli flags and tumbling, bloated bodies, the corrugated tin roofs of Bedouin shacks spinning in the current like a top, the debris of the West Bank on the move. Head scarves now wrapped around the legs of dead Palestinian women somersaulting by, children, men old and young, piled together in an endless chain of corpses, pushed and pulled by the waters southwards. The still living clung desperately to wood, planks, and other detritus torn from their homes, others to the occasional trunk of a tree, a few grasped inner tubes, hoping against hope to survive the storm. A veritable army of humanity, dead and barely alive, together raced helplessly towards the Gulf of Eilat and onwards into the Red Sea. In the cruelest of ironies, their course would in time pass nearby the holy site of Mecca, because of the storm no longer distant from the refigured Saudi coastline.

Concerned with the political aftermath once the storm and flood ended, the IDF cut off the Negev transmission. They feared that the resulting fallout would falsely claim that the Jews survived, while the Palestinians were left to perish. The IDF knew from bitter experience that in the region, reason rarely prevailed, emotion almost always trumped logic, even in a shared disaster of such enormity.

The reality, the truth was that both Palestinians and Israelis lost their lives, the dead from both entwined; those living along the Jordan from Galilee's tip to the Green Line had drowned as well. The television screen blanked, replaced by a test pattern. Paolo switched to CNN but their onsite coverage had ended, replaced by a talking head, filling airtime, jabbering from the safety of CNN's high and dry Atlanta studios.

"The whole damned country's heading south, Angelo, and we don't need the TV to tell us what we know. This place could collapse, too, you know. Sandstone's not granite and Tiberias sits on a fault line ..."

"No need to remind me.•We'll be safe, Paolo. We'll be safe," Angelo repeated confidently. "You must place your faith in God. And hope Dimona's safe," he added, "or we're all lost."

Several days would pass before everyone learned Dimona and its atomic reactor near Beersheba at the entry to the Negev had emerged from the catastrophe dry and unscathed. Luck, good fortune, preserved by fate. A tidal wave washing through its nuclear power plant would have resulted in a critical melt down, its consequences more dire than ten Chernobyls, the Holy Land rendered an uninhabitable wasteland, a macabre peace between its warring parties finally achieved.

Paolo grunted, non-committal, his faith less in God than in himself, his survival skills. Irreligious to a fault, he saw no profit in argument, or contradicting Angelo. Pointless exercise, sophistry at best. Let him believe what he believes, he decided, if it comforts him.

* * *

The greatest storm ever recorded had in a few days transformed the Middle East's topography, and beyond the coastlines from the southern tip of Israel to Iraq, from Iran eastwards to and through the Indian subcontinent, and finally the islands of Indonesia. While the alarming forecasts of global warming's impact predicted a profound alteration of the coastal regions in this extended tip of Asia, few could entirely grasp the import of the reports of the mass dislocation of millions, the destruction and death, numbers that rivaled those lost to the Black Death. The mind, unaccepting, simply shut down when confronted with such staggering figures. But what the catastrophe presented to the observer was a vast remaking of the world, a harbinger of the future, a future where most of the world's population would live as they had since ancient times, less than a hundred miles from the water, the patterns of settlement near the oceans and seas and along the world's rivers.

Images of chaos and destruction were not novel to a jaded world. We'd grown inured to disasters. They had become commonplace, expected, practically scheduled events. The world experienced catastrophes on an annual basis, predictable as the seasons, captured live by cell phones and television cameras, hurricanes in Florida and the Caribbean, the swath of devastation in Katrina's wake in New Orleans, earthquakes in China, Turkey, and Iran, the tsunami in Southeast Asia, all offered up *ad nauseam* by scores of network and cable stations for the tireless viewer. These were all memorable as was, for the true believer, the biblical Great Flood. Since for most of the world's population

65

these events occurred elsewhere, not in their own backyard, they were by that very fact unthreatening. But this was something new, something viscerally frightening, something almost impossible to conjure with, a global scale disaster, the scope of which no one could have predicted. The two Italian scholars, with their keen knowledge of the past, knew instantly that the forces of nature had changed their and everyone's world forever.

CHAPTER EIGHT

On Day Four, the storm over Israel weakened, losing its force, the rain turned from an incessant heavy fall into a persistent drizzle; the storm's lethal winds, according to the weather station's anemometer atop a peak in the Edom Mountains, were more than those experienced during a category five hurricane. A new category would have to be created. The winds, exceeding two hundred twenty-five miles per hour with even higher gusts, brought with them storm surges greater than seventy-five feet. The once-shrinking Dead Sea, where tourists floated upon its mineral-rich surface and plastered their bodies with its healing mud at the lowest point on earth, thirteen hundred feet below sea level, was unrecognizable. It had been restored to what it may have been during the time of Christ. The forty-six-mile-long sea ran across the valley, separating the Edom and Moab mountain ranges, swallowing anything and everything that once surrounded it.

When daylight broke on the fourth day, US, Russian, and Israeli spy satellites peered from space, transmitting images back to their respective home bases. What could not be seen from the ground was defined by the images from space. Vast portions of the Negev were no longer desert but sea and there was little to distinguish the Dead Sea funnel that ran down through the Gulf of Eilat into the Red Sea. The waters had reduced arid Saudi Arabia to three-fourths of its pre-storm landmass, replacing land with a surrounding sea that linked the Red Sea to the Persian Gulf which also had increased its width, obliterating all its southern coastal towns. Oil production in Saudi Arabia, Iran, and Iraq ceased, their facilities and those in Kuwait and the Gulf States were lost to the salty waters, swamped, no longer functioning. They would ultimately recover but their recovery would be measured in months, not days and weeks. The blow to the oil-producing nations was profound, the ripple effect of such a loss portending a worldwide economic collapse, an imminent reality. A halt in a dependable oil supply from the Middle East foretold factory shutdowns, transportation disruptions, spiraling costs for everything produced under the sun, and all that followed such disasters— violence, anarchy, mass movements of population— a scenario that was being played out simultaneously in the world's major financial capitals, east, west, north, and south.

At the UN, which had been in continuous session since Day Two of the storm, world leaders met in the glare of cameras, deliberately speaking in measured, calming terms, forced smiles creasing their reassuring faces. Behind the scenes, where all major decisions were made, recovery plans were put in motion, aid packages constructed, verbal agreements concluded to staunch an odds-on global meltdown. Yesterday's bitter enemy or *demagogue du jour* knew he or she could ill-afford such a consequence. A worldwide recovery plan was mercifully taking shape with stellar speed.

The fate of Jerusalem, the jewel in the crown of the world's three major religions, concerned many, not least among them Dr. Paolo Pisa and Father Angelo Lorenzo. Had it survived as the IDF reported? Were the fates kinder to it than they were to other, lesser holy sites in the neighboring nations? It was with great relief that they learned later in Day Four that its ancient walls, built by the conquering Muslims a millennium earlier, protected it. The ravines siding the Mount of Olives had flooded; King David's city was under water. But the thick, stone walls of the Old City held firm and withstood nature's wrath. As in Tel Aviv, the windows of many of the hotels were blown out, as were many of those of the Knesset. But the destruction was comparatively minor, the damage done to the city's western sections reparable. Jerusalem, with the notable exception of the washed-away Arab market running through the *Carda,* the city's heart, suffered little in comparison to other towns and cities, its casualties miraculously limited to one hundred twenty-six lives.

The lights dimmed in the Radisson, brightened, then dimmed again, the portable generators still hit-or-miss. It would be several hours, perhaps even days, before full power to Tiberias was restored but at least one could be thankful that the incipient panic that rose with the Galilee's waters had dissipated. Through the softening rain, Paolo could make out the silhouettes of the tourist boats, their diesel engines fired for three days running, all the nautical skills of their captains employed to keep them afloat and underway, if only sailing in circles. The water hadn't receded significantly nor would it for no one knew how long. It lapped against sides of the lakeside structures, the fallen trees and the streets strewn with glass Paolo had seen just yesterday deep under turbid flow, no longer visible. The water had leveled off at a height where it was now possible for the smaller of the tour boats to sail parallel to the Radisson's first floor terraces and take on passengers to rescue.

Over each room's intercom, the hotel manager could be heard calling all to attention. "There is no need to panic," he announced. "The worst of the storm has passed over us," he continued, stating the obvious, "and the boats will evacuate us to safety. "

"Safety?" Paolo arched an eyebrow, quizzically. "Where's safety?"

"You must put your faith in God and the Galilee pilots," Angelo said, resting his hand on Paolo's shoulder. "Be more optimistic, my friend."

"I'm by my very nature a pessimist. Or more precisely, I'm a realist. It's in our bloodstream. This is a maybe, maybe not situation we're faced with here, this so-called evacuation to ... safety?" he snickered, squinting, "My father was a pessimist, used his wits to survive. He lived to return to Rome, worse for wear surely, but alive, in his ninth decade now. The optimists? Their ashes are mixed together in mass graves in Poland. Always keep a suitcase packed, Angelo, because you never know what's coming next."

"Perhaps you're right." Angelo's shoulders slumped with fatigue. "I'm tired and admittedly ...frightened."

"We both are. Let's get our stuff together for the cruise to ... safety," Paolo chuckled sardonically. "Just essentials, cell and umbrella and one change of clothes."

"And my Bible," Angelo said. "I need nothing more."

* * *

As they walked down the dimly-lit stairs to the first floor landing, joining the single-file of guests boarding the boats that would ferry them from the Radisson, Paolo managed to connect by cell to his parents in Rome. The news was both good and bad. They were safe, dry, though Rome was a debris-ridden mess, the Tiber's flooding the immediate cause. Its bridges did not give way, fortunately, but floating cars had piled up in waterlogged Vatican Square. North and west of the Alps, the sun shone brightly but Holland's enormous sea dikes, built after the great North Sea flood of 1953, were overtopped and failed, the North Sea submerging much of the lowlands. More than a third of the country, including The Hague, was under water. Belgium's port of Ostend, but for its cathedral's roof and spire and the northern coast of France, including the lower stories of the fabled seaside monastery at Mont St. Michel, lay under the ocean's waves. While the Arno had swept through Pisa and Florence, as they already knew, the art treasures had been previously secured. The Leaning Tower leaned a degree or two further but no more, the repairs made years earlier proved to be adequate.

"You should see this mess yourself, Paolo," Guido exclaimed. "Boats, army boats in the streets, patrolling for looters. What looters? What's left to loot?" he asked absently.

"Looters always find something, Pop. Who knows what'll float and where it comes from and who it belongs to? Wet fingers can be sticky, too."

"The Jerusalem factory's ruined, all that olive wood, the boxes ..." Guido's voice trailed off.

"So, the factory'll dry out and you'll replace what's lost. There's still plenty of wood left in Israel. I haven't heard of anyone building an ark ..." Paolo joked. "It'll dry out, don't worry. This is a desert, remember? We've got the workers, Pop, you'll make more boxes ..."

Long retired, Guido in his own mind thought of himself as still in the mix, still working although Paolo's brother and Sandro's son had assumed direction of the business a decade ago. But Paolo, dutiful son that he was, would never consider disabusing his father of his fantasies. Denied them, Guido Pisa would die.

"How is the priest, Paolo, how is he doing?"

"Fine, Pop, but he's not a young man ..."

"Neither are you, Paolo," Guido reminded him.

"I'll call you when we reach Jerusalem, Pop," Paolo laughed, ending the call, turning to Angelo. "Did you get through?"

"Yes, yes, they're fine, the both of them. He's complaining about the Euro and what it won't buy. I've heard this song before, the one about the Frankfurt bankers manipulating the rates, etc. He thinks they're all Nazis in silk suits ..."

"That generation, they never change. My father goes on about the pope, calls him HYP."

"HYP?" Angelo seemed baffled.

"Yes, the Hitler Youth Pope ..."

"That's unfair," Angelo bristled, defensive, his face flushed. "The Holy Father's a good man, a fair man. Those were the follies of youth in a hell that permitted no choice ..." He hesitated a moment, then waved his hand, annoyed with himself. Two no longer young men, standing together in a dim hotel stairwell awaiting rescue, drawn into talking about their parents and the emotional baggage carried with them. "Ah, why are we talking about this anyway? We're becoming like them, fighting the old, unwinnable battles ..."

"It doesn't matter how old you are, or what you've accomplished," Paolo said. "If you're Italian, you may be a prince but in the end you're still a little boy to them."

Angelo smiled, nodding.

* * *

One by one the guests crossed a makeshift plank onto the boat, helped by the hotel staff and a contingent from the Israeli navy that managed to make its way to Tiberias. The boat's bow pointed north, rising and falling slightly, secured to a brace of terraces by cables, its steel hull grinding against the hotel's wall. All aboard were issued life jackets and instructed to grab the rails firmly. Angelo was assisted aboard and given a seat towards the wheelhouse.

"You'll be fine, Father," the sailor said. "Everything's under control."

"Bless you, son," Angelo said reflexively.

A half hour later, the boat fully loaded, the cables were cast off and the deck-mounted Japanese diesels roared to life. As the boat slowly gained headway, successfully fighting the southward running current, sailors with long, steel poles took up positions in the ship's bow, pushing aside the tangle of debris as they turned west on Ha-Yarden Street, past Tiberias' industrial quarter and the abandoned bus station, before turning again onto Yehuda Ha-Levi where the captain cut the engines back to idle. Behind the newly created shoreline, IDF half-tracks, the desert warfare personnel carriers, were parked, waiting to take the disembarking passengers and those in the following boats to higher ground, up in the muddy hills to the government quarters. One of the several tanks deployed by the IDF as backup should the half-tracks lose traction climbing the hillsides' soft earth was already in service, towing a stalled half-track behind it.

Fifteen minutes later, they all found themselves in the main government building before a long table handling the registration of the evacuees. Each was given a boxed lunch, a cup of coffee, and instructions.

"Families and friends must stay together," a young soldier said, "and make sure you go to the assigned building."

When Angelo's turn came to register, he handed over his passport.

"Ah, an Italian," the soldier said. "From Rome, I'll bet."

"Yes, from Rome," Angelo replied, aware that his clerical collar probably gave him away.

"Lovely city," the soldier said.

"I hope it will remain so."

"It will," the soldier winked. "It's eternal, isn't it?"

The passport scanned, the computer spit out an ID bracelet.

"Put this on your right wrist, Father."

"Just in case?" Angelo asked.

"Just in case. But as you can see," the soldier said, "the rain's practically gone, some lingering showers maybe, nothing more."

Paolo's turn came and he produced two passports.

The soldier glanced at both, then studied Paolo's face, asking, "Which is it? Israeli or Italian?"

Paolo groaned inwardly, concerned that he would once again be subjected to a time-wasting interrogation.

"I'm just kidding, Dr. Josephus. I know who you are,

you're the TV guy, the art specialist. My mother loves you."

The soldier was preparing to continue the conversation when he was interrupted by a senior officer.

"Cut the bullshit, Tal. Are you blind? Look at the line already ..."

The soldier punched in the information and moments later Paolo was securing his bracelet as well.

The Israeli nationals were shunted off to a local school, the foreigners to the courthouse, where they were given blankets and, for those in need, dry clothing.

Angelo asked an IDF soldier if he thought it appropriate for him to ask those in his group if he should offer up a prayer of thanks.

The soldier grinned, saying, "Of course, Father, this is the Holy Land after all."

Most in the group, mainly the Europeans, a clutch of Japanese, and a gaggle of Korean Christians on a pilgrimage, urged him on. The Orthodox Jews from Antwerp, in Israel on a buying trip, shrugged their approval. Sensitive to the larger group's diversity and loath to offend, Angelo decided against offering up a Mass. Instead, he chose something more ecumenical, something more inclusive.

He introduced himself, careful not to reveal that he was part of the Vatican's inner circle or why he was in Israel. He concluded correctly that all would assume that he, like them, was either on a pilgrimage or merely touring. He reminded his audience in a voice riddled with exhaustion, that, "the will of God is greater than our own and we were among the most fortunate ... the flood which has brought so many so much suffering has not discriminated between the good and the evil." Then, remembering the words of John Paul II, he continued, "Perhaps we've been poor stewards of the Earth but out of this catastrophe there will certainly come a healing ..."

He looked up then, surveying the group, and opened his Bible. His first reading was from the story of Noah, his last taken from the Book of Job. He ended his brief sermon by offering heartfelt thanks to the Israelis who had "risked their lives to save us all." As a priest, he felt it incumbent upon him to recite the Nicene Creed, that in Christ all could find salvation. And prayed that none among them would be offended by his words. If there were objections, none were voiced as the room fell silent, the believers' heads bowed in prayer in the small building high above what remained of the modem city of Tiberias, near Cana where Jesus had performed his first miracle, as told in John 2:1-11 the changing of the water into wine.

The service over, Father Angelo Lorenzo collapsed onto one of the many army cots supplied by the IDF, his tattered Bible his pillow, his intent to hear Confession thwarted by fatigue, and fell into a deep, dreamless sleep.

The skies had rained themselves empty, the heavens from Germany to Italy to Greece cleared as another front, this one originating in Kazhakstan, pushed down from the north. The storm had passed.

CHAPTER NINE

From civilization's dawning, the world's people settled along the coastal regions and the river valleys, guaranteeing themselves access to water. This pattern continued well into the nineteenth century when the advent of the steam engine and the structuring of a reliable transportation system permitted populations to move beyond their immediate sources of water. Even today, if one views the Earth from space, this pattern of settlement continues, from Australia to Asia, through Africa, along the Mediterranean and Europe, even in North America and South America. The majority of the world's people still live less than a hundred miles from a body of water, whether it's a major river, a sea, or an ocean. All human settlement, whether it be in Europe, the Arabian peninsula, Southeast Asia, Indonesia, or the island chain of Japan, is thus subject to nature's whims, vulnerable to the incursions of the warming seas and oceans. Stories of the wrath visited on humanity by the waters that surround us fill human history.

* * *

At many conferences, some attended by either Dr. Paolo Pisa and/or Father Angelo Lorenzo, the participants were constantly warned of the potential consequences of the measurable warming of the globe, particularly the waters that covered most of its surface. The attendees at these highly publicized meetings— scholars, government officials, UN representatives, Nobel-winning scientists, the usual suspects— were informed and warned time and again that the world's peoples were in imminent danger, that a global catastrophe would produce tens of millions of refugees.

Over fine wines the world's experts discussed the surge of populations since the beginning of the nineteenth century when it was estimated the world held a billion souls. History told us that the world's population had always grown but nature had inevitably restored the balance, kept such growth in check through famine and pandemics such as the Black Plague that wiped out a third of Europe in the thirteenth century.

By 1927, the world's population had reached two billion, thirty-three years later, in 1960, three billion, fourteen years later four billion. By 1999, four billion had blossomed to five billion. Arithmetic progression had been supplanted by geometric progression, the time span between each added billion shrinking rapidly. Alarmingly, the life-sustaining heavy industries created to meet these burgeoning populations' needs and demands caused a heating up of the earth's atmosphere. In turn, this warming of the atmosphere ripped gaps in the Earth's protective ozone layer. Worldwide weather patterns were consequently altered, the warming atmosphere causing a steady, inexorable melting of the North Pole and breakdown of the North and South Atlantic glaciers. This, in turn, caused an incremental rise in ocean and sea temperatures and their levels. Startling aerial shots of emaciated polar bears stranded on breakaway ice floes bore witness to what none could deny. No advanced scientific degree was needed to draw the obvious, grim conclusion about mankind's future on earth.

Father Angelo Lorenzo had always adhered to the belief, supporting Rome's position, that the furthering of life on Earth was paramount, that nature would, as it always had, restore the balance even if the world's population doubled again by mid-century. But along with other foreigners jammed in the courthouse, the past few days had badly shaken his faith in nature's restorative balancing act. All around him voices discussed, argued, and speculated. Some, a very few, disputed or dismissed global warming as the primary cause. Many of the American Jews were defensive, attributing it to cyclical weather patterns, ignoring the industrial nations' role in adversely affecting these weather patterns. Many of the Dutch and German tourists assumed the moral high ground, placing the blame squarely at the feet of the US, China, and India for heating up the world with inordinate greenhouse gas emissions, their unchecked materialism, their obscene hunger for profits, ignoring their own and their European neighbors' complicity in bringing on the calamity.

From the back of the room, an American voice

denounced all of Europe as "one big pain in the ass, especially the French. If it wasn't for us ..."

Paolo glanced at Father Angelo, shaking his head in a show of dismay and disgust, knowing how the speaker's sentence would end, like the priest, an unwilling, trapped listener, wishing he were elsewhere. The old arguments, the calumnies, the finger-pointing, running around the deck as the boat sinks beneath them, no thought of rescue but searching instead for someone to blame for the misfortune. What drivel, he thought, why can't people think things through? It's all been documented; global warming had achieved the status of an article of faith and yet even among the educated, the intelligent, there were doubters, Flat Earthers. He believed the cleric would probably agree.

The Japanese and Korean visitors maintained a polite silence, finding the name-calling foolish, rude, while an Orthodox Jew with a diamond-filled briefcase chained to his wrist opined that the storm was surely the judgment of God, punishment for all our mindless hedonism. Two weeks earlier, Father Angelo Lorenzo might have joined his voice to that of the merchant. Two weeks ago they all— believers, doubters, and disbelievers— lived in a different world.

* * *

As the senseless debate around them ebbed and flowed towards no conclusion, on the generator-powered television a BBC reporter was painting a dismal picture for the world's economy in the near future. On the eve of the storm, the price of a barrel of crude oil had settled at $116. At the close of business on the fifth and last day of the storm, it had rocketed to $300. Nearly all of the pumping stations in Saudi Arabia, Iran, Kuwait, and Iraq were underwater, he repeated, and over half had exploded, belching black, lethal smoke into the air above them.

"By the most optimistic estimates, it will take months before the stations are online and pumping again," she said. "Russia, Nigeria, Venezuela, and those unaffected areas of Azerbaijan are working up to full capacity to supply as much of the world's needs as is ..."

In Washington, the president announced that he was

ordering the immediate release of oil from the strategic oil reserves to alleviate the crisis. He announced he was on his way to appear before Congress and demand that all environmental constraints on offshore drilling and mining of shale be lifted until the emergency was over. America applauded and by day's end, the protective restrictions so carefully crafted over several decades were set aside by a compliant Congress. The NYSE, which had dropped precipitously during the storm— over 1,600 points on the third day alone— recovered immediately and climbed to within forty points of its pre-storm high within two trading days, mostly on the strength of the major oil and oil service companies' projected gains.

Next to appear on the screen was the UN's Secretary-General, surrounded by representatives of the world's major religions. The scene was as impressive as it was reassuring to many watchers.

"This should have happened a hundred years ago," Father Angelo whispered to Paolo, as the UN chief proceeded to tell the world what most either suspected or already knew.

"All estimates of human losses are of course based on unconfirmed reports our office has received," the Secretary-General's voice flat, emotionless, "but permit me to reveal what we know at this time. Before I do so, I have with me the exalted personages from ..."

As each was introduced, he or she offered prayers conveying the essence of their particular beliefs. Only the clergymen from China and Vietnam were dressed as civilians, a nod to their doggedly secular nations. But they, too, presented a message similar to the others. The world was broken and it was imperative that all governments must work together to repair it.

More reports drifted in. Lebanon had lost twenty-five thousand people; Bangladesh, with its 360 mile-long coastline, suffered the loss of nearly six million out of its populace of one hundred twenty-seven million. Death had reduced Pakistan's population of one hundred thirty-eight million by five million, while in Iran and its neighbor Iraq, two hundred thirty thousand and eighty-five thousand succumbed, respectively. No news emerged from Oman on the Musandan Peninsula nearby the Straits of Hormuz. Saudi Arabia, with much of its twenty-one million inhabitants living in towns hugging its shoreline, had imposed a news blackout and scrambled all incoming satellite transmissions. Outside estimates conservatively predicted the kingdom's losses at 2.8 million Saudis. While all the estimates were by their very nature at best rough, none could seriously discount how staggering the cumulative end count would be.

As the Secretary-General, like a metronome, ticked off the statistics, each was met with "Oh, my God!" sobs, and other expressions of grief and disbelief in the crowded courthouse.

The television screen suddenly went black as one of the generators failed.

"It's a small mercy," the priest, sighing, said within earshot of Paolo. 'The news is ...unbearable."

"A *mitzvah*, the failing of a generator, but a short-lived one. It'll be up and running again in a minute. His point is well taken, millions gone, why is he persisting with this tolling? Enough already. No one's sitting here keeping score ..."

"I have to leave this room, Paolo, and get some air. I'm having difficulty breathing ..."

"I understand. Here, take my arm ..."

The priest gripped Paolo's elbow and stood, following him slowly through the door to the still-slick sidewalk fronting the courthouse.

"We're in for a very rough time, Angelo. Governments always move at a glacial pace. Warnings as we know are sloughed off until the wolf, so to speak, is nudging the door open, ready to spring. Instead of grabbing a shotgun, most times they grab a broom. Impending crises always seem to be met with ineffectual half-measures." Paolo snorted with contempt. "This isn't an impending crisis, is it? This is a crisis, *the* crisis, the worst the world's ever faced."

"Well, I wouldn't go so far as ..." Angelo began to say, but Paolo pressed on, as if he were lecturing a student or addressing a stodgy conference, gathering steam, waking them up, intent on presenting his thesis, what the future held for them all.

"The storm's unleashed what the Germans call *Einwandern,* immigrants, millions, tens of millions of them, in fact, to contend with. It may translate as "immigrant" in literal German but it's used as a pejorative, meaning something, um, unkosher, something vaguely illegal. You can imagine the reception they'll receive, huh? Who'll feed these *Einwandern,* house them, put them to work? At what? Who and how, and how quickly? Do you see the opportunity all this offers our terrorist pals among others, this unleashing of chaos? It's dizzying. Angelo, *amico mio,* you may be in unwitting agreement with bin-Laden or the Hassid in the courtroom on this one, that this is all God's punishment, the will of Allah, Yaweh's wrath, the price of Westernization, whichever, take your pick. Our allies, our good friends in America ... they know, they know the price of oil is the least of what's facing us."

His piece said, Paolo paused, drew a deep breath.

"Always the pessimist, Paolo, as I've said before," Angelo said. "Well, I'm not sure I'd agree with bin-Laden even on this matter. It wasn't unforeseen, admittedly, and perhaps it could have been averted if we'd paid heed to the Holy Father's warning not so many years ago ..." He looked directly at Paolo, drawing his companion's attention to his words. "But that's, if you'll excuse my clumsy metaphor, water under the bridge. Why would God punish so many of the innocent for the sins of others? Yes, I know, the Holocaust, the Black Plague ... History serves to contradict faith at every turn but there must be a greater purpose in this, somewhere ..." The priest was faltering, tentative, at pains to convince himself that he truly believed what he was saying. Was he now only reciting a lesson learned long ago, one that had lost its force, its meaning, its inherent truth? "Perhaps some good will come of this, Paolo."

Paolo looked away, gently disengaging himself, studying instead the brightening afternoon sky.

CHAPTER TEN

By the time the men returned to the courthouse, its power had been restored along with the television picture. The Secretary-General had turned to the Middle East, broadening the context to underscore his remarks. He noted that once more the entire region had been torn apart, this time by nature, not warfare. He named the areas hardest hit, the cities bordering the Tigris and the Euphrates, the states situated on the Arabian Sea, the oil-rich nations that made up the United Arab Emirates. The Secretary-General noted that while the suffering inflicted by the storm was unequal, suffering was suffering, the only difference a matter of degree.

Israel's neighbor Jordan experienced several serious population dislocations, the onrushing waters carrying most of the overflow below the Golan Heights to the north into the Wadi Rakad, the Yarmuk, and the Jordan River itself. Further south, the southern branch of the Yarmuk, the Kabbok, the Amon, and the Zered poured into the great rift. Amman lost several of its buildings to flooding but most residents made their way to the tablelands above the eastern bank of the Dead Sea.

The rocky Jordanian heights rose almost a mile in some areas while through the canyons that separate them the waters wended their way into the gulf. The Jordanian port of Aqaba ducked the damage visited upon its wealthier Israeli twin, Eilat, sitting beyond the razor-wire border fence a few, short kilometers to the west.

"Close call, eh?" Paolo said to the Israeli soldier standing next to him. "Abdullah and the rest of the royal bunch must be thanking their lucky stars. Or Allah."

The soldier acknowledged the comment with a polite nod.

The Iraq War's refugees, hundreds of thousands still living in tents two years after major hostilities had ceased, were less fortunate. Even experts declined to guess how many went missing when the Tigris and the Euphrates turned their campsites into watery gravesites. The Mediterranean coastal strip from Latakia in Syria to Haifa in the south was drummed down by the storm. The most conservative death toll numbers posted topped thirty-eight thousand. Beirut, still recovering from the 2006 war between Hezbollah and Israel, the rubble cleared from its boulevards, the shell-pocked buildings repaired and refaced, would have to rebuild again.

"Ships with medical supplies and food are on their way from France," the Secretary-General said, adding hopefully, almost absently, "I understand that all the coastal cities are not beyond salvaging and repair."

The next face behind the UN's lectern was Egypt's ambassador, a portly man clearly reluctant to deliver the devastating picture of his nation's fate. Most of Egypt's seventy-five million citizens continued to cluster as they had done since ancient times along the Nile's banks. But the Nile was, as were the other rivers, an ever-present sword of Damocles, liable to fall upon those who planted the fertile fields it irrigated. Tie undone, sweat covering his brow, the ambassador leaned into the microphone and, with a slight tremolo shaking his voice, confirmed that the news from his homeland was "not good. The flooding that began in Nasser in the south gained too much ... "he paused, gathering himself. "The Aswan Dam ... it held." Turning to the Russian ambassador, he permitted himself a small, appreciative smile. "But it was ultimately breached. The momentum of the waters has caused a breach in Cairo's walls and I just learned it has also spread through to Alexandria. The delta is ..." He stopped abruptly, his composure gone, and handed the microphone back to the Secretary-General. Lowering his eyes, the ambassador sank into his seat.

The Secretary-General turned as an aide mounted a map of Israel on an easel beside him and handed the diplomat a pointer. Gaza and the West Bank were delineated by a green line.

"The Israeli ambassador informed me that the rapidity with which the storm struck prevented his government from assisting in Gaza's evacuation," he said, looking down at his listeners from the podium. A murmur of disapproval swept through the hall, many doubting the ambassador's explanation of the evacuation delay in spite of the evidence of their own eyes. "The ...," he paused, searching for a neutral term, "the

82

predicament in Gaza is similar to that of Ashkelon and Ashdod," he continued, tapping the pointer on those northern Israeli cities. "The wall of seawater swept across the plain, trapping everyone in its way. But with the storm's slowing, efforts are underway to transfer children and the elderly to temporary shelters near Beersheba."

"How many died, sir?" a reporter, identifying himself as a representative of Canada's CBC, asked.

"No one can say with any accuracy ..." "A, uh, ballpark figure, sir, please?"

The Secretary-General winced, unwilling to venture a guess.

"Sir?" the reporter pressed. "A number?"

"I'm afraid I can't say," he responded plaintively. "Do numbers really matter anymore?"

Normally unflappable, he was, like many of his compatriots in the yawning hall, beginning to unravel. "It saddens me to inform you that Gaza is no longer habitable. So from that statement you can draw your own conclusions."

The reporter turned off his recorder and sat down.

"Earlier in the day I met with officials of the United States, Russia, Sweden and Norway. Each has agreed to absorb a substantial number of Gazans. Norway will accept 25, 000 as will Sweden. Russia and the United States will take in twice that number although we've yet to work out the details." He turned to the Israeli ambassador. "We do not need another refugee crisis in the area to add to the one we've always had," he stated pointedly. "A fleet of ships sailing under the UN flag are being dispatched to Ashkelon to bring those willing to safety ..."

The negotiations had been conducted in the greatest secrecy as are all negotiations of such import between Israel and its neighbors, neutral or hostile. So the announcement came as no surprise to the Israeli ambassador who had been key to securing the Israeli government's approval of the plan earlier in the day.

In the Tiberias courthouse, someone commented sourly that "We're finally rid of them." The remark was met with loud disapproval from a middle-age French couple nearby.

"Do you know what you're saying? That's what they said about us seventy years ago."

"So what? This is different. They're different from us."

The Frenchman began to answer, then decided to let it go, sighing and passing his hand over his face, as if trying to erase what he'd just heard.

"What's happening in Israel?" someone shouted at the screen, as if the Secretary-General was present in the room. "Tell us what's happening here?"

"What does he think's happening?" Paolo said angrily to Angelo. "All he's got to do is look around."

All one need do is recall the previous days in Tiberias or listen to the television reports for a general picture of the storm's depredation. Apparently the shouter needed official confirmation, his mind like many of his compatriots closed off, incapable of imagining or accepting the worst, the reality that they faced. In fairness, they were confined within the four dun-colored walls of the courthouse's main courtroom. And like soldiers in trenches aware solely of their immediate surroundings, they knew only what had happened around them. Israel's television stations had been placed under the IDF's authority and that authority was exercised to censor, cognizant that any report of weakness or details of destruction might embolden Israel's enemies to launch a preemptive strike.

The odds of such an external assault, or even an internal uprising, were minimal, less than zero. Considering the nations of the Middle East had suffered massive losses of life and property and military hardware, even the thought of an attack was preposterous. Half the West Bank and almost all of Gaza were floating bone yards. But the ever-cautious IDF concluded that reducing the odds even further was the most prudent approach. At the very least, it bought time to plan and organize a defense should one of their enemies decide to pursue such military folly.

On the screen, the Secretary-General again tapped the map of Israel. Suddenly, the censors acted, terminating all transmission. A message appeared on the blank screen, confirming that the report had, for security reasons, been censored. Other channels were tried but each posted the same message. Using their satellites, the IDF ordered the jamming of as many Arab stations as they could, knowing all the while that their efforts to blanket the Middle East with a total shutdown would be futile.

"Jesus Christ," an IDF soldier exclaimed in English,

throwing up his hands in disgust, instantly grasping what the IDF was up to, the reason for the shutdown. "What are they doing? Do they think the Arabs can't phone the information in from London? Or Paris? Or New York? Even if they can get through which is doubtful. And what're they gonna do, the Arabs, send their tanks? What tanks? Now? What, Hezbollah's fleet of rowboats? Everyone's trying to save themselves! Arseholes!" A rumble of agreement spread through the crowd. As if the IDF censors overheard the soldier, the television picture magically reappeared to a smattering of applause and sarcastic remarks from the gathering.

"Someone must've seen the light. I mean, how stupid can you be? What are they worried about?," a woman said, "We're all in the same boat"

* * *

At the UN, the Secretary-General was describing the loss of several buildings in Tel Aviv's Bauhaus Quarter and the consequent loss of life both there and in the seafront hotels. Pointing to the map once more, he drew a circle around the Sea of Galilee.

"A blue basin, the sea is twelve miles long and six miles across at its widest point. The waters from the mountains flowed into the sea, then into the Jordan Valley, through to the West Bank, spilling into the Dead Sea ... Jordanian authorities provided us with an estimate: two hundred thousand dead but ...," he paused, searching for a phrase to put a positive spin on the profoundly negative number, "estimates are often exaggerated. I would prefer to call it a guesstimate." He smiled, a hopeful note in his voice. His listeners shifted uneasily in their seats.

"So to say," one whispered.

"Within the 1967 Green Line ..." The Secretary-General was interrupted as a sheet of paper from the Israeli ambassador was handed him. Reading aloud, he said that while material damage in the area was great and dislocations plentiful, "less than ten thousand Israelis were killed, perhaps less, those limited to the towns in the Lower Galilee, along the coast, and Afula in the Jezreel Valley..."

"Those numbers sound low," Paolo said.

The IDF soldier, British-born with a Manchester accent, the one who'd voiced his anger at the censors, responded.

"I spoke with my brother this morning," he said, holding up his cell phone as if verifying he'd actually done so. "He's a damage assessment guy, works for an insurance company when he's not called into the emergency communications center in Tel Aviv. He said once the wind velocity increased past 180 kph, thousands fled to the bomb shelters. In spite of warnings to the contrary, they're airtight, just in case of a gas attack. They proved to be floodproof, too. Lucky ducks, that bunch. Most of the others made it to the high rises, the ones built with Jerusalem stone, rock solid like Masada, not like those shitholes the Palestinians throw up," he added contemptuously. "They're no better than the tents they used to live in. A lot of people cut by glass but better to bleed, eh? If you're not bleeding, you're dead, right? Jerusalem's pretty much okay, my brother said. Some mudslides in East Jerusalem, the Arab market, yeah, but everything's pretty much still standing."

Paolo was weighing what the soldier was telling him, trying to slice through his youthful bravado and conjure an image of what might greet them when he and Father Angelo Lorenzo finally reached Jerusalem.

"The Negev's one unholy mess, my brother says, almost a complete washout, never figured out why people are crazy enough to live there anyway. Farmlands are pretty much gone, useless, but what he says is interesting. We got drenched here, yeah, but east and west the water rocketed through but once it recedes, maybe early next week, Sodom and maybe even Gomorrah will rise above the waters again ..."

"Yes, Genesis 19, Verses 24-28, an appropriate reference for this disaster," Father Angelo chimed in.

The soldier rolled his eyes, the priest having completely missed his lame joke. Onscreen, the Secretary-General confirmed in detail the intelligence the soldier had received from his brother, that the walls of the Old City had withstood the storm, that the Old City save the market were safe, and the Western Wall, the Temple Mount, and Jesus' purported last resting place were soaked, needed pumping out, which had already begun. In Bethlehem and Nazareth, the Churches of the Nativity, the Annunciation, and the Basilica needed extensive repair and renovation but structurally they remained sound. All were spared the fate of countless other of the Middle East's holy sites. Even Mohammed's Tomb in Mecca was allegedly half-submerged but since the Saudis refused onsite reportage, including helicopter flyovers, the tomb's true condition remained shrouded in mystery. No Western nation still dependent on Saudi oil would dare make public satellite photos taken from space until given the green light by the House of Saud.

The Secretary-General turned a reporter's query about Mecca away with a shrug of his shoulders, referring him to the Saudi ambassador sitting in the first row.

"I've heard nothing further," the diplomat responded dismissively. "Has the Hajj been cancelled?"

The question was as provocative as it was rhetorical. A quick look at the aerial photos answered it. Mecca could only be approached by air. Or boat. The storm and its attendant floods effectively cancelled the annual pilgrimage of flocking Muslim millions. But the Saudi envoy stayed the official course, masking the reality with bravado and continued denials.

"I've had no confirmation that it was cancelled," he replied.

"I suppose then Satan's safe from another stoning this year," the reporter murmured, unheard by the TV audience though just loud enough for his seatmates to hear and chuckle over.

The Tiberias courtroom fell silent as the Secretary-General stepped back to the podium, checked his watch, and began droning again, finally turning the stage over to the leader of the Greek Orthodox Church to offer a universal prayer. As they sat back down on their cots, Angelo spoke first.

"Listen, even the drizzle's stopped."

"Amen, Angelo, God's been good to us."

"Is that really you speaking, Paolo," he asked, unsure, his brow creased with doubt, ' "or are you having fun with me?"

"It was me. It's been a long day, longest I can remember."

Sleep was virtually impossible. Amid the snoring and the oversized court clock ticking off the seconds like minute hammer blows, neither man could drop off.

Paolo turned on his side, addressing the priest.

"Are you still up?"

"I can't sleep either, too many distractions here. It reminds me of summers when my parents sent me off to camp, up near Balzano by the Swiss border. It took an eternity to fall asleep."

"When you're young, four seconds are an eternity. At least it always was for me." As the room darkened, both men slept fitfully, minds wandering, chewing on the what ifs that made up their pasts. Father Angelo Lorenzo had been blessed with luck his entire life. His only brush with death came when a wall in a dig at Megiddo collapsed moments after he passed along it. Three had died but Father Angelo emerged unscathed but for a bruise where an errant brick had struck him, knocking him cold for an hour or two. For this, he often offered profuse thanks heavenwards. He knew in his heart that God's hand had reached out and brushed death aside for Angelo Lorenzo that day.

As a respected churchman, and an archeologist of considerable reputation, he had made the Holy Land, as had Paolo Pisa, his life's work, obsessively studying every aspect of it. There were times he believed he knew every stone, every water tunnel, all of subterranean Israel, so to say— its prehistory, how fact and legend intertwined and were absorbed into the Book of Revelations itself.

In the darkness, in his half-wakened state, he took stock of his life, its meaning, his work. The dinners at the Vatican, his love for the late Pope John Paul II struggled with his difficulty accepting the way the Church's old guard was pushing that beloved pontiff unceremoniously towards sainthood a mere six years after his death. He felt bothered by the unseemly haste.

"Are you still awake, too, Paolo?"

"Haven't slept a wink," he replied, his eyes wide open, inclining his head in the direction of a snoring German couple three cots away. "They sound like buzz saws, those ..."

"Our soldier friend isn't doing badly either," Angelo whispered. "And he's asleep standing.

"When I was in the IDF I learned how to do that, too," Paolo grinned. "It's useful in times like these. Ah, I can't wait to get out of here."

"Patience, Paolo," Angelo said quietly, as if he were advising a student. "Tell me, if we'd have been swept overboard during the rescue, and we had drowned, have you thought of what you'd want the world to remember of you?"

Paolo pondered for a moment, then replied, "It's a game

for aging men, isn't it, these thoughts, for those of us with more behind us than we care to admit and an uncertain future ..."

"*Tempisfugit*. That's the meaning of the skeleton in the Vatican's main hall, the one with the hour glass. A constant reminder. Life's temporal, the Church eternal. No need to remember what will always be there ..."

"Not that old saw, Angelo, please. We're only grains of sand, specks in God's eye? Listen, Schliemann will always be remembered for his discovery of Troy, his illuminating of how the ancient world operated, giving us Homer, too. But us, well, I'll have to give you that. All the books, the television, the fame is ... temporal. We dig, we find oil lamps, mosaics, whatever, admittedly some important discoveries but ..."

"I won't be remembered, Paolo, I'll make no great discovery, something my name will always be attached to. No Dead Sea Scrolls for me, I'm afraid."

"I believe you've just committed the sin of pride," Paolo needled him. "But your secret's safe with me."

The soldier they thought asleep was now standing above them.

"People are complaining, please be quiet," he said in his normal speaking voice, waking the woman on the cot behind Paolo's.

"Sorry," the cleric apologized.

Both men got to their feet and fumbled their way towards the dimly lit courtroom door. Once outside, they found two chairs as a waning moon peered from behind a cloudbank, illuminating the men's faces. Nearby, a guard's cigarette glowed.

"Have you never thought the same thought, Paolo?" Angelo continued, pressing.

"Of course I have, countless times. Just the one big one, that's all I want, all I need. If I was religious I'd have made a deal with the Almighty ... using the name Moshe Josephus, of course."

"You shouldn't joke about such matters, Paolo," the priest scolded him.

"It's only half a joke, Angelo. Like you, I've been at this for nearly half a century. We occasionally though not often trod the same path, you and me. Great acclaim, honorary doctorates, television interviews, whatever. I've read Josephus' *The Jewish Wars* to the point where I can almost recite it by heart. Sometimes I think of it as my personal *Torah*. If I was confident it wouldn't cause another world war, I'd dig for Herod's treasures, right where the Temple was destroyed, under the Dome of the Rock. As a kid in Rome, my father used to point out the bas-relief on the Arch of Titus, with the Roman soldiers carrying sacred vessels and candelabra into the city, the victors' spoils. Imagine how much else they made off with, from the Priest's Court, from the Holy Place by the nave, from the Court of the Women. But even invading armies always leave something behind, fragments, artifacts, perhaps writings they deemed useless, impossible to peddle, not worth the effort to steal. Or maybe like the scrolls someone secreted something somewhere, some treasure hidden in a hideaway. I'm only speculating but …"

"Speculation often leads to discovery, my friend."

"Can you envision what the Temple looked like from the Judean hills, Angelo? A Jewish version of the Vatican or the Pantheon. Seven years, that's all, seven short years before it was razed. I've been told that the few Jews who live off the Algerian coast still wear black stockings in mourning …"

"I hadn't heard this," the priest interjected. "Interesting how faith persists in such unusual, out-of-the way places. An island off Algeria …"

"Josephus writes— I'm sure you've read this, Angelo— that Titus came to the gates and offered to spare the Temple and the city, to strike a deal. He spoke directly to a Hellenized Jew, Pineas, the Temple's treasurer. Pineas figured if he gave Titus gifts, particularly gifts made of gold, the Temple would be spared, Jerusalem would be left in peace. Pineas misjudged Titus' greed. He accepted the gifts and added them to the swag, whatever he could get his paws on, including the contents of the Holy of Holies and whatever he could mine loose from the subterranean passages and wherever else his armies marched. But, still, he couldn't have carried it all off …"

"I've asked many of my Vatican colleagues if these relics removed from the Temple are in our collections or hidden away or if one could trace them. Everybody tells me no. If they ever existed, they've long since disappeared. In fact, in 2007 a sonar search of the Tiber was conducted …"

"Yes, yes, I know," Paolo cut in. "We brought it up on

the King show last year, remember? Some rusted Fiats, a German personnel carrier, one of our WWII tanks and one of theirs, old *lira* with Mussolini's image stamped on them, mainly worthless junk. Nothing more ancient than an Olivetti from the Thirties with half the keys missing," he laughed. "Nothing from the Temple, though. I'm not a suspicious man, Paolo, but if my friends know something or know someone who knows something, they're sworn to secrecy, secrets they'd never share with me .... Greed's a terrible sin but it's probably more common than any other we commit ...."

"Given the pressure exerted lately on so many great museums to return art acquired by, um, questionable means, so many works of suspect provenance. And with few exceptions, the museums' resistance, the kicking and screaming, well, what else can we attribute it to? Art stolen by the Nazis, much of it hanging on private collectors' walls or hidden in bank vaults in Europe, in Asia, probably in America, too, all kept from public view. Museums the world over, the Met in New York, the Belvedere in Vienna, others throughout Europe and elsewhere, all having to return purloined works to their rightful heirs. These, the last century's thefts, are almost dwarfed by the theft of national treasures during imperialism's heyday. Egyptian stele, Cleopatra's Needle, standing in New York's Central Park? If these so-called European conquerors could have figured a way to do it, they'd have trucked the Parthenon, the Sphinx, whatever could be moved, home with them. One of these days, the British Museum will have to give back the Elgin Marbles. But I'm sure they've got enough in the basement to cover the discolored walls where they're now bolted in ..."

"Yes, agreed, "Father Angelo said, nodding his head. "You certainly won't get an argument from me."

"And if lsrael recovered the Temple's treasures, do you think for a moment they'd display them in the Israel Museum alongside the Dead Sea Scrolls? Not one chance in a million they would. No, the ... ultra-orthodox," Paolo's face contorted as he spit out the words, "they'd want to rebuild the Temple exactly where the Second Temple stood, where the Dome of the Rock now stands. Remember the uproar when the Israelis began replacing the rotting bridge that crossed to the Temple Mount, the protests, the rock- throwing, a baby *intifada*. And over what? A safety issue, nothing more, a bridge that could snap like a twig at any moment. If the Palestinians viewed that as a provocation, what do you think the decision to rebuild the Second Temple would spark? Not only in Israel but throughout the world of Islam?"

"It's something neither of us want to contemplate, of that I'm sure. But, then, the ultra-orthodox are gaining in political strength, and numbers, as we in the Church have always known, count mightily when it comes to political decisions."

"True enough, but it's not something we'll have to deal with decisively, so to say, for a few years yet. And who knows yet how this storm and the floods will alter the political landscape. Ah, we can argue the political prospects into the next decade. Frankly, I'd rather concentrate on our immediate prospects, what we might come up with. That water channel, the one cut through stone under Jerusalem?"

"Yes?"

"I'm more than convinced Pineas and his friends managed to smuggle out valuables— how many, worth how much, that I don't know. Given the time, whatever they salvaged probably dates back to the First Temple, the Temple of Solomon or— maybe I'm fantasizing here— Moses himself."

"Go on," the priest urged, drawn in by Paolo's conjectures.

"You just have to know where to put your shovel. Why did we come here, Angelo? Some workers found a manuscript, under a seat in an ancient theatre, perhaps a passion play from the era of Paul. We won't know until we examine it ...." Paolo was suddenly taken up short. "My God, what if it's lost? That possibility escaped me ...."

Angelo was reassuring.

"The storm, for all intents and purposes, was kind to Jerusalem, Paolo. I believe you're worrying unnecessarily. I'm sure it was stored in a safe, secure, and dry location."

"Yes, of course, of course." Paolo breathed his relief. "My pessimism kicked in again, that's all."

"You were saying ...."

"I'd put my shovel in the Kidron Valley's gravel, below the First Wall or near the Pool of Siloam where the tunnel exits from the platform under the First Wall. For the sake of argument,

92

say I found copies of the Tablets or a copy of the Genesis Scroll. But it'll be tricky, this sort of dig. It's sacred ground ..."

"I know," Angelo said. "It's a huge necropolis, perhaps thirty feet deep in parts, and the graves are arranged in layers that precede Herod's rule. And, since the seventh century, it's been a Muslim grave site..."

"But what a find it would be, eh? The find of a career, every other find either of us has made paling before it .... Sorry, I was getting carried away. Had to censor myself from elaborating when King put the question to me. Fame is often a welcome gift but I don't want you to think fame is all this is about, Angelo."

"I never said it was, Paolo. I am, though, very curious about what you do think this is all about. For you, I mean. What's it all about for you."

Paolo cleared his throat, marshalling his thoughts, warming to his subject.

"Israel's provided me with a profession, one that it's unlikely I could've had elsewhere and one that has ... that goes to the very core of who I am or who I think I am. I want to return something, something more than attractive coffee table books that decorate people's living rooms. This country, as much as Italy, is my land. Like Rome, for me Israel's eternal. As a people, we've echoed over time in a way unmatched by others, a chain from ancient times to today, a chain almost broken by Hitler. I know you believe, believe deeply in the Resurrection and what it offers those who believe in Jesus. For us, the Jews, the state of Israel represents our resurrection. Our people have been resurrected and our history, more than bleached bones and fragile artifacts, is the foundation upon which Israel rests. What I'm saying in too many words is that my late-in-life's dream is a dream of return. Or more precisely my returning with unbounded gratitude something priceless to my land, a gift from its own history. And you, Angelo," he added softly, "I know you don't wish to pass forgotten. Have you a dream, a wish to see fulfilled before you pass?"

"I can't say ..." Angelo replied, open-palmed, the first light of dawn shadowing his face. His friend's question perplexed him. Paulo Pisa had a unique ability to discomfit Father Angelo Lorenzo with queries that unleashed in him a nagging doubt. His dream, his wish doubtlessly mimicked in part Paolo's but he left it unspoken. Yes, he, too, longed to make a discovery so significant that its notoriety would assure him lasting fame while bringing honor and glory upon his beloved Church. But he'd assured himself that if he expressed his dream in such terms he'd look the fool in Paolo's eyes, even though he believed all men on God's earth shared a desire, however inchoate, to be remembered. He had almost dismissed Paolo as a showman, a glib mountebank. He realized now that he'd been sadly mistaken. This sudden diffidence was underscored by his realization of his misperception, what he believed, who the man actually was. What Father Angelo had just heard was an unsought confession. Behind the courtier's easy manner, the striking looks accentuated by the punishing desert sun, behind the veneer projected by Dr. Paolo Pisa to the world, there stood a deeply religious Jew.

If only he'd been more comfortable with his own desire for immortality, even in that limited way most men of stature— Father Angelo Lorenzo was surely a man of stature in his world— are recalled, referenced in encyclopedias, a list of websites when Googled, a book or two on a library shelf, their discoveries or their accomplishments noted, however briefly. What matter if their lives were reduced to a few lines? Surely such a wish couldn't be considered prideful by any objective measure.

Angelo dipped into his shirt pocket, picked out a cigarette, fired it up, drawing deeply.

"You smoke, Angelo?"

"Even a priest has his vices. Only once a week, though."

"Once a week?"

"Well, one pack a week then."

Both men laughed as they stood looking down upon Galilee's waters, shimmering in the early morning light, the shoreline extending hundreds of yards beyond what it had been days before.

"My father came to Israel regularly after the war," Paolo reminisced, "looking to set up a factory to process the olivewood artifacts, although to this day I'm sure he was looking for something else, something he couldn't or wouldn't define. Even before we settled here, he'd bring me along, only me, the second born. My siblings, even my mother, weren't invited to join us. The rest of the family found it odd, him choosing me over my older brother." Paolo shrugged. No explanation for his father's action suggested itself but for Paolo, the puzzling choice was one for which he would be eternally grateful. "What he was searching for, beyond a factory site, I can only make a stab at. He couldn't or wouldn't define it but I suspect he was on a quest for a connection to this land; something within himself drew him here. Although I do believe whatever it was, that which he couldn't put in words ... whatever it was, he wanted me to share it. Maybe he figured just by my being here, by observing, by listening, by sensing what surrounded me, it'd spark that connection, that sense of belonging, an affinity for the land. He's spare with his words is Pop, not a bit like me, very precise. Otherwise he's Italian to the core."

Paolo smiled at the recollection.

"He'd bought an old British Army jeep, drove like a lunatic and scared the hell out of me, still a child, up and down the coast, back and forth, west to east, wherever what passed for a road then existed. Zionists of the old school, Sabras, Europeans, displaced persons released from the Cyprus camps, a babble of tongues. Yiddish was by necessity the most common language although wherever you went you'd hear different dialects, scores of them ..."

Paolo swept his hand northwards, towards the Golan Heights, the high ground, the primary bargaining chip in the on-again, off-again peace negotiations with neighboring Syria.

"Remember the Hula, the lake north of Galilee?"

"Of course," Angelo said, "it was drained and the Dan and Paneas rivers were diverted."

"Which was why the flood moved with such speed. It was like pouring water from a bucket into a smaller bucket. Instant overflow. If the Hula had been left alone and the rivers followed their natural course, the flood might have at least been slowed. I'm sure it seemed a workable solution to the irrigation problems then, but ..."

"Disasters are always followed by ifs, Paolo. I don't know whether the story's apocryphal but the US Army's Corps of Engineers years ago had plans on the board to straighten the Mississippi ..."

"And cut a canal across Florida, too," Paolo added. "Why

is Man so intent on changing Nature's natural course?"

What neither man could see from their perch above Galilee was the terrifying extent of the flood's devastation. The lifeblood of the forests, their protection against erosion, the thousands of trees twisted and torn from denuded hillsides, joined by the precious topsoil, all sent hurtling southwards. Replaceable, yes, but not easily. Years would pass before the forests and the land around it were restored. In the eerily quiet morning, the two modern survivors of a flood of Biblical proportions silently surveyed the landscape.

Father Angelo sighed deeply, a compulsion tightening its grip on him as he struggled against it. Why not respond to Paolo's question? What profit is there in maintaining this gnawing silence? What is left to hide? His cigarette had died. He let it fall to the wet ground, crushing it beneath his sandaled foot.

"No danger of a forest fire," he said lightly, glancing at Paolo.

"None, Angelo."

"Paolo," he began slowly, his voice betraying a nervousness he rarely, felt, not even when offering up his sins in the confessional. "What I'm revealing to you I've never revealed to another soul."

Paolo nodded slowly, encouragingly, placing a welcoming hand on Angelo's arm. "You've said you're seeking a discovery rooted in your people's history, in the soil of the Jewish people. I share the dream but for reasons that are different from those you've chosen. I've read Sigmund Freud extensively, a good if not particularly observant Jew, more secular than religious, as you of course know. But he was a man content with his inner self, comfortable in his own skin as few of us are." Father Angelo's words flowed in a torrent now. "I count Sigmund Freud among my heroes. Hard to believe, I'm sure, but among his most acute observations, there's one that pertains particularly to men like me, priests, men of the church, celibates. Freud wrote that when one gives up life's natural pleasures, there must be substitutes. Perhaps those weren't his exact words but his meaning was clear. I don't want to be remembered as a good priest, true to his vows, a man who advised and dined with popes, or even a scholar with several highly-regarded, dust-gathering works to my credit. That's my other self, so to say."

"This dream, more like a *hope* of mine, may sound prideful and perhaps it is." Angelo paused, as if reconsidering what he was about to reveal. "But before I join the Lord, I want to live up to my name, my names— Michaelangelo Urban Lorenzo. One an artist, which the descriptive term 'great' is too pale, too inadequate; the second a pope, a Medici." Angelo averted his eyes, unwilling to catch Paolo's, fearing a look of disbelief, or worse, of ridicule from the younger man. There would be none. Paolo Pisa would not presume to judge Father Angelo Lorenzo. He well understood how persistent the dream of immortality was.

"Like you, I want to make one significant find, a find that will make my name famous, and bring honor and glory to the Church." He was almost stammering now, searching for the proper word or words to conclude his confession. "Some discovery so that my name will echo through time, a discovery that has to do with the death of Jesus." Father Angelo Lorenzo crossed himself mechanically. His face was drawn, his features pinched, clearly exhausted by disclosing his innermost desire to his companion.

"Do you have a target, an objective, something you believe could be uncovered, unearthed, retrieved?" Paolo asked, with no trace of irony.

Father Angelo pondered a moment, puzzling out an answer, a precise, unadorned answer to put before his friend.

"I would hope to find that one object, if God wills it, something from the Last Supper, and use the object as a cornerstone to ..."

"Give me a concrete example, Angelo," Paolo interrupted. "You're being vague. Which object? There were many ..."

Father Angelo cleared his throat, then continued.

"The *Crux,* the True Cross, the *Crux Immissa* or *Capitata.* Such a Cross, you know, replaced the hanging tree, the *infelix arbor* or the *infelix lignum,* the accursed tree. How delightful, how lovely it sounds in Latin, doesn't it? *infelix lignum."* Angelo added, "Mellifluous term when spoken, a sweet sound that to our ears disguises its true purpose."

"Nothing's lost in translation if you understand Latin, Angelo."

"Still ..."

"If I remember my lessons in the history of the Church, wasn't St. Helena accorded the honor of finding the True Cross?"

"Yes, yes, I know, it's Church dogma but I question it, that the Cross found by St. Helena was, in fact, *the* True Cross. But who am I, a lowly priest, to question such an accepted tenet of our faith?" Angelo parted his hands as if offering a benediction, a distinct, sarcastic tone to his reply.

"Now you're being disingenuous, Angelo," Paolo teased him. "You're hardly a lowly priest ..."

"I suspect you know well the story of the Cross, the fate of the Passion's symbols, the nails, the hyssop, the dice, the hammer, the crude ladder used to remove Jesus from the Cross, the crown of thorns ..."

Paolo was intimately familiar with the story of the Latin Cross as was every scholar of the era. Each detail had long ago been learned by heart, as one learns a prayer or a favorite poem. His own closely guarded opinion held that the artifacts from the Crucifixion, notwithstanding a landslide of bogus claims to the contrary, had been strewn centuries before to the four winds. But as a scholar, he was aware no proof existed to support his theory, either. Paolo decided to remain a willing listener, a sounding board for Angelo, as the priest slowly unwound, relaxing, at last in his element as he described the evolution of the legend of the True Cross.

"May third is the day on our Christian calendar celebrated as the day of The Invention of the Cross. Legend has it that Helena, the mother of Constantine, sailed to the Holy Land in 326 A.D. in her seventy-ninth year and, with the help of an elderly Jew, located the holy places that we revere today. Helena was said to have had at least three Crosses unearthed, each later confirmed by Byzantine ecclesiastical historians as true Crosses from Golgotha or Calvary. Each was verified by touch, and because of their provenance, each was claimed to have divine healing powers.

"The bishops of Jerusalem, Cyril and his successor, Macarius, further confirmed the Crosses' authenticity. The Church of the Holy Sepulchre was ordered built by Constantine to commemorate the discovery on the site deemed to be Golgotha, and a piece from one of the three Crosses placed within it. St. Helena's Chapel of the Invention of the Cross is situated there, of course. The remaining artifacts were packed off to Rome. The

Church of Santa Croce in Gerusalemme, the Roman basilica whose floor is covered with soil from Jerusalem itself—hence the name, was raised within her palace walls by Helena to house the relics. A so-called piece from the True Cross, a bent nail, bone fragments, a thorn or two, and the other alleged relics from the Crucifixion are still on display. And a finger from St. Thomas ... although I have my doubts," he added, smiling at his own quip. "The Crosses have had a checkered history, as you well know. One of the Crosses was carried off by the Persians in 614 A.D., and was ultimately returned to Constantinople, finally 'reappearing' miraculously in Jerusalem. That Cross later disappeared during the Saracen invasion of the Holy Land and St. Louis purportedly brought another of the Crosses to Paris in the thirteenth century. It's all quite a ... as the English say, a mingled yarn." Father Angelo paused, rubbing his eyes, trying to dispel his weariness. "Even the wood with the Cross maker's markings I.N.R.I that mocked Jesus as the 'King of the Jews,' that piece, too, with its Hebrew and Latin inscriptions, was sent by Helena to her son. In a Papal Bull, Pope Alexander II authenticated it but no one has seen it in generations. I certainly haven't."

Paolo asked a scholar's question.

"What wood was used? I've never come across a reference ..."

"Who knows?" the priest replied. "Jerusalem was covered with olive trees, cypress, pine, cedar, palm. Likely cedar, if I was to venture a guess, since it's as hard as rock."

"Probably," Paolo agreed. "Pine's too soft, olive trees are too small. There're not enough of them to make such a Cross. And the Romans were in a hurry. Aside from the one in Santa Croce, and the one in the Duomo in Milan, what happened to the other nails?"

"With the help of the old Jewish guide— by 300 A.D. many Jews had returned to the Holy Land— our history informs us that Helena recovered four nails. On her way back to Rome, her boat was caught in a storm. To calm the waters, she threw one of the nails overboard and miraculously the storm passed. We could have used a few miracle nails this week, eh? The fourth nail, or the nail believed to be the fourth nail, is in the cathedral in Treves in France. Some say there were fourteen nails, but that's patent nonsense. It does account, though, for the occasional claim of a fresh discovery of yet another 'true nail.' Fourteen nails? Absurd. The Romans weren't building bookcases, after all. They were crucifying bodies with as much haste and as little effort as possible. Four seems a reasonable number to me and to many of my colleagues even though Rome agreed long ago to set the number at three, two for the hands, one for the feet. It's the depiction of the Crucifixion we're familiar with from the great works of religious art. But if Jesus' feet were separated, as a few of us think they were, a position the Greeks refer to as *suppedaneum,* then four nails it would have to have been."

"The sun's up, Angelo, let's go get some coffee."

"Yes, finally, praise God. I must say my morning prayers but you go in, and I'll join you in a few minutes."

CHAPTER ELEVEN

Inside the courthouse tables had been arranged and food and coffee served. Paolo waited for Angelo before pouring himself a cup. Angelo appeared just as a senior IDF officer stood before the group and began rattling off instructions in English while the junior officers translated what he'd said into Hebrew. The cadence of his voice and the rings under his eyes testified that beyond their courtroom oasis, the situation in Israel was problematic. He sounds American, thought Paolo.

"Shalom! My name is Colonel Adam and when we get going, I'll be accompanying you. You'll be in good hands." He stopped momentarily to laugh to himself. Apparently he finds his own words amusing, Paolo thought. "I needn't tell you we've suffered extensively but the damage will be repaired and what needs to be, rebuilt," the colonel said confidently. "We haven't been washed into the sea and since you've all been glued to the television, you have a pretty good idea how bad it's all been and what we're facing. To make a long, long story short, if not painless, as I'm speaking ships are anchoring off Gaza and evacuating Palestinians, planes are ferrying supplies to the ravaged nations, and billions of dollars are being sent by the World Bank to speed the recovery. For reasons I can't get into here, our government has rejected all offers of assistance ..."

"Too many strings attached," Paolo said, under his breath.

"You'll all be our guests here for another night," the colonel went on, a statement that was greeted by assorted groans, "until we've cleared the roads. Tomorrow you'll be bused to the hotel where your luggage and whatever belongings remain, will be stacked by the hotel's entrance. After you collect your possessions, you'll reboard the bus and be taken either to a hotel north of Tel Aviv or to Ben-Gurion Airport. Lufthansa's providing gratis transport to Frankfurt ..." The colonel was interrupted by applause from the German and Dutch tourists. "Or, if you prefer to fly another airline, we'll try to accommodate you ..."

The group passed the day whiling away the hours. Prevented from returning to Tiberias because of the waters, they wandered about the courthouse grounds, peeking in windows, using the government-issued cell phones to call home. Luck favored some while others cursed in their own tongues, their connections home faulty, inaudible, or inexplicably terminated. A few used their blankets to lie in the sun. By the day's end, photos were being shown, addresses exchanged, grandchildren boasted about, family stories told and retold. Just before dinner, a young IDF soldier was handed a camera by one of the Japanese tourists and asked to take a group photo. All sixty, even Paolo Pisa and Father Angelo Lorenzo, amidst laughter, wisecracks, and playful shoving, took their places for the shoot. The soldier, who looked as if he wanted to be elsewhere, focused, clicked the shutter, returned the camera to the bowing Japanese, and hurried away. By ten that evening, most of the group were asleep in the darkened courtroom.

Standing in the doorway, Colonel Adam spoke to a Canadian-born IDF captain. "They don't know how lucky they are, this bunch. They can thank God they came here instead of India or ... pick any place, Ron. The world's been turned upside down, the chaos is indescribable. It's just the start, count on it. We'll be on full alert until the Messiah returns, I can guarantee that."

Adam's companion laughed as he brought a match to his cigarette. "That long, eh?"

"Maybe even a day longer," the colonel added, snickering. "And wouldn't you know it, goddamned Hamas is screaming for blood, that all this is Allah's will, a message to his people to rise up and drive the Jews into the sea ..."

"Hamas boilerplate," the other officer replied. "Same old Hamas 'follow me, I'm right behind you' bullshit."

"Maybe so but they're all over Al-Jazeera and Al-Arabya commanding the Palestinians to stay put, telling them that it's 1948 all over again, that if they leave, they won't be permitted to return, and so on."

"Once Gaza's evacuated, Hamas loses its constituency. Of

course they're going to tell them to stay, what do you expect? What's Fatah saying?"

Adam laughed. "What else? The opposite. Clan warfare. One says 'tomato,' the other says 'tomaaahto.'" He drew out the word for effect as Ron smiled. "At least Abbas' head isn't buried up his ass. He's ordering them to use common sense, to board the IDF trucks and the Red Crescent ambulances. Tells them not to worry, they'll be driven to the Ashkelon docks, the promised landing craft will be there, waiting for them, and so on …"

"Do you think they'll listen? Better still, obey?" Ron asked.

"What choice do they have? They've got to go somewhere, they can't tread water, and none of the Arab countries are reaching out ..."

"Same old. No choice really."

"Gaza's swamped. The boats'll take them to the Greek islands and Cyprus, and they'll be sorted out and off they go."

"Cyprus, huh?" Ron said. "History repeats itself ..."

"Yeah, but this time the refugees are getting shipped to the US, to Germany, to Scandinavia, whoever okayed taking them in. A free ticket out to the new Promised Lands ... maybe a hundred opted for relocating in the West Bank. Their televisions must've failed. There's not much left there either. Ramallah's halfway to a ghost town; so're Nablus and Bethlehem. Jenin's badly banged up, too, uninhabitable..."

"No wonder Hamas is shitting bricks. Once the Palestinians get a whiff of what breathing space's like, they'll never want to return." He swiped at an ash that had fallen on his uniform.

"Don't bank on it, Ron, your homeland's a strong magnet ..." the Colonel's voice trailed off.

"You can't help but feel for them, the poor bastards. They're always being betrayed, always beaten down either by us or Fatah or Hamas. Their leaders are worse than worthless. Well, maybe something good'll come from this because it can't get much worse, for them and for us."

"Point taken, Ron."

The UN confirmed early that morning that approximately five thousand armed peacekeepers from unaffected nations had been allocated to keep order in the West Bank and along Gaza's border with Israel proper. The request came from a most unusual source--the Vatican, which quickly grasped the urgency of protecting its countless interests in the Holy Land. Further upheaval, bloody conflict and strife benefited no one, least of all the Church, and its eternal presence there. The Secretary-General was required by UN rules to put the request on hold pending Israel's approval. Inasmuch as it came at the behest of the Pope and politics being politics, Israel was expected to give the nod later that day. It was seen by Jerusalem as a win-win situation. An all-too-rare public relations coup for once. And the peacekeepers would free up thousands of IDF troops for emergency duty elsewhere in Israel.

Before he stepped away from the rostrum and exited the UN's pressroom, the Secretary-General announced that a mass immunization campaign against hepatitis, cholera, and a host of other waterborne ailments had begun under the auspices of the World Health Organization. With epidemiologists warning of the danger of lethal epidemics that could rival medieval plagues, all affected European regions and those immediately accessible areas in Asia and the Middle East were targeted for immediate medical intervention.

* * *

In Tiberias, monster military bulldozers, normally used by the IDF to plough under the homes of Palestinian terrorists and their families, were now put to more peaceful use, clearing the downed trees, the overturned cars, the utility poles, and other wreckage from the storm that blocked the town's sewers. The cleanup spread the fetid reek, carrying the overpowering stench of decay to the noses of the guests, more than a few retching as they rushed to reclaim their belongings from in front of the Radisson and reboard the buses.

The waters from Israel's northern border region still poured through the southern valleys but at a far slower, almost stately rate now. The ancient religious center of Safed remained dry, filled beyond its capacity to serve all those who fled there in the storm's first days. But the arrivals from the flood zones, Arabs and Israeli settlers alike, and from elsewhere in stricken Israel, somehow made do until a modicum of normalcy returned.

In the higher elevations, the death toll was comparatively low, most losses attributed to coronaries and natural causes. While thousands of Israelis perished, their numbers paled beside the Palestinian losses. In the ensuing weeks, when more accurate estimates using surviving civil records were released, it was reported that twenty-one thousand, two hundred and fifty-nine Palestinians had died, most of them in the Gaza Strip, and two hundred forty-two thousand, three hundred twenty-one were now either homeless or heading for relocation either in Europe or the United States and Canada.

A drumbeat of manufactured outrage dominated Arab television for a week after the evacuation of Gaza's residents began. Heated accusations that Israel failed to open the fences between itself and Gaza and the wall separating it from the West Bank cities were repeated *ad nauseum* until the UN itself interceded and provided visual evidence to the contrary. The effort to project the truth of what had come to pass was futile until, in an unprecedented act, Saudi Arabia and the Gulf States weighed in and publicly supported the UN's version of events. The oil producing nations along the Persian Gulf recognized immediately the advantages of discretion in this time of international chaos. Pride was swallowed, the daily policy of broadcasting hatred and enmity towards the so-called "Zionist Entity" was suspended, if only temporarily. What was essential to their ultimate survival, the House of Saud and its neighbors realized, was renewing the flow of oil as rapidly as possible and with it the immense wealth its sale to the infidels, east and west, brought the Arab kingdoms. Further disruption could very well bring the kingdoms to their knees, placing them at the mercy of the Islamic fundamentalist terror movements within their own, storm-reduced borders.

In concert with the US, the IDF, and the Egyptian government, itself under constant threat and harried continuously by the resurgent Muslim Brotherhood, combined to jam the Middle East's airwaves, cutting off all satellite transmissions from Iran and Hezbollah's Syrian station. A handful of Hamas pirate radio broadcasts were also knocked off the air. As further insurance against inflaming the faithful to undertake another disastrous *jihad*, advanced, Chinese-created software was employed to quarantine normal access to the Internet; websites were scrambled, and downloading information was eliminated for the duration of the emergency. The mullahs' familiar cries for vengeance and calling upon Allah to visit death on the infidels were shouldered aside, their rants suddenly gone from the airwaves. In their place, Arab viewers, all Middle Eastern viewers, in fact, were treated to repeated showings of the IDF's rescue efforts, the opening of the gates, and the Palestinian's Red Crescent ambulances and Israel's Mogen David working seamlessly together, treating the storm's victims and transporting them to field hospitals set up in higher elevations. Those Palestinian storm survivors who'd decided to stay in Israel praised the rescue services' combined effort.

The fundamentalist prophets were checkmated, bombarded with images that cried out to be censored. The irony of the situation was made complete when the mullahs in Tehran ordered their own satellite receivers jammed, erasing visual evidence of their sworn enemies cooperating as Iran's television screens faded to black.

CHAPTER TWELVE

Oil production, five months after the storms had passed, barely reached half of its pre-flood output. The pipelines connecting the storage centers to the offshore supertankers were still undergoing around-the-clock repair. Kuwait's infrastructure was wrecked, the oil fields at Al-Kuway and Al-Ahdi producing well under their normal capacity. The floods had gifted Bahrain with an unwanted inland sea as they did the once-arid regions of Saudi Arabia's Wadi, Dwasir, and Tal'if. Every sheik in every sheikdom planted along the Persian Gulf choked back panic. Fear and confusion was the order of the day for the fabulously wealthy. They watched helplessly as the gulfs' wells sputtered, pumping air, the oil-grounded fortunes they had from birth taken for granted plummeting precipitously. The World Bank predicted darkly it would be eight years before the oil industry fully recovered.

One of the few positives to emerge from Iran's loss of its primary source of revenue was its overnight tumble as the Arab world's premier military power. As a threat to its enemies, real and imaginary, Iran was weakened considerably, if only temporarily, as a force to be feared. Unlike Dimona in Israel, in addition to crippling its oil production, the storms partially destroyed Iran's nuclear facilities, inoperable for what the CIA analysts determined was a minimum of four months. Iran's army could no longer rely on its supply train and its air force, fuel-starved, was grounded. Its frigates and destroyers huddled together in the harbor at Bandar Abbas. And its small fleet of swarming attack speedboats. Half its number were unseaworthy, damaged during the storm, their hulls stove in and floating belly up, turned by the storm to flotsam.

Militarily, for the immediate future, Iran was prostrate. But for how long? It was a question no one, certainly no one in the West, could comfortably answer.

While Iran's weakening was regarded by the West as a positive, as with many positives there were corresponding negatives. No oil meant those nations dependent in part on Iranian exports would have to seek another source of supply. And its crashing oil revenue served to aggravate Iran's persistent unemployment problem. While the official figures provided by Tehran hovered around fifty percent, the UN's economists cited a considerably higher number, in the neighborhood of eighty percent, exacerbated when Iran's oil industry collapsed and millions more were thrown out of work.

The directors of the CIA and the NSA were summoned to the White House for what had recently become two-a-day briefings, including weekends.

The CIA chief laid the latest intelligence on the president's desk. The president began thumbing through it. Three minutes later, he looked up, catching both men's eyes.

"So this then is the latest intelligence estimate?" he asked.

"Yes, sir. It's still warm." The director acted in a formal manner even though he and the president were nodding acquaintances at Columbia in the early eighties. The Oval Office often had that intimidating effect, even on the closest of friends. Even seated, the president was imposing. A tall man, over six foot two, proving again the adage that height was always an advantage in American politics.

The president allowed himself a brief smile.

"Is this true then, Hank?" he asked. "The mullahs view this mass exodus as a positive, that all these people running for their lives is a good thing, good for Iran?"

"Yes, sir," the CIA director nodded. "Our intelligence comes from an unimpeachable source, midlevel, Tehran itself."

"It's analogous to the Cuban situation in '80," the NSA chief chimed in. "When Fidel stood on shore waving bye-bye to all those Marielitos. Added a few thousand from his jails and nuthouses ..."

"Mental institutions, please," the president corrected him. "'Nuthouses' went out with Harry Truman."

Both intelligence officials laughed reflexively.

"Sorry," the NSA head replied. "But I see the mullahs' point and I think Joe here probably does, too." His colleague nodded his agreement. "Less mouths to feed, less discontent, and so forth. Their problem becomes someone else's problem. PDQ."

The NSA man was nothing if not elliptical in his judgments.

"What about their goddamned nuclear program, where's that stand?"

"Down but not out," the CIA director said. "With their employment problem 'solved,' so to say, and the dissidents unable to mount any sort of opposition with their supporters having, like Elvis, left the building ..."

The president interrupted.

"Yeah, got it, got it," he said, slightly irritated. "Answer my question. What about their nuclear program? 'Down but not out' doesn't cut it. How long is 'out?'"

"Our best intelligence estimates figure four months at the earliest, six at the outside, to get back online again."

The president sighed.

"I suspected as much. Now what?" He ran his hand over his graying hair. "Any way we can disable it entirely, for, say, eternity?"

"Too risky in my opinion, the situation throughout the Middle East being what it ts. Everyone would know we were behind it, even if we weren't behind it. Too many repercussions. It's probably a headache we don't need now ..."

"Of course," the president said, standing. He circled his desk, and sat on its edge, signaling the meeting was over. "Just speculating. Forget I even mentioned it."

"Forgotten," both men responded, almost in unison.

"And Hank, call your Mossad buddy when you're back at Langley. Tell him hands off Iran. Make sure the message is unequivocal. And make sure it's clear that this message comes from me and that it reaches the prime minister before tomorrow. No fancy stuff; repeat, no fancy stuff or no aid. If they cross us, they'll end up sitting *shiva* for the deal." The president smiled at his own remark.

"Consider it done, sir," the CIA chief chuckled. "They won't be happy."

"Can't please everybody, can you? But I'd bet my last nickel Jerusalem'll understand our position. Okay, gentlemen. See you later. Anything crops up before six, you know where I live."

"Some way to celebrate your re-election, isn't it, sir?"

The president nodded, his smile brief, then gone, as he turned back towards his desk.

* * *

The intelligence estimates and scenarios were remarkably accurate. In Iran, there was a porous safety net, no palpable welfare infrastructure which storm victims could count on to help them muddle through, no long lines snaking around a government unemployment office. Tehran was neither Washington, Paris, London, Madrid, nor Berlin. With nowhere to turn, no jobs to be had, even before the roads were passable, hordes of desperate Persians streamed out of the region, overwhelming their still-suffering Middle East neighbors.

The UN hastily organized a rescue operation, using its influence and pressure from the Western governments to gain acceptance of its efforts. Camps were set up inside several affected countries but from the outset it was clear the UN and some of the rulers were working at cross purposes. Each Middle East nation faced its own, internal refugee problems. Who needed the starving masses from next door? They only spelled trouble. The unwelcome UN camps were spare, the shelter they provided well intended but slapdash, hardly resembling the tent cities that normally sprang up in crises of times past. The few in number fortune favored found shelter under a sea of tarps supported by tent poles with primitive sanitary facilities sufficient for half their number.

Little could be done to slow this human flood short of a military response. Although the reports were unconfirmed, their number and the minute detail they offered lent them credibility. Eyewitnesses claimed that heavily-armed border patrols within sight of some camps opened fire on several large groups of Iranians trying to cross into Turkey, killing scores, including children. Tens of thousands were driven back under the fusillades. Similar tales of violence and assaults against refugees emerged from witnesses along Iran's common border with Syria and Iraq.

It was an indisputable fact that the poorest countries in the Middle East were chronically overburdened with high birth rates and excess population. And, as there was a limit to how many in this crisis could be given refuge in neighboring nations, there too was a limit to how many agreeable Western nations would accept. The prescribed limit had been reached within two

110

weeks of the storm's ending. Hundreds of thousands had already been welcomed into the Nordic countries, Canada, and the United States, each physically unaffected by the catastrophe. But the boat was now full; the gangway had been removed and stowed; all seats were occupied; there was no standing room, none.

Who knew how and when the turmoil that gripped the area would lift? No immediate, life-saving rescue formula was forthcoming from any quarter. The obvious options had heen exhausted. And now the unmentionable was being bruited about in each global power's inner sanctum. Triage, the last-resort medical term. An ugly term yet an appropriate one, describing precisely what would come to pass as the crises multiplied. The storms and floods had created a global emergency. Millions had died and millions more had been cut loose, dislocated, abandoned. The tragedy that befell the stricken areas begat further tragedy, the victims as always the innocent, the helpless. Everyone could not, would not be saved from their fate. All who could assist did assist but the endgame had become crystal clear: passive triage was unavoidable. The unsettled situation east of the River Jordan would just have to sort itself out in time. Triage.

* * *

Predictions warning of the total collapse of the West's economies, almost free from the near-death grip of the 2008-2009 worldwide recession, failed to materialize. The severe initial damage, resulting from the fuel shortages, had been somewhat alleviated. By using his executive authority, the American president ordered the release of three-quarters of the Strategic Oil Reserves in the storm crisis' early days, effectively averting a national shutdown. The offshore drilling program approved by Congress in 2008 and renewed in 2011 had done expectedly little to ease the fuel shortages. Analysts estimated it would be another eight years before a drop of crude was loosed from the ocean floors. However, Mexico increased its production and, thanks to its government's foresight, the new refineries constructed and on line around Tampico and Vera Cruz handled the increased flow effortlessly.

Venezuela increased its exports as well. After its bellicose,

111

anti-American president Hugo Chavez was deposed in a bloodless coup in 2011, its foreign policy under a new, friendlier civil government towards its northern neighbor warmed considerably.

In the end, American money spoke and spoke loudly. Tankers sporting all the flags of convenience sat at anchor, clogging Caracas' harbor, awaiting its complement of Venezuelan crude to carry north to the coastal refineries that dotted the Gulf of Mexico's shoreline from Texas to Louisiana.

Norway, Russia, Azerbaijan, and Nigeria, the latter having resolved its oilfield labor problems, served as England and the European Union's main oil suppliers. The demand from the industry-intensive nations was considerable but resolving the crisis brought on by the floods proved unexpectedly manageable. Europe dropped into a brief economic recession but, contrary to the dire forecasts, the recession was relatively shallow because many of the member states had developed and had been exploiting alternative energy options for just such emergencies. While wind and solar power as a general, dependable energy source was barely off the drawing board, nuclear energy remained a major energy supply source. Much of France's power still came from nuclear plants and England drew heavily on nuclear energy as well. As one-time supporting players in the Soviet bloc's grand design, Eastern Europe's new member nations, even after Chernobyl, never abandoned nuclear energy. Its upgraded nuclear plants had outlived its defunct Soviet sponsors by more than two decades now.

Coal mining was revived slowly in the extensive but often-idle coalfields of Poland, Belgium, northern France, and Germany. Smokestacks were fired up throughout Europe. With the fresh combination of energy resources— oil, coal, and nuclear— put into play, save a few initial missteps, within eighteen months the European economies would be humming along if on a considerably reduced track. The one burning question that overrode all others? How long would it be before they recovered their pre-storm prosperity?

* * *

Once the storms ended, the US Congress was called into emergency session as the senators drifted back from their

Thanksgiving hiatus. The overriding issue, the only issue to be addressed, was the energy crisis. Under immediate consideration was the new energy bill, approved by the House before the recess and reconciled by a joint House/Senate committee, then sent up to the Senate for approval. As with all major pieces of legislation, it was debated at length on the Senate floor. None present that day could remember when all the US Senate's members were present as they were on this day. No pairing off, no vote trading, no abstentions. Each of the one hundred members were prepared to vote either yea or nay.

The first to speak, to a full Senate, was the Republican senator from Wyoming, a long-time supporter of his state's powerful coal industry.

"In a perfect world," he reminded his colleagues, "I'd vote for every measure that would support renewable energy resource development. But this isn't a perfect world. We've just crawled out from under the worst recession this nation's suffered since the Great Depression. And now the world's been hit with these storms, these massive floods. I wish it were otherwise, but it's not. Clean energy is expensive, less available, and in short supply. We need to support what we already have in almost inexhaustible supply. Which is why I urge you, all of you, to vote 'Yes' on the bill before us. Let's pass it quickly, overnight, just as we did the storm and flood refugee bill."

His short piece said, the senator yielded the floor to his Democratic colleague, the five-term senator from Illinois, a seasoned if long-winded orator, an intimate of the president, much sought after for his moderate, rational positions on a wide array of issues.

"Coal's called the 'dark fuel' for a reason," he opened. "And I accept that coal, more than any other energy source, is responsible for global warming. It's not a theory it's a proven scientific fact, a particularly ugly truth. No question. But coal's a tough habit to kick. And who knows, maybe the storms and the floods that followed were the result of global warming. I certainly think they contributed and contributed heavily. Who's more responsible, us or the Chinese, for the planet's warming? The Canadians, Germany, the Eastern Europeans? Does that matter now, when we're all crammed into the same leaking boat, faced with another economic meltdown? Pointing fingers is a zero sum game, doesn't solve the immediate problem." He paused for effect, trusting his words would sink in and sway the votes of the members who vehemently opposed the bill. "Look, you know my record. I'm a consistent sponsor of renewable energy source mandates and there's no reason why we can't have both, is there? When the renewable energy resources bill comes before us again, it will once again have my support. And this time I predict it will pass easily. Voting for the non-renewables bill doesn't cancel out next session's renewables bill. As my good friend from Wyoming pointed out, this isn't a perfect world. The storms and floods made it more imperfect. We need fuel to run our factories, our transportation system, whatever that fuel turns out to be. I wish we could depend on non-renewables to fill the need but the reality is we can't, we're just not there yet. Does anyone here today want more of our factories to relocate? They will, you know, and with them will go more American jobs.

"No one here wants a repeat of the near-crash of four years ago. I realize there'll be political consequences down the road. But nothing we do here today is set in stone. It can be re-examined, revised, or revoked by Congress down the line. Remember, this is a two-year bill. So let's swallow the bitter pill and keep American manufacturing and our jobs at home. We've got to remain competitive in an increasingly competitive and hostile world, more so after this catastrophe, and do whatever it takes to keep the engines stoked— whether it's coal, nuclear energy, shale oil— whatever we need."

The congressional measure to provide tax incentives and research funds for oil shale and tar sands extraction, rehabbing idle nuclear plants, and coal-to-liquid production was naturally and vigorously opposed by America's environmental groups and their allies in Congress. They deemed continued tax breaks and further underwriting of non-renewable energy sources shortsighted, a temporary fix to an intractable problem that, with a little political courage, could have been solved long ago. That it was harmful to the environment was accepted by all. The arguments on both sides of the issue were familiar, repeated so often that it was a rare congressperson who couldn't repeat both sides *verbatim*.

And so it went, occupying the Senate for another four hours, the back and forth, but the end was foreordained. When the bill-granting incentives to the non-renewable resource

114

producers came to a vote, it passed by a large, bipartisan margin.

* * *

Jerusalem recognized the potential pitfalls of accepting the massive aid package, even from its staunchest ally, the United States, which was forthcoming within a week of the storms' end. The Israeli premier and her coalition were resistant at first, the strings attached seemed more like ropes. And as a right-wing commentator quoted in *The Jerusalem Post* bitterly noted: "From ropes nooses are fashioned." But the situation in Israel was dire. The nation's losses, in terms of life and infrastructure, were incalculable. In the more recent past, it could afford to dismiss demands made by the US and the European Union regarding all the political and social issues that it contended with daily. The settlements, the peace process, and Israel's own nuclear program were the foremost concerns of the world powers. All were potential sparks that could ignite a region-wide war that would make the bloody 2006 Hezbollah-Israel conflict look more like a border skirmish.

Intense jawboning by Israel, the Palestinians, the US, and the EU had resulted in what it always had, a stalemate, no movement towards the resolution of these central issues.

But the time for jawboning was washed away by the floods. The catastrophe of November, 2011 radically altered more than geography; it shifted the political terrain. Under extreme pressure from the US, backed by Brussels, Israel was given no choice. Take it or leave it as it is written, the premier was told in no uncertain terms: you have ten days, no wiggle room, and the clock's running down.

Behind closed doors, cabinet members insisted that Israel be given more time before accepting the aid offer. Her housing minister suggested she adopt a hard-line negotiating position on some of the pact's demands. Another cabinet member from the opposition party, a strident nationalist, the son of pre-WWII German immigrants, jumped to his feet, calling the US's either/or position a *Diktat*.

"I know from *Diktats!*" he declared.

The premier's steely, blue-eyed glare caught his eye.

"Diktat?" she repeated, turning it into a question, a look of

distaste on her face.

"Diktat? You know from *Diktats,* Goldmann?" She often used her opponent's patronymic if displeased, a time-tested tactic that never failed to diminish rivals. "You're making no sense, which, for you, isn't unusual. Stop acting like an ass and sit back down," she commanded, adding, "And get yourself a calendar. This isn't 1938, it's 2012!"

The prime minister's humorless, barracuda smile and her sharp features gave her the aspect of a nineteenth-century American pioneer schoolmarm. She had only been in office two months when the storms hit and she acted, as in all matters and emergencies, decisively. It didn't harm her increasingly formidable reputation that she had once been in the employ of the Massad, either. Or that she was the exalted David Ben-Gurion's niece and bore the family name. Israeli wags had lately refashioned a line once used to describe England's Margaret Thatcher in referring to their own prime minister, that she was the only cabinet member of either sex to use the men's room. Even her most hardened opponents would have been at pains to disagree.

Although the room in which the cabinet met was supposedly soundproofed for reasons of security, the bodyguards posted before the doors and the media swarm huddling in the corridors nearby heard unintelligible cries of outrage, muffled threats, and thumping which they attributed to fists being pounded on the conference table within.

"What's that sound like to you, Ilan? To me it's like a head being smacked onto a desk, eh?" one of the bodyguards quipped, winking at his partner.

"Sounds like it to me, Nahum. With her, maybe it is." He smirked at the notion.

"I wouldn't put it past her," the first bodyguard said, laughing loudly. "Maybe the target ought to check his underwear. It might be time for a change."

But, tellingly, none of the coalition's ministers— left, center, or right— stalked out, so progress towards a resolution apparently was being made. At the end of the seven— hour marathon session, the prime minister's position— it is an emergency, Israel must take the aid as offered, it is a matter of our survival— prevailed by a slim majority. Before adjourning and revealing the decision, in an effort to console the opposition within the cabinet, the premier pointedly reminded the gathering that nooses can always be slipped. The government survived intact but each official at the session knew that defections and support would be remembered, markers kept, each dealt with at the appropriate time by the prime minister.

"All's hardly lost, ladies and gentlemen, the storms solved the problem of Gaza for us," she remarked sarcastically as the meeting ended, as always every strand of her short, lacquered black hair, remained in place.

The general outline of the agreement required that the aid money be used in a specific manner, the manner to be determined by the donor, the USA, which would administer the aid as well. The amount of aid approved was never quite made public, the figure fudged in politispeak to address the American government's "political concerns," as it was delicately put in an Israeli government press release. Both governments, Israel's and the US's, knew that American generosity towards its stalwart Middle East ally had lately turned into a bipartisan political hot potato, with the minority Republicans taking the lead, pointing out that the US had already agreed to accept hundreds of thousands of homeless Middle Easterners.

"What more do these people want? We took those Palestinians off their hands," the Senate's Republican minority leader declared. "How much can we afford to give, to do for them? Really, haven't we done more than anyone could reasonably expect?" Senior Democratic senators and party leaders in the House of Representatives began to echo the Republicans' concerns.

It was clear in Washington that discretion regarding the financial aid package's price tag was more than ever a political necessity. In days, the president himself intervened, intent on avoiding a public battle and, worse, a logjam. He recognized that an opening to resuscitate the moribund Middle East peace process was, on the heels of the catastrophe, presenting itself. With the Palestinian and Israeli sides weakened considerably and both deeply in need of assistance, the US could and would dictate the pact's terms before the money began to flow. A window of opportunity in the Middle East never remained open for very long. And the president, as a former member of the Senate's

Intelligence Committee, was an astute and experienced observer of the Middle East's political dynamics. He was not about to let this window slam shut on his fingers because of a Senate squabble. Through a combination of personal charm, undisclosed promises, and a display of arm-twisting which, according to Washington veterans, was unlike any seen before in the Capitol, the Oval Office managed to tamp down the incipient opposition to the offer of assistance. The aid package was approved, *viva voce,* three weeks to the day after the storms had ceased.

Under the plan, a joint Israeli-Palestinian economic zone was to be created. The zone, with Jerusalem as its heart, would spread ten miles around the city, to all four points of the compass. All settlement activity was to cease immediately, all unapproved settlements removed, and a minimum of half the government-approved settlements disbanded. Work permits were to be issued without delay to a quarter of a million West Bank Palestinians to expedite the entire nation's reconstruction process. The Palestinians would, in turn, replace the foreign workers from Eastern Europe and Asia who had replaced them during and in the years following Arafat's second *Intifada.* The US and the EU agreed to underwrite the return of the foreign workers to their countries of origin as soon as was "humanly possible," as it was so stated in the agreement. The deal effectively created, *by fiat,* hundreds of thousands more instant refugees, just as the UN mandate to partition Palestine did in 1948, these new refugees added to those who had fled Gaza during the storms.

The majority of the foreign workers objected to voluntarily returning to the lands they had left to seek work and survival in Israel. But what could they do, what choice did they have? As with all aspects of the enormous aid package, the repatriation of the foreign workers wasn't open to negotiation. Their fate was decided by political realities brokered in Washington and Jerusalem. Hard times demanded hard choices.

In Israel, the decision to accept the aid package on America's terms was almost unanimously unpopular. The foreign workers were much preferred to the local Palestinians. What danger to life and limb did these foreign workers represent? The expulsion of so many Palestinian laborers after the second *Intifada,* the importation of foreign workers to replace them, the building of the separation wall, and the sealing of the borders was seen by many Israelis tired of living with the ever-present threat of another car bombing or a drive-by shooting or a brutal, random stabbing, as an unintended blessing. As the signatures of the American Secretary of State and the Israeli foreign minister were affixed to the agreement in a quiet White House ceremony, the return to Israel of the *pre-Intifada status quo ante* was, most feared, assured.

A Tel Aviv radio station hastily ran a call-in poll, capitalizing on the nation's intense interest in the agreement with the US and its terms.

"The prime minister claims 'all's not lost.' What do you, our listeners, think? ... yes or no?"

The station's switchboard lit up like a Roman candle and flashed for ninety minutes before an overload caused a brief power failure, shutting it down. The tally taken just before the system short-circuited had the "No" voters running a miserable and distant second to the "Yes, all's lost faction," the latter outnumbering the former by approximately four to one. When the station returned to the air, the announcer approached the results Talmudically.

"Well, on the one hand, we'll see," he droned. "On the other hand, maybe we won't."

Hard times had indeed required hard choices. In his own way, the minister named Goldmann had been correct in his assessment of the deal. What the US had presented Israel with in return for aid, no matter how it was polished and buffed by the diplomatic communities of both states, was, pure and simple, a Diktat.

* * *

In the West Bank, Hamas, its political base gone with the Palestinian exodus from Gaza, had wisely begun to mute its inflammatory rhetoric. Work permits, jobs and equal pay with Israeli construction workers supplanted demands for the right of all Palestinians to return to their historic homeland. Recognizing the weakness of its political position, undercut even further by the absence of significant financial aid from its Islamic allies, aid that evaporated faster than the water receded from the flooded territories, the Hamas minority in the West Bank grudgingly aligned itself with the majority Fatah as a junior partner. Like the non-Palestinian guest workers, the embittered Hamas leaders realized they had no choice.

Perhaps the Israeli minister's use of the German term *Diktat* was also appropriate when it came to Hamas submitting itself to Fatah's dominance. Hamas would, after all, have little say now in the formulation of Palestinian policy. A political crumb here, a financial crumb there, all the trump cards were held by Fatah. Whether Hamas could in time salvage something from the political limbo into which it had fallen, maybe plant and develop in the West Bank political power of the sort they once wielded in Gaza was an unknown, a question mark. Who knew what the future held? And if their future was left to Fatah, as the Israeli government presumed and trusted it would be, Hamas would be forever hamstrung, abandoned to the mercy and largesse of its uncompromising, arch enemy. The mistakes Fatah had made in Gaza would not be repeated in the West Bank. Hamas's command of the Gaza populace would be non-transferable to the West Bank.

Never say never may be a durable political truism, proving itself time and again throughout history. Dormant sometimes passes for dead. But if it was to be realized in Hamas's case, an awakening would be a long time in coming. The Israeli prime minister's parting words would perhaps come true. With Hamas crippled, the premier's judgment was a harsh one, but all was in fact hardly lost. And perhaps in the end, wherever and whenever that might prove to be, the agreement wouldn't return the nation to that spiral of daily violence and uncertainty common a half-decade past. Perhaps the feared noose, the *status quo ante,* would be slipped. With the new US-Israel agreement in place, for the Palestinians, perhaps a new day was actually dawning. Perhaps.

* * *

JERUSALEM

11

THE SECOND TEMPLE PERIOD

*Jerusalem in Herodian Period Based on the writings of Flavius Josephus
on the eve of Roman destruction of the Second Temple — 70 A.D.*

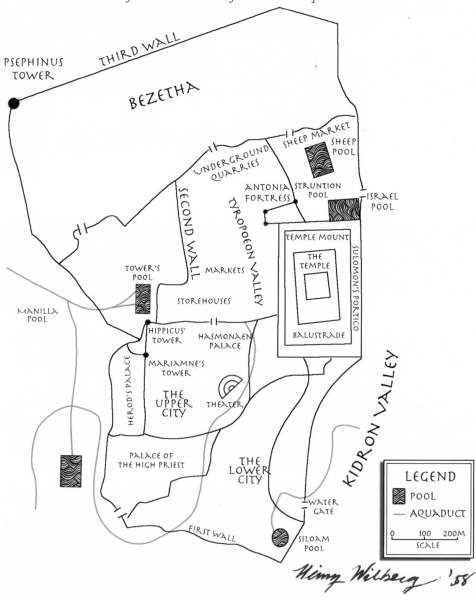

PSEPHINUS
TOWER

THIRD WALL

BEZETHA

SHEEP MARKET

SHEEP
POOL

UNDERGROUND
QUARRIES

ANTONIA
FORTRESS

STRUNTION
POOL

ISRAEL
POOL

SECOND WALL

TYROPOEON VALLEY

TEMPLE MOUNT

THE
TEMPLE

SULOMON'S PORTICO

TOWER'S
POOL

MARKETS

STOREHOUSES

BALUSTRADE

MANILLA
POOL

HIPPICUS'
TOWER

HASMONAEN
PALACE

HEROD'S PALACE

MARIAMNE'S
TOWER

THE
UPPER
CITY

THEATER

KIDRON VALLEY

PALACE OF
THE HIGH PRIEST

THE
LOWER
CITY

WATER
GATE

LEGEND

POOL

AQUADUCT

0   100   200M
SCALE

FIRST WALL

SILOAM
POOL

Henry Wilberg '58

122

TOMBS OF THE KINGS

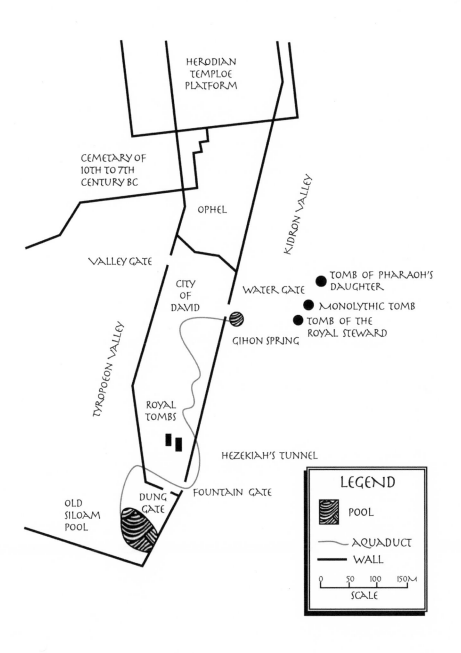

HERODIAN
TEMPLOE
PLATFORM

CEMETARY OF
10TH TO 7TH
CENTURY BC

KIDRON VALLEY

OPHEL

VALLEY GATE

TOMB OF PHARAOH'S
DAUGHTER

CITY
OF
DAVID

WATER GATE

MONOLYTHIC TOMB

TYROPOEON VALLEY

TOMB OF THE
ROYAL STEWARD

GIHON SPRING

ROYAL
TOMBS

HEZEKIAH'S TUNNEL

FOUNTAIN GATE

DUNG
GATE

OLD
SILOAM
POOL

LEGEND

POOL

AQUADUCT

WALL

0   50   100 150M

SCALE

PASSAGES, CISTERNS, AQUEDUCTS, CONDUITS BENEATH THE TEMPLE MOUNT AT 70 A.D.

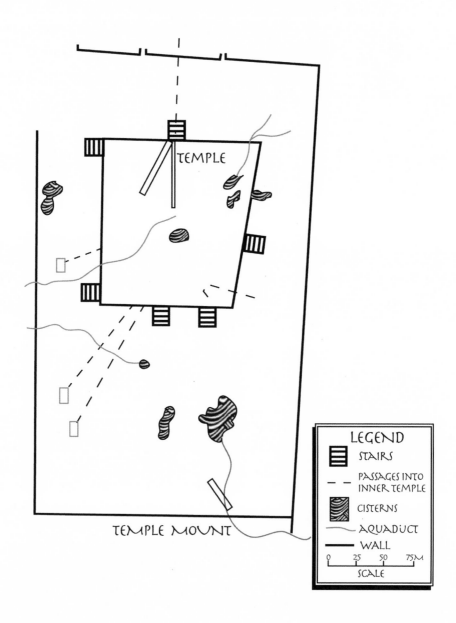

TEMPLE

TEMPLE MOUNT

LEGEND

STAIRS

PASSAGES INTO INNER TEMPLE

CISTERNS

AQUADUCT

WALL

0   25   50   75M

SCALE

SURVEY OF ENTRY AND PASSAGE WAYS (AQUEDUCTS, CONDUITS, SEWER LINES, ELECTRIC, ETC.) BENEATH MOSLEM QUARTER AND TEMPLE MOUNT

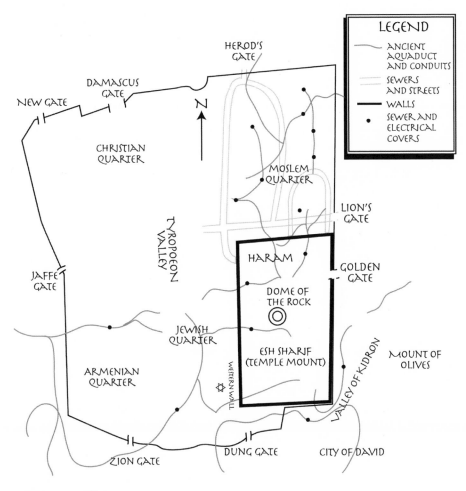

CHAPTER THIRTEEN

The miles-long convoy of yellow American-made school buses rattled along the coastal road that bordered the Mediterranean from the Lebanese border in the north towards Rafa, at Gaza's tip, in the south. They turned eastwards, driving at a snail's pace to avoid the washed-out Beit Netofa Valley. Turning north again, they headed to Deir Hana and past Sakhnin to the crossroad that marks the beginning of the Beit Kerem, the valley itself now framed by mountains of mud. More huge bulldozers like those they had seen in Tiberias churned mightily, straining to push aside the storm's debris, making the road passable. From Beit Kerem, the buses turned right, and moved on toward Akko and the coastal road once more.

The effects on the coastline that had been battered with winds in excess of 175 miles per hour and the waves that had gathered their momentum far out to sea and washed over all the natural and man-made structures stretched to the horizon. The Med had risen and leveled all the roadside and beachfront homes, the storms' winds punching out the windows of the high rises and seaside hotels, just as the houses inland along the rivers and the Galilee had become victims of their waters. A sparkling sea of glass had become an uncomfortably familiar sight to the busses' passengers. So too had the occasional loud pop, signaling the loss of a tire and a further delay as the grumbling passengers exited the disabled bus while the convoy halted and the flat was repaired.

Dr. Paolo Pisa peered out the bus window at the long inland lake that appeared in the storm's wake, drowning the miles of fish hatcheries that supplied St. Peter's fish to Israel's markets and restaurants.

"We'll drain it," Colonel Adam said from across the aisle, anticipating Paolo's question. "Give it a month or two. Fish can be quickly replaced."

How American, Father Angelo thought. All problems solvable in no time, in the wink of an eye. Problem? No problem.

The priest's deep doubts counterpointed the IDF colonel's boundless confidence.

In Netanya, a citrus center settled in 1929 turned now into a seaside resort and overpopulated by Russian immigrants, they glimpsed what they would encounter as they approached Tel Aviv and what they had already experienced in Tiberias. The beaches had, as they had elsewhere, been washed away, the pleasure boats, cabanas, chaise lounges and beach chairs floating aimlessly in the surf while nearby teams of Orthodox Jews searched for the bodies of the drowned.

"See the glass," the colonel said, pointing. "The big panes are from the upper floors, the piles just below the lower stories, they crumble like windshield glass. The Passover bombing in 2003, it was just over there ..."

An army of Palestinians worked the dozers, dumping their loads into waiting trucks. "Nothing's wasted here," Colonel Adam said. "All that glass, it'll be recycled. In two weeks, you'll be drinking Coke from bottles made from it."

The buildings looked blasted out like those targeted by suicide bombers, but they withstood what Nature had thrown at them. Their lower stories were, like New York's Empire State Building, built from granite, some faced with marble like Rome's ancient structures. Israel had prepared itself well against an air attack though a repeat of the biblical-sized flood hadn't ever been even a remote consideration.

"Jesus, it looks like Miami after Hugo," one of the American tourists exclaimed.

"Worse," his wife added.

"Worse than Katrina," a third said. "Far worse."

Similar observations and the predictable, mindless "which was worse" opinions and disputes filled the air as the evacuees' bus neared the outskirts of Tel Aviv. Paolo raked his fingers through his hair, imagining similar chatter taking place in each of the buses, thinking all the while— What was left to say? Did it matter which was worse?

* * *

The massive day and night cleanup was clearly underway throughout Israel. The exception was the still-impassable Jordan

Valley, which remained for the most part underwater. Government projections conservatively predicted the central valley would become accessible within three weeks, which, to the displaced, was little comfort. Three weeks would seem an eternity. Elsewhere in the Holy Land, the scale of the cleanup was enormous, day and night, as no effort was spared to expedite the nation's return to normalcy. Klieg lights illuminated the work sites, giving them the appearance of shadowy, B-movie sets. Cleanup brigades arrived in vast numbers, trailed by streams of construction vehicles. The debris was methodically being scooped up, from fragments to boulder-sized chunks, piece by piece, and deposited in the trucks' beds to be carted away to temporary landfills. There it would be sorted and ultimately used in the nationwide reconstruction process. The extent of the destruction made the cleanup painfully slow going, the perpetual traffic jam caused by the comings-and-goings of the dump trucks further hampering swift progress as cars, buses, and vans skirted around them. But even with the unavoidable interruptions, a start had been made.

In the biblical land famed for its miracles, few expected miracles. Maybe, as Colonel Adam maintained, the fish farms surrounding Netanya would soon be reopened, replenished and operable, shipping their product region-wide. It seemed doable, even to the doubting Father Angelo, certainly it contrasted with what he and his bus-mates had seen on their tortuous journey to Ben-Gurion Airport. What it would take to repair and resurrect the nation's damaged infrastructure, its towns and cities, was beyond simple comprehension. Even with the will and money available, what was not beyond doubt was the time it would take to perform the staggering task of reconstruction. No one on the ground believed it would be less than several months before Israel was returned to a semblance of what it had been before the storms and floods struck.

* * *

By the time they reached Ben-Gurion, the upper story windows of the three-star hotel to which they were assigned had been replaced. Outside, another of the mountains of trash built from furniture, clothing, handbags, computers, large and small televisions— all the measures of material success— was being moved aside by the ubiquitous bulldozers. The hotel lobby itself was far the worse for wear, its carpet spongy, waterlogged and curling at the corners.

"As you can see, gentlemen," the desk clerk was saying, "we're pressed for room so I assume you won't mind sharing?" The questions were rhetorical. "Twin beds, of course?" the clerk added smugly.

"On a high floor, please," Paolo responded, glaring at the clerk, "a room with windows ... and running water. Um, no pun intended."

The clerk ignored Paolo's riposte.

"Breakfast room's open at 6.30, Dr. Josephus. Have a good night."

"Thank you," Father Angelo said, taking the room key, following Paolo to the elevator.

The room was small but adequate, with a view of the airport's sprawl, a far cry from the luxury hotels to which both men had become accustomed. Colonel Adam had warned the disembarking passengers that Tel Aviv, unlike the higher reaches of neighboring Jaffa, had taken the brunt of the storm head-on, so they were unloading close to the airport to avoid any delays leaving Israel.

"An old guy, a German, told me Tel Aviv looks like Berlin the morning after Kristallnacht. Dizengoff probably still looks like Kristallnacht ..."

"Well, at least we're not in the center," Father Angelo offered. "I suppose we can give thanks for that small mercy."

Neither man passed much time in Tel Aviv with its numberless nightclubs, its oyster bars and tattoo parlors, the malls, the crowded beaches and looming beachfront hotels, and its jabbering herds of American, Canadian, European, and Asian tourists, all intent on adding yet another land, another checkmark next to their "been there, done that" list. Father Angelo always thought of Tel Aviv as a third-rate Gomorrah. He guessed that Paolo, as a fellow Roman, shared his view of the city.

For Guido Pisa, Tel Aviv was always an afterthought. A flyover city, an upstart, an overnighter. A necessary, modern city haphazardly tossed up to accommodate a growing population's needs, Western tastes, and modern inclinations. For Guido Pisa, only Jerusalem mattered, and he imparted his love of Jerusalem to his son, Paolo. Only Jerusalem connected the whole of history—Jewish history, Roman history. He separated Jerusalem in his mind from Israel itself, for knowing in his heart that but for the destruction of Jewish life in Europe, Israel would have remained a neglected British colony, good for little more than citrus exports, a narrow stream of religious pilgrims, and a hardship posting for British soldiers. He once confided in Paolo that but for Hitler, "who would have gone there, a bunch of Russian and Polish Zionists in ridiculous hats."

Paolo, for his part, loved Israel deeply, for it was his second homeland and, like his father Guido, he recognized Israel as a necessity, a haven for his people, their last best chance for survival in the bloody wake of World War II. But Paolo Pisa was, again like his father, more a Roman Jew than an ardent Zionist, in tune with his Jewish neighbors in the Tiber district.

Father Angelo Lorenzo was less flexible in his biblical interpretations than his colleague. As such, in an odd turnabout, Father Angelo proved himself a more outspoken and fervent Zionist and lover of Zion than was Paolo Pisa. His Zionism had in the past rankled more than a few of his superiors within the Vatican hierarchy and had at times slowed his advancement into the innermost circles of the Church. His detractors had earlier decried his obsession with Zionism. But their voices were muted now, their opinions dismissed. Father Angelo Lorenzo's scholarship and notoriety, while perhaps paling besides those of Dr. Paolo Pisa's, had so elevated him as an unassailable personage within the Church that his carping critics lost their audience, many eventually shunted off to a third-world diocesan dustbin.

The aging priest's attachment to the Holy Land went far deeper than his work as a biblical scholar. He believed in his heart and soul that God had spoken directly to the ancient Hebrews, telling them that this land, Israel, was their land, theirs alone. For Father Angelo Lorenzo, the Jews of the Diaspora had simply returned home. Case closed, as the lawyers say. Israel was, after all, the land of Jesus Christ. And for the priest the Israelis were brethren, somewhat wayward to be sure, but brethren nonetheless and the protectors of the land that begot the Savior. And as the protectors of the Holy Land, the Israelis assumed the sacred obligation of preventing its falling into the hands of others.

When the Vatican finally recognized the state of Israel,

Father Angelo Lorenzo rejoiced, considering the recognition as a restoration of the natural order of the universe. He could never quite grasp why it had taken so long to choose the proper moral course of action. He did acknowledge that it was an ongoing struggle for Christianity to survive in the sea of hostility that was the world of Islam. For the Church, he was well aware that the policy that insured its survival was always the paramount consideration.

Yet appeasing Muslim sensibilities made little sense to him. What gain did appeasement bring to the Church in Nazi Germany? Subordination and lasting shame.

Appeasing the Muslim world would not alter or diminish the Church's position in the Holy Land. The Church would remain a privileged entity under all Israeli governments, whichever way they leaned politically. Yes, there would be incidents, violence in other Muslim nations, even in Israel itself. But the Church had survived far worse and would do so again, Father Angelo believed, unto eternity.

He was delighted that the pope had arrived at the same conclusion. For Father Angelo Lorenzo, Israel was the resurrection of the People of the Book in their biblically-ordained Promised Land.

* * *

Lying in their separate beds, enervated by the day's events and again unable to sleep, both men spoke of what they might encounter when they returned to Rome.

"When you're surrounded with as much devastation as we've witnessed here, it obscures the imagination, Angelo. Can it be any worse at home? Nothing I heard on the news provides a clear picture. Or maybe I just don't want to think about it. Or maybe I can't ..."

"I don't think it can match what's happened here," Father Angelo, ever the optimist, replied. "We're not sitting on the sea, after all, and for once during this millennium, Rome seemed prepared ..."

"Never believe what you hear, Angelo. The only thing we prepare for in Italy is dinner. It would truly amaze me if what they claim was true, that the artwork, rare books, whatever, were secured. I'd prefer to wait for the damage estimate, weigh how honest it is.

Followed by the inevitable fall of our five-hundredth post-war government."

"True to form, Paolo, you're very consistent," Father Angelo laughed, adjusting the pillow and clasping his hands behind his neck. "Well, this time I think you'll be proven wrong, all your fears will go unrealized ..."

"From your mouth to God's ear, Angelo. I hope you're right," Paolo paused, "this time."

"Colonel Adam told me that he'd been officially informed by his superiors that the lDF declared strict martial law in and around Jerusalem and in the Negev, that all looters, even Jewish looters, will be shot?"

"Where was I? I didn't hear him say that?"

"At the pitstop south of Netanya. You were on your cell with your ex. I forgot to tell you ..."

"Right. Yes, well, the Messiah will return long before the IDF shoots Jewish looters. Arabs, yes, but Jewish looters ..." Paolo's face suddenly darkened. "Well, maybe, who knows? Times change. This situation's unique and if the government loses control, anything could happen, nothing short of all hell breaking loose. Anyway, the rumors are flying. What's true, what's fantasy, it's become harder to distinguish between the two ..."

"Maybe the flood's unearthed ... God knows what. So much here's been turned upside down, who knows what'll surface? Perhaps the floodwaters broke open ancient graves or tombs and freed up the treasures or whatever the dead had buried with them?"

"Angelo, Angelo, you know that's a pipe dream, my friend, an old wives tale," Paolo said, shifting uncomfortably, the bed creaking under him. "Those old Jews were buried naked as the day they were born, wrapped in winding sheets, tossed in wooden boxes, and sent off to meet Yahweh. Some of the lucky ones, at least. No, I think if the IDF's cracking down it has more to do with the Palestinians pouring in from the West Bank"

"It's martial law all over the Middle East, in Iraq, Iran, Egypt, Jordan, Syria, Lebanon, everywhere ..."

"We're only talking degrees here, Angelo. It's always martial law somewhere in the region. The difference lies in its severity. Whatever the case, we can watch them sort it all out on TV from Rome tomorrow evening. I don't know about you, but I could certainly use a decent meal," Paolo said drowsily, as Father Angelo began to recite his bedtime prayers again.

It was 2 A.M. Paolo Pisa and Father Angelo Lorenzo had talked themselves out, at least for the night, as each dropped off into deep, dreamless sleep.

At 3 A. M., the phone rang, jangling both men awake. Father Angelo propped himself up, blinking the sleep away, concern creasing his brow as Paolo reached over and grabbed the receiver. Clearing his throat, he mumbled his "hello, who's this?" into it.

The voice was familiar but in his groggy state Paolo couldn't immediately place the voice.

"Moshe? Is that you?"

"Yes, who am I talking to?"

"It's me, Dov."

Dr. Dov Rosenberg, the Director of Antiquities at the Israel Museum in Jerusalem. Dov, whose Italian was a comical Hebrew and English mélange with vowels tacked onto the end of each word for effect, a man with energy the equal of Paolo Pisa's or, as Paolo was known in Israel, Moshe Josephus.

"Forget about flying home. You're not being evacuated. I've cancelled your and Angelo's seats on the Rome flight. Sorry, short notice. No time to explain. Something's come up, something urgent and I need you both here for a couple more days. One of my aide's is picking you up at 9. So set the alarm. See you tomorrow ... I mean, later."

"What's so urgent about the papyrus and the box, Dov? We can always come back, you know," Paolo had said before he realized he was talking to a dial tone.

CHAPTER FOURTEEN

Dr. Dov Rosenberg was world-renowned, preeminent in his field, an authority not only on the Dead Sea Scrolls but on nearly everything unearthed in Israel from the day the ancient Hebrews walked out of Sinai onwards. Like Paolo Pisa, he was lauded by most and decried by many, his preemptory manner often offending, attracting detractors as a lightning rod attracts lightning. Much of the criticism had little to do with his scholarly efforts. In the cutthroat world of archaeology, religion, art, and archaeological digs carried out in wilting heat mixed with huge, insatiable egos, the players often played the game by a fluid, sometimes questionable set of rules. Conflict was inevitable, particularly with a government that claimed the land under its feet was God's gift, the same God who spoke directly to Moses, to the People of the Book.

Dr. Dov Rosenberg's doctorate was awarded by Harvard University and, although he was given instant tenure at various universities, his true love was his Directorship of Antiquities at the prestigious Israel Museum. Listing his academic accomplishments would probably fill the Tiberias phonebook. Like Paolo Pisa and Father Angelo Lorenzo, his papers and books were respected by and the envy of even his bitterest rivals.

He was commonly referred to as just plain "Dov," except by the grandees in the chairs of Judaeo-Christian or Judaic Studies in major American universities where he was called "The Deli Man." Dov was on a first name basis with all the stars in archaeology's galaxy. He counted the legendary IDF general, Yigael Yadin, he of the Dead Sea Scrolls, among his mentors. The curators of New York's Met, the British Museum, the Louvre, and the Alte Pinothek in Munich, to name-drop but a few, were all close colleagues. Dov was personally responsible for several of the substantial gifts that elevated the Israel Museum to world-class status.

His personal charm, when he chose to turn it on, came

easily. He convinced the wealthy, those who preferred an annex on which their name was chiseled, one that could be viewed with Google Earth, of their gift's significance. It had more resonance— Dov's favored term— eternal resonance, Dov would insist, than a mere tree planted in a memorial forest. So what if the donors lived elsewhere? Who cared if so few even owned so much as a housekeeping flat in Jerusalem or Tel Aviv? Or visited once a year or every two years? Where the money came from was irrelevant. What counted in the end was the endowment to the museum. The endowment was a mitzvah, the mitzvah, a generous gift to the Jewish people.

Dr. Dov Rosenberg could trace his own roots in Israel back more than two centuries, when his great-great-great-great grandfather, Chaim Rosenberg, left Russia's Pale of Settlement on a swaybacked horse, a day ahead of the latest pogrom with the curses of his rabbi father and the tearing of the older man's sleeve echoing in his ears, and made his way to the border of the Ottoman Empire. The horse keeled over dead south of Constantinople so Chaim pressed on by foot, arriving in the flyblown Palestine sinkhole penniless, ragged, and blistered.

Chaim Rosenberg married and prospered, trading horses as he had in Russia, expanding his business to include camels and goats. His was hardly an empire but his honesty and forthrightness was spoken of admiringly, his name honored even among the local Arab and Bedouin tribes. The Rosenbergs' Israeli lineage served Chaim's descendant Dov well when he was on a fundraiser in New York or in negotiations with Arab or Bedouin families over this or that valued artifact. Even among the extreme elements of Hamas' and Hezbollah's lunatic fringe, it was said that when the Jews were Inshallah pushed into the sea, the scholar who understood Palestine's essence, Dr. Dov Rosenberg, was to be spared Islam's sword.

Dov was an odd duck, to be sure. Shaped like a ten-pin, his pendulous gut overlapping his belt, he was a shade over five and half feet tall. His hairline had retreated long ago. The fringe of white above his ears was a sad reminder of the bird's nest of hair that was once as plentiful and as wild as Einstein's own and looked as if it hadn't seen a comb since the Six Day War. The collarless, faded work shirt he wore several days running, stained with evidence of past meals, and the baggy harem-like pants, the cheap sneakers, and the tobacco-yellowed fingers completed the disheveled portrait.

But in that large head resided an encyclopedic knowledge unmatched by any other. Once, when at an international meeting in Los Angeles, Paolo Pisa overheard an American colleague refer to Rosenberg as "The Deli Man," he came to his friend's defense.

"Unlike you, Sam, Dov can explain the menu in every language spoken around this table. And, Sam, use a fork to pick the pickles out of the dish, not your fingers which look as if they haven't been washed since the last dig ..."

An uncomfortable silence descended on the dozen assembled scholars, all now intently tucking into their sandwiches, averting their eyes from Paolo's chastened target. Paolo often smiled at the recollection, noting how he'd never again heard Dov called "The Deli Man." At least, not within his earshot.

* * *

At precisely 9A.M., a tan, armor-plated Hummer was idling in front of the hotel. As Paolo Pisa and Father Angelo exited the hotel, the driver, a ramrod-straight IDF major, greeted them with a "Get in, gentlemen" as if they were being placed under arrest. The Hummer was filled with electronic equipment, an Uzi sat between the two front seats, and a German shepherd perched at attention behind the driver, the back seat's third passenger.

"Don't worry," the Major said, laughing, "the dog hasn't eaten anyone since we left Gaza last week. You can pet him, he's a good boy." He reached over and scratched the dog's head.

Father Angelo winced, inching further back into his seat, relieved when Paolo seated himself next to the dog.

As they pulled away, Paolo tapped the driver on the shoulder.

"Do you know what this is all about, Major?"

"Dov didn't say, something about another discovery maybe?" he said, then, qualifying his response, "I really don't have a clue. He doesn't tell me everything."

"We should've known," Father Angelo chimed in, turning to Paolo. "Leave it to Dov and his mysterious ways. If he's not expansive, he's vague. There's no middle ground, no in between ..."

"He probably thought we'd figure it all out with that whisper of info he gave us about that box and the parchment. Grab the next flight, fly in ... 'Fill in the blanks yourselves, boychicks!' Everything's life and death with him," Paolo said. "Some way to speak to his elders, hmmm?"

"Dov is nothing if not paternal. Probably acted the same way towards his parents when he was growing up." "Parents? Grandparents!" Father Angelo enjoyed the thought of a teenage Dov holding court, instructing his elders in the ways of the world. He leaned forward and tapped the driver on the shoulder.

"Major, when do you think martial law will be lifted?"

"It's impossible to say, Father. Everything's too ... uh, what's the English word? Unsettled." He shifted in his seat, touching the Uzi as if it was an amulet. "You can see for yourself," he said, pointing out the window, as they drove past Ben-Gurion airport.

"It's a very busy place, has been since yesterday. Flights in and out, around the clock.

Supplies come in, people leave. We can only hope that at least the Israelis return.

Between Hamas and Hezbollah, the economy, Iran, people are tired, now the floods, the pressure's constant ..."

"Your accent's not Israeli," Father Angelo remarked.

"I came here from Odessa in 1987," the Major volunteered, more conversational now. "I took a crash course in Hebrew, never learned it in Russia, never even heard it before I emigrated. I was in the Russian military, in the artillery, and now here I'm again in the military. Once a soldier, always a soldier, I guess. In Russia they'd send you to East Germany to keep an eye on the Germans or to Sakhalin, that hellhole of an island we captured from the Japanese in 1945. Just in case the Japanese were planning another sneak attack." His tone was sharp, sarcastic, the months spent on Sakhalin still galling to him. "Here it's better, much better, if only because you can go home every night. It's better for morale ..." The major paused, arranging his thoughts. "Martial law, that was your question, yes, Father? Looting, not so much, the usual storefronts, car radios, whatever can be sold or traded off quickly. The government and the IDF's main concern's for the historical sites. They didn't want another Bagdhad," he said, referring to the wholesale looting of Iraq's museum treasures following the American invasion in 2003. "And believe me, the Jews are as bad as the Arabs when it comes to the black market. From what Dov told me, you two know more about black market relics than most ..." The Major's voice was drowned out by the deafening roar of a KLM 747, laden with supplies, on its landing approach towards one of Ben-Gurion's outer runways.

As the plane touched down and the noise diminished, Paolo spoke up again, "Dov's too free with his compliments."

"We can do only so much," the Major continued, "monitoring who comes in and who leaves, checking cars, old Arabs on donkeys ... 'scut work' I believe the Americans call it. And now with the borders open ..."

As if to underline the major's words, a casual glimpse out the car window confirmed how precarious the situation had become, how the flood had compromised Israeli security. Occasionally a jagged, storm-breached gap in the separation wall appeared, blocked only with large coils of razor wire dumped to stall any population influx. The rusted and burned-out supply trucks and cars lined up along Highway I's shoulders, a junk yard monument to the heroes of the 1948 independence struggle, were sunk deep into the mud and sodden earth, only the tops of their cabs visible.

"The Jordan Valley ..." Paolo began.

"The Jordan Valley?" The Major shook his head. "Un-in-hab-i-table." He pronounced each syllable as if it was a word he'd just learned.

The Hummer began its climb towards Jerusalem, past Sha'alvim, through the narrow Atalon valley and the Arab hamlet of Abu Ghosh. In the near distance they could see the high-rises of the new Jerusalem's skyline.

"It still gives me butterflies, Paolo, the same as I felt the first time I visited almost forty-four years ago," Father Angelo mused. "The Holy City, the city on the hill ... We came at Easter time, a bunch of young seminarians, wending our way on the Via Dolorosa to Calvary, praying at each of the fourteen stations of the Cross. When we placed our rosaries on the Holy Sepulcher, I wept. We all knew then we'd made the right life choice, giving ourselves to Christ." Father Angelo reached over, holding his rosary out to the driver. "This is the same rosary, Major, the same one. Perhaps it saved me in Tiberias ..."

"Perhaps," the driver said, noncommitally.

"I was a kid, maybe ten, when we landed at Lod," Paolo interjected, adding his own reminiscence, "a few years before you came, Angelo. It was August, the weather was brutal. Not much around Jerusalem, mostly low buildings, crowds of Arabs, on foot or sitting sidesaddle on the donkeys, Polish Jews in the fur hats." Paolo leaned back against his headrest. "It was so damned hot I was sure their heads would melt."

The driver joined Paolo, laughing in concert at the memory, adding, "Hasn't changed much, has it, Dr. Josephus? Peculiar bunch, keep to themselves, reproduce faster than the Arabs, and manage to get themselves exempted from the military ... some deal these guys worked out," he said sourly.

"Those are the rewards of political leverage, Major. It's not just them and it's not just here, it's the same the world over. They were never my father's favorites, never saw one in the store, the first one Pop and my uncle opened, a hole-in-the-wall a few meters from the Jaffa Gate, over on David Street," Paolo continued. "The store's still there, turned into a grocery now, fruit in crates for sale out front. I loved it here back in the day, even if the city was split in two, the eastern part verboten if you were a Jew, me hanging out with Pop's workers and their kids." He closed his eyes, conjuring up the scene from memory.

"They used to take me around, dressed me up just like them so no one would know who I was. I had a little Arabic, enough so everyone thought I was just another street kid which was how I viewed myself back then. Never got caught, either. Saw all the sites in the Muslim quarter. I knew every part of this city, the Christian, Armenian, and Jewish quarters, of course, like the back of my hand, still do. Old Jerusalem, the Muslim quarter, it was pretty rundown, the Wailing Wall, the graves on the Mount of Olives, even the Temple Mount, everything looked shabby. Preserving the past wasn't very high on the agenda, anyone's agenda in those days, the ... 'good old days.' Seemed like there was a lot less personal conflict and hostility then, but maybe I'm reminiscing through a kid's rosy memory filter ... 1967 ... yeah, the war changed everything."

"A magic time," the driver said, keeping his voice neutral. "But I wouldn't know of such things ..."

Fifteen minutes later, they were descending on the still rain-slick road past Yad Vashem, the Holocaust Museum. Father Angelo, as he always did in reverence, unobtrusively crossed himself. The Hummer turned off Herzl, drove past the Presidential Park, past the Knesset, turning finally into the roadway adjoining the Billy Rose Art Garden, with its Picasso, Rodin, and Henry Moore sculptures and where a slew of gardeners were replanting the storm-tossed and uprooted trees, shrubs and bushes. The Hummer edged into its reserved space fronting the Israel Museum.

* * *

Dr. Dov Rosenberg shot up from his chair, a Turkish cigarette hanging from a corner of his mouth, and came around his desk as the two men entered his capacious office. He looked as he always did; though diminutive and heavyset, he appeared somehow physically larger, in fact, than he actually was. Twenty years earlier, when he was barely forty, the odds on his being dead within six months were short - the odds makers predicted his final moments, lying in a heap atop his beloved Negev sands, his last words an order barked at a subordinate half his age. Odds on Dov Rosenberg's survival were no longer given. In his sixty-second year, Dov was assumed by many to be immortal. In Tiberias, when Dov's name arose during one of his and Father Angelo's rambling conversations, Paolo opined that, "unlike the two of us, Angelo, Dov will have his own tomb, like the Patriarchs." It was said in admiration, without a hint of envy. Father Angelo hastened to agree.

"Moshe," Dov virtually shouted, hugging Paolo, simultaneously reaching out to shake Father Angelo's hand. His voice sounded like a buzz saw, drowning out all around him. "I thought you and the Father were casualties, the hotel had collapsed ... But Dov knew better, didn't he?" He tapped his brow for emphasis. His habit of referring to himself in the third person was in working order. "'God didn't want two old Romans, certainly not you two, it wasn't your hour." He glanced from Paolo to Father Angelo. "You were in safe hands, Moshe, with Angelo as your guardian angel, no? We've got miracles here that Angelo believes in. So, what, you walked here over the waters or you parted them?"

"We took the bus, Dov," Paolo grinned at Dov's exaggeration.

"I was a little bit worried about you two. I even checked the survivors' list on the computer," Dov interrupted, continuing as if he was alone in the room, playing out his familiar routine of jabs and teases. "I had a look at your passports, they put them on the TV screen." He wrinkled his smallish nose with distaste. "You,

141

Angelo, you look okay, you never change, must be the holy water. Or the famous Vatican kitchen I read about in Gourmet Magazine ... Moshe, on the other hand, take some free and much needed advice from an old friend with your best interests at heart. Get a new photo made. You look an old Italian, like your father, the olivewood king ..."

"I am an old Italian, Dov ..." Paolo laughed loudly, unable to contain himself. "We're all getting on, the clock's running down ..." "Moses lived to 110, Moshe," Rosenberg reminded him. "We should be that lucky."

He cut the banter and turned serious. "I'm sorry I couldn't say much on the phone but, you know, the IDF censors ..." He shrugged, palms open, beseeching, his meaning clear. "Okay, enough with the shmoozing," he said, grabbing his rumpled jacket and struggling into it. "We're going for a short ride."

CHAPTER FIFTEEN

The cigarette dangling from the museum director's mouth burned down near extinction as he shoved his bulk into the Hummer's back seat, bumping the German shepherd towards the middle. Father Angelo grabbed the opportunity to seat himself up front next to the major while Paolo sandwiched the dog between himself and Dov. The German shepherd sighed audibly.

Dov grabbed the dog's ruff and rubbed it vigorously, saying, "I remind you, my canine friend, that rank has its privilege so shove over."

They drove rapidly, across Wingate Square and up Jabotinsky Street, the collected pools of water below the Zion Gate's entry to the Old City parting easily before the oncoming Hummer, to the crest of the large hill called the Mount of Olives, looking down upon the Kidron Valley. It is here on the Mount of Olives where the world's more religious Jews wish to be buried, resting in peace with the remains of the Prophets Haggai, Zachariah, and Malachi, the latecomers now among the first to greet the Messiah on his return to Earth and first in line to travel the shortest route to Heaven.

As it is for Judaism, the Mount of Olives is considered sacred ground by the pious of Christianity. The Chapel of the Ascension, within the courtyard of a mosque, is believed the point from which Jesus ascended to Heaven, a few meters from the Church of the Pater Noster where Jesus instructed his disciples in the Lord's Prayer and upon whose walls is inscribed the prayer in forty-four languages. The Mount of Olives is replete with the history of Judaism and Christianity. Here, too, sits a Franciscan church where Jesus wept after experiencing his disturbing vision of Jerusalem's destruction. Also on the mount is the Garden of Gethsemane, and the Basilica of Agony where Jesus prayed the night before his arrest by Pilate's soldiers, and the Tomb of the Virgin which houses an underground vault where Joseph and Mary are purportedly entombed.

But Dov Rosenberg's urgent call of the night before wasn't intended to offer Paolo and Father Angelo a private tour of an area whose meaning and history they were themselves intimately familiar with. As the major was angling the Hummer into a tight parking spot, Dov was already instructing the scholars to exit the car.

"Get out and follow where my finger's pointing," he said preemptively. "You know the Valley of Kidron as well as I do. There's Mount Ophel and the Mount of Contempt, there, you see?"

"Yes, Dov," Paolo answered, slightly exasperated, standing now behind Dov, Father Angelo to his right.

"At the storm's worst, that second day, the wall of water, the flood crested, etching a new groove through the valley, the cut's maybe fifteen feet deeper now. Look over there, the tombs of Absolom and Zachariah, they're on their sides ... what a damned Schande." Rosenberg shook his head sadly.

"We see," Father Angelo said. "The IDF's roped off the entire valley." Below them, ribbons of orange tape boxed the Kidron in, with squads of IDF soldiers posted at both ends of the valley.

"This was all predicted in the Book of Joel," Father Angelo reminded them. "It's right here in the Kidron Valley that the judgment will be rendered on Resurrection Day. 'Let the heathen be awakened, and come up to the valley of Jehoshaphat, for there I will sit to judge all the heathen around me.' It is commonly believed that the Jehoshaphat referenced in Joel was in fact the Kidron Valley."

"I don't believe we're there, Angelo, at Joel's Day of Resurrection, at least not yet," Dov replied excitedly, drawing a last, deep drag from his cigarette before casting it aside as the smoke streamed from his nose. "But the flood's produced a sort of resurrection for us. Under Absolom's tomb, all that survived the destruction in 70 A.D., we discovered another tomb from Herod's reign, a chamber, still sealed ..."

Dov's declaration riveted both Paolo and Father Angelo's attention. Both men stared intently at their host. "Well, Dov, what's in it? Why all the suspense?" Paolo asked impatiently, as anxious as a child shaking a wrapped birthday gift.

"Haver! Haver! Patience!" Dov said, swatting away Paolo's question; he had barely recited the preface to his story. He would not be Dr. Dov Rosenberg if he was not given to grandiose exposition and he'd only just begun to unravel this tale. Whenever

Dov got wound up spinning a story, it would be stretched out for effect, inevitably dubbed by him as the discovery of the millennium, a discovery so significant the Earth would, if it could, stop spinning on its axis. Both Romans knew the drill. They were as they had been more times than either cared to remember in Dov's thrall, condemned to await the denouement at the time of his choosing, Dov's revelation of what treasure or treasures the waters had brought forth.

"Remember four years ago, the dig that uncovered the massive tunnel, the drainage canal under the Western Wall? That was nothing, peanuts, compared to what's washed up now. The goddamned heavens opened up and ... well, you know, this I don't have to tell you, you were in Tiberias. Anyway, when the storm let up a little I drove to the museum— ten miles an hour, the water was up to the fenders— to check the damage to see if I could assist the rescue teams. Some leakage but nothing major, thank God, and everything was under control. You saw, the walls haven't completely dried out yet. That was the Friday, third day maybe, of the storm. I rechecked on Saturday when the rains had stopped. Still dry but the new housing down the hill showed serious damage, most all of it seemed reparable."

Dov coughed, cursed cigarettes in general, pausing to catch his breath before proceeding.

"Then it all became clear, the extent of the damage, what had happened. The low-lying areas around the old walls of the city, just above the Sultan Suleiman part of the wall, the Garden Tomb. The water had rushed in from the Wadi El-Joz to the south and west, past the YMCA and to Morasha. The crest of the wave, how broad it was no one can figure, rushed due south from the wadi and sliced through the Kidron and past the City of David ..." He nodded towards the half-submerged, spongy section below them.

"'And?" Paolo said, hoping to prod Dov towards the story's conclusion, wondering how much longer the telling would take. What was it the Americans always say in the face of such lengthy disquisitions? Cut to the chase. That was it, cut to the chase. But Paolo knew the request would be fruitless, to ask Dov Rosenberg to cut to the chase. Dov was deaf to entreaties once he'd worked up a head of steam.

"'So when the waters began to recede," he continued, "the IDF, figuring there'd be chaos and looting, called me for advice. I insisted that the Kidron be sealed off immediately, who knew what would be unearthed with the ancient graves torn open, and that it be placed under twenty-four hour military guard. They agreed and told me to have a look-see myself, see if there was anything else. Ah, I've gotta sit down ..."

Dov found a bench and dropped onto it. Reaching into his jacket, he pulled out a handkerchief and mopped his sweat-dampened brow. Father Angelo, relieved, took a seat beside him, exhausted from listening to Dov. He'd had that effect on many a visiting scholar. Paolo half-sat, half-leaned on the low wall opposite, hands clasped before him, squinting as the sun rose higher above the hills of Jordan to the east.

"Where was I?" Dov asked rhetorically. "Oh, yes, well, I drove over in the Hummer and inspected the site." He gesticulated toward the Hummer against which the Major was reclining, the German shepherd seated at attention by his feet. "Absolom's tomb was lying on its side, maybe five meters from its original site. In fact, nothing was where it was supposed to be. Everything had shifted. Then I saw what appeared to be the top of a room, a chamber of some sort, made from sandstone like the Temple itself. It was probably there before the tomb was erected but we'll know more later, when the archaeological team examines it more closely. To expose it so we could access it, I had the workers dig around its perimeter. Took the better part of a day. The room's height is a little more than six feet, like Moshe here, with what looks to be a thick oak door, blackened like soot, of course, with its brass hinges intact. The chamber itself faces the Dome of the Rock. It's sealed with what I believe is lead so we didn't want to take a chance of damaging its contents, if there were contents, by prying it open without knowing what was inside."

"So?" Paolo cued.

"So you look before you leap. I called the museum and they rushed over the sonar device. It's like the ones doctors use for internal examinations, with a small digital camera on its tip that transmits the images to a computer. The minister okayed me drilling a hole through the door and ... what I saw was a storage area, artifacts stacked neatly, lead boxes on the floor. I tell you I felt like the wind was knocked out of me, that I was having a coronary, my heart was pounding so much ... I knew in that instant exactly how Howard Carter must've felt when he discovered Tutankhamun's

146

tomb ..."

Paolo could no longer contain himself.

"Dov, the suspense is killing us. What's so hush-hush? So you found an ancient chamber filled with artifacts, so what?"

"Look, you know how it is around here." Dov looked left and right, as if a spy might be hidden in their midst even though the entire area was under military quarantine. Satisfied that no one was eavesdropping, he went on. "After that fiasco with the Dead Sea Scrolls, the ad in the Wall Street Journal, looking for a buyer? Remember that, the disgrace?" he sputtered.

"Who could forget?" Father Angelo said, shaking his head in dismay. "Once we knew what it held, we cut through the door seal and entered. I've now had a chance to examine several of the boxes. That's all I can say now."

Paolo grimaced, then groaned, knowing speculation would lead them nowhere. They would learn what they needed to learn in Dov's own good time. This was not the first instance Dr. Dov Rosenberg had called upon the two men to verify a find. Nor was it unusual for European scholars, Dr. Paolo Pisa and Father Angelo Lorenzo often among them, to request Dr. Dov Rosenberg and his team of experts from the museum to examine and confirm a find of theirs. In 2009, Dov had brought his people to Cologne in order to determine whether a dig had in fact unearthed the oldest known synagogue north of the Alps, a synagogue so old it dated to the era of Hadrian. If Dr. Dov Rosenberg confirmed a find, for those in the scholarly community his approval was tantamount to the pope having pressed the papal seal onto an ecclesiastical letter.

* * *

Dov's cell phone jangled, cutting through the mid-morning silence on the Mount of Olives. The conversation was one-sided unless one counted Dov's repeated "yesses" and "right aways" as conversation. As he rang off, a slightly rattled Dr. Dov Rosenberg signaled the driver that they were all to return to the museum immediately.

As the Hummer descended the hill, Dov turned to Paolo.

"My apologies, Moshe, my orders come directly from the Minister himself. He's holding me personally responsible. And you two, both of you have to sign a document pledging yourselves to

147

absolute secrecy. No conferences, no academic get-togethers, no casual leaks to loved ones or trusted aides, nothing is to be said or written about any of this unless the Israeli government grants permission to go public. Absolute secrecy. Absolute." Dov's face was stern, as serious as either Roman had ever known it to be.

"Which minister called, Dov?"

"That's not important, names. He's not quite a government minister but his mandate comes directly from the prime minister. He has no portfolio, as the British might say, but he might as well have. He's always referred to as 'the Minister.' When he says jump, you ask 'how high?' Which is all you need to know about him."

* * *

"Your office is a dump, Dov," the Minister snapped, standing ramrod straight, his height equal to Paolo's, his fists balled atop Dov's paper-infested desk. "You don't need a security team, you need a cleaning staff ... How the hell do you find anything in this, this ... ashpah, this mess?" The sweep of his hand sent a sheaf of papers fluttering to the office's floor. "And what took so long? The country's in chaos and I have to wait for you to finish your Cook's Tour? You were supposed to be here a half-hour ago." His cold, blue eyes fixed Dov's until the museum director averted his and looked away.

"But ...," Dov began to protest, then stopped himself. The Minister waved away the stillborn complaint as one might an annoying child's whine. He was comfortable in his position of power. He didn't suffer fools nor did he brook opposition, particularly if his opponent was a civilian. The Minister sat atop the political pecking order, the type of Israeli who made and maintained Israel as a reality, a sabra who had fought valiantly in every war since 1973. A former general who had risen rapidly in rank, he was handpicked by the prime minister, her first appointment after she'd cleaned house, relieving those she referred to in public as "the weaklings"— the general staff that mishandled the 2006 conflict against Hezbollah— of their commands. Long overdue, most in the prime minister's kitchen cabinet agreed. In private, her term for those who botched the military operation was far harsher and unprintable.

Neither Paolo nor Father Angelo had ever seen Dov

contrite. In the Minister's presence, he positively fawned. The Minister drew two identical folders from his briefcase, each bound in red imitation leather stamped "Confidential" in gold leaf on their front, with the names of each Roman imprinted below, their photos under their names. Father Angelo's read: Michelangelo Urban Lorenzo, S. J., The Vatican, Italian National; Paolo's read: "Dr. Paolo Pisa/Dr. Moshe Josephus, Dual Nationality, Italian National/Israeli National.

Both men had signed pledges before, oaths of secrecy, statements defining and detailing conflicts of interest, legal documents stating they would publish nothing without written permission in preparation for a dig or remove so much as a bottle cap from an excavation site. These were the rules of the profession and while some colleagues had violated them, the black market in Judaica and Christian relics commanding as they did such absurdly inflated prices, the austere, icy expression on the Minister's face left no doubt that the Israeli government would enforce the agreement.

"These documents obviously contain complex legal clauses and you're welcome to read them before you sign. But the bottom line's obvious, yes?" Both men nodded. "And if you violate anything in the agreement— a phrase, a clause— you'll pass whatever short years are left to you in a jail in the Negev. And Father, the Vatican can't and won't help you. You do remember the immortal words of Joseph Stalin when your Pope Pius angrily protested Russia's occupation of Eastern Europe and demanded they withdraw, don't you? To refresh your memory, he asked 'How many divisions does the pope have?' You see my point, don't you?" The Minister expected no reply.

Father Angelo looked stricken.

Seeing his friend's discomfort, Dov attempted to intervene.

"Boychick," he addressed the Minister, "there's no need ..."

"As for you, Dr. Pisa or Dr. Josephus, whichever," he continued, ignoring Dov, "don't even dream that for a moment we'll respect your Italian passport. For me, it's nothing more than a coaster to put under my beer glass. All that matters to me, to us, is that you're also an Israeli citizen, which is how, if it's necessary, we'll judge you. Capisci? Any questions?"

Silence.

"Okay, sign the last page. Dov will witness your signatures," the Minister said, handing Father Angelo an ancient Waterman pen dug out of the marble holder half buried on Dov's cluttered desk. Paolo followed suit.

"Nice hand, Dr. Josephus," the Minister remarked, admiring Paolo's signature, smiling almost imperceptibly for the first time. He checked his watch and frowned. "Well, I know we can trust both of you, you've flawless reputations. And do excuse my rudeness," the last said more as an order than a request, "I've a great deal on my mind and more on my plate." He neatly tucked the signed documents into his briefcase. "So if you'll excuse me, gentlemen, duty calls. I'll see my own way out ..."

After he'd left the office, Dov said, "I never heard him apologize to anyone for anything before. Not that anyone around here has more than a nodding acquaintance with the word 'sorry.' You must've made a positive impression on him, Father."

"And he on us," said Father Angelo, still unsettled by the Minister's brusqueness.

"Well, everything's apparently kosher so we can begin," Dov said, relaxing, clearing his throat and fingering his pockets for his cigarette pack. "I didn't bring you two here on a wild goose chase. What we've found," he said, lighting his cigarette, and pointing it at Paolo, "might be the greatest find in the history of our people." Arcing the cigarette towards Father Angelo, seated opposite, he said, "The older brothers of your church."

"The greatest find?" Paolo's brow wrinkled with doubt.

The Italians knew Dr. Dov Rosenberg was given to histrionics at times, but in the end he always delivered, so he had their full attention. "Yes, the greatest find," Dov repeated, "pending the results of all our tests."

"Tests on what, specifically? And has the testing process been expedited?" Father Angelo asked. "I, for one, would like to return home ..."

"The Minister assures me that the testing on the find is proceeding with all deliberate speed. We don't want to keep you here longer than's necessary. Whether or not it's completed, you'll be flying out in two days at the latest. Listen, I know he offended you but believe me it wasn't personal. He is what he is and he's in our corner, which is what's important. So, yes, the tests are being conducted as we speak, in the utmost secrecy, of course, at Dimona. If it all proves out, they'll confirm a connection between what was found in Tiberias and the contents of the room we discovered in the Kidron."

"Yes, go on," Paolo urged, leaning forward, hoping to avoid another long-winded explanation, mindful of the earlier one on the mount. He mourned inwardly when Dov began again.

"Let me elaborate. Because of this disaster you weren't able to examine the box, the one with the date corresponding to 60 in our era. It's the old Judean dating system but roughly the years match up."

'That's true, Dov," Father Angelo confirmed. "It's the same year or close enough to it."

"Okay, let me continue," Dov said as if he was being prevented from doing so. "There was a second box, discovered at the same site."

"Another box?" Father Angelo choked out.

Paolo was caught off guard.

"Why didn't you ..."

"We couldn't tell you, not then. We needed your signatures, Moshe. Security, first and last," Dov said casually, angling his head towards the space lately vacated by the Minister. "I had no choice, none. You understand, don't you?" He didn't wait for Paolo's response. "We've had a couple of look-sees since. The first box is relatively minor. Our specialist in ancient Aramaic verified that the manuscript in the second box appears to be the First Gospel According to Matthew ..."

Father Angelo blinked rapidly and gripped his chair's arms. His head was swimming. "My God, Dov, are you ... are you sure?" he stammered, his voice breaking, "I-I mean, isn't there a ... margin for error here? After all ..."

"I know, I know. Questions, questions. Relax, Angelo, I know what's going through your mind. You want to phone the pope immediately but you can't, so relax, sit back and listen to what I've got to say. The manuscript we've discovered details the life of Jesus, his lineage from birth, his youth, the escape to Egypt, his baptism, and later his temptation and his early ministry. His sayings and the Lord's Prayer are included as well. Even what some Jews call the familiar cast of characters— Barabbas, Pilate, the Pharisees— they appear, and in this case, it's not a joke. The place of the praetorium is mentioned, the Temple, Gethsemane, Jesus' bearing the Cross to Golgotha, his death on the Cross the moment he became the Christ, his burial, his resurrection ..." Dov paused, winded. "It's all there. Look, we all know Matthew by heart. And, yes, earlier dated copies have appeared and other Gospels have been found in Egypt, too. More tests are needed but our best experts are inclined towards authenticating this manuscript as genuine, the true Gospel According to Matthew."

Paolo Pisa remained dubious.

"What makes this manuscript different from any of the others put forth over the last five hundred years? This could easily be just another medieval 'nail from the true Cross' scam or one of the hundreds of 'arrows' that allegedly pierced St. Sebastian ..."

"Yes, yes, Moshe, I know, I'm aware of all the phony manuscripts, the fake burial boxes containing the bones of Jesus, 'relics' made last week in China, I'm familiar with all that," he said huffily, sensing his authority was being questioned. "Maybe some even came from Guido's stores, eh?"

Paolo's look challenged Dov, his eyes demanding a retraction. None would be forthcoming. Paolo let it lie.

"When the storm gained force, I phoned the Minister," Dov went on, "who immediately had a military truck commandeered and ordered the dig site manager to personally drive both boxes here, just in case. Believe me, this manuscript is different, unlike any we'd yet seen. Not the text, that's fairly similar. It's the presentation that differentiates it from the others. This rendering is in the form of a play. It could have been performed in the theatre in Tiberias where the workmen found it, in situ, left behind or hidden for reasons we'll probably never know. Or maybe it was just forgotten. Sometimes the only explanation is a painfully simple one."

Amen, simple, Paolo thought.

"What's more than likely, though," Dov continued, "is that the Gospel was performed as an entertainment, probably before an audience consisting of Greeks and Jews who still considered the Nazarenes just another Jewish sect. What this isn't is a couple of fishhooks buried in a house in Tiberias, attributed by the credulous to Peter. Only faith supports that claim."

"True, very true," Father Angelo acknowledged.

Dov walked past both men, approaching the crenellated silver-gray covering that fronted a quarter of his office's far wall. Pressing in a code on the keypad next to it, the covering slid slowly away, revealing the double, steel doors of a large vault. After entering a second code, the three heard a sharp click, then the thick steel doors slowly parted, opening inwards on tracks.

"The latest in security technology, a gift of the German people, so the card said," Dov joked. "Latter-day reparations, one might say."

Inside the climate-controlled vault, there was floor-to-ceiling burnished steel shelving lined with treasures of the ancient world. Selected statues, large and small, from the Canaanite period, artifacts from the Phoenician era and the reign of David, and rows and rows of Crosses, among other priceless samplings, some allegedly dating to the time of Abraham, were all neatly arranged in chronological order, almost filling the vault from top to bottom.

The trove, its very extent, was breathtaking. Paolo didn't wonder long why in all the years they'd worked in Israel that neither he nor Father Angelo had been aware of this vault's existence before now. Remembering that smoking inside the room was forbidden, Rosenberg pinched out his cigarette.

"You're the first ..." Dov said, searching for an appropriately neutral word, "um, 'outsiders' ever permitted through these doors. It's not a question of trust, Moshe, Angelo, it's more an issue of ... security." Dov shook his head, annoyed. "Yes, security. That's the blanket word, the catchall word we use, to trigger the veil we draw across whatever, whenever someone in one of the ministries wants to shield something from the public eye. Or worse, the world's eyes, no matter how absurd it is on the face of it. Well, maybe the museum's not the best example but ... ah, you know what I mean, no? More paranoia we don't need. It's beginning to border on messhugas, this top-to-bottom security obsession. And the storms, they only made it worse. So now, boychicks, now that you know what will happen to you if you breathe a word, the 'dire consequences' that made you wet your pants, you've got clearance. Here, put these on." He handed each man a pair of white cotton protective gloves, slipping on his own, and lifting the lead box from a near shelf.

He carried the box to a table several meters inside the vault, put it down and removed the cover. He gingerly removed the manuscript and opened it gently. "See, it's in the form of a play, a Greek play. That word," he said, pointing, "it means Chorus and that ... that means Strophe, reason and anti-reason ..."

"We both read Greek," Paolo reminded him quietly.

"... the world of the fates, our inner thoughts, the world

153

Freud explored," Dov said, talking over Paolo. He then carefully turned to the portion in Matthew that surrounds Pilate's condemnation of Jesus to death.

With the kind of stylus used to read the Torah so one's finger did not touch the word of God, Dov traced Pilate's words to the crowd gathered below his window: "Whom do you want me to release to you? Barabbas or Jesus, he who is called the Christ? And the crowd yelled 'Give us Barabbas.' Then what shall I do with Jesus who is called the Christ ... and they shouted, 'Let him be crucified.'"

He then pointed to the Aramaic word for Strophe, reading aloud, "'Pilate, he is an innocent man, the only son of God, he is The Christ, our long-awaited Messiah, our King. If you let Him live, He will reign over us, all of us, for He is the Son of God. In the name of Rome, use your power to save Him so He can save us.'

"Here," Dov went on excitedly, pointing with the stylus, "Antistrophe holds another view. 'Pilate, he is an imposter, this is all a clever trick by the People of the Book. Your gods are supreme, the God of the Jews cannot be seen, that is why you are here in the name of Rome. Let him die, he has violated the law of the Prophets of the people you rule in the name of Rome. God cannot have a son, domains cannot be mixed, let him die on the Cross.'"

"I think this is a hoax, Dov. We've seen this sort of thing before, a Passion Play so soon after Jesus' death. No, sorry, I don't believe this. This manuscript is nothing more than a clever forgery."

"No, Paolo, with respect, I believe you're wrong on this ..." Father Angelo objected.

"Gentlemen, let's not debate this now, please," Dov cut in, raising his voice above theirs. "We're not on a panel in Cambridge or Rome. We've got plenty of time to hash this out privately, between ourselves, but let's let the lab make the final call on the dating.

I've read this several times in its entirety and, yes, there's little here that we've not heard before, including the condemnation of the Pharisees." Dov returned to the manuscript.

"'Pharisees, hypocrites! Because of you, the Kingdom of Heaven is against men, woe to you ...' It's not our purpose to debate the origins of anti-Judaism or anything else today. Let's just focus on the manuscripts. Please."

"I agree," Father Angelo said, adding, "that was Matthew

23:13."

"Yes, we know, Angelo. Even some Jews know their New Testament."

"I needn't be reminded of that, Dov," Father Angelo bristled, a hurt look on his face.

"I meant no disrespect, Angelo," Dov replied, squeezing the priest's arm gently, smiling. "I know you need no reminders. Apologies."

"Dov," Paolo said, "you said 'manuscripts.' Are there more?"

"Sorry I failed to mention it before. There's another, a second document. It was in back of the first, on a single piece of parchment and in very good shape. Thank God for lead boxes," he exclaimed. "It's in Hebrew, in the ancient script. We haven't had it decoded yet."

"It's from the same period, before the Temple's destruction?" Paolo asked.

"Probably," Dov said, lifting the glass-enclosed parchment from beneath the first manuscript. "It's here where the story begins to come together. I doubt we'll ever know definitively who wrote this, all of this is so preliminary though, but there are ... hints ... in other sources. Josephus comes to mind, and Tacitus. No love lost between those two. As you both know, in his Annals, Tacitus believed the Jews originated in Crete and took their names from the Cretan mountains. He rejected the idea of one god and found our religion mean and tasteless. He laughed at our burial of the dead but oddly he appears to have respected the Jews' contempt for death. What more can we say, Tacitus was a complex fellow, a true Roman and one cruel bastard."

"Tacitus," Father Angelo said, longing for a cigarette to occupy his fiddling hands, "was no friend of the new cult. Yes, he was Roman, with a Roman's vision of the world which, in that era, considered Judea a sixth-rate province, a constant thorn in Rome's side ..."

"So what's the connection between the two, Dov?" Paolo asked, gesturing towards the manuscripts. "In capsule form?" He surreptitiously checked his watch.

"That, you know, I don't know how to do, Moshe, but ... I'll walk you both through it as quickly as I can. I believe it was written just before the final assault on Jerusalem in the summer of 70 A.D.

155

when Titus thought the Jews would surrender. He gave them their chance and Pineas responded by showering gifts on him from the Temple's inner rooms and the treasury. I'm half convinced this parchment contains directions, a roadmap of sorts ..."

The dubious expression had returned to Paolo's face. The condition of the parchment raised a red flag, and the deep black lettering, slightly different in shape than modern Hebrew, hadn't bled into the page itself. Dov noted Paolo's and Father Angelo's questioning looks.

"Don't worry, I've seen my share of parchments from this era and they held up pretty well. It's not a hoax, this piece ... well, not at least at this point. You've seen the parchments downstairs, the ones on display in the museum. Many are in fragments, the result of being rolled into ceramic jars and sitting for two thousand years. This one came out of an airtight, sealed box buried ten feet under a tomb, unmoved since Herod ordered it built." Dov paused, looking at both men. "Look, we're by nature skeptical, remember? We've handled scores of hoaxes since Yadin presented the Dead Sea Scrolls. This parchment wasn't rolled but flattened out so it was no problem putting it between these two pieces of glass, magnifying it a little." He tapped the glass with the stylus. "The author ... let's call him a scribe, but I think he was more than a mere scribe. Whatever he was he was in a hurry. Some of the Hebrew letters almost connect but not clearly ... I think this was done deliberately, with considerable forethought."

Dov ran the stylus over what he termed "the title," in deep, black lettering twice the size of the rest of the text.

"This seems to translate roughly as 'The Accursed Tree,' the Latin infelix lingnum obviously. Both the Romans and the early Christians used this phrase, the place where criminals were nailed and died in agony. The crux was never a Jewish form of execution."

"So then it is an early Christian document," Father Angelo said.

"Wait, Angelo, listen, there's more." The unlit cigarette clamped between Dov's teeth fell to the floor.

"Seneca and Cicero used that phrase, too," Paolo noted.

"Yes, yes, Moshe, let me continue," Dov stammered, clearing his throat.

Paolo was sympathetic. He thought, yes, the first scholars who examined the Dead Sea Scrolls probably experienced the same

156

sort of hesitation, of anticipation at what they were privy to.

""'Our only child was speared,'" Dov began, "'on the accursed tree planted on the top of a skull above the Star and the Black Eagles below. He could not escape from its thorns and cried out in pain. Below strong men laughed and did not offer to help as they pointed to the Child. His blood dripped on his mother. She and her Son cried out to God in the heavens for help. Only silence as the strong men walked away. They told her that her Son was being punished for what they did not know and the accursed tree was his fate. Her Son died on the accursed tree since he was a transgressor of the rules. Later other men came to help and climbed the tree and cut him down. His blood was upon them. He was laid to rest not far from the tree in a tomb of stone in keeping with his traditions. Three days after the morrow, she saw her child as if in a dream. He told her to cut down the tree in fours like the corners of the earth. It must be buried since it has my blood. When the rooster ushered in the Sun, she came back with four men and cut the downed tree into fours. It was hidden under two slabs of five. Here it rested until the Black Eagles returned with branches dipped in oil to fire the limestone. The keepers of the tree sailed it to the land of the dead below the olive trees to the place where a Father was transgressed by his Son who had violated one of the Ten. On the Four Corners of the Earth rested the wisdom which the first son had obeyed and the second had transgressed. The tree had become Holy and in what was a dream, others now read from the Place, the lime will melt into the wood, the Star will set and the Eagles will perish, then the Four Corners of the Earth will be One. That Day will come when the Waters of the Jordan cleanse the land and the accursed tree will be called capitala.'"

"Capitata . . . capitata," Father Angelo repeated as Dov finished his reading, swaying unsteadily, one hand clapped to his brow, the other reaching out for support. "Capitata ..." Paolo caught the priest as he began to sink, steadying him, his arms around Father Angelo's shoulders. "Dov, slide that chair over here," he said, easing Father Angelo onto it.

The priest was breathing heavily, his hand clutching the Cross about his neck.

"Our Father, who art in Heaven," he said weakly, "hallowed be his name ..."

Paolo and Dov gaped at Father Angelo, fearing he was

157

suffering a seizure. The priest was mumbling now, rocking softly, the remainder of the Lord's Prayer, barely intelligible, thanking God repeatedly for "His miracle." Paolo and Dov had seen the same sort of religious display many times before in Jerusalem. Christian pilgrims making their way along the Way of the Cross during Easter, the Christmas throngs, the aged, black-clad women rubbing their rosaries on the marble slab where Jesus reportedly lay, prepared for burial. They were all witnesses to an unswerving, deep belief in their own faith, their expressions differing little from those shown by the Hasidim of the Mea Shearim ghetto. According to the Hasidim, God had spoken to them directly, saying, "I have chosen you to be special to me ... and Israel is your land." For two thousand years, the two faiths had lived parallel, occasionally intersecting lives with little benefit for the Jews, lives that more often passed each other like ships in the night. Both knew God was the same God for both yet each climbed a different mountain, one in a faith rooted in the past, the other in a faith grounded in the future.

However much Father Angelo walked in both worlds, the secular world of the scholars and the religious world of the church, his faith in the end superseded everything. As he crossed himself, he wondered if either Paolo or Dov understood why he was overcome. He suspected they did.

"I'm ... I'm okay, fine, just fine," he said, the color returning to his face, allaying their concerns. "It's all a little overwhelming ... for me."

"Are you well enough to continue, Angelo?" Dov asked solicitously. "We've more to see in the larger vault downstairs, the crux immissa, the capitata and the limestones it lay under for two thousand years."

"Of course, of course, even if I had to crawl." he said gamely. "Would you give me a hand, Paolo?"

The three exited the room slowly. Once Dov had secured the vault's doors, he reached into his pocket and extracted his half-consumed cigarette, flicking off the burnt end. Lighting up, he turned back to Father Angelo and Paolo.

"Now you see why we had you sign those documents? What you've seen is overpowering, isn't it? It leveled you, Angelo, yes? And it would be almost impossible to keep such a secret without legal constraints, yes?"

Father Angelo permitted himself a small smile and nodded.

Dov coughed up a lungful of smoke, staring at the cigarette squeezed between his nicotine-stained fingers.

"These will kill me one day, boychicks, mark my words. Angelo, if it makes you feel any better, I've got my own confession. When I first read the parchment, it made me dizzy, too, so you're not alone."

"Why do we need the cryptology boys to decode what's obvious, eh?" Paulo asked. "The star is Jerusalem, the Black Eagles the Romans, the mother Mary, and the son Jesus the Christ. Where's the puzzle?"

"Brilliant, Moshe, just brilliant," Dov teased.

"We've found the Latin Cross, and the 'stones of five,' the tablets, which, if the document proves to be valid, were removed from the Temple about the time our misguided Pineas bribed our pal Titus with all that tribute. And this you're going to keep from the world? Again, why? Are you out of your mind, Dov?"

"Maybe we are, Moshe, but this discussion, too, can wait. All in good time. Follow me."

As they left Dov's office, Father Angelo grabbed what appeared to be a common staff leaning against the office wall to balance himself.

"Careful, Angelo. It may look like a typical walking stick— I forget where it's from or whose it was— but it's worth over a million. Dollars, not shekels."

CHAPTER SIXTEEN

As they descended the several flights to the bowels of the Israel Museum, the Romans walked slightly slower and out of earshot behind their escort, giving them a moment to confer about the situation they'd found themselves in.

"There's something about this that disturbs me, Angelo," Paolo said, *sotto voce.*

"Which is?" Father Angelo whispered.

"Why did they call us to confirm the finds? They've a boatload of experts here, men like Natan Goldin at Hebrew University, the people at the Rockefeller, Manfred Fisher from Goettingen, he's spent his life here and he's Germany's foremost authority on such objects ... I suppose we should be flattered but it leaves me bewildered.

Honestly, for all my years here, and for as long as I've known Dov, I just can't get inside his or their thinking."

"It bewilders me, too. On the one hand we had to sign off on that secrecy oath, on the other we're asked to provide our views, our expert opinion yet breathe a word of it to no one. I'm half puzzled, and half insulted." Father Angelo grasped the walking stick a little tighter as they reached the sub-basement, the cavernous area below the room where the Dead Sea Scrolls were on display.

"They're certainly not like us, are they, these Israelis?" Paolo's question was less a question than a statement of fact. By his silence, Father Angelo clearly accepted it as such. A small woman, perhaps in her thirties, whom Dov referred to as his assistant, awaited them. "Shalom," she greeted them, unsmiling.

The four stood before a massive, polished steel door, twice as high as it was wide. On its front was a legend in German and its Hebrew translation: "A Gift from the People of Germany to the People of Israel." It was dated 1964. Under the date was the name of the manufacturer, Karl Hausmann & Soehne, Frankfurt-Main, BRO.

"All these gifts ..." Dov clapped his hands in mock

celebration.

Two dials, combination locks, secured the door, between them a timer behind bulletproof glass. As Dov dialed the first set of numbers, his assistant turned her head away. Once Dov turned the handle to the left, he looked away and the assistant entered the second set of numbers, turning the handle to the right.

"This ritual of rituals, this safe drives me crazy. Every two months we receive new combos from Tel-Aviv along with a new assistant." He jerked his thumb in the assistant's direction. "All sent separately. King Solomon and Herod had their holy of holies. This is the modern one, overseen by me, Dr. Dov Rosenberg, the new high priest, the keeper of the keys to the kingdom ... or at least the combinations to it ... Ah, behold, the Panzer of safes, voila!" He extended his arms in presentation, as the doors quietly opened. As he pushed a green button on the jamb, the steel bars opposite the door released and slid slowly back.

Paolo had seen similar security arrangements and vaults in the basements and, more often lately, mountain repositories of the world's great museums and banks where treasures are normally stored and added to in times of crisis. After 9/11, Paolo had been asked by the Met in New York to validate newly acquired pieces from the Flavian period. He accompanied the treasures in an armored truck from the Met to the Federal Reserve downtown. Fearing terrorists might strike the Met, the more important pieces were to be relocated there and exact copies put in their place. Here in the Federal Reserve's impregnable vault he recognized original paintings and sculptures he previously believed he had viewed elsewhere, along with artifacts from earlier eras, and gold bars, all stamped with the Nazi Adler perched atop a swastika, chockablock and coded. But the Federal Reserve's storage room was almost dwarfed by the room they were about to enter. The Israel Museum's vault was a museum within a museum, a perfect square approximately two hundred feet long and just as wide.

"This, my friends," Dov announced grandly as they entered, "is our Fort Knox. It was built at the height of the Cold War, the materials and construction used the same as you'd find in missile silos. Layers of steel and concrete, a self-contained building under a building. Or, in this case, under the gardens. Of course, we could've built this ourselves but it was part of the deal with Bonn."

Neither Paolo nor Father Angelo invited a detailed history

162

of the doors. What transfixed them were the long rows of rooms faced with gold-enameled, cage-like barriers, each more than an inch thick and adorned with the seal of the State of Israel. It was a sight neither man had ever seen before. As they walked along the aisles, they began to appreciate the enormity of what was secreted there, hidden away from the world, under the holy city of Jerusalem. The shelving, in infinitely greater quantities than Dov's office vault upstairs, contained treasures they viewed only in photos, many in black-and-white from another age. On the sturdy steel barriers to each room, each shelved article's provenance was affixed and behind these plaques was another identifying label indicating where and when the artifact was found. Fort Knox had its gold; the Israel Museum had enough art and archaeological treasures to underpin the shekel.

"Angelo, you look surprised," Dov said, noticing the priest tapping the locks on the room barriers.

"You miss nothing, Dov," Father Angelo smiled.

"We use old-fashioned keys which, when turned, connect to our computer network. If you play with that lock, you'll be gassed."

"No, not true, it can't be true!" Father Angelo gasped. 'That's a bad joke, Dov."

"No, no, it's not a joke, Angelo. When the prime minister toured the vault after it was installed, he questioned the security and was told of the gas. Legend has it that he shouted 'Rip it out and send it back! Today.'"

Father Angelo blanched. "Why . . . why wasn't it removed and returned?" he asked.

"Once the PM calmed down, the system was explained to him in detail. He was told several Western institutions had identical systems installed, so he finally accepted the, um, efficacy of gas as a last resort backup. It was touch-and-go but in the end he swallowed hard and even praised the security system, avoiding any mention of the gas, of course. Imagine if word of this had ever gotten out," Dov said. "We'd have had a revolution on our hands. That was then, though, and this is now. Security is all but a word to the wise, boychicks." Dov pressed a finger to his lips. "No word of this leaves the museum."

It was virtually impossible to grasp and absorb what both men saw in the rooms framing the corridor leading to where they would examine the finds. They felt satiated, overwhelmed by the collected riches arrayed before and around them. A bas-relief from Ramses II, dated ca. 1304-1237 B.C., basalt stelae from the 15th century B.C., Egyptian sarcophagi, a grouping of medieval Haggadah, a pocket Bible printed in Renaissance Italy, Sumerian art, proto-Canaanite works from the 12th century B.C., terra cotta from the 6th century B.C., ossuary boxes from nearby Mount Scopus, Nabatean clay statues from Petra in Jordan, entire mosaic floors dating from the Roman occupation, oil lamps inscribed with either Jewish or Christian symbols, marble chancels, tombstones from Germany, Russia, and elsewhere inscribed with Hebrew characters, menorahs by the score, wooden Torah arch doors and finials from Algeria to India, Purim rattles, and in its own room, an ivory pomegranate from the Temple of Solomon.

As they neared their destination, Paolo stopped and pointed to a scroll under glass.

"I thought that was upstairs - the Isaiah Scroll, Dov?" Paolo said.

"Upstairs is the copy, this is the real thing. We moved it down here when Arafat started with his intifadas. Washington suggested we move it again during their Iraq war.

We have another gift from the Germans, buried deep in the ... hills. Its location is so secret that even I don't know where it is."

"Sure, Dov, as if you didn't know," Paolo laughed, shaking his head. "I don't know, Angelo doesn't know, but you? You know."

"Well, Moshe, maybe I have an idea where it might be," Dov said, grinning back at him. "Remember," he added, wagging a finger at both men as they stood before a second, smaller inner vault, "you signed the pledge."

Dov and his assistant repeated the door opening ritual, one looking left, the other looking right as each spun their respective dials. As they walked through the portal, a cursory glimpse revealed even more of the nation's valuables but not what they'd came to examine. The walls of the smaller vault were lined with crux immissa, more than either could count. Other Crosses, the T-shaped crux commissa or ansata, were represented in quantity along with Crosses from the Knights Templar. Below the Crosses lay stone tablets, each etched with the Ten Commandments in ancient Hebrew or Latin or the common people's tongue of Aramaic.

It was in the muted lighting of the anteroom that the

scholars immediately recognized one of the finds they had suddenly, urgently been summoned to examine, to validate. The four pieces of the capitata, the crux immissa, discovered in the Kidron, had been reassembled on the slate floor.

Father Angelo crossed himself reflexively, knelt, and kissed the shaft below the traverse bar, once more reciting the Lord's Prayer. He was this time in full possession of his faculties. He had done what any true believer would have done when confronted with an object of such religious magnitude. Completing the prayer, he used the staff to rise slowly to his feet, his eyes still fixed on the Cross.

"The Renaissance painters seemed to have gotten it right, Angelo," Paolo said, placing his hand on the priest's shoulder. "The capitata appears approximately twenty feet long, give or take a few inches, the traverse bar slightly less than half that."

"Yes, it seems to be," Father Angelo concurred. "Larger than I thought it might be, actually." His voice trembled as he spoke, his heart thumped, and his pulse began to race as he studied the Cross. The priest took a deep, calming breath as Paolo continued his comments.

"Look here," Paolo said, pointing to where the bars had interconnected. "It's notched with two holes. The two were probably connected with wooden bolts. And there, the black ring circling the vertical section, the darker wood below, say, five feet of it leading to the base. I'd bet it was sunk into the ground, maybe stabilized with a concrete base of some sort to hold it upright."

As seasoned archaeologists, both men had eagle-keen eyes and long experience where visual measurement was concerned.

"The ancient Romans were always great engineers," Father Angelo said, steadier now, "even when dealing with death." He fingered the nail holes at the ends of the traverse bar, feeling the air rushing from him. "If Jesus' neck was at the place where the two beams crossed ..." he said, barely above a whisper, leaving the thought unfinished.

"If it was Jesus," Dov said, "he was a large man, over six feet tall, a giant for that era. Our forensic people plan to test the wood for blood."

"Just as I thought, the Cross is cut from cedar," Paolo said definitively. "No olive tree could make a straight staff a third this length."

"You know your woods, Moshe." Dov poked Paolo. "You must've listened to your father, maybe a little, hah?"

"More than a little, Dov." "What about the Romans' sign mocking Christ?" Father Angelo asked, "The one that appears above his head in the paintings—I.N.R.I. Jesus of Nazareth, King of the Jews?"

"Nothing found, nothing confirmed, nothing verified," Dov replied briskly. "You can see for yourself, Angelo. There's only a small hole in the shaft, but who knows if it's a nail hole and if it was, did it hold a sign, the sign? Maybe the Romans hung the sign around Jesus' neck for all to clearly see? After all, whoever was crucified on this Cross was well above the ground. Perhaps we're taking the Biblical description of the event too literally. Could it be the sign didn't exist in the first place? Maybe it was a figment of an early painter's imagination and was picked up by his successors, becoming a necessary ingredient in all subsequent depictions of the crucifixion ..." Dov paused for a moment but Father Angelo merely stroked his chin, lost in his own thoughts, knowing what he knew. Unshaken in his faith and beliefs, it was clear to Paolo, if not to Dov, that Father Angelo had sealed himself off from Dov as their host launched into his various conjectures and interpretations.

"Let's move on," Dov said impatiently, as if he was a tour guide keeping his charges on a tight schedule. "We can return to the Cross later."

As they moved to the far end of the second vault, Father Angelo took hold of Paolo's arm. "This is all so draining. Imagine, the capitata ..." He could barely say the word.

"Forgive me, Angelo, but it all seems too neat, too ... tidy."

Paolo's closely-held professional tenet, the one he lived by, that faith was no substitute for hard evidence, was shared only in part by his colleague, even less so after Father Angelo Lorenzo came into physical contact with what could very well be the True Cross. What more sacred object could there be in Christendom? Father Angelo's carefully nurtured appetite for skepticism in most matters disappeared, his desire to accept as actual what he had just seen nudging his doubt aside.

"It makes sense to me, Paolo ..."

Paolo began to speak, then shrugged, knowing instinctively argument was futile.

At the end of the room, Dov had stationed himself before a

small table. It was, judging by its markings, covered with a large cloth from the Byzantine Period.

"Before I remove the cloth, let me say a few words," Dov said.

"Only a few, Dov, please, not another history lesson," Paolo pleaded, "it's not as if we're unawares ..."

Before Paolo could finish, Dov interrupted, soldiering on.

"You don't know what I'm going to tell you, Moshe, believe me. The so-called Tomb of Absolom, beneath which these artifacts were found? It's nothing more than a gravesite of an unknown, a mystery man, a 'who knows who.' Whoever was inside, it wasn't King David's son, Absolom. Didn't know that, did you, Moshe?" Dov crowed, triumphant. "It's for the tourists, this myth, entirely without basis but what could it hurt, eh? It makes for what everyone calls a 'photo opportunity,' another entry for the 'My Trip to Israel' album. The tombs in the Kidron Valley were in reality the tombs of wealthy Jewish families in the Herodian period and the one popularly called 'Absoloms' was probably from the family of Hezir. All the recovered evidence is here, in the vault. But tradition rides roughshod over evidence, right, Angelo?" Dov challenged. Father Angelo ignored the baiting, his silence a signal for the director to continue. "So the tomb remains misidentified, but who cares? What's more important is what we've discovered in there. The Hezirs apparently ordered the tomb's base hewn from rock with that additional chamber, perhaps for further burials, in which we made our discovery. My guess is that the Hezir family was well connected, members of the Second Temple's upper crust. Their line vanished with the destruction of the city so no more is known of them or their fate. We've determined, though, that the Hezirs were hardly followers of the Jesus cult or any of the 'messiahs' that kept cropping up in the century of Christ's birth. They were more likely Pharisees and at least one of them sat on the Sanhedrin. If the Cross we've just seen, still a big 'if,' is the Cross on which Jesus was crucified, it somehow fell into the Hezirs' hands and, to keep it from Jesus' followers, it was simply hidden away in that stone safe deposit box."

Dov was incapable of reducing essential information to bite-size nuggets, the import of which scholars of Paolo Pisa and Father Angelo's rank would readily grasp. Not a chance. Dov was an inveterate lecturer, unfolding information as if he was peeling an onion. Paolo and Father Angelo were beaten into submission under the director's torrent of words. Their sighs and polite smiles served as a white flag of surrender.

"Yes, please continue, Dov," Paolo said unnecessarily as if there was the ghost of a chance Dov would do otherwise.

"What's important to understand," the director said, "is the atmosphere in Judea after Herod's death and the events that followed from it. The Sadducees ran the show, as you well know, far too self-satisfied and conniving for their and their fellow Jews' own good. The deal they cut with the Romans they believed was the best deal to be had. It exempted the Jews from the Imperial Cult, providing them with a sort of 'special relationship,' as one might say today, with their rulers. They were the power brokers within the Temple, one of their number the Sanhedrin's high priest - this we know from the New Testament, from Mark — a position comparable to, say, a modern CEO. Jesus's growing popularity represented a palpable threat to their sway so they reacted as any entrenched group might, they moved against him and his followers.

"Pontius Pilate recognized the danger and, as the Roman procurator in Judea, was certainly an active and willing collaborator in Jesus's demise. Who needed more *zores,* this time from a wandering lunatic fancying himself the Messiah? Judea was overrun with these sojourners heralding the apocalypse. It was an uncertain time, to put it mildly. Pilate's governing responsibility was to keep a lid on the restive Roman province, ever on the point of disintegration, something Titus later found nearly impossible to do. As if Jesus' pronouncements weren't unsettling enough, the Pharisees, emphasizing the oral traditions, held the Hellenized and Romanized Jews in contempt. Nothing personal, Moshe," Dov laughed. "Only citing facts. And who can forget the Samaritans up north, clustering around Mount Gerizim, apostates with their own temple, intermarrying with Gentiles?"

"The meaning of the parable in Luke 10," Father Angelo said.

"Correct. Add to the simmering cauldron the Essenes, with their roots in the Maccabees' revolt, announcing they were the 'true Israel,' that they were God's elect. Daniel 7:13— awaiting Judgment Day and the arrival of a heavenly 'man.' Is it any wonder Pilate thought these people, all of them, Jesus included, were more than slightly crazy?"

"One can almost empathize with Pilate," Paolo began to say.

"One, perhaps, but not this one," Father Angelo interrupted, folding a hand around his crucifix.

"All this being said," Dov continued, "when Titus arrived less than four decades after Jesus' crucifixion, a true judgment day arrived. I suspect that some, no, many believed that the end of days was nigh with the destruction of the Second Temple. The small but growing cult in the north, in the Galilee, well, they probably believed it as well but they would, as we know, survive. Whatever and wherever the truth lies, it all remains speculative. We've found as yet no other documents but God only knows what other documents might later turn up? It's been less than a week since the storms ended. We're far from dried out. Well, whoever hid these artifacts we recovered knew of their inestimable value. Like the Jews during the Babylonian Captivity, believing that they too were facing the end, extinction, they wrote everything down. A footprint in the sand wouldn't do; they wanted posterity, if there was to be a posterity, to remember them. Well, I'm digressing," he said, reaching down and removing the covering from the black marble table.

Paolo blinked rapidly, dumbstruck. Dov's assistant, whose first time this was in the vault's inner sanctum, and Father Angelo stared, wide-eyed.

Before them lay two small tablets, limestone pink, in mint condition. They seemed as new as the day they were cut from local stone and, according to tradition, sent to an inscriber. The lettering and characters were formed in the same fashion as the form used during Herod's reign. The letters revealed the divine words given to Moses on Mount Sinai.

The four, instead of moving forward, took a step back as if they'd encountered a force field.

"This just cannot be," Father Angelo gasped. "The capitata in one room, and the code of conduct before us." Without being asked, Paolo brought Father Angelo a chair. "This just cannot be," he repeated, as he lowered himself into it. "This must be a dream, a hallucination."

"It's not, Angelo," Dov assured him. "And put your gloves back on. These tablets, I suspect, were in the inner sanctuary of the Second Temple. They were probably removed from the wall with a crowbar-like tool. You can see the pry marks on their undersides," he said, lifting one, then the other, and turning them over.

"They were found exactly where the Tiberias manuscript indicated they'd be located, on the so-called four corners of the earth, with the capitata."

"So if you were a strict interpreter of the manuscript and pursue the inherent demands in the manuscript, then the Dome of the Rock is to be destroyed and a new temple, the Third Temple, built on the site."

"Your Jesuitical training has held you in good stead, Angelo," Dov remarked. "You've followed the dots to their logical conclusion. The implications are staggering, no? Imagine how this news would be greeted by the Orthodox, the Hasidim, to say nothing of the world of Islam. Holy War is too tepid a term, unsuited to what such an action would bring down upon all our heads."

Dov glanced at Paolo. "Moshe, you're skeptical?"

"I said to Angelo before that this all fits together too neatly; the tablets seem new. Nothing's convinced me that this isn't a masterful hoax. The cisterns and the water channel beyond the Royal Portico, the channel that leads out to the Kidron under Solomon's Portico, it's still there. While Pineas was delivering the lucre to Titus, who's to say some other official wasn't ordered— or even took it upon himself— to chisel the tablets from the walls while his accomplices carried off the four pieces of the Cross. But Josephus wrote that the X Roman Legion had the city surrounded and remained encamped later when Jerusalem was renamed Aeolia Capitolina. Jerusalem was enclosed within a tight circle years after the Temple was destroyed." Dov was listening intently, slowly shaking his head in disagreement. "So rather than unequivocal answers we have more questions, no?" Paolo continued. "Where the Second Temple stood, the Romans erected their own Temple of Jupiter and raised a statue of Hadrian. I can see smuggling out the tablets, but the Cross? Dov, it doesn't fit beneath a robe or toga. It needs a squad of strong backs and certainly absconding with it under the Romans' eyes and noses would have attracted attention. Too far-fetched, no, couldn't have happened."

"Okay, obviously we can't accurately reconstruct what happened," Dov countered. "You're a scholar, a scholar of this time, Moshe, the era whose history is clouded with contradictions,

170

yes? When the Temple was put to the torch, documents were naturally destroyed, the records of Jesus' trial, for instance, as was everything else that was perishable and in the conflagration's path. Listen, we know from our own history that money can often buy whatever you want and in too few instances it bought some Jews their lives during the Holocaust. For hard cash there was always a Nazi to look the other way. Those few Jews fortunate enough to make the proper connections and pay the Kopfgeld, the price, slipped away to freedom and a future. So why is it a stretch for you to conceive of the obvious, Moshe? Is it impossible to believe that a lowly Roman soldier or soldiers guarding the temple gates were above being bribed? The legionnaires were in it for booty, too, right? The lion's share was going to Titus and his generals so the legionnaires, like the Crusaders and the Nazis after them, they had to look out for themselves. Not so strange, so unthinkable, eh? Human nature. Say the guard or guards were handed a bag or two of gold coins to take a break, a stroll while a few Jews dragged some wooden beams from the Temple?"

"It's still a stretch for me, Dov ..."

"Moshe," Dov said forcefully. "I got a call from the IDF a few hours after the flood washed through. You're going to tell me someone broke the seals around the Absolom site in the midst of the chaos and mud, put the Cross and the tablets in the room, resealed it all, called the army, which, in turn, phoned me with the discovery? Too neat? How the Dead Sea Scrolls were found, that was too neat, also? Coffee table books, they're neat, too neat, but not what we've come up with here." Dov finished, his voice softening.

Dov's cutting remark stung as sharply as his first jab. In spite of his years in Jerusalem's streets, his Israeli passport, his army service, his time on the digs, Paolo had never quite entirely reinvented himself in an Israeli mold. He remained a well-bred Roman, as thin-skinned as his priest colleague. As part of the respected merchant class, when push came to shove he was subject more to the affectations of the business elite than to those of the peddler or fishmonger. Dov did not suffer from similar affectations or presumptions. His tongue was sharp and he used it often to obtain the desired effect. As quick as he was to insult, he was swift to soothe ruffled feathers as well.

"Moshe," he said calmly, "not everyone who shits on you is

an enemy and not everyone who pulls you from the shit is a friend. This may sound like a crass Israeli joke but it's also Dov's 'Third Commandment to Live Life By.' Make a note, boychicks."

"It's my nature, Dov, to question even basic assumptions. But I suppose you have a point," Paolo said, "however clumsily you phrase it."

"Touche, boychick," Dov laughed, the tension between the two dissipating. "Why don't we just assume the artifacts are genuine and will soon be confirmed by the lab people. The Tiberias manuscript is, of course, the key. If that's verified, everything flows from it, right? But if it's a clever forgery - which Moshe here half – believes - well, . . . it's a hoax then and I'll look the fool. As soon as we learned of the find, I contacted the Minister who, I suspect, contacted both Interpol and the CIA. The Minister's people are interrogating, or should I say 'interviewing' the men who found the manuscript. Or, as the Minister prefers to say, 'Mossad is asking the appropriate questions.'"

"Who are they, the men who found the manuscript?" Father Angelo asked.

"The one's an electrician from Tiberias, a Christian, I think, the other an Arab-Israeli stonemason from Nazareth. Their backgrounds, computers, phone logs, everything about them is being checked and double-checked. From the little I know, they seem unlikely hoaxers but ..."

Both Paolo and Father Angelo knew well that the word "interview" was, like much in Israel, a mask that hid an uncomfortable reality. In the wake of the storms and floods, the intractable problem of tamping down the illicit trade in stolen artifacts took on a new urgency. The upheaval in Israel was an unexpected convenience, lending instant credibility to a hoaxer's claims that what he or she was offering was authentic, the real thing— found treasure, so to speak— its sale thus legitimate. The government foresaw the illicit traffic easily multiplying tenfold overnight. The prices such sales could bring in private sales or on the block at Christie's or Sotheby's rivaled the skyrocketing prices they, and other auction houses, received for museum-quality artwork.

In the cutthroat world of the drug trade, the product is sold, then consumed. In this world, the cutthroat world of original artifacts, *objets* d'art could sit for generations in an alarmed vitrine in

172

a North London estate, or in a Palm Beach mansion, or a Rhine villa, or a Saudi Arabian palace, their provenance hidden from the larger world.

Only a small portion of the art treasures and artifacts stolen by the Nazis were ever claimed and recovered. Who was left to claim or recover them? Renoirs, Cezannes, Durers, Titians, Klimts, Rembrandts, all the masters, secreted away. It has variously been reported that a purloined Chagall hangs over the bar, between two elk heads, in the private den of an unindicted Nazi functionary's family in his Bavarian hunting lodge. Before his death, his wife, children, and grandchildren were forbidden entry. Only the surviving members of his former army unit— now all gone, too— were allowed through the door and treated to a viewing.

And little effort is required to imagine the organized theft that ensued after the collapse of the Soviet Union in 1990; or the disappearance of Iraq's treasures following the American invasion in 2003. In the academic world of archaeology, there was only one set of rules and trust was at its core.

For their part, illegitimate traders and hoaxers knew the dire risks of engaging in and getting caught illegally selling artifacts or perpetrating a hoax in Israel. If the perpetrator was caught, he wasn't booked and put before a civil judge and jury. He suffered the same fate as he would if he stole a glass jar from an Egyptian dig or a Babylonian artifact during Saddam Hussein's reign. To put the matter to rest in Israel, if the artifact was genuine it would be confiscated and quietly salted away, the culprit jailed and punished without benefit of a public hearing. Occasionally— no accessible records were kept— to cover all traces of the theft or hoax, the luckless perpetrator was, as he was in Egypt and Saddam's Iraq, murdered, his wares destroyed.

"Think, Moshe, think of what all this could be worth. More than a Vermeer, more than the Prussian Jade Room carried off during the war. But it's less the money than what it could be traded for, yes? How many missiles, how many suitcase nuclear devices would the manuscript or the tablets or the capitata buy? No one knows, but one is too many and a couple would do enough damage to fulfill our enemies fervent wish of wiping us from the face of the earth."

"I shudder to think of the capitata or any of the finds being held hostage," Father Angelo said.

"Yes, Angelo, and as much as it disturbs us let's admit that they'd be considered far more valuable than two dozen human hostages. But why are we here, Dov? Israel's got more experts on the Second Temple than it has violinists. What about Yagdin here or Fischer in Germany?"

"We're keeping the circle watertight, Moshe. I know we're neck deep in experts, this is not news. Our computers are filled with the names and histories of people we may one day need. You two, you're the right fit for the situation. To be precise, you're the world's leading authorities. Or close enough to the top - the authorities at the head of the authorities' list. Angelo's a member of the Vatican's inner circle and you're 'world-renowned'— how I hate that phrase!— a scholar and a TV personality. Who could ask for more if a find of such world-shaking importance needed authentication? I've known and worked with each of you, albeit separately, for decades. And your differences hardly escape me, either, but my gut instinct tells me that as a team ... well, it will work. I chose you, not the Minister, not a Knesset committee, not some Mossad official, I chose you two."

"You flatter us, Dov," Father Angelo said, blushing slightly.

"Remember your history, boychicks. The future can't be left to chance. I'm sure the Pentagon has impact studies on global warming's effect, on the mass movement of refugees, among other eventualities. So do we, our plans and scenarios, and you can be sure ours are similar. The future arrived last week with the storms. We thought the change would be gradual, say twenty years or more, but it wasn't, it was overnight. Look at what faces us. Total disruption of oil, tens of millions homeless, unemployment in the hundreds of millions, more critical in the hostile Arab sea that surrounds us. Sure, there'll be cooperation in the West and in Asia but the reality is we're heading into another Great Depression. Borders are closed, governments clamping down and all that follows such repressive actions. Given the 'every man for himself' economic situation, in spite of the cooperation lip service, it wouldn't surprise me if when push came to shove, even the US would loosen its ties with us."

It was a side of Israel neither man had fully appreciated. The Israel that was a nation of long-term planners, viewing each situation from all angles, addressing it with Job-like patience. Terrorists knew they were never safe, never in the clear. The

174

Mossad busied itself hours after an attack, tracing them, setting the traps that would eventually spring and bring them to ground. Time was relative; success was essential. Or, on a grander, international scale, like the Jesuits during the Counter Reformation, insinuating themselves, bringing foreign nations and their leaders into their confidence, convincing the major and some minor powers of Israel's centrality to Western civilization's survival, thereby securing for themselves their own survival. Planning and patience were Israeli watchwords. The equation had proved out for more than sixty years. Whether it would continue to do so was made moot by the storms and their aftermath.

The assistant's cell phone rang. After answering it, she handed the phone to Dov. He listened, nodded, and rang off. "The Minister ... He's on his way back." He returned the phone to Ruth. "Thank you, Ruth. You'll have to excuse us ..."

CHAPTER SEVENTEEN

When they returned to the director's office from the subterranean vaults, the Minister was already there, pacing behind Dov's desk.

"Take a seat, gentlemen. You, too, Dov," he said, clearing his throat. "What I'm going to tell you falls under the secrecy agreement you signed earlier. Israel's public face— the boys in the tanks, the scholars in uniforms, the bikinis on the beach— visuals meant to project a comfortable Western image of our society, visual propaganda put forth to a dubious world no longer works as it did after 1967. Not unsurprising, to be sure. To some extent, it was successful in spite of the efforts of the other side to paint us as something else. But we must acknowledge that to a degree they too succeeded. In the end, though, we learned who our friends and enemies were and on whom we can count in a crisis. The counting can be done on some of the fingers of either hand, of course," he said.

Dov chuckled, looking down, flexing his own fingers, and nodding.

"As Dov has already told you, we have a blueprint, plans in the works that will go a long way to ensure our survival in a way the IDF and the weapons at our disposal cannot. In a nutshell, our strategists have concluded and the prime minister concurs that we must court the West in its search for its Judeo-Christian roots as a bulwark against the Islamic onslaught. We've done some of that for decades, these brotherhood conferences, the hands-across-the-sea efforts, the late John Paul's 2000 visit and the current pope's, um, controversial 2009 visit, but this ... this is, this must now be a full-bore operation."

Father Angelo absently touched his Cross as Paolo inched forward, to the edge of his seat. "This is intriguing, yes, but where do we fit in? What do you need us for?" He swiveled around, glancing at Father Angelo.

"I'm not finished," the Minister said, lifting his hand slowly, palm outward. "The international situation, even before the storms, presented unexpected opportunities. All one need do is consider the election results in France, in Germany, in Austria, and England among others, Denmark for one. Multiculturalism is fine for nations with a common thread. The US can handle it, not without problems, of course. Which is why they could accept a quarter of a million mostly Muslim refugees without blinking twice and without too much of a popular uproar, considering. It's a country of immigrants, or so goes that trite phrase their political candidates drag out every few years. Their population's fluid, there's always work of some kind for the willing, so they absorb and make do, even with the complaints. Israel's got people from over one hundred fifty different countries who sometimes, like immigrants everywhere, don't fit in. The thread here is more tenuous than in the US because we're younger and very small. But we need people so we have to make do, too. Our other common thread, which we haven't pressed nearly enough, is a far larger one, our historical connection with Christianity. You see what's happening in Western Europe, no? In your own beloved Italy? Their core populations are in free-fall and who's filling the population gap? It'll be more so now with their homes and livelihoods disappearing with the floods? So what's to be done?"

"I see where you're heading with this, Minister," Father Angelo said, thinking ahead, a perturbed look on his face.

"No, Father, it's not what you're thinking," the Minister replied. "As a Jew I would never demand the mass expulsion of a people even though the far-right lunatics scream for it in the Knesset and in their shuls. But as the Germans say, there has to be a middle way. Our planners thought the middle way was inclusion. Let the Muslims build their mosques, let their children attend madrassahs. Lend a hand, maybe there'll be a positive payback, a peaceful integration. But the resistance on both sides doomed it, reduced it to a fantasy. Nations, in the end, in order to survive, must share a common experience and the inclusion policy, well ..." The Minister grimaced, his belief that the plan failed written indelibly on his face.

"The storms would have undermined this scheme anyway, Minister," Paolo said, "even if, against all odds, it worked. Gaza for one is gone, empty, done for. What now? The Gazans will want to return one day, everyone does, to their homeland."

178

"This much is true. But our think-tank geniuses predict that there will shortly be an EU-wide border shutdown. A less obvious 'wall of separation' than we have here. Those who made it through on compassionate grounds will be given short-term visas while the EU governments formulate a longer-term policy. Which the geniuses believe will be wholesale deportation in the guise of 'repatriation.' With 'loans,' which no one ever expects to be repaid, to ease the blow. Then the EU 'wall' will become permanent. Jerusalem's Law will have traveled far and wide."

"Jerusalem's Law?" Paolo asked.

"What happens here, soon spreads," Dov chimed in. "We had the suicide bombers - first a few, then several and, finally, an epidemic spread well beyond our borders. Ask the Americans how easy it is to prevent a suicide attack. Look at the walls they build around their embassies. Try to come within two hundred yards of their White House ..."

"We built a 'wall of separation,' a fence, call it what you like," the Minister cut in. "Whatever bullshit term you use, the proper one is 'iron curtain.' It's open now for humanitarian reasons but it will be closed if, as we expect, things get out of hand. And they always do. Trust me, deep down our gesture to the Palestinians is as unpopular here as any gesture we've put forth. It's only a matter of time before the regret will set in. What Muslims have and what Jews and Christians lack, though, is patience."

"Where is this leading then, Minister?" Father Angelo asked.

"I'm getting to that, Father. You were here with John Paul, yes, as an adviser?"

Father Angelo nodded, knowing full well that the Minister knew more intimate details about his life than did the members of his own family.

"After his visit, after his act of contrition at the Western Wall, after he referred to us as 'the elder brothers of the Church,' we saw an opening, a scenario. It's a policy that we've been developing for over a decade with no set date, obviously, to pursue it. Theoretically, it was well within the realm of realization. It played well on paper, but what it lacked was the essential element without which the policy couldn't be put it into play. The finds, should they prove authentic, are that element, brought forth by the floods, what the lawyers term 'an act of God.' The finds will confirm what most in the Western world have been taught to believe but many doubt and refuse to accept, that Israel is the Holy Land, and the find's proof - a glittering gift from a favoring God."

"Are you beginning to understand your role, boychicks?" Dov interjected. It was abundantly clear now to both Romans that Dr. Dov Rosenberg was more than a celebrated, jovial, if disheveled, antiquities expert and museum director. His acumen went far deeper than his public role. His earlier deference to the Minister was apparently theatre--good cop, bad cop. An "Aha!" moment. The Romans grasped this now. Dov's keen nose, an uncanny ability to sniff out character flaws in others while performing in his role as circus master, had proved invaluable in the past. Which was why it fell to him to choose two among scores of renowned archaeologists who would best serve the Israeli government's intentions. Paolo Pisa and Father Angelo Lorenzo's expertise in Biblical artifacts was almost less important than their impeccable scholarly reputations. The find's authenticity would be verified by others within Israel, but external, independent validation was imperative. The eventual announcement of such discoveries by the Israeli government and the familiar Israeli leitmotiv, the theme that now the discoveries prove beyond a reasonable doubt that Israel is the Holy Land, would be met with doubt and suspicion worldwide. It was the Romans' unassailable reputations, particularly the cleric's, that would give the claim enormous support and further the Israeli government's survival-through-outreach policy.

"All great scholars," Dov reminded them, "dream of a legacy."

Father Angelo felt his throat go dry, making it difficult to swallow, as Dov rattled off the names of the greats and their finds - Schliemann of Troy, Howard Carter and King Tut, Arthur Evans' work at Troy.

"They're all remembered, on every archaeologist's lips, their names in all the texts. You'd be inhuman if you failed to think of lasting fame. Rich people put their names on buildings, on research centers. Have you ever seen a research center called 'Anonymous?'" Even the Minister laughed at the remark. "Scholars are different. Their books are fleeting fame but a find associated with their name, well, for us that's like Salk's polio vaccine, Einstein's theory in physics, the great Michelangelo, your namesake, in the world of art. Finding what we've found is ... I can't think of a better term than legendary."

180

Lighting up a cigarette, he glanced up at the Minister, who waved for him to continue.

"Jews are never trusted and don't even try to contradict me with puny examples that serve to prove otherwise. They prove nothing. For every one you toss at me, I'll toss a thousand back at you. Yours may be well meaning but we know what we know, remember. We no longer labor under illusions. If we had, we'd be long gone from here." He took a drag on his cigarette and exhaled sharply. "If we, as Israelis, announced immediately after the floods we'd uncovered the True Cross and the tablets, try to imagine what the world's reaction would be? 'Another cheap Jew trick, a hoax, trying to get in good with the goyim,' or 'How much are they selling them for? Discount for cash? You can never trust them, any of them!' meaning all of us, and so forth and so on, ad nauseam. Remember in 2008 when our colleagues unearthed the fortifications above the Valley of Elah, where David slew Goliath? The lines of text found on the pottery there? There're still a number of other ... colleagues," Dov virtually spit out the word, "that continue to deny the existence of David's kingdom. So, if the Internet's exploding with accusations about how the openings in the Gaza fence and the separation wall are just another Israeli trick, well ..." Dov raised his hands in surrender, retaking his seat.

The Minister began to speak.

"Neither of you need worry. I assure you we won't embarrass you or compromise your careers or in any way leave you hanging out to dry. If the finds prove to be a hoax, all we've lost is a few days and even the hoax will go unmentioned. By all of us, yes?"

Both scholars nodded their assent.

"But if they're legitimate, if the Cross and the tablets are genuine," the Minister said, "you'll have two simple options. To step away and maintain your silence or join us, cooperate with us. Just a 'yes' or a 'no' to Dov. Understood?"

"Understood," Paolo said, Father Angelo echoing him.

"Father, what we're asking of you is as important to your Church and the world as it is to us. Hundreds of millions may ignore the Pope and his homilies, true enough, but many millions do listen and follow Rome's dictates. The Church catches enough ears and for your part we know you had John Paul's ear and assisted him with his statement on the Jews ..."

"Minister, I'm only ..."

"... and you were part of the transition team when he died, may he rest in peace, and, even though you disapprove of the haste, you're still on the committee that's placed him on the fast track to sainthood, and you met with the new Pope three times already since August of last year ..."

"But the Vatican is the size of a postage stamp, Minister." Father Angelo's hand closed tightly around the staff. He was feeling overwhelmed by the Minister's persistence. "Its world moves slowly, guided by centuries of protocol, tradition, and its own chain of command. His Holiness' schedule is set in stone, two years in advance. His world's choreographed to the minute. I'm merely a priest ..."

"Please, Angelo, spare us the humility, you're far more than that," Dov said.

Father Angelo's face reddened. He averted his eyes.

"Accepting praise is no sin," the Minister added, smiling his jawbreaker smile, "no need to feel embarrassed."

"You just don't make an appointment with the leader of a billion Catholics, walk in and tell him a story. He's not your local dentist, after all. He's the Supreme Law Giver, the leader of the Church, his authority derived from God through Christ Jesus to Peter," he replied heatedly, surprising himself with his own boldness.

"Yes, yes, Father, we know, all well and good," the Minister said patiently. "All we're asking is that you weigh the options I've presented to you after mulling it over with Dr. Josephus. For two minutes."

The Minister walked over and stood above Paolo.

"And you, Dr. Josephus, you will remember your roots, won't you, where you come from? And I don't mean Rome or your family's olivewood business." The Minister allowed himself a brief smile. "We need your international renown. You're a, uh, 'beloved' figure thanks to the media coverage you've courted for decades, yes? A TV heartthrob, all those culture vultures adore you. The books, the appearances, well, I needn't tell you who you are ..."

The Romans could almost hear the bolts shut in the psychological vault the Minister and Dr. Dov Rosenberg had placed them in. Carrot and stick, spider and fly, an old game, expertly and naturally played by masters of the game. What reasonable alternative did they have? Why would either man decline to cooperate if the finds were true? The earthshaking, once-in-a-millennium discovery would indeed both alter and confirm the world's perceptions and beliefs and benefit Israel as the site where the find was made as well. Sacrosanct Israel. If the plan unfolded as the Minister described it, it would be a masterstroke of true genius.

Without admitting it openly, both Paolo Pisa and Father Angelo Lorenzo knew they were entrapped. The attraction was too great for either man to refuse his cooperation, the downside seemingly minimal.

"These grand schemes always have a code name, don't they?" Paolo asked facetiously. "Or am I reading too many thrillers in my spare time?"

"Are you on board, Moshe?" Dov asked, his eyes narrowing, his face stern.

Paolo looked over at Father Angelo. The priest shrugged non-committally.

"Yes or no?" Dov pressed.

"Yes ... for me," Paolo said.

"Yes," Father Angelo followed, slightly hesitant. "Yes, you can count me in as well."

"Good," Dov said, rubbing his hands together appreciatively.

"In May, 2007, as we all know, an Israeli team located King Herod's tomb near Hebron in ancient Judea. A large piece of mosaic flooring, almost pristine, was uncovered in one of the cages. Richly decorated, yellow, blue, and so on; you've seen the photos," the Minister said.

"We've named this mission 'The Herod Mosaic,'" Dov stated boldly, stubbing out his cigarette.

The name delighted Father Angelo.

"Yes, what better symbols! The blue can represent the Cross, the color of Heaven where Constantine saw the Cross. The yellow can stand for the Tablets, God's holy words carved in stone. You know, Michelangelo used color this way ..."

The Minister smirked.

"Yes, of course, Father, if you wish to view it that way - or any other way, please do. But the code's colorless, I'm afraid, a code, 'The Herod Mosaic' are merely cover words for our operation, nothing more."

Father Angelo blushed, chastened for his own childlike

enthusiasm.

"It has an appropriate ring to it, though, Minister," Paolo hastened to add, coming to his friend's aid, "The Herod Mosaic. Yes."

As he shook both men's hands at the museum's entrance, the Minister said, "The flood's also uncovered Noah's Ark."

"What?" Father Angelo's jaw dropped.

"I'm just kidding, Father," the Minister said as Dov ushered the scholars towards the Hummer. "We've ticketed you both on the Rome flight the day after tomorrow but you're being rewarded for your efforts. Two nights at the King David to enjoy yourselves. You've earned it, gentlemen." The Minister sounded as if he was awarding prizes on a quiz show. Paolo recognized the Minister's hearty kudos for what they were— insincere— but he didn't feel insulted by it. The Minister was what he was and his comments and jibes, as Dov said, were never to be taken personally.

"When we need you back here, Dov will be in touch with you. Enjoy your freedom," he said as he turned back into the museum.

* * *

The King David Hotel was legendary, built in 1930 by the British when Israel was still a Zionist dream and the nightmare of the Holocaust awaiting the Jews of Europe just over the horizon. It was British headquarters during their Palestine Mandate and a prime target for the militant Israeli underground, the Irgun. In July, 1946, the front of the hotel's right wing was blown apart by Irgun guerrillas. The death toll: ninety-one. British officers, enlisted men, and innocent civilians. Collateral damage. Within two years, the British withdrew their occupying forces, its mandate ended. By 2012, though, its fabled past an effaced memory, the stately King David itself remained, reborn as a luxury hotel. Looming over it as well as the structures in the partially buckled adjoining streets, the omnipresent gigantic Klieg lights hung from cranes, illuminating the several worksites where bulldozers labored to clear the lakes of mud and debris.

At the reception desk, Father Angelo turned to Paolo.

"The Minister is a type familiar to me, Paolo. He's not a rare bird, I can assure you. I've seen his kind in the Vatican, quite a few

184

times and no, I won't name names. If my Vatican compatriots hadn't taken the holy orders, they'd most definitely have risen to the upper levels of the Mafia," he said, smiling, adding, "Do you think we're doing the right thing?"

"Does it matter?"

"I suppose not." Father Angelo fiddled with his Cross. "Good will come of it, though, I'm sure. I will pray for our success and ... safety."

CHAPTER EIGHTEEN

Within memory the hills and valleys surrounding the Old City were home to grazing sheep; Arab olive growers lived side-by-side with Jews who could trace their family histories back to the Arab conquest of 640 A.D. that ended the Byzantine Period. Greeks, Syrians, and Turks lived nearby as well in settlements in the small, impoverished province of the Ottoman Empire. Their homes were not far distant from the Old City's walls, a crumbling memory of the glory of Jerusalem that lived in reality only in the imaginations of those who had never lived there. In many ways the hilltop city differed little from the walled cities that dotted the landscape of Europe eastwards to the Urals. Many of the roads still in use were built by the Romans and, as the Ottoman Empire sunk further into decline, the province of Palestine— the name given it after the Romans destroyed Judea— fell into a desperate state of disrepair.

In the minds of the faithful, Jews and Christians, Jerusalem remained the golden star. It was here where Solomon built his temple and where the Second Temple of Herod was built and razed. Jerusalem is mentioned no less than six hundred times in the Old Testament. It was here where Jesus preached and for his efforts was crucified and later resurrected as the Christ. It was here where he was buried and around his reputed tomb so many churches known collectively as the Holy Sepulcher rose, protecting the sacred ground of his days on earth. It was here, where the Dome of the Rock now sits, where the Prophet is said to have ascended into Heaven. This, the third holiest site in Jerusalem, was the fountainhead of the world's three major faiths.

The Jerusalem captured by General Allenby's army in 1917 contradicted its depiction in Renaissance paintings or in the colorized postcards sent home by religious pilgrims, the Heavenly City peopled by old Jews praying at the Western Wall, while above floated an imaginary God. Or the pious trudging from station to station on the Way of the Cross. What the paintings and postcards did not show was the dirt, the poverty, the crumbling houses, or the rubble at the base of the city's walls where large sections had collapsed over time.

General Allenby's victory in the midst of the Great War was a bright spot in a dark and bloody year. The march into Jerusalem was a harbinger of a future that still lived in Western imaginations, the Holy City in Christian hands at last. The defeat of the Ottoman Empire brought its carving up, the spoils doled out to the victors under the Mandate System. Palestine was absorbed into the British Empire. In 1917, the Balfour Declaration committed the United Kingdom to "look favorably," if vaguely, upon the creation of a Jewish homeland in Palestine. Twenty-seven years later and a world war that left them shrunken and virtually prostrate, their status as a world power drastically reduced, the British exited Palestine.

After the First World War only ardent Zionists arrived in Palestine, a handful of the world's fourteen million Jews. Along with the British they began to transform the Old City but most of the time and money was spent on building the protectorate's infrastructure elsewhere, particularly along the Mediterranean coastal plain. In the 1930s, thousands more arrived, mainly Jews driven from Hitler's Europe. They clustered primarily in Tel Aviv and Haifa. Following the Allied victory in Europe in 1945, Palestine's population grew apace, in the face of armed British hostility and opposition, with survivors of the Holocaust. When David Ben-Gurion declared Israel's statehood in May, 1948, the population numbered more than six hundred fifty thousand. Around the Old City, apartment houses began to rise, supplanting the sheep meadows and olive groves. Jerusalem was expanding slowly, but until the Six Day War, it remained little more than a small city, split in two between Israel and Jordan, with the Jordanians in control of the eastern section and the Second Temple's western wall.

The Six Day War rearranged Israel and the world's perceptions of the Holy Land. The eastern half of Jerusalem and the River Jordan's west bank fell under Israeli control. The bitterness of the Palestinians, their expulsion or exit according to one's own reading of history, was compounded by the crushing defeat inflicted on the Arab armies in 1967 and Israel's subsequent occupation of formerly Arab territory.

188

In the distance, the Palestinians watched helplessly as homes, high-rises, and hotels rose rapidly in Jerusalem, as they had in Tel Aviv. And the tourists poured in - at first Jews from the United States and Canada, later British, Germans, Russians, and the ubiquitous Asians. The city was modernized, it seemed, overnight. In Israeli eyes and soon in the eyes of Jews worldwide, Tel-Aviv was Israel's center but Jerusalem, the city on the hill, was its capital, its heart, its soul.

* * *

The card, written in Italian and accompanying the gift basket, read: "Welcome To A New World. The Suite And All Your Needs Are Compliments Of The Thankful People Of The Holy Land, The State of Israel." It was signed Jehuda Ben-Jehuda. Paolo wasn't surprised that the Minister had taken such a name, "the Jew of Jews." It all seemed somehow so fitting, so appropriate, assuming of course that it really was his name.

The phone rang. It was Father Angelo remarking on the luxury they'd been visited with. "It's almost sinful," Father Angelo said, half-jokingly.

"I think, Angelo, that we're at the start of a long journey filled with sin. This is only the beginning."

"In the vestibule of Hell, then, Paolo, is this where we are?"

"Not quite yet," Paolo said lightly, "but if it is …"

"Bite your tongue, my friend."

In the hotel's dining room overlooking the British Gardens, they ate well, comfortable in their companionship and relieved to be away, if only in body and for an evening, from the Minister and Dr. Dov Rosenberg.

"To be young again," Father Angelo said wistfully, a propos of nothing in particular, his tongue loosened by a second glass of wine. "I was in love once …" He permitted his words to drift away.

"And yet …" Paolo prodded.

"And yet," Angelo replied, finishing Paolo's thought. "And yet I chose the Church instead. Do you think men and women of our world somehow jettison those inner feelings? I had my doubts in seminary, the other seminarians ... we all had them. In my father's house, offering a son to the Church was, well, it was like pushing a son into medicine or into law or into the world of scholarship. Almost a reflex action."

"I understand what you're saying," Paolo said, returning the priest's smile. "Our worlds in many ways run parallel."

"Have you read John Paul's biography, Paolo?"

"Yes, of course. I hadn't expected to find it so but I found it fascinating."

"He had the love of a woman before he took the priestly vows. As did I when I chose the priesthood myself. I'm not in any way comparing us beyond my trifling understanding of what he went through, too. It was a difficult, extremely painful decision at the time as I imagine his must have been. I wrestled often in the early years with what I'd done. But I realized, even as a young seminarian, that by choosing a calling that combined my pastoral work with scholarship ... it's what we know Freud called repressed desires, the rechanneling of energy ... in the end it suited me perfectly."

"I know something about love lost, Angelo, of redirecting myself, rechanneling what was left of me in my love of, shall we say, popular adulation. Yes, yes, I know, a sin but one I've learned to live with, to accept. The Minister read me, read *us,* I believe, accurately."

The nearby lobby clock chimed in a new day.

"Midnight already? Let's call it a day," Father Angelo said, his face showing his fatigue. "I want to see an old friend at Notre Dame tomorrow, after early Mass."

The streets around Notre Dame near the New Gate in the Old City on Hatzahazim Street were still being cleared. The traffic was stop-start, cars and trucks worming their way, redirected by detour signs. Although martial law had been relaxed during the night, the taxi returning Father Angelo followed a circuitous route back to the King David. As he entered, the clock struck noon. Paolo awaited him, seated in a lobby armchair, reading the day's *Jerusalem Post.* As he approached, Paolo folded the newspaper and laid it on an adjoining table.

"How's your friend?" he asked.

"Old, worn out, tired of the violence, and now the flood. Alberto's an Italian from the Tyrol, a bronze medal skier at the

190

1964 Innsbruck Winter Olympics, the one for which they trucked in snow. This morning he looked like a ghost, but I suppose so do I. Sometimes." Father Angelo shook his head sorrowfully. "Well, at least the Mass restored me. "Are you up to paying a visit to Heinz Wilberg?"

"Heinz Wilberg?"

"Yes, he's the son of one of my father's first salesmen. When my parents fled Rome in 1943, my father's always claimed their escape was successful because of his own exquisite sense of timing. Absolute nonsense, pure myth."

"How so?" Father Angelo seemed puzzled.

"The salesman, Wilhelm Wilberg, hawked our wares, the music boxes, the freshly-carved 'artifacts' in Germany from the Holy Land. He used a blind, another company's name, just to be on the safe side, when Hitler came to power. The Bavarians, in particular, bought this kitsch by the trainload and Wilberg was always calling Rome for more stock. The irony's laughable, no? Wilberg was half-Jewish. His older brother, Helmut Wilberg, was the German General Staff officer who dreamed up the concept of Blitzkrieg. Another irony. He was among thousands of *Mischlinge* in the new Reich's military. Helmut Wilberg advanced rapidly, finally ending up on Erhard Milch's staff in the Luftwaffe."

"Yes, Milch, I remember the name. The Lufthansa chief, half Jewish so it's rumored, protected by Goering ..."

"The Nazi heirarchy, even Hitler, would review photos, determine who looked Aryan enough to pass as one, and pronounce the lucky *Mischling* worthy of a *Deutschblutigkeitserklarung,* a certificate of pure German blood. I've read that about a hundred and fifty thousand *Mischlinge* served in the military. Even the killer Reinhard Heydrich, the chair of the Wannsee Conference, he was part-Jewish."

"History has more gaps than facts, I'm afraid," Father Angelo said.

"It was my family's good fortune that Wilhelm Wilberg's son, Heinz, was in the *Wehrmacht* and stationed in Rome when SS divisions were ordered south from Poland in 1943 to 'cleanse' Italy, render it *Judenrein.* Whether he was tipped by his father or his uncle, he won't say nor does it matter. But Heinz phoned my parents and said simply, 'Go south. Tonight.'"

"How did he end up in Israel?"

"After the war, Wilhelm Wilberg was released from a British POW camp and returned to his job with my father. Heinz wandered away from his unit in late April of forty-five, burned his uniform, rejoined his father in Munich, and tossed his weapons and medals into the Isar. He took an engineering degree at the University of Munich. But the atmosphere was suffocating, surrounded by murderers and often taught by them - so much so that he'd often wake up choking, gasping for air. Everyone around him was linked in a conspiracy of silence, saved from proper justice by the outbreak of the Cold War. The Nuremberg Trials barely scratched the surface - well-intentioned, a legitimate effort, but it all was basically a show. They caught some big fish but most slipped the noose. Like Goering, cheating the hangman by buying himself a quick and easy exit with a cyanide capsule, thousands who should by rights have been tried and convicted for war crimes submarined their way to safety. Whether they remained in Germany or Austria or France, wherever, or escaped to South America or the Arab countries ..."

"Yes, ODESSA, the 'ratline.'" Father Angelo looked away. "I've read the Vatican documents, Paolo."

"And as much as Heinz pleaded his case, he couldn't gain entry into the US, not in 1948. Granted, thousands changed their identities, lied, and slipped through the net, mostly minor actors in that murderous drama. But Heinz refused to do so, to alter his name, who he was, who he might have been. His family name was burned into the American watchlist; it made Heinz Wilberg anathema. There was no way he could or would explain it away, this ... this 'stain.' Israel needed engineers, decided to look the other way and opened its doors. Heinz wasn't alone, unique. There were others as well. Some would even return to Germany for *Wehrmacht* reunions. Insane, no? Well, hard times again, hard choices but in Israel's case and Heinz's, the right choice was probably made."

CHAPTER NINETEEN

In the taxi on the way to Heinz Wilberg's apartment, Paolo continued to expound on Wilberg's past.

"He knows more about what's under this city than anyone in the world. From the fifties and halfway into the sixties, Heinz directed the project to run sewers and phone lines under the Old City until the advent of fiber optics made copper wiring obsolete.

He's been under the Dome of the Rock, in the old cisterns and the ancient water tunnels. Whatever had been found there during those years, Heinz found. And probably kept some for himself, too."

"Can he be trusted? We're bound by the agreement, you know." Father Angelo said.

"I'm not dense, Angelo. I'm sure the Minister knows my father and Heinz were friends, that my family's indebted to him. The Minister's got eyes and ears everywhere, too. Cameras on lightpoles, maybe a car following us. We're never out of sight, believe me. All we need be is circumspect. No need to elaborate or go into minute detail, right?"

"I suppose," Father Angelo said, unconvinced and visibly apprehensive.

Heinz Wilberg's apartment was just as Paolo remembered it from his last visit in 2004. It was frozen in time, a living room lined with floor-to-ceiling books arranged by topic, as if it was a library. Civil engineering texts shared shelf space with anthropological studies, history with literature and a variety of non-fiction, each neatly tagged and in alphabetical order. Heinrich Boell, Fischer, Goethe, Grass, Thomas Mann, the greats and near-greats, along with a smattering of English-language classics that sat separately in a smaller bookcase. On the cocktail table, piles of news magazines - *Time, Newsweek, Der Spiegel,* and Hebrew journals as well.

On the wall, framed photos stared back at Paolo and

Father Angelo. Wilberg's grandfather, Prussian-stern in his spiked helmet, a photo taken somewhere along the Western Front in 1916. His uncle, the general, his tunic sporting the Knight's Cross, adjoined the photos of Wilhelm Wilberg with friends in Paris, circa 1942, and an undated wedding photo featuring Heinz's parents and maternal grandparents in the high collars and flowing dresses of the period. Predictably, photos of Heinz Wilberg in uniform were absent from the assemblage gracing the wall.

For Father Angelo's benefit, the increasingly frail Heinz Wilberg gave them a tour. Old maps of Palestine under Ottoman rule lined the foyer corridor. In the parlor, the vitrines held oil lamps, jars, jugs, shards from digs.

"All these pieces are Herodian," Wilberg commented matter-of-factly.

On the far wall of the parlor, a mounted set of officers' sabres, one from each of the world wars; another display case held beer steins, thirty-nine in all, each representing a German state during the glory days following reunification under Bismarck. For Paolo, Heinz's apartment brought forth a memory of his former in-laws apartment in Tel-Aviv. Teutonic to the core, on the surface untouched and uninfluenced by new surroundings and new times.

One can only wonder what's in the closets, Father Angelo thought to himself as Wilberg pointed to a large, framed photo of himself in an IDF uniform, astride a tank during the Suez Crisis of 1956.

"In those days," he explained, "the tanks were powered by Czech engines, from the old Skoda plant in the former Goering Werke ..." Wilberg turned to Paolo.

"You needn't have called ahead, Paolo. Few people beat a path to my door these days," he said. "Shall we continue in Hebrew or English, Father? My Italian is almost unintelligible."

"English would be better for me, Dr. Wilberg."

"Only if you call me Heinz, Father," Wilberg chuckled.

"Then you must call me Angelo."

Wilberg nodded approvingly.

"Paolo, you look wonderful. Natural disasters seem to agree with you. What brings you here? You never said. By the way, I saw the interview you gave to *Deutsche Welle* last month. Very impressive."

"Thanks, Heinz." Paolo had forgotten Heinz Wilberg's style of communication. Peppered questions, one riding on another - a born interrogator.

"And your father phoned the other day. Making sure I rode out the storms and flood."

"He considers you another son, you know that."

"Yes, yes, I do," he said, dismissing the flattery. "Angelo, I'm sure Paolo's told you of our connection so there's no need to travel that rutted road. I have to say, though, that this is the first time a priest has visited my home. And me a born Catholic ..."

Father Angelo's face betrayed his surprise.

"You seem amazed, Angelo. I'm one-quarter Jewish. As you can see, it's that percentage that won out in the end." Wilberg's cobalt-blue eyes twinkled.

He reached over and removed three books from a shelf. Paolo noticed they bore Father Angelo's name.

"Would you do me the honor, Angelo, of signing these?"

"Of course," Father Angelo agreed, somewhat taken aback as Wilberg handed him a pen.

"Don't be upset, Paolo. I have a couple of yours here as well. Love the illustrations ..."

By mid-afternoon, the conversation turned from the past to the present. Paolo couched his and Father Angelo's mission in the vaguest of terms.

From a chest in the map room, Wilberg pulled a stack of hand-drawn maps of the Old City. "A few years ago, a Hasidic rabbi showed up at the door announcing he'd heard from another rabbi that I was the 'map man,' the one who knew Jerusalem better than he, the rabbi, knew the Pentateuch. He rambled on, walking right past me into the apartment, declaring that some day the Dome of the Rock would be the home of the new temple. That set off warning bells. This *rebbe* and his bunch spelled trouble, big trouble and I wasn't having any part of it, this Third Temple nonsense."

"What'd you do?" Paolo asked.

"I feigned dementia, began acting confused. He seemed not to notice. Then he pointed at the map cabinet, demanding to know what it held. I told him 'old photos' of Deutschland in as heavy a German accent as I could muster, but he persisted. He wasn't hearing because he'd stopped listening. I thought my next move might have to be goose stepping smartly around the room, but thankfully it didn't come to that. It was all I could do to finally shuffle him back out the door." Wilberg smiled at the recollection of the incident. "And you two, you want to resurrect the temple also?"

"No, Heinz, not quite yet." Paolo laughed. "The government called us in to evaluate a mosaic they'd just uncovered near the new staircase to the old Temple Mount constructed in 2006."

Wilberg slid open a third drawer, removing a set of maps identified simply, in Hebrew and English, as *Old* City, *Subterranean.*

"Today it's all done with computers. Draftsmen need not apply. In the late 40s, an old professor of mine washed up here, too. And he wasn't even a quarter-Jewish. Strange, eh? I knew he'd spent two years in Dachau in the late thirties as a political 'undesirable,' a Red. A *Geruecht,* a rumor had it he was Adenauer's cellmate when the Russians stormed Berlin and set him and several others free. Who's to know where the truth lies?" Wilberg shrugged. "Anyway, it was he who etched the copper plates for these for the Israeli navy." Wilberg unrolled the crinkled map and laid it out on a drafting table. Pointing with a pencil stub, he explained how the cisterns were built at the Dome of the Rock under where the Second Temple stood.

"Think of these tunnels as trees. From the trunk, say, the tunnel itself, they branch to the cisterns, which empty into pools both inside and beyond the city's walls. In the time of the Second Temple, there was a pool in the Kidron. It was called the Siloan pool and provided water for the City of David to the southeast. Cisterns were the major source of water supply. This wasn't Rome or Paris with their miles of tunnels, remember, and there was only one Roman aqueduct on the coast south of Akko, so cisterns were the answer.

"Look here," Wilberg said, tapping the map. "See the 'X' marks that were put there by the mapmaker Warren when the underground was traced for the Ottomans? Imagine doing this with the only light coming from oil lamps and torches and the imminent danger of a tunnel collapse at every turn. I'd have hated to be in Warren's shoes when he inched his way through this maze.

"By our count, there are thirty-three cisterns. The temple needed a considerable water supply for purification baths as well. Most of the cisterns were connected to the tunnels but not all were used for water collection and distribution. Numbers nineteen, twenty, and thirty served as passages to the Temple Mount. In Herod's era until the Temple's destruction, one could access the Tyropoeon Valley, today's Warren's Gate, and enter the temple, perhaps even the treasury itself. Hard to say, unfortunately, but definitely a possibility. Today, the temple's treasury lies under the entrance to the Dome of the Rock. All of these were sealed by the Arabs after their invasion in the seventh century.

"Numbers one and three were used by the priests to leave the temple through the north wall. Number ten, here at the bottom of the map," Wilberg tapped the spot, "this cistern led under the Royal Portico, just to the right of the Halda Gate."

He straightened up and arched his back.

"Age makes you stiff in the wrong places yes? There was a time … ach, I'm wandering, sorry. Where were we? Ah, yes, when we first started laying the cables, we wanted to avoid digging new tunnels since it was still Jordanian land. Out of the blue, in nineteen-sixty if I haven't confused my dates, David Ben-Gurion phoned me."

Wilberg stopped in mid-thought, apparently recreating the conversation in his mind.

"One thing about the Israelis," he continued, "is they know everything about their people and old Ben-Gurion naturally knew everything about me. For him, people were either useful or useless and I was curious as hell to find out what he wanted of me. I had no clue. Ben-Gurion's appearance was disarming, 'grandfatherly,' like the Americans say."

"I only know him from photos," Paolo said.

"But you do know that behind that benevolent look was a steel will that broke many men far stronger than me, no?" Wilberg looked at Paolo.

"So I have heard."

"What he wanted was for me to run the telephone line to Amman, what was later called a 'hotline,' just in case."

"How could that be done?" Father Angelo asked. "It was enemy territory ..."

"False passports, a German-speaking team, phony permits, dollars to 'befriend' whoever needed to be 'befriended,' the usual time-honored methods. It sounds harder to do than it was. The line wasn't connected until after nineteen seventy-three, of course, but when what we'd done became known, the late King Hussein secretly congratulated Golda for our, uh, ingenuity."

"Or *chutzpah?*" Paolo smiled.

"Or *chutzpah,*" Wilberg nodded, laughing. "Like Adenauer, Ben-Gurion thought in historical terms, in connections past and present, that history was the wellspring of all politics. If I found anything of real importance under the Old City, I was to deliver it to him in person. No intermediaries. He then asked me an odd question. 'Wilberg, · he said, 'could anyone have gotten out of the city during the siege?' I thought he was talking about nineteen forty-eight. 'No, Wilberg, not nineteen forty-eight, the summer of seventy A.D. when Titus set the city ablaze.' I said it was possible and sketched a rough map for him, showing him what I just showed you, going north from the Temple as the priests had or via cisterns five and ten, then descending through the last, thirty-three, for instance, would bring you outside.

"Ben-Gurion then asked me if it would have been possible, for example, to remove treasure from the Temple unnoticed. I said it was possible, tricky with the Roman soldiers stationed all around, but possible. If the pieces were large, they would have to be dismantled since the tunnels wind and are, as you know, narrow and in some places no more than three or four feet high. Anything bigger than a child would have to be pushed or dragged, the pusher or dragger crawling through the tunnel. Smaller treasures, well, a bribe could grease the skids and out you go. But this is all conjecture."

Father Angelo was rapt, staring, totally absorbed in Wilberg's tale, missing its import, but Paolo began to feel a growing sense of disquietude. Heinz Wilberg was clever and canny but while he wasn't party to what the two of them had seen in the bowels of the Israel Museum, he was describing accurately and in detail how the finds could have been removed from the temple's treasury.

"What the old man wanted more than a telephone line

was a probe, to see what evidence could be unearthed to legitimize the claim that Israel was in fact the ancestral home of the Jewish people. He longed for a significant discovery to prove beyond doubt that there was in fact a covenant with God awarding in perpetuity the land of Israel to the Jewish people. Such a discovery, he claimed, would sweep away any questions about Israel's legitimacy, its right to exist where it exists. The Dead Sea Scrolls were significant but it was not enough." He paused. "But even Ben-Gurion knew there'd always be bitter opposition to any claim and, no matter the material evidence, the argument would never be won. It seems it will never be enough," he said softly. "Every inch of this country is contested. And will continue to be, yes?" It was a declaration, not a query. "Ben-Gurion said to me, 'Wilberg, the scrolls are one thing, Eichmann's trial another, good publicity. Every pot, every shard with the seal of the Israelites is like a "land deed" that also helps us. We need to continue proving our legitimacy, we have to have something more, every day, to show the world that we belong here, that it is as it was written in the Torah.

"But," he repeated, "it will never be enough."

David Ben-Gurion's words, related by Wilberg, virtually echoed those of the Minister and Dov Rosenberg. Clearly what they were involved in, what they agreed to assist in, went to the heart of what Israeli policy was from the beginning. If Wilberg was as suspicious of his guests as they suddenly were of him, that he too was part of the grand scheme, the probing, he did not let on. An old soldier, a survivor like Paolo's parents, even if he wore a German uniform, he knew to hold his tongue. Which was probably why Ben-Gurion trusted him.

"Beer, my friends?" Wilberg asked.

"Maybe just one," Paolo said, "then we must be going. We're on the evening flight to Rome."

As Wilberg poured their drinks, Father Angelo posed a question.

"I'm, curious, Heinz. What did you in fact dig out when you cut the trenches for the telephone lines? Where would you look if, say, Ben-Gurion returned and gave you an assignment?"

Sly, Angelo, sly, well-done, Paolo thought, hiding his smile.

"I wondered when you'd ask me, Angelo," he said,

199

handing both men sweating beer steins, Bayern for Paolo, Wittenberg for the priest. Paolo marveled at how the man always seemed a step ahead, anticipating. But then, Heinz Wilberg was a survivor.

Wilberg thought for a moment, then drew another map from the cabinet and spread it on the table. "Here, take a look. There are all kinds of hidden vaults and chambers. There were some near the Pool of Israel by the Gate of Remission. And the Serpent's Pool, and in the Kidron Valley below the Jewish and Muslim burial grounds. There're a hundred feet of bodies stacked like cordwood around the Pillar of Absolom and the Ophel site. It was a complicated task, let me tell you, digging through there. We had to contend with the gravesites since the government wanted all the lines buried in East Jerusalem, near the Mount of Olives. No surface lines so we used sonar, actually, which expedited the dig but only a bit. When we reached the Pillar, we hit solid rock.

We broke three of the digger's cutting blades. With little room to maneuver, we had to dig around the Pillar by hand before we could press on. And what do you think we found, eh?"

"I can't imagine," Paolo said, scratching his head, trying mightily not to act eager and astonished.

"A burial vault. We marked it on the map, here, by the other 'X.' If I had to look, maybe I'd look around there."

Father Angelo hoped Wilberg hadn't heard his sharp intake of breath. An unintended confirmation of sorts, 'X' marking the spot where the museum's *capitata* and tablets were uncovered. Paolo still couldn't dispel his doubts. Could Heinz Wilberg be toying with them, knowing what they knew, really testing them? On whose behalf? The Minister's? His own curiosity? Or were these suspicions misplaced?

"But then there were so many vaults," Wilberg said, "one no different than the next, so there's no reason for me to think one is more special than another. I suppose if I had to, I'd say by the Pillar's a good starting point. I'd forgotten about all of it until a week or so ago. A neighbor of mine, still in the reserves," he thumbed rightwards, indicating where the reservist lived, "a guy about fifty. He was called up in the flood emergency and sent to the Mount of Olives. The government feared looters and secured the valley. By the time my neighbor got there, the valley was

200

flooded and filled with open graves, an invitation to thieves if ever there was one. And you know how rumors go viral, yes, especially around here? Ancient graves equal gold is some fools' minds so the IDF was probably right to worry about a looters' stampede even if nothing but rotted winding sheets and blackened bones were scattered around. But the IDF locked Kidron down in time and focused on the area around the Pillar where most of the graves are."

"So we've read," Paolo said.

"Floodlights and digging around the clock, trying to put everything back into a semblance of order. Sorry to report, Angelo, that the prophecy of dry bones turning up did not come true and there've been no TV reports about the reappearance of the Messiah so …"

"I would have heard, Heinz. I'm an avid watcher of the news." A polite smile accompanied Father Angelo's rejoinder.

"Although," Wilberg continued, "there was no less than a brigade of soldiers reburying the damp bones of the dead from three millennia ago. As well, I might add, of those planted a few weeks ago. A dismal business, no?"

Paolo concluded Wilberg was less intent on probing further into why he and Father Angelo were in Israel. Their flimsy, diversionary tale of having to validate a discovered mosaic appeared to adequately explain their presence. Wilberg in the past would certainly have been more persistent but now, in his eighty-eighth year, he was more often lost in reminiscing, dropping names, and braying about old times, an old man's passing of his shortening hours, very much like the scholars' own fathers. Clearly Wilberg was unaware or uninterested in what they were really about. Just a visit to an old friend, a little brain-picking, whiling away the hours before flight time. It was all a coincidence, but an eerie one, inasmuch as Wilberg had more than fifty years before been within an arm's length of the finds. Paolo exhaled slowly. How much history might have had to be rewritten had Wilberg and his men broken into the vault a half century earlier and made the discovery. Another meaningless historical "if," Paolo thought, as he placed his emptied beer stein on the coffee table.

"We have to be off, Heinz."

"Well, you must come again, preferably not to visit my

grave, eh? On the Mount of Olives?" He laughed. "I may be what the Americans call 'spry' but 'spry's' a temporary state, don't you know? Do give my regards to your parents and a fond hello to ancient Rome." He seemed drifting into reverie. "I haven't been back since 1943 ..."

* * *

As the Romans stood before the taxi rank awaiting a cab, Father Angelo turned to Paolo.

"Heinz did say nineteen forty-three, didn't he?"

"Yes."

"The *Wehrmacht* wasn't in Rome in 1943. They were being redeployed. It was the SS and the *Waffen* SS units, the shock troops - they were the shock troops sent to round up the ..."

"Yes, Angelo, but not quite," Paolo cut him off. "There were *Wehrmacht* units in Rome then but honestly I don't know if that's the uniform Heinz wore. Nor do I care. They know, the IDF and everyone else who's supposed to know such things. 'Useful and useless,' as Ben-Gurion himself declared more than once. If Goering said 'I'll decide who's a Jew,' is it a quantum leap to imagine Ben Gurion saying 'I'll decide who's a Nazi?' Heinz has proved himself useful and the good he's done outweighs whatever bad may or may not be attached to him."

ROME
III

CHAPTER TWENTY

The same mountains of mud and debris greeted Paolo Pisa and Father Angelo Lorenzo as their taxi exited Leonardo da Vinci's airport sprawl and headed northeast towards Rome, thirty kilometers away. Scores of ever-present dozers worked to clear the pile-ups that framed Autostrada 91 and in several sections spilled onto the highway. In classic Italian fashion, it seemed the supervisors outnumbered the workers eight to one. That singular aspect of Italian life seemed not to have been affected by time or the catastrophe.

Approaching the city's inner reaches, detour signs metastasized as they neared the Piazza Mazzini. The cabbie adeptly slalomed his way into the city before informing his passengers that they'd have to hoof it the last few blocks since the Tiber's overflow had made further progress impossible.

'This is it - as far as I can go. I'm sorry, Father, but what can I say? It was worse yesterday, you should've seen it," the cabbie said by way of both apology and offering hope for better days to come.

"I'm glad I didn't," Father Angelo replied, handing the driver several Euro notes. Chaos on Italy's roadways and in Rome, in particular, was hardly unusual, nor worthy of comment. The floods, though, made chaos a cornerstone of daily life. The flight and the events of the past weeks left the men both exhausted and enervated. But the obstacles they'd overcome and what they were involved in made the prospect of a walk home hardly noteworthy, no more than a minor inconvenience.

Father Angelo made his way to the Vatican-owned complex near Hadrian's Tomb, his three-bedroom apartment, compensation for a life of selective poverty— a concept that never failed to amuse the aging priest— was more than a welcome sight. An errant thought invaded his mind. He felt inclined to drop to his knees and kiss the floor of the flat's vestibule as the pope always kissed the tarmac upon his return to Italy from abroad. But he quickly discarded the bizarre notion, dropping instead onto his leather sofa. Fifteen minutes later, he was fast asleep.

Paolo Pisa's penthouse had been cleaned and prepared for his arrival earlier in the day by his parents' housekeeper. It had become a tradition and Paolo had ceased asking, sometimes begging, his mother to unburden the elderly cleaning woman from this task.

"Mama, I know how to use a vacuum," he had pleaded. Like his father, his mother had her ways and was not to be dissuaded. Unspoken surrender to her wishes ultimately prevailed.

As usual, the apartment looked as if he'd never left. Everything was in its place, where it had been the day of his departure. His new mail was sorted and stacked neatly atop his antique roll-top desk. When he glanced out the window and was greeted with the familiar sight of the Pantheon, he knew at last he was home.

Like men in a foxhole, whose immediate parameters only extended to the edge of the next foxhole, both men only vaguely appreciated the enormity of how the topography of the Middle East and much of Asia had been changed. The bits and pieces gleaned from the 24-hour news cycle certainly gave them more than a sketchy picture of the disaster's extent. Israel, after all, hadn't been spared. And Paolo's imagination could certainly extrapolate from the particular to the general, from where he'd been and what he'd seen to what he might eventually discover staring at the images on his computer screen. Yet it was only when he powered on his computer and Google-scanned the earth from a mile above that all the havoc was brought home full force. It was almost incomprehensible, defying the normal diet of exaggeration that the news channels spat forth. For the better part of an hour, he sat staring, speechless, a myriad of thoughts and questions racing through his head. The permutations were endless, the implications enormous. He imagined Father Angelo found himself in the same sort of quandary, trying to match and reconcile the reality of what they'd come home to, to what they now knew and the adventure they had embarked upon, to the drastically altered world they'd left a short time ago.

The days and weeks that followed were mercifully

uneventful, filled with visits to family, conversations with publishers, reviewing other writers' works, responding to messages, and the chores of daily life. In the midst of the swirl, the Herod Mosaic remained foremost in their minds, though, never far distant from either scholars' contemplations. Several times a day each checked his e-mail messages for word from Jerusalem, either on Paolo's iPhone or, in Father Angelo's case, his Vatican-issued BlackBerry. Nothing. No word. Silence.

Christmas came and went as did New Year's Day. Rome was unexpectedly gripped in a seasonal freeze on the 15th of January, 2012, the mountains of debris barely reduced by then, turned by the foul weather into impassable icebergs, choking not only the Eternal City's streets but the Tiber as well.

Both Paolo Pisa and his Vatican colleague prepared for a major international meeting of scholars in New York, long in the planning, and dedicated to commemorating the discovery of the Dead Sea Scrolls. It would not be heavily attended, the November storms had seen to that, but the turnout would still be respectable. As major presenters, Paolo and Father Angelo daily exchanged comments, mindful of stepping on each other's academic toes and particularly aware of the querulous sharks who would people the audience, each anxiously awaiting the Q and A that would follow each scholar's lecture to score obscure points. Paolo was to speak for a half-hour about the "Historical Implications of …" a simple task, a walkover, a talk that could by given off the cuff. Father Angelo, assisted by two other priest-scholars, was to chair a panel on "The Vatican and the Future of the Dead Sea Scrolls."

"There's no place like New York in February," Paolo remarked sarcastically. "The icy wind off the Hudson, what a delight, what more could a couple of aging scholars ask for?"

They ran down a list of cities to be avoided, if humanly and professionally possible, once the snow flew.

"Perhaps Chicago would've been a better choice?" Father Angelo laughed.

"Or Cleveland?" "Don't forget Oslo." "'Or Moscow."

And so on.

Although he frequently participated in these meetings, Paolo abhorred most of the other participants, many of them with little hands-on experience on difficult digs, no deep brown desert tan, no dirt under their fingernails to speak of. These scholars chose instead to confine their on-site efforts, the comfort of research libraries sufficing to advance their arcane theories and their careers.

Unlike Paolo, Father Angelo couldn't afford the luxury of contempt. The path he walked was a more treacherous one, his opinions and conclusions subject to intense scrutiny and disapproval on the one hand by the Church, on the other by rivals within the academic community. How many times had he heard a Vatican colleague express a wish to lay hands on one of the original scrolls, even doubting *a priori* their authenticity? It had lately become dogma in some Vatican quarters to question Israel's assertion that it had released every scintilla of information relating to the Dead Sea find.

Even more disturbing to the Church was the occasionally proffered idea that Jesus was connected to, even an integral member of, that strange apocalyptic Judaic cult, the Essenes, that lived in Qumran where the scrolls were discovered in 1947. And it was from the Essenes that his teachings and his ministry originated. And what if in his extensive research in the era Father Angelo Lorenzo concluded that it was true, that Jesus was, after all this, merely another Essene? What then? It was a prospect he was loath to even contemplate. It sent chills down his spine, caused his throat to constrict. His swift excommunication would be the least of it.

Such notions as an alternative explanation of Jesus' origins, even if they failed to gain significant traction in the academic world in which they all— believers and non-believers— traveled, deeply offended the Vatican's sensibilities. The mere airing of such ideas and where they could inevitably lead, the conclusion that Jesus was part of a dissident group and not unto himself unique, the Son of God, was considered dangerous, threatening to the Church's very *raison d 'etre,* tantamount to anathema.

Their flight was scheduled to depart late morning from Rome to JFK. The flurries that deposited a thin coat of snow on the streets overnight had melted away. On their way in the Mercedes limo to Leonardo da Vinci, separated from the driver by sound-and bulletproof glass, Father Angelo reminded Paolo that Dov Rosenberg was listed among the presenters. In fact, he was the main attraction, charged with delivering the opening speech to the conference.

"So perhaps he's waiting to see us face-to-face before ..."

"Well, he hasn't been scratched. He's still on the program. And I considered the possibility that we'll all be together in New York as the reason for the silence. But I've got to admit my nose is way out of joint with our pal Dov. Not a peep, not even a 'wish you were here' postcard, nothing, *niente.* We've been sitting here, both of us, for nearly two months on pins and needles. I thought we were central to this whole ... project. What happened to keeping us up to speed, calling us? I mean, a find like this, all the damned secrecy, the pledges, worse than the Sicilianos with their blood oaths, the Mafia with that *Omerta* nonsense." Paolo looked out the rain-spattered window as the limo crept across the slushy Tiber and headed southwest.

"Like the Church, Paolo, I'm sure Dov has his reasons ..."

"Dov's always been contemptuous of the IDF's and the government's absurd levels of security and secrecy, their bizarre 'eyes only' policy. Whatever Dov's 'reasons' are, even if he's under the Minister's thumb for one reason or another, he's never been one to take government orders so seriously. It's like he's been dropped into a black hole. He could've at least given us a hint, a heads-up, no?"

"Maybe they decided to proceed without us," the priest conjectured. "I doubt it, Angelo, not after all that *Sturm und Drang* ... "

The conference's opening day and his subsequent visit to Washington would represent for Dr. Dov Rosenberg twin triumphs in his long and storied career. He had been invited to the United States as a guest of the American government. In his role as Director of the Israel Museum and head of its vaunted Antiquities Department, he was to announce new revelations resulting from the deciphering of the ancient texts. Later in the week, he would travel to the Capitol and present a reconstructed "page" from one of the scrolls to the American Secretary of State at the Washington National Cathedral, the first ever to leave Israel, a gift from the people of Israel to the American people.

The ceremony, followed by a gala dinner at the Kennedy Center, would be attended by the President of the United States, several of his cabinet appointees, Congresspersons from both political parties, many governors and big city mayors, philanthropists and deep-pocketed political contributors, media moguls, a smattering of Nobelists, Western ambassadors and UN diplomats, A-list political operatives, the leaders of every major and some minor American Jewish and Christian organizations, along with a cohort of lobbyists from various Zionist and pro-Israel Christian fundamentalist groups. It promised to be a grand, unforgettable, and glorious affair.

"Let us pray mightily, Angelo, that Dov had the forethought to have his hair trimmed and also to leave his sneakers and that favorite sweat-stained shirt at home in Jerusalem," Paolo said, his annoyance at Dov melting away, replaced by his growing anticipation of seeing him again. So many questions came to mind, each screaming for an answer.

"The Almighty, while he may be aware of Dov's sartorial missteps, might not wish to interfere in this case," Angelo smiled as the limo slowed to a stop at curbside by Terminal C, International Departures. "He may not feel it's in his power to do so. In my considered judgment, He may believe it's best to leave Dov to his own devices and dress code."

CHAPTER TWENTY-ONE

As Paolo and Father Angelo awaited their turn at Alitalia's business class check-in, nudging their bags forward, the priest's BlackBerry vibrated. He drew it out, checked the caller ID, and placed it against his ear. An instant later, his face paled, his breath shortened and he swayed. Clutching one of the stanchions holding the velvet ropelines, he steadied himself.

"What is it, Angelo? Paolo's face wore a look of concern.

The priest's eyes darted upwards, seeking the terminal's bank of television screens, fixed as always on the international news channels, BBC, CNN, RAJ Uno, and Euronews. He tried to raise his hand and point but he couldn't; it was as if what he'd heard drained all energy from his body. Paolo and several other of the flight's passengers had looked first at the priest, then, following his lead, gazed at the television screens above their heads.

Staring back at the viewers, a dour newscaster delivered the report in terse, grave sentences.

"This just came across my desk," he was saying, lifting a sheet of paper, as the words flashing "Breaking News" ambled across on the crawl superimposed on the screen below his desk. "Our Jerusalem bureau has just learned that Dr. Dov Rosenberg, the Director of the Israel Museum and one of the world's leading authorities on Biblical antiquities, has been kidnapped. The Israeli government has provided no further details of the abduction, nor the suspected whereabouts of Dr. Rosenberg. Dr. Rosenberg was scheduled to deliver a paper at a major conference in New York City this week and was later to present to the Secretary of State a …"

The unceasing din and hum within the terminal joined a stream of boarding announcements and gate changes, drumming out the newscaster's final words. As a photo of Dov Rosenberg replaced the newscaster's image on the screen, Father Angelo, visibly agitated and panicky, turned to Paolo.

"That was Cardinal Zaccaria, he told me ..." The priest's words rushed from him in a torrent. "We have to return to Rome, Paolo, I have to go back. I - I don't know what to do, this is so distressing, what's happening, I'm feeling confused ..." He placed a hand on his brow and kept it there. His face was mottled, the color returning to it slowly. "Paolo, what should we do?"

"Keep calm. You're not making a great deal of sense so take a deep breath and slow down. Did the Cardinal say anything else, has he heard something from Jersualem?"

"No, nothing." Father Angelo shook his head.

"We've got no facts, Angelo, barely a bulletin, a few sentences, a headline. You're right, though. Let's go back, they'll cancel the conference anyway, that we can be sure of. Without Dov, what's the point of holding it. Jesus! What next?"

As they made their way to the taxi rank, Father Angelo asked, "Do you think it's connected to our ..."

"Of course," Paolo said, his voice tinged with irritation at his friend's inability to connect the obvious dots. "How could it not be? Someone's onto what's in the vault. You don't think only the five of us knew about the find, do you? The tablets, the mosaic, the Cross, they all came from somewhere, yes, the site? The tablets might fit in a briefcase, the mosaic, too. They could've been tucked away unseen, it's an outside possibility, though at the very least it's far-fetched. But the Cross? No, many, many more eyes saw it than our little coterie of ... *cognoscenti.*" Paolo snorted when he said the word. All those efforts to keep the circle unbroken around the find and now this!

"To get it from A, the site, to B, the museum, they needed strong backs, no?" Paolo paused, letting what he was saying to Father Angelo sink in. "Unless you think Dov performed the Stations of the Cross and dragged it back himself ..."

"No need to patronize me, Paolo," Father Angelo said quietly.

"I'm sorry, Angelo. This is ... is profoundly upsetting, I know, for both of us. This looks bleak, worse than bleak. Why would anyone kidnap Dov unless they thought he could be pawned for something invaluable, eh? We know the link between Dov and what's invaluable, what's in his keep, yes? No mystery here."

"Who would do such a thing?" Father Angelo wondered

212

aloud.

"Plenty of suspects, Angelo, take your pick. How did it happen? A word here, a word there, a whisper, a secret not kept, a slipup, loose lips, someone says something to someone else, an abduction plan's hatched. The why, I think, is clear, but not the details of the how. Ah, somehow Dov must've let his guard down, that much I'm sure of.

Damn it! I'm no stranger to arrogance, Angelo, but it comes at a cost, there's always a reckoning."

"True enough," the priest said, his composure returning. "Dov's very headstrong, addicted to taking chances, isn't he?"

"Yeah, always the first to complain, always thumbing his nose at security, telling anyone and everyone how suffocating it was to do his work under such conditions. It'll all come down to ... What the hell did he do, what the hell did he do? Ah, we're just beating our gums, stumbling around in the dark."

"It's probably a renegade Palestinian group," Father Angelo speculated. "They're the most likely to ..."

"We don't know that, Angelo. Why not a bunch from the Israeli lunatic fringe?" Paolo countered. "If one of them killed Rabin, what's to keep them from grabbing Dov for who knows precisely what reason? If it was those fools, they'll announce their reasons soon enough. They just love the televised posturing, the drama and the list of demands, the 'or elses.' It won't make much sense in the greater scheme of things, and even they know it won't change anything but they'll press on, these madmen, in the name of whatever and 'justice,' or whatever they define as justice."

"Their concept of what 'justice' is," Father Angelo echoed, "yes, that red herring. They could've been infuriated at Dov's removing a national treasure from the Holy Land, you know, and even more disturbing, gifting another nation with it."

"I'd never thought of that. Could very well be." Paolo pondered a moment. "It'd certainly provide them with a motive. It doesn't take all that much to set them off."

"This is all so sad, Paolo, isn't it?"

"Tragic's more like it. Since the government accelerated the bulldozing of those illegal settlements last January, the opposition to the policy's numbers have grown. Remember when a few of the crushed trailers were dumped into the sea by Eilat, past Dolphin Reef, to create an artificial reef like they did with that old 6'1mboat, the *Soufa*. A lot of fanfare. The Minister for Tourism standing by, smiling, directing the operation, glad-handing, the usual. Even the mayor of Aqaba was there, figuring if it worked out, there'd be tourist spillover for his city, so what could it hurt?" Paolo said. "The minister said 'more European tourists will now think of Israel instead of Egypt when they consider booking a dive trip.' Well, what with the storms, the joke was sadly on her. The trailers were probably washed down past Hurghada, on their way to the Sudan and points south."

"The best laid plans," Father Angelo remarked absently.

It certainly sounded like the sort of scheme the Minister might have put into motion, the artificial reef, but Paolo knew that the reef was the least of what enraged the settlers, a minor insult among several more major ones, imaginary and real, bouncing around in their vengeful minds. It was more the heavy-handedness in the way the government was dismantling and plowing under the illegal settlements that sparked protests, that ramped up the violence, the threats of retribution, and maybe in the case of Dr. Dov Rosenberg, brought about an unintended consequence.

"I just pray no harm comes to him," Father Angelo said.

"He'll need more than that, Angelo, that's what worries and terrifies me ..."

* * *

Air traffic into and out of Leonard da Vinci was surprisingly light for a weekday, the crowds sparse, the wait for a cab mercifully short. They said little on their way back to Rome, their conjecturing exhausted, their mingled thoughts kept to themselves. In less than an hour, they were back in Rome, at Father Angelo's apartment, seated on the antique two-seater settee opposite the priest's flickering TV, awaiting an update from Jerusalem.

As the weather report ended, RAI's camera panned the crowded wood-paneled room in Jerusalem's press center. It was SRO as the crush of reporters from the world's press elbowed and jostled each other for the coveted positions fronting the lectern that sported the Jewish nation's crest. It was where

Israel's first prime minister's niece, Dora Ben-Gurion, was about to appear. Two security men emerged from the shadows, dressed in plainclothes, sporting dark glasses, and wired to ear buds. They assumed positions on opposite sides of the podium. From a doorway off to the right, the prime minister entered, briskly following a third armed security officer, a bull of a man a head shorter than his charge.

She bore little if any resemblance to her illustrious uncle, physically or in demeanor, so little that some even questioned if there was a familial relationship at all, whether the patronymic was, in fact, an affectation, a political ruse. And only rarely, unlike her uncle, did a smile crease her thin, sharp-featured face. In a land of less than eight million, where every citizen believed he or she knew better how to run the country, where all governments - left, center, or right - became unpopular overnight, often through no discernible fault of their own, Dora Ben-Gurion still retained an astonishing approval rating of over half the nation's voters.

She had come to power the previous September, two months before the storms. Public opinion grudgingly came around, admiring her steady handling of the flood crisis in this land known for crises. Her determined recovery and reclamation program, with assistance provided by the IMF, the US, and the EU, had cushioned part of the crushing catastrophe. By any objective accounting, the world's economic experts judged that Israel had fared better in the aftermath than its Arab and some of its distant Asian neighbors. And while a complete recovery wasn't more than a hope-filled glimmer on the distant horizon, the steps taken to repair and restore its infrastructure had, by mid-February, 2013, put Israel firmly back on the road to eventual normalcy. Or what approximated normalcy in the region.

"*Shalom*, " she said, her face haggard from fatigue, her voice harsh, rough. "Yesterday, Dr. Dov Rosenberg, the Director of the Israel Museum, was kidnapped on a road leading from Jerusalem. They were driving a white van that was then abandoned at the site of the shooting. Dr. Rosenberg was to leave later this week for an important meeting in America. His driver, Major Yuri Abramov, was mortally wounded and died early this morning at the Hadassah Hospital. Before he died, Major Abramov informed us that a gang of perhaps six attackers surrounded their van and opened fire. Major Abramov returned their fire, killing two of the assailants, before himself being overcome. We are establishing the identities of the dead, one of whom it appears was wanted for illegal gun smuggling by the Palestinian Authority. It is unknown whether Dr. Rosenberg himself was injured or where he's being held. An extensive manhunt for Dr. Rosenberg is continuing."

At that moment, the Minister appeared at the Prime Minister's side, whispering into her ear.

"Look who just showed up, Paolo," Father Angelo exclaimed. "I don't believe that man even casts a shadow ..."

"It doesn't surprise me," Paolo replied equably, his hands folded in his lap. "Notice how purposefully vague the Prime Minister's being? I doubt we'll learn much from this briefing."

"We are searching for a gray Toyota Hi-Lux with *Haifa Movers & Freight* painted on the driver's side door," the Prime Minister continued. "It was reported missing or stolen in early December. The tag number appears on the screen ..."

In the front row, an internationally known TV reporter's hand shot up, expecting to be called upon first as was the usual practice, her two-part question already formulated and ready to be voiced. The Prime Minister glanced at her momentarily, then away, ignoring her frantic hand waving, as well as the shouted questions of other reporters.

One, an inquiry from the back of room, repeating the rumor circulating that the flood unearthed some significant artifacts, caught the premier unawares, causing her to wince almost imperceptively and visibly stiffen.

"We won't be entertaining any questions on this matter but my office will keep you updated and informed," she said dismissively, adding that "We've alerted the Palestinian Authority that this emergency requires us to close the security fence which, as you all know, for humanitarian reasons we ordered opened following the floods. For the moment, let us extend our nation's sympathy to the family of Major Abramov and our prayers for the safe release of Dr. Rosenberg. Israel appreciates your interest and your attention."

Cries of complaint and the chirping of cell phones trailed the Prime Minister as she, the Minister, and the security officers exited the room, the door closing quickly behind them.

* * *

"Well, I suppose she had to say something, even if what she said we could've gotten off the Internet an hour ago." Paolo's voice betrayed his disappointment and distress. "She was being more than circumspect, Angelo, there's a helluva lot more to this than the snippets we heard. No news is no news. What was Dov up to, where were they going?"

"Maybe it's just a coincidence that the van was attacked? You know these things've happened before on the roads outside Jerusalem. Hitchhikers killed, terrible things ... And in the aftermath of the catastrophe, someone looking to make a ... a score, an easy one." Father Angelo was secretly pleased with himself that he remembered the American slang word. "Maybe that's all it was, a horrible coincidence. Maybe they took Dov because they think Dov might be worth some money to someone. Paolo, we shouldn't let our imaginations run away with us."

"It doesn't figure, Angelo. You're being far too optimistic. As they say in Israel, and I'm sure you've heard this, all the optimists remained in Germany after nineteen thirty-three, the pessimists left for Palestine. This is no simple hit-and-run. A half dozen armed guys? One or two, maybe, but not six or however many there were. If it was just a simple robbery, why not just grab their wallets, steal the van, and leave them by the roadside? If you didn't know him and took a look at Dov, do you think he looks like someone who's worth more than fifty *shekels?* No, this was planned, someone knew something and said something. Less important is to whom that something was said."

CHAPTER TWENTY-TWO

At 6:30 p.m., Jerusalem time, RAI broke into its scheduled programming and returned to its news coverage of Dr. Dov Rosenberg's abduction. The Italian newscaster announced that each of the major media's Jerusalem bureaus had received the tape she was about to play directly from a group identifying itself as Fatah al-Islam. In the run-up to the tape's showing, she noted that while Fatah al-Islam was a shadowy, underground splinter organization active primarily in Lebanon as an adjunct to Hezbollah, it had lately gained a tenuous foothold in the West Bank, too, a growing threat to the ruling Fatah Party. Its long-established links to Hamas, she continued, and to the more radical clique of ayatollahs in Tehran itself were known to the West's intelligence communities even if its leadership remained concealed. Fatah al-Islam's tactics mimicked those used by al-Qaeda in Iraq during the American occupation.

"These guys learned their lessons well, from the masters," a former CIA head said grimly, following the tape's partial showing during an appearance on one of America's Sunday morning gabfests.

Tapes received by Western news organizations often showed last-minute testimonials by suicide bombers, threats of wholesale slaughter, and, most disturbing, images of beheadings of those referred to *proforma* as "enemies of Islam." The tapes' intent was crystal clear - to strike terror into the heart of its Western viewers and thus weaken the viewers' and their governments' resolve to do battle with them. Although Fatah al-Islam believed in the inevitability of their cause's triumph, the ultimate conquest of the West by the forces of Islam, the logic behind their tactics, to soften the West, was faulty and in fact had the opposite effect. It succeeded only in hardening it and driving Fatah al-Islam and its allies further underground.

The Western networks and cable stations, including *al-Jazeera* and *al-Arabiya,* refused to transmit images of the actual executions. If one had a taste for gore, however, the murders were readily available without commentary on several Western and militant Muslim groups' official websites.

The brief introduction over, the tape began to roll. The picture was grainy, the product of a first-generation video recorder, the sound scratchy. In a small, almost bare, non-descript room, a large, full-bearded man, in full *sayyid* regalia - black turban and robes - sat cross-legged upon a large cushion, framed by two standing bodyguards, each wearing a ski mask, with swords tucked into their sash belts and AK-47s held across their chests. Tacked to the wall behind the seated *sayyid* was a magnified map of Palestine with the Dome of the Rock at its center.

"Inshallah." An Italian language translation ran along the bottom of the TV screen. *"Inshallah,"* the *sayyid* repeated. "Thank you for your guidance in our *jihad* against the infidels, the Crusaders who we evicted long ago only to be replaced by the perfidious Zionists who now occupy our holy land with the assistance of their lackeys or the Great Satan."

The bodyguards repeated in unison the *sayyid's* praise of Allah, raising their weapons above their heads for emphasis.

"His accent's not Palestinian," Father Angelo remarked. "It sounds like a learned second language."

"Yes, yes, that's not his mother tongue. The inflection's off. What do you think, Angelo? I'm thinking Farsi, no?"

"It could very well be but why is he running this show?"

Paolo shrugged, then began to speak but the words didn't come. His mind suddenly blanked. He felt uneasy, a squirming in his stomach, the outcome of the kidnapping unthinkable, yet if history was any guide, inevitable. Both Romans stared intently at the screen, riveted, unable to turn away as the *sayyid* droned on, his voice a monotone.

"We have in our hands, *Inshallah,* holy objects sacred to those who paved the path for The Prophet and then foolishly rejected him, choosing instead the law of the prophet Moses and accepting their false Messiah in the place of the True Prophet. The Great Flood that lifted the holy objects from the sands is Allah's judgment upon them. His disgust with the way their pollutants have fouled the earth, their quest for wealth, their mindless pursuit of material goods, their smokestacks, their ripping of the treasure from our soil to fill their coffers ..." The sayyid shook his finger at the camera, scolding, yet his flat tone remained unchanged. "This is the judgement of Allah upon the West that has destroyed his work in the Heavens ..."

"So much jibberish, he's making no sense."

"He doesn't have to, Angelo, the script's familiar to his followers, and mindlessly accepted. It's rote," Paolo replied, though he had to admit the message the *sayyid* parroted would, with a little rephrasing, sound very much like the late Pope John Paul's dire warnings. Had Angelo, he wondered, noticed the striking similarity?

The *sayyid* glanced down at his notes, then continued, "Allah will wreak His special vengeance upon the royal family of Saud, they who have already suffered mightily in the Great Flood by His will and must continue to suffer for having violated the laws revealed to the Prophet Mohammed by the Angel Gabriel in the Tablets of Heaven. *Jihad* is the holy obligation of every Muslim. *Jihad* is not the call to murder that the Zionists, through their media puppets, claim it to be. We, the true followers of the Koran, will achieve our goals in the struggle, it is the will of Allah."

The *sayyid* looked off to his left, the camera jerkily following his gaze and then pulled back for a wide-angle view. His bodyguards then moved towards the previously unseen Dr. Dov Rosenberg. The camera then moved in for a close-up shot. Rosenberg was slumped on the room's tiled floor, his legs splayed before him, propped up by a third bodyguard. He appeared to either have been drugged or nearly prostrate with shock. His eyes were glassy, his face swollen. There was no movement to his limbs; his hands lay flat, palms facing upward. He was alive but immobile.

An indecipherable sound came from Paolo's throat as Father Angelo gasped, his breath catching, both rendered speechless by what they were seeing.

"Allah is merciful and forgiving but not in the way the West understands," the *sayyid* said. "Muslims do not deny that we are a part of a common chain that began with the People of the Book. We share a common heritage and our city of Jerusalem is the fount of the great faiths. There is a core of holiness there and within this core are holy objects ..."

Paolo shifted on the settee, crossing, then uncrossing his

legs, rolling his eyes, as the *sayyid* wandered off on another tangent. Father Angelo remained at the edge of the settee, his body tense, his fingers interlaced across one knee, his eyes never leaving the TV screen.

"There is a rumor afloat in the Zionist Entity," the *sayyid* was saying, "a rumor kept from the world by the Zionist niece of the infidel who drove the Palestinians from their lands, and her Zionist slaves. The Great Flood washed up from our land sacred objects hidden from the world by the Zionist Entity's so-called government and its leaders. They are not fools, these satanic spawn. They understood long ago that the great lie of the Holocaust, perpetuated by generations of Zionists and their cowardly allies, had run its course, the doubters outnumbering the believers of this calumny. And now, to save themselves from the implacable will of Allah, they must replace their Holocaust myth with another myth, convincing the West that the Zionist enclave is the true Holy Land and must fall forever under its armed protection."

The *sayyid* turned away from Dov Rosenberg, whose name he chose not to nor needed to mention, and pointed to a far corner of the room. The cameraman pivoted around, his camera now focusing on the area behind him. There, arrayed on a threadbare green carpet, lay what he called "a piece of their so-called True Cross of Christ and some tablets of Moses from the Temple of Herod."

It was unusual for Islamic fundamentalists to ever mention the Second Temple, their propagandists regularly asserting that, like the Holocaust, Herod's Temple was also a myth, an imaginary figment concocted by the Zionists to further their goals. The Romans were baffled as to why the *sayyid* had deliberately referred to the Second Temple, what he had meant by it. Had it been a slip of the tongue, meaningless, or did the mention carry a deeper meaning?

The *sayyid* seemed to be winding towards concluding his remarks. He turned again towards Dr. Rosenberg, pointing once more.

"This Zionist pig is the director of the so-called museum, a warehouse that is filled with valuables stolen from the true followers of Islam." Again the wagging finger was shaking in Dr. Rosenberg's direction. "He has admitted to the Zionist Entity's

222

theft of our people's treasures. He has also provided us with documents asserting the relics our freedom fighters liberated from the Zionist thieves are true relics." His facial expression remained immutable, his voice stilted, ending as he had begun, "In the name of Allah, the Compassionate, the Merciful …"

Glancing up at his bodyguards, he watched as each drew the sword from his belt as the tape ended, its worldwide audience watching in horror, left hanging over Dr. Dov Rosenberg's fate although few believed he would survive. There would be no televised execution although an execution was almost a certainty. Executing Dr. Dov Rosenberg on international TV would serve no further purpose. Why fulfill the Western world's dire expectations, its insatiable taste for the grisly? Leave them instead to imagine the worst, such images far more powerful than the reality.

Fatah al-lslam had achieved what it had set out to do with the broadcast. It had captured the world's attention with its amateurish ten-minute tape. The gauntlet was thrown down. There would be no "Now back to our regular programming" announcement by the networks and cable stations. In its place there would be round-the-clock-coverage, breaking news bulletins by the score, millions in the viewing audience crowded around their screens. All eyes were turned towards Jerusalem. In the wake of the tape's telecast an infinite number of questions surfaced, not the least of them was how would Israel, how would the world react to this latest outrage, what would they do now in the midst of the economic chaos, the environmental catastrophe, and the population dislocation that still held them in its grip?

* * *

It would later be revealed why Dr. Dov Rosenberg was where he was when he was taken by a gang of Fatah al-Islam militants. The forensics team assigned to determine the provenance of the original relics requested that they be brought to Dimona for final confirmation of their findings. Because of the inestimable value placed on the relics, the team volunteered to dispatch an armored convoy for their transport. But Dr. Rosenberg, the investigative report read, insisted in no uncertain terms that he bring them to Dimona personally. He was reluctant to part with the relics out of his sight; he would not be dissuaded. Inasmuch as security wouldn't be compromised since what they possessed was unknown outside of perhaps a handful of trusted signatories to the secrecy agreement, the Minister threw up his hands and relented, giving Dr. Rosenberg permission to personally accompany the relics to Dimona.

Although the museum director objected strenuously to the Minister's insistence that an escort would be required once the relics neared Bethlehem - Rosenberg reasoned that a cavalcade of armored vehicles would only attract undue attention and raise questions - he acceded in the end to the Minister's demand. As an afterthought, the Minister suggested that the operation take place after ten in the evening when the road was lightly traveled. Dr. Rosenberg, according to the report, raised no objections, remarking that he was "a night owl anyway."

The van, driven by Major Abramov, with Dr. Rosenberg and the relics aboard, was to converge with its armed escort two kilometers beyond Ramat Rahel. It was perhaps three hundred meters before Ramat Rahel that the daring and perfectly coordinated attack occurred. The strike upon the van was lightning fast, less than a minute from the first shot to the getaway, and carried out with uncharacteristic precision on a traffic-free road.

Moments later, the van with the priceless relics and Dr. Rosenberg U-turned and headed back towards Jerusalem, leaving two Fatah al-Islam assailants dead and Major Abramov bleeding profusely from several bullet wounds by the roadside. It would forever remain a mystery, despite the Massad's best "efforts," as to how Fatah al-Islam came by the intelligence that allowed them to waylay Dr. Dov Rosenberg's van and escape.

* * *

The banner headlines screaming across the world's TV screens and special editions of its major newspapers were all variations on one theme: "True Cross and Tablets of Moses Found." The rare, more skeptical media organs added a question mark at the headline's end but they were few. It was apparent, too, that Dr. Dov Rosenberg's predicament would soon be reduced to an asterisk when compared to the discovery of the

True Cross and the Tablets of Moses. How could it not in such momentous circumstances?

It was late into the moonless Roman night before a political analyst on a small Italian cable channel pieced it all together. At the heart of the story was an intricate plot that he outlined in the starkest of terms. Blackmail, pure and simple. Fatah al-Islam's intent, unspoken by the *sayyid* but as clear as a bright summer day, was to blackmail both Israel and the West, dividing them, thus rendering Israel vulnerable. Of course, this plan differed little from hundreds of others hatched by Muslim militants since Israel's founding, all similar in their overriding aim-isolating Israel and ultimately driving it into the ground or into the sea.

But Islam's radical movement finally had in hand something far more valuable to move their master plan forward. It wasn't an unfortunate IDF soldier or two, a minor diplomat, or even a famous scholar like Dr. Dov Rosenberg to auction off, another unlucky pawn in endless, tortuous negotiations that might drag on for years, eventually resulting in the inevitable trade-off, the release of a few hundred Palestinian prisoners.

Such an endgame was a pinprick, a baby's step, hardly something that could be considered a mortal blow, a great victory by any standard. And the news of it would be relegated to page eighteen in the major dailies and perhaps appear once, near the end of the hour-long television newscasts, and after the first viewing not at all. Four or five news cycles down the pike, the world-renowned Dr. Rosenberg, dead or alive, would rate barely more than a mention on the all-news channels outside of Israel.

No, this time the monetary value of what the terrorists held was not only immeasurable - the very symbols of the Western world's major faiths - but their recovery by the West was absolutely essential. Would the West accept the loss of the earthly evidence that symbolized and confirmed the foundation beliefs of Judaism and Christianity? Such a decision by any and all Western leaders was inconceivable. Fatah al-Islam's leaders and their sponsors knew this instinctively. And they counted on another, absolutely critical element giving their plan more than a remote chance for success. The entire scheme hinged on the Israeli government's intransigence and its prime minister's refusal, facing

225

the onslaught of American pressure and European threats and arm-twisting, to make concessions to retrieve the tablets and the Crosspiece from the Cross.

CHAPTER TWENTY-THREE

The theft of the relics and the frenzy of politicking that would follow on its heels weren't uppermost in the minds of Paolo Pisa or Father Angelo Lorenzo. It was no great leap of logic to grasp that the Fatah al-Islam thugs had squeezed, by either force or drugs or a likely combination of both, every ounce of information out of Dov Rosenberg. His nearly lifeless appearance on the tape clearly said as much. The kidnappers were hardly strangers to violence and torture and neither Paolo nor Father Angelo believed Rosenberg could withstand either, particularly when administered expertly by his captors.

"It's likely that Dov gave up our names, you know," Paolo said. "We'd be on the top of the list."

"And whoever else is involved, too." Father Angelo nervously ran his hand through his hair. "One can hardly blame him for …"

"Of course, neither of us would've, could've held out or behaved differently." Paolo's voice dropped a few decibels. "Dov's a dead man even if they chose not to film and show it. Which they'll surely do at one point. I don't mean to sound heartless, Angelo, but he's done. They've got what they wanted from him so he's disposable, like an old shoe. They'll do him like they did Daniel Pearl, dump what's left of him somewhere in the Territories and send a chop-chop video to the networks."

Father Angelo nodded grimly. "Do you think we should try to contact the Minister or …"

"How would we go about that? Where do we start? We're supposed to be sort of, um, incognito, waiting for the 'call,' like some sort of deep cover agents from an old thriller. If this hell we've gotten ourselves into wasn't turning into a monstrous tragedy, the theatricality of it all might be amusing. But it's not, is it? Not one bit. Anyway it's more likely that the Minister will contact us. If he still has any use for us, that is. We're floating around in limbo."

"What about your friend Wilberg? I think he wasn't so innocent, so unawares. All those old maps, his government connections, his— I must say this, Paolo, so please don't take offense— the doddering routine as if he was failing which even to a casual observer he wasn't. I didn't buy his act that he was ignorant of everything that's happened since the Yom Kippur War."

Paolo nodded slowly, his brow furrowed in thought, a look of foreboding darkening his face. "Angelo, turn on your computer, please."

"Why?"

"Just turn it on. I want to check something out."

The computer quickly logged in to Father Angelo's home page. Paolo seated himself before it, typed "Wilberg" into the search engine, and pressed "enter." Several hits appeared immediately, the most recent a link to the February 24th edition of the *Jerusalem Post,* two weeks earlier.

"Jesus Christ!" Paolo said, pounding his fist on the desk, tipping over Father Angelo's pencil holder, sending its contents clattering to the floor. "What is it?"

Paolo pointed to the article, excerpted from the newspaper's Local News section that now filled the screen. In a shaking voice, Father Angelo began reading the short piece aloud over Paolo's shoulder.

"The Jerusalem police reported the murder of Dr. Heinz Wilberg during a break-in at his apartment in the Yemin Moshe district. Wilberg, an engineer and former IDF tank commander who served during the Suez Crisis, directed the government's telephone line installation program during the 1950s and 1960s. He is survived by a son, William, of Haifa, and two grandsons. William Wilberg told police he believed the killers may have been after his father's priceless map collection. A police spokesman said the investigation is ..." No further information regarding Wilberg's map collection was provided, whether it had been stolen or whether the apartment had been ransacked. Nor was mention made of Wilberg's uncle, the *Blitzkrieg* planner General Helmut Wilberg, at least not in the spare, online edition. A small mercy, Paolo thought.

Father Angelo, overcome with dread, found himself

unable to continue reading. "My God, Paolo, do you think Wilberg's killing is also connected to ..."

"It had to have been. Which means we may move up one slot on the hit list." Paolo's stab at humor fell flat. "Sorry, Angelo, I know this is no time for joking ..."

The priest appeared not to hear him. His fingers were rubbing his temples as if he was trying to massage away a headache.

"What I think, Angelo," Paolo continued, "and please humor me here, is that the Israelis will inform the Vatican and the world that two of the foremost scholars, us, viewed and verified the relics ..."

Father Angelo looked up. "Conversely," he said slowly, "they might announce that we examined them and decided they were just another clever hoax, that what the terrorists stole is worthless, meanwhile dealing quietly to retrieve them."

"Yes, I agree, that's a diversion they could use, and then wash their hands of the whole matter. But then why all the secrecy, Dov's midnight ride with only those two pieces in the van? Why? What was that about? Without the Crosspiece and the tablets, it would be Israel's word against Fatah al-Islam's with Israel trying to prove the negative and Fatah al-Islam flooding the airwaves with denials of Israel's denial. And then they'd have to parade us before the world's camera and we'd have to deny what we believe to be true. Would you be willing to do that?"

"You know I wouldn't, Paolo."

"There're too many questions raised and none answered if they declare it a hoax. Confusion and debate over whether it's real or not certainly isn't what they want. Listen, no matter how this turns out - the grand plan, Ben-Gurion's grand plan and the plan of his niece - for it to work at all depends not only on the relics being what forensics and we believe they are, but on possessing the relics themselves. With each new generation memory fades and fails. The relics become Israel's supreme bargaining chips with the Christian world and, if and when push comes to shove, Israel and only Israel is accepted by a billion believers as the Holy Land."

Father Angelo rose from the settee and began to pace around the paneled study. He pinched the bridge of his nose, his eyes half-closed, deep in thought. Paolo recognized the look, that of a scholar working out a seemingly intractable problem, bringing his prodigious thought processes to bear. The priest was well-schooled in the *"Verstehen* Approach" to history which he explained to his dubious colleagues as little more than "putting yourself in the shoes that walked before you, adjust for time, place and intelligence, and you will come to understand the past." It was an approach that served him to advantage in the modern world, too, in the world of the nearby Vatican where *Omnia ad majorem Dei* gloriam - All For The Greater Glory Of God - was also subject to occasional adjustments, with God on the one hand, the secular Caesars on the other, a balance the ultimate result between the two.

"However much Jerusalem tears apart the West Bank," Father Angelo was saying, "they know the search is futile. They have already accepted that Dov is dead, no doubt a rabbi's ready to recite *Kaddish* over his remains. That is sadly a given."

Paolo lowered his eyes, nodding.

"I must apologize, Paolo, for what I said before. I don't know what I was thinking. To declare it all a hoax serves no one, least of all Jerusalem. There can be no seeds of doubt planted. What's paramount now is the retrieval of the Cross and the tablets. Remember, in times of crisis such as these, religion plays a major role and these objects, particularly these objects, have the power to unite us all, Christian and Jew. We've both seen the faithful flocking to the holy sites to view and even touch objects deemed holy..." he paused, smiling slightly, adding, "whether or not they actually are. Imagine yourself a true believer presented with the opportunity to even glimpse the True Cross ..."

"Or the tablets," Paolo said.

"Yes, the tablets, of course," he added. "I'm afraid we're in a complicated, an almost impossible situation here, my friend. As I intended to remind the audience in New York, the Vatican wasn't exactly overjoyed when the Dead Sea Scrolls were discovered and interpreted. Rome's applause was muted. What they did not want to hear was that the Messiah lived among the Essenes. It ran contrary to the official line. Christ, for the Church, has always been unique. The Church, its very foundations, are constructed of tradition and doctrine. I fear that when it comes to the True Cross, they're likely to affirm that they have its pieces in Santa Croce in Gerusalemme, in the St. Chapelle, and, forgive me, I forget where else, along with the nails and the wooden marker in both Hebrew and Latin."

"You're thinking Rome will call the find a hoax?" Paolo was incredulous.

"I'm afraid so, even if the Cross is verified by an army of scholars and experts and even if we testify in support of their claim. You musn't forget that the De-Judaification of Jesus is a process, inexorably moving forward for almost two thousand years and nothing, but nothing, will reverse it. John Paul's position on the Jews and Israel was hardly shared by many in his inner council. And with John Paul gone ..."

"But what about you, Angelo? You'll stand up for what we both know, won't you, if it's the truth? You agreed you'd refuse to deny the truth if Israel declared it a hoax," Paolo reminded him.

Father Angelo pondered for a moment before proceeding.

"I won't be permitted to appear publicly and whatever I say in private will be debunked, quietly but determinedly. I will be de-fanged, so to say, marginalized. You must understand how significant an event this is and how it threatens the Vatican's hegemony and control. No, the Curia's already closed ranks." He was speaking with the growing confidence of a man now firmly in his element, grasping all the weight and meaning of what had been placed on his and Paolo's shoulders. "They'll issue an official statement, allegedly authored by me and couched in abstract, indecipherable terms. I defy you to find anyone able to break the code and with any accuracy convey my opinion. And as a priest, what can I do? What leverage do I have? Allies? None. The motive behind the Church's reaction is to subject the finds to question, at least the discovery of the True Cross, without offending the Jews, Israel or Christianity in general. A kernel of doubt thrown into the mix, to protect its franchise. The world will view it all as an honest effort to take the wind from the terrorists' sails, turning the tables on them, making them look even more like the murderous fools they are. Surely you don't for a moment think the pope welcomes a Muslim fundamentalist regime on Israel's doorstep, do you?"

"No, not at all, but how will they address the issue of the tablets?" Paolo asked, his fascination with Father Angelo's prediction of the Vatican's machinations growing. "One find's real, one's not? It won't fly."

"They're not interested in the tablets. Wrong church, wrong pew, as the Americans say. They'll 'defer' to the judgment of Israel's rabbinate and Rome's chief rabbi will concur, mark my words. Even if the Tablets are verified, the Church has a quiver full of muddling and dizzying explanations for the appearance of an *ersatz* Cross. In times of confusion, people often shut down, their brains overloaded, and stop paying close attention. Eventually, the questions will fade and disappear, the public's attention span being what it is, not what it ought to be."

Father Angelo had outlined the Church's case as a skilled Jesuit might be expected to do, elaborating as he unveiled it further. All ecclesiastical efforts would be aimed at obtaining no other verdict than a judgment of "not proven." Paolo conceded to himself that the priest's arguments were compelling, and that he was, for once, feeling slightly out of his depth, unsure of how to handle what he now felt was sure to come.

"Both of us will shortly be invited to the Vatican, Paolo," Father Angelo was saying. "You'll be treated with the utmost courtesy and civility, with an occasional flattering remark thrown in for good measure. I know these people, known them my entire adult life. They're expert at this sort of friendly meeting and they've already done their homework. They know you're a Roman, of course, but you'll be asked if you prefer to be called Dr. Josephus. This is intended to discomfit you, a not-so-veiled message to confirm they're aware that you'll support the Israeli position while at the same time subtley questioning your loyalty to your homeland."

"I wouldn't expect otherwise." Paolo's response, though, sounded hollow to his own ears. He really didn't know what to expect.

"Meanwhile, I suspect the Minister himself is trying to get hold of us, we being the rare eyewitnesses to the finds. He'll play on your heritage, first as a noted Jewish scholar and then as an Israeli citizen to come forth and verify them. But he doesn't know you're here nor does your family; they all think we're on the New York flight. So after failing to reach you, he'll try to contact me. His contention will play to my reputation for honesty and forthrightness - his words - as a Biblical scholar, and that I will

232

surely verify that the relics are the originals. But he won't have a chance, at least not before we've had our Vatican 'audience.' My cell phone's unlisted and all incoming calls to this apartment are routed through the antique Vatican switchboard - they're promising to upgrade to a twenty-first-century system sometime in the twenty-second," he chuckled softly, "so the Minister's chances of breaking through quickly are less than minimal, although my impression is that the delay will be short."

"And when he does he needn't play on anything with me, Angelo. I'm willing to testify and verify the find," Paolo stated firmly.

"Yes, I know, but let's not lose sight of the immediate danger Wilberg's killing and Dov's kidnapping has placed us in. Your friend Heinz Wilberg is dead, murdered, and we don't know why exactly. The official story strains credulity. But we do know it has something to do with the discoveries, don't we? We could rack our brains from now till doomsday and come up with no other logical reason, yes? And whoever murdered Wilberg must have us in their crosshairs as well."

"So where does this leave us?" Paolo shivered involuntarily.

"Between the proverbial rock and an increasingly hard place. This is a chess game playing out at the highest level. They're the kings and the bishops. Us? We're the pawns. As you said of Dov - we're also disposable."

CHAPTER TWENTY-FOUR

A familiar voice coming from the television caused Father Angelo to shift his focus. Filling the screen's frame was Pietro Cardinal Zaccaria on the Vatican channel diligently planting seeds of doubt about the objects hijacked in Israel that set the world's media, blogs, vlogs, and websites abuzz.

"While we have yet to receive the full details, just because a terrorist cabal claims to have in their possession a part of the True Cross and the Tablets of Moses, well ..." the self-assured cardinal paused as a teacher might, awaiting his students' full and undivided attention. All the media's subsequent questions were deftly parried, the cardinal the reigning Vatican master at providing the vaguest of acceptable replies that deflected any follow-ups. Like Father Angelo, Zaccaria was in his mid-60s, of medium height and slightly stoop-shouldered. His face had a vulpine aspect and his unblinking eyes betrayed the acute, fearless intelligence of a missionary.

"Do I need remind everyone that throughout the Church's and the world's history there have been an interminable series of infamous hoaxes?" His arms were outstretched now, his palms open in supplication, the very model of Jesuitical reason. "The so-called vessels containing the bones of our Lord Jesus Christ, the 'diaries' of the genocidal maniac Hitler - a forgery as you will recall that landed its perpetrators in a German prison - the Piltdown Man in England, and the many, many splinters from the many, many false 'True Crosses' that crop up from time to time." He reminded his faithful listeners that there were long-verified pieces of the True Cross under the Church's protection, residing there in Rome, in Italy, and in France.

"In previous eras, some asserted that the Cross itself would self-multiply, *ut detrimentia non sentire.f,' et quasi, intacta permeneret.* Imagine," he smiled, shaking his head in staged disbelief. "Perhaps it is this long-discredited notion that the terrorists are attempting to once more put forth in a transparent attempt to gull us as did earlier tricksters." He shrugged, pausing again for a moment's reflection, then continued, "History's replete with examples of similar swindles, far too numerous to list and waste more of everyone's time with, and this sideshow may well be among them. Unless proved otherwise"

"Who is this man, Angelo?" Paolo asked. "I'm not familiar with him."

"You could say that he's the Minister's *Doppelganger.* Our ... I should say the Church's 'Minister.' He can be a very rough customer, not the kind you'd want to cross swords with. He is what Cardinal Ratzinger was to John Paul, the keeper of orthodoxy and doctrinal purity, the crusader against modernity and the claim that other religions are equal to ours. An opening salvo, that's what that was, opening shot across the bow."

Paolo felt an encroaching dread witnessing the Vatican's official response. It was remarkable and unsettling how the Church would and could muster all its energy to rapidly confront this threat to its hegemony, and clearly set itself on a potential collision course with Israel.

* * *

The phone call came from Cardinal Zaccaria's office at 10 p.m. As he had prophesied, Father Angelo was summoned to appear at the Vatican the following morning. "Would the Father kindly request Dr. Pisa to join them as well?" the caller asked rhetorically. A car would be awaiting them outside the residence at 7:50 A.M. "Sharp" was understood but left unsaid. A Zaccaria request was always answered affirmatively, without hesitation. Father Angelo was still a servant of the Church, its magnetic field overpowering, and for the priest, his obedience a confirmation of the Jesuits' adage: "Give me the child, I will give you the man." The script was following a predictable course.

"This is new territory for you, Paolo," Father Angelo counseled. "They will, as you might expect, attempt to divide us, but don't allow them to intimidate you."

"I've never been intimidated by them before and don't plan to start now. It's too late in the game." Paolo's courage sounded as it was, surface deep - a certain queasiness at the prospect of a meeting with the pope himself unnerved him.

236

* * *

At the appointed time, a black Mercedes C-Class sedan idled at the curb, waiting as Paolo and Father Angelo exited the building. Behind it, a police car escort was parked, its blue rooflight spinning and flashing, its engine humming, its occupants watching as the two men climbed into the sedan.

It was a very short ride from the residence to the Vatican, a walk that Paolo and Father Angelo could easily have made in less than ten minutes. That a car had been dispatched for their transport wasn't particularly unusual, although the occasions Father Angelo had been brought to the Vatican from his flat by an official car were rare. It certainly added a certain gravitas to the cardinal's summons. But the police car? That was unusual, giving both men pause, underscoring Father Angelo's perception that they may indeed be in danger for their lives.

The driver turned right onto the broad Via Della Consilazione, the Basilica with Michelangelo's dome now in full view, ahead of them the Piazza San Pietro even at this early hour filling with pilgrims and tourists long before the opening time. The car edged its way past the square and Pope Leo II's Santa Stefano, towards the Palazzo del Govematorato, the hi-winged, long and narrow building that housed the Vatican's administrative offices, a disharmonic, inflated 1930's Mussolini era construction.

Once inside the building, they were met by a page who led them towards a large oak door - a Swiss guard on either side - the Vatican's heraldic crest prominent on its upper panel. As the page eased the door open, Father Angelo entered first, followed closely by Paolo. At an overlong, highly polished conference table, two cardinals sat on one side, balanced on the opposite by Cardinal Zaccaria and a civilian, a prosperous-looking man in a dark, well-cut business suit from Armani's latest collection. A bottle of mineral water and a glass had been placed before each man. At the table's head sat the pope, Benedict XVI, a smallish man dressed in the flowing white robes of his station, his hair snowy white under a silken skullcap. Father Angelo was familiar in varying degrees with everyone in the capacious meeting room.

The pope beckoned and he approached, dropped to a knee, and kissed the pontiff's ring. As Paolo Pisa came forward, the pope stood and offered his hand in greeting.

"Your Holiness, I'm overwhelmed by this honor," Paolo stammered.

"It is more an honor for me to welcome you and our Father Angelo Lorenzo. It's not often that I'm in the presence of celebrated Biblical scholars such as yourselves," the pope said, his Italian slightly tinged with the gutteral Bavarian inflections of his youth. "I have come to know you only through your outstanding works so it is more than a pleasure to meet you in the flesh, so to say, even if the occasion is somewhat ... unorthodox." A thin smile creased the pontiff's face, his clear blue eyes never leaving Paolo's. "All you've done to enlighten the public in an age when so much nonsense bombards us daily is to be commended. As is, of course, the groundwork you've done for the Church in Israel." As if on cue, the others seated around the table applauded politely. "Please be seated."

It was evident that the pope had been well briefed. Paolo was deeply impressed by the pontiff's almost casual demeanor and his unmistakable aura of command, in sharp contrast to the martinet he had been portrayed to be by a hostile press before his acension to the Throne of St. Peter and later after his commentary on the world of Islam. The pope exhibited the mannerisms and command of a highly successful CEO with a lifetime appointment - which, in truth, he was.

The first of the cardinals introduced was John Cardinal Murphy, bluff, florid-faced, a corona of steel-grey hair encircling his large head. Seated at the pope's left, Murphy, an American, New York-born, was an authority on holy objects and his books were known to both visitors. Because of his ecumenical background, he was the natural choice to become the Church's unofficial liaison to the Israeli government following the Holy See's recognition of the Jewish state in 1993. Inside the Curia, he was nicknamed "The Fireman," effectively tamping down the inevitable brushfires that arose between the Jewish community and the Church over various and sundry issues. Cardinal Murphy's fluent Hebrew was brought into play whenever the occasion required it, providing him with unlimited access and acceptance within the Jewish community and its several, sometimes conflicting, organizations. His many awards from the American Jewish Congress, AIPAC, and B'nai B'rith provided the wall decor for his office. Murphy, like Father Angelo Lorenzo, was a Zionist and like the priest his allegiance and obedience was above all to the Church.

To his left sat Etienne Cardinal Desereaux, a pensive man with a sallow complexion and sunken cheeks, a contemporary of the pope's, and a Biblical scholar as well. Like Cardinal Murphy, he was closely aligned with Europe's Jewish communities, particularly France's, Europe's largest. Cardinal Desereaux was highly regarded in Jerusalem for his counsel in matters concerning the influx of Muslims into his native country, always trying to balance its threatened Judea-Christian heritage.

"By the way," the pope asked, turning to Paolo. "Do you prefer to be addressed as Dr. Pisa or Dr. Josephus?"

"Inasmuch as we're in Italy, in the Vatican itself, I'd prefer the former," Paolo replied crisply, mustering as innocent a tone as he could, silently thanking Father Angelo for the alert.

"Very well then," the pope said, placing his palms together. "Dr. Pisa it is. Here on my right is Cardinal Zaccaria, whom you all know or know of, and to his right, Dr. Frederico Fanelli. Dr. Fanelli directs our scientific research laboratory and is primarily responsible for acquiring, verifying and evaluating the objects and relics found in our museum." Smiles all around.

Cardinal Zaccaria spoke first, relating to the assembled the ordeal their guests had undergone during their days in Tiberias, the pope adding that "You're both quite fortunate with so many succumbing to the storms and floods." He shook his head in dismay, sighing as he did so. "So many died, so many innocent souls ..."

Cardinal Zaccaria waited for the pontiff's words to fade before continuing. After Cardinal Ratzinger's elevation to the Holy See, Zaccaria was selected to be the Church's public face, its spokesman -- the pope's personal choice. He came from great wealth, a product of the Piedmont merchant aristocracy in Italy's north. In the nineteenth century, his family's banking empire was a major provider of the funds that supported Italy's successful reunification movement. And in conjunction with the now-defunct German-Jewish Bleichroeder banking house, the Zaccaria bank loaned Chancellor Otto von Bismarck the monies he required to forge the disparate German states into a nation.

Pietro Cardinal Zaccaria was an international player, frequently called on of late. Deeply conservative, he was respected and feared by more than a few within high government circles worldwide. As one having the pope's ear naturally would be.

"I was deeply saddened to learn of Dr. Rosenberg's kidnapping, a man I'd met on a number of occasions," he said, addressing Paolo and Father Angelo directly. "I can only pray that this will all be resolved favorably and that Dr. Rosenberg will be released unharmed. That his wife, having survived Treblinka, should now suffer this is unconscionable, almost inconceivable. I am sending her a personal note ..."

Paolo couldn't but notice how smoothly, how pitch-perfect the kabuki of putting the guests at their ease was acted out, how effortlessly all the bases were touched by the hosts. Although the encounter ahead promised to be difficult, the sentiments expressed could not but be appreciated by Paolo. Despite his awareness that the pope, any pope, attends no meeting unless its script has been infinitely choreographed, Paolo marveled at the flawless execution of this dance. Like any great corporation, the Church's innermost circle closes ranks if faced with a challenge to its exclusive patents. How else does one safeguard as flawless and omnipresent an operation as the Holy See?

Father Angelo, if asked, would echo the assertion that the pope's public image of blessing the faithful multitudes in the Piazza San Pietro or, as John Paul II was wont to do, kissing the ground at each stop during his circumnavigations of the globe, were only two facets of the papacy. The world was familiar with the public pope, the carefully crafted image of an elderly, kindly man of God offering benedictions from his balcony. The pontiff's daily life was necessarily more complex. It was filled with a swirl of meetings, strategy sessions, reports from the Church's far-flung outposts, and often turgid position papers presented by one or another faction within the inner circle itself. Issues were debated heatedly and decisions arrived at collectively. But in the end, when all the voices were quieted, it was always the Vicar of Christ who bore the enormous burden of the final say.

Central to the Church's operating system is its doctrine.

In the seventeenth century, the astronomer Galileo was accused by Church inquisitors of heresy for concluding that the earth revolved around the sun, the heliocentric theory directly contradicting Church dogma at the time championing the geocentric theory which had the sun revolving around the earth. Doctrine could be modified and had been over time but often it could take decades or even centuries before a significant tenet of faith was reversed. It wasn't until 1992 when Pope John Paul II officially conceded that the earth revolved around the sun, expressing regret as he did so over the Church's mishandling of the Galileo affair. This was little consolation for Galileo who breathed his last in 1642. On the other hand, Father Angelo knew this glacial movement, this obstinacy, was part of the Church's proven appeal down through the ages. The faithful could in increasingly uncertain times count on its continuity in a rapidly changing world.

Before Cardinal Zaccaria could continue, Cardinal Murphy interrupted. "Excuse me, Cardinal. May I offer a word?"

"Certainly, John, "Cardinal Zaccaria said, smiling genially, "please go ahead." Paolo wondered if even this interruption was rehearsed as he attempted to catch Father Angelo's eye. The priest, seated opposite and at the elbow of Dr. Fanelli, was looking in the pope's direction as the pontiff glanced at the wall clock. Paolo shifted awkwardly in his chair.

Cardinal Murphy cleared his throat "Dr. Pisa, you and Father Lorenzo are the reigning experts in this field and have had the good fortune to examine the objects in question. It's not our intention to debate their authenticity in their absence." Murphy placed his hands flat on the table. "And as you're aware, we approach holy relics somewhat differently. Be assured, gentlemen, that this is not an inquisition ..." Dr. Fanelli barked a sharp laugh at the remark which brought a near-laugh from the pope himself. "The TV's reportage for me is highly suspect, every word I hear from it I take with a shaker of salt," he said. "Listening to an eyewitness's report directly, from authorities of your and Father Lorenzo's stature, well, that's a completely different story. It's why we're all convened here today."

"Would you begin, please, Dr. Pisa?" Cardinal Desereaux interjected, leaning forward, the first words he'd spoken since being introduced to Paolo.

"Yes, please do," the pope seconded, his hand half-raised, signaling them to proceed.

Paolo and Father Angelo exchanged quick glances, the priest nodding. Paolo took it as his approval to relate for both what had come to pass during their few days in Israel.

"It's best I first present an overview, beginning at the beginning, which should put what occurred and why it occurred in some sort of context." Paolo's voice steadied, his equilibrium, shaken earlier by the unfamiliar surroundings and the uniqueness of his audience, had restored itself. As it always did when he was called upon to perform. It mattered not that he found himself suddenly thrust into the midst of the Vatican's ruling hierarchy. A performance was a performance. He had years of public and televised appearances tucked under his belt - even if in this case it was to be a command performance for the pope and his most trusted aides.

"'We were both invited by Dr. Rosenberg to examine an ancient manuscript found by workmen in a stadium near Tiberias. I'll detail the manuscript's contents in due course," he said, aware that the churchmen knew nothing of the so-called Passion Play nor the poetic map directing them to the finds. Cardinal Murphy scraped his chair closer to the table, placing his elbows on it, his hands clasped together. The pope steepled his fingers, listening intently, his face a mask of curiosity.

Inasmuch as the relics had fallen into terrorist hands, Paolo no longer considered himself or Father Angelo bound by their agreement. The theft made the find public, and had given them flexibility, rendering both scholars' written vows moot. Yet he still felt it incumbent upon him to show some circumspection in his description, fudging whenever he thought it necessary to do so.

"The stolen objects were housed in an impenetrable vault below the Israel Museum and access is by invitation only. The vaults were undamaged by the storms and floods. Father Angelo and I both witnessed the four pieces of the Cross, arranged symmetrically, along with the two stone tablets said to be from the Second Temple."

"Were you confident it wasn't another hoax?" Dr. Fanelli asked.

"Whenever I'm brought in to verify a find, I'm by nature

skeptical. If I wasn't, then I shouldn't do what I'm doing. I approached these objects as I do all discovered relics, Dr. Fanelli, with my normal skepticism."

Dr. Fanelli appeared, if only temporarily, satisfied with Paolo's answer. Nodding, he settled back in his chair.

"But when Dr. Rosenberg related to us how the objects were discovered," Paolo said, "pending extensive testing, I left convinced an extraordinary, to say the very least, find had been made. Insurance companies, as we all well know, refer to storms and floods as Acts of God. One might even say that the discovery— what preceded it, what made it possible— were Acts of God."

Nice turn of phrase, Father Angelo thought admiringly, even if a bit overdone. "So," Cardinal Murphy pressed, "these objects then, the objects displayed by the terrorists, were the finds you both examined, the pieces allegedly from the Cross and the stone tablets?"

"As best as I can determine, but honestly, I was distracted, unable to focus properly. And when I got hold of myself, my eyes were glued on Dov, slumped there like a sack of grain ..." Paolo paused, awaiting a reaction. The cardinals and Fanelli all nodded gravely.

"Please continue," the pope urged.

"We were sworn to silence regarding the finds by Dr. Rosenberg and an Israeli government representative - standard procedure with discoveries of such potential significance."

"Who was this representative, Dr. Pisa?" Cardinal Zaccarias voice had a sharp edge to it.

"We were never formally introduced," Paolo said, grinning. "I'm sure he has a name but it was never revealed beyond Dov referring to him as 'the Minister.' You may have seen him during Prime Minister Ben-Gurion's press conference yesterday. He appeared while it was underway, whispering in her ear near the end of the ..."

"We can always review the tape," Cardinal Murphy said, turning to an agreeing Cardinal Desereaux, "although his name's not important. We just prefer that all loose ends are tied up, no matter how minor they may at first seem. I'm sure you understand, Dr. Pisa."

"As an archaeologist, I certainly do," Paolo responded.

Across the table, Father Angelo smiled.

"Is it fair to say Jerusalem was involved in the discoveries from the start?"

Cardinal Zaccaria asked.

"Cardinal Zaccaria, I'm a scholar, not a diplomat, but in my extensive experience Jerusalem's always involved in archaeological issues. Whether they're permitted digs or accidental discoveries, Jerusalem's hand is in from the very beginning. When it became clear that the floods following the storms had caused extensive dislocation in the burial ground on the Mount of Olives, martial law was declared immediately to prevent looting and ransacking. The entire area was cordoned off in less than two hours."

The pope raised a question: "Dr. Pisa, the holy sites, was there much damage? Did the waters do great damage in the *Carda,* the heart of the Old City?" The pontiffs brow wrinkled, his concern evident. "As you probably know, many things are kept secret, even from the Pope."

Father Angelo chimed in, assuring the pope that no, the damage to the holy sites in the central city was minimal, praise God.

"We can offer up prayers to our forbears that they had the foresight to build Jerusalem on a hill."

"Yes, we should, we must," the Pope said, a smile in his voice, inviting Father Angelo to go further, to offer his thoughts.

"Your Holiness, a wall of water can uproot whatever lays in its path, even if it was buried for thousands of years. The furrows the flood cut were deep, wide, and extensive in number, reshaping the topography worldwide, as Dr. Pisa has noted. In the Kidron Valley, it was no different. Dr. Rosenberg brought us to the vault where the objects were found under the pillar. He confirmed that when he was first shown the vault, it wasn't entirely visible and it was still sealed. This doesn't rule out a hoax, but if we assume the finds are real and verifiable, the puzzle remains. How did they end up there in the first place? In fact, we checked with an expert on the maze of tunnels under the Old City, the tunnels from Herod's era …"

The pope raised a hand, interrupting Father Angelo in mid-sentence, and silencing him.

"Father," he said, his eyes narrowing, his fair skin flushing, his accent more pronounced. "We all know the True Cross was found by St. Helena. My history tends occasionally to be somewhat rusty but Dr. Fanelli has prepared what we know to be true from original documents held here in our library." The pope turned towards Paolo. "As a scholar of the era, Dr. Pisa, I'm sure you're familiar with the documents in question."

Paolo nodded in agreement. Yes, he'd seen and examined the documents. As documents, *per se,* they were original. But they were opinions, judgments made by believers. Hence, what they contained, what they purported to validate, was still open to question. To accept the documents' judgment without an afterthought was to stumble headlong into the classic logical fallacy *trap---argumentum ad verecundum-relying* on authority, absent of factual evidence, to support your argument. But Paolo knew better than to engage his hosts-wolves in their own lair, metaphorically speaking— colloquy. It would lead nowhere, offer no resolution. Better to keep one's tongue and concentrate on the issue at hand.

"The Cross St. Helena found," the pope continued, his voice firming, "was verified by four Byzantine ecclesiastic historians"— the pope emphasized *ecclesiastic* as if the mere mention of the word clinched the pontiffs *prima facie* case--"and was later affirmed and supported by Cyril of Jerusalem, Ambrose, and Chrysostom. This can all be found in Tillemont's and Jortin's works. Do I mispeak, Dr. Fanelli?"

"Never to my knowledge, Your Holiness," Dr. Fanelli hastened to say, playing to a T his assigned role as papal echo.

Father Angelo flinched, rebuked and flustered by the pope's apparent disdain for what he'd said. The Pope's summary rejection stung as painfully as if the pontiff had slapped him. If he'd read the pontiff's reaction correctly, even the remotest possibility the finds might be real was unthinkable, unworthy of consideration.

"Perhaps Dr. Pisa should elaborate," the priest said, slinking deeper into his chair, regretting his words, wishing vainly for instant invisibility.

"Your Holiness, Cardinals, Dr. Fanelli," Paolo jumped in, "there's a key to this mystery. There were in fact two manuscripts that Dr. Rosenberg requested we examine and analyze. The first appears to have been a rendering of the Gospel according to Matthew. It's structured as a passion play and is structured not in the style we're familiar with but in what we've come to know as the Greek dramatic style." Paolo described the chronology of how the manuscripts were uncovered and in brief detail what they contained. "The second piece is what might almost be termed a roadmap, taking the form of a follow-the-dots poem." Paolo reached in his briefcase for the folder that contained his notes.

As he read the poem he'd reconstructed from the ancient Hebrew into Italian, he could sense a pall descending on the room. When his recitation was completed, the only audible sound was the persistent ticking of the clock on the room's far wall. The pope, Dr. Fanelli, and the cardinals were staring at him in silence.

The uncomfortable stillness was broken finally by Cardinal Murphy who was ostentatiously scratching his head in wonderment.

"Forgive me, Dr. Pisa, for sounding like a doubting Thomas, but all of this sounds too ... convenient," he said in a slightly querulous voice. "You're claiming that the first passion play ever written, along with a ... a guide or clues written in verse, were found together in Tiberias by a couple of workmen? And a few days later two of history's most significant finds were unearthed?"

Paolo said nothing, his and Father Angelo's discomfort almost palpable.

"In the Brooklyn neighborhood I come from," the cardinal said, switching to English, "this story you've told is called a *bubbe meisse,* an old wife's tale."

"I remember that term, a Yiddish phrase," the pope said softly, "from before the nightmare years." His eyes were half-closed, as if searching his memory for lost recollections.

"It's just too pat, gentlemen," Cardinal Murphy continued, addressing Father Angelo as well. "It's implausible is what it is." The cardinal began massaging his neck to release imaginary tension.

Silence fell again, all eyes turned towards the pope, each man anxiously awaiting his comments. Often during high-level meetings these papal pauses seemed endless but the cardinals and the inner circle had accommodated themselves accordingly. The pope was thoughtful, slow to judgment. He might adhere unswervingly to Church doctrine but he willingly considered dissenting views on a whole range of non-doctrinal issues. More than likely he would weigh and reject those views but he did listen, converse, and consider. Soon after his assumption of the papacy, those with whom he came into daily contact recognized and accepted the pope's complexity. He was a combination of the modern, scholarly intellectual and the traditional churchman, someone who characteristically thought deeply before speaking. Any notion that age and the demands of the position were taking their toll was sorely misplaced.

Finally, he spoke.

"Often, as I learned long ago, it's best not to rush to judgment," he said, his eyes surveying the group, fixing in the end on Paolo Pisa. "Our world is rooted in a timelessness that is transcendent, its traditions attached to fixed moorings. Our faith is our anchor much as is the faith of the Jewish people who gifted us with Mosaic Law that we over time adapted and universalized. As my beloved predecessor often commented, it is the Jewish people who are the older brothers of the Church. But I am digressing ..." The pope smiled slightly, perhaps enjoying the growing consternation plastering itself onto his cardinals' faces. "Who among us could have envisioned that tunnelers building an underground beneath the Vatican would discover the bones of St. Peter? Who could conceive of a Bedouin boy wandering into a cave and stumbling upon a canister in which a piece of leather would speak of a destroyed world in the time of Our Lord? Do we all recognize the parallels in what we've been confronted with here?"

The Church's foremost princes and Dr. Fanelli grew pin-drop silent, their faces apprehensive. They had expected the pontiff to join them in their stated disbelief, in the end graciously thanking Father Angelo Lorenzo and Dr. Paolo Pisa for their time and efforts. In effect, a "thanks" but a "no thanks," unequivocally rejecting as did Cardinal Murphy moments before the Kidron discoveries as no more than an ingenious hoax perpetrated by parties unknown. They had, all of them, presumed, assumed, and consequently misread, as had the relieved Father Angelo, the pontiff's line of thinking.

"We needn't rush, there is time enough," the pope

247

continued. "Our relations with the Israeli government are by and large quite warm and our unity in the face of a growing Islamic fundamentalism that threatens not only Israel but the Church itself, no more directly than in the Holy Land itself. You're all cognizant of the severity of the threat and what it means if the forces of fundamentalism gain sway, exercise the upper hand, aren't you?" he asked rhetorically.

The pope took a moment to sip from the glass of water before him.

"For the moment, we're unsure that the discovered objects will be recovered but in my experience the Israeli government ... I am convinced that back channels have been opened in an effort to retrieve them."

Paolo knew then that the Pope had already been made privy to intelligence he and Father Angelo could only guess at. Zaccaria, Paolo figured, had his ear to the ground and would be the first to hear, the Pope the second to know.

"If the items are recovered, we will request of the Israelis that a joint team of experts - ours and theirs - test them."

Murmured yesses from those at the table.

"It would avoid potential conflict, Your Holiness," Dr. Fanelli said, stating the obvious.

"It is true, is it not, Dr. Fanelli, that specialists can date letters on a piece of ancient marble by the shape of its chisel marks?"

"Yes, absolutely," Dr. Fanelli answered. "We can even determine the composition of the ink used on parchment. Highly sophisticated computer programs have pieced together fragments from the Dead Sea Scrolls ..."

"Quite astonishing," the pope said, shaking his head. "Yes, quite astonishing. Sadly, these are the most difficult of times and they will worsen. I'm afraid it is not news that in an age of moral relativism - and our faith under siege, faced with unique challenges - it is paramount that we continue to assert the roots of our Judea-Christian civilization." The pope's gaze came to rest on Cardinal Zaccaria. "Cardinal, all this being said, it's imperative that the Israelis be made aware of our desire to share with them the testing of the objects if and when they're recovered."

"It's a request I'm sure they will welcome, Your Holiness." Cardinal Zaccaria was his reassuring self. "This is certainly no cause for dispute," he said, in a veiled reference to the thorny, ongoing issue of Pope Pius XII's canonization which, though muted, remained contentious.

"Good. Let me be firm that whatever the outcome, we will not alter any pillars of our faith."

The lines of papal authority had been clarified, a tentative direction established, a course outlined. Turning to his guests, the pope looked at one, then the other.

"This unfortunate situation with all its ramifications is quite delicate."

Paolo and Father Angelo understood the pope's message. No oath need be taken, no agreement signed. Discretion was imperative.

The pontiff turned his attention to the French cardinal, Desereaux.

"Perhaps, Cardinal, you can encapsulate for me what's in your report on the 'earth's desecration' "— the term the pope used for global warming—" that landed on my desk this morning. I've had no chance to even riffle the pages yet, today's schedule being what it is."

"The Western governments appear more inclined in the face of the catastrophe to take more proactive positions ..."

The pope cut Desereaux short. "One could not expect less, surely. What I devoutly wish to hear is that they're 'committed.' 'Inclined' leaves open too many doors, too many escape hatches. We've seen what runaway industrialization is doing, the willful ignorance of governments. We will have to progress more rapidly, use whatever means are at our disposal to apply pressure, Cardinal Desereaux. This is no longer a dismissible theory, the storms and flood proved otherwise. Like John Paul, I believe deeply that we have lost our sense of stewardship, for one another, for the world that God gave us." The pope looked at each man individually. "The teachings of the prophets, the disciples, and our Lord Jesus Christ must remain our only guide if we intend to save our planet. We've seen what the flood did to Italy - every morning I still see and hear the workmen clearing the mud from our very doorsteps."

Cardinal Zaccaria tapped his writswatch.

"Yes, yes, I know, another meeting," the pope said impatiently. "They can wait a few moments. Dr. Pisa, could you remain behind, please?"

"Of course, your Holiness," Paolo said as the others filed from the room.

The aide who had initially ushered them in reappeared, carrying one of Paolo Pisa's works, handing it along with a Mount Blanc to the pope.

"I'm a fan of your works, Dr. Pisa, I have them all in my personal quarters. If you would grace me with a signing ..."

"It would be my ... honor," Paolo said, taken aback, his face showing a mix of pride and slight embarrassment. Over the decades, he had become used to readers' adulation but this unique request could hardly compare. As he inscribed his signature, a faint tremor shook his hand. No small wonder, he thought to himself.

"Thank you," the pope said, handing the signed copy to the aide. "Dr. Pisa, you know that you and Father Angelo are sailing in very troubled waters."

"Yes, I'm afraid we do."

"Look after each other," he said.

And with a paternal pat on Paolo's back, the pope turned and left the room, head bent slightly, his robes trailing as he slowly made his way down the yawning hallway to his next meeting.

At the palazzo's main door, Cardinal Zaccaria was speaking with Father Angelo. As Paolo approached, both men turned to face him.

"I know your mention of the Tiberias manuscript's discovery triggered something in His Holiness. He's an acclaimed scholar, quite an intellect actually, but nothing fascinates him more than the mysteries surrounding a discovery of this sort and all it implies. But as you've heard, he's quite practical, too, as fervent a defender of our faith as all who came before him. Which is to be expected. It's a difficult balance, keeping the Church first and foremost and at the same time addressing the concerns and interests of the temporal powers that often conflict with ours ..."

A security officer opened the Governatorato's outer door for Paolo and Father Angelo.

"I can imagine," Cardinal Zaccaria added, "with the turmoil of the past few days - the abduction of Dr. Rosenberg and the theft of the objects - you both must be fearing for your

250

safety. I've ordered additional security at the apartment complex, by the way. As you've no doubt realized, a limousine ride to the Vatican never goes unnoticed. The *paparazzi* aren't the only eyes out there. And the Fundamentalists, as has often been said, have boundless patience. They bide their time, searching for our weak points as predators might, culling a herd. Theirs is a primitive approach and it's difficult to combat because our defenses are porous and they're not always impenetrable. Theirs is a threat that doesn't speak with one voice and it is, as we've learned, unpredictable, closed to reason or accommodation. We're separated from these devils by more than geography and politics," the cardinal said, his voice hardening as the door began to close. "We're in the twenty-first century, they remain in the fifteenth, and therein lay many dangers. Be very careful."

* * *

The phone console's red message light was blinking incessantly. Father Angelo raised the receiver, pressing the message button as Paolo turned on the television. The phone message was from the Minister, his call finally allowed through. What he said was simple, direct, repeating almost to the word what was being headlined simultaneously on RAJ Uno: The live feed showed only a half-circle of Israeli police vehicles, a Magen David ambulance in its midst, its attendants securing the ends of a sheet covering a shapeless form on the ground. For Paolo and Father Angelo, no identification or confirmation was required.

Dr. Dov Rosenberg's battered body had been found twenty meters from the shoulder on the main north-south road near Hebron. His hands were still bound with duct tape. Decapitated, his head was nowhere to be found. The sign pinned to his blood-drenched shirt read that he had been convicted of *moharabeh-crimes* against Islam and the state and he had, by the will of Allah, been executed.

ISRAEL

IV

CHAPTER TWENTY-FIVE

Cardinal Zaccaria's ominous warning had chilled both Paolo and Father Angelo to the bone. First Heinz Wilberg, then Dov Rosenberg. Connected? Probably. It stood to reason. Or connected not at all? Questionable. Too coincidental. Neither man knew for sure. There could no longer be an argument but that the two Romans were on the terrorists' shortlist, marked for execution for reasons that remained elusive to both. Why should it matter that Wilberg had an impressive map collection of the Old City among his other treasures? Or had run tunnels under the Mount of Olives? Why had Rosenberg's directorship of the Israel Museum put him in harm's way? *Moharabeh?* Crimes against Islam and the state? Which state? Had their own mere association with the victims made them guilty of an unspoken crime, one that was punishable by death by irrational enemies? Neither man could fathom why their colleagues were murdered or why they themselves were apparently facing a death sentence.

Any doubts about the danger they were in were dispelled by the police escort that accompanied their car back to Father Angelo's apartment. And any lingering questions evaporated as the Vatican's limo was waved through the police cordon blocking off both ends of the street. Four *carabiniere* greeted their return— two seated on folding chairs, two standing sentry by the complex's doors— machine guns at the ready, cigarettes hanging from their lips. To Paolo the level of security seemed more suitable for a head of state.

After hearing the Minister's phone message and the simultaneous announcement of the discovery of Dov Rosenberg's beheaded corpse, Paolo and Father Angelo's attempts at coherent conversation became painfully halting. Disorientation, fear, and anguish set in. What little had to be said, had already been said.

At six in the evening, the Minister called back. After exchanging *proforma* commiserations with Father Angelo over Dr.

Rosenberg's death, he requested the phone be handed to Dr. Josephus.

"We need you both back here as soon as possible. Several Vatican masterpieces for display in Jerusalem are being transported tonight. I've arranged that you accompany them. The plane's estimated departure time is eleven p.m." The Minister's preemptory tone was familiar. He hadn't made a request or extended an invitation. He had issued an order.

Before Paolo could respond, the Minister assured him his belongings would be collected from his flat and sent on Alitalia's morning flight to Tel Aviv.

"A car will pick both of you up at nine-thirty. Enjoy dinner." Click. "This is pure insanity, Paolo," Father Angelo said.

"I'm not disagreeing with you," Paolo replied.

* * *

If the Romans didn't know better, who could blame them for having thought they'd mistakenly landed in the midst of a soccer field during a World Cup final. The excruciatingly bright lights that illuminated one of Ben-Gurion's military runways were blinding. The shadowy outlines of the two panel trucks sent to carry the Vatican masterpieces to the Papal Bible Museum for the small exhibition sat idling nearby. When the lumbering transport landed at three a.m., the Minister, accompanied by four aides, was already on the tarmac waiting to welcome them. As they deplaned, perfunctory introductions were made, all the names passing the groggy Father Angelo and Paolo in a blur. Moments later, they were all hustled into a retrofitted, unmarked Hummer and driven to their sleeping quarters, a faceless building on Allenby Street, a block off Magen David Square.

The Minister jokingly referred to the building as a five-star hotel for "friends of Israel. And others." The Romans remained blank-faced, insecure, unconvinced that the level of security would be adequate.

"You'll be safe here," he assured them, smirking away their concerns, as he opened the door to their room. "We've a meeting at nine tomorrow morning, so try to sleep." He began to walk away, then turned, tapping his forehead as if he'd forgotten something. "By the way, my name's not Jehuda ben-Jehuda, but

I'm sure you've already figured this out by yourselves. It"s Zvi Bar-Levi."

"Then you're ..." Father Angelo began.

"What I am is, for want of a better title, the coordinator of special operations."

"Which means?" Paolo asked.

"Which means nothing," Bar-Levi replied, smiling mirthlessly. "See you at nine." He turned on his heels and returned to the elevator.

The new, unfamiliar surroundings robbed Father Angelo of sleep. When he rose at seven, he had no recollection of having even dozed and momentarily thought he was still in Rome. Paolo caught a couple of fitful hours that revived him as much as did his morning shower.

The TV early morning news reported the usual, a stray mortar shell lobbed from somewhere outside of Nablus fell with little damage and no injuries, the hunt for Dr. Dov Rosenberg's killers had produced no new leads, a question raised in the Knesset regarding the Prime Minister's handling of the crisis ended in a shoving match, and a fresh video from Fatah al-Islam, threatening for the umpteenth time to destroy the "Zionist enclave," had been received by the station manager at his home. No mention was made of the missing relics. News wise there was no news.

At 8.50 a.m., Bar-Levi appeared at their door to accompany them to a heavily-guarded, non-descript building on Pinsker Street. The low-ceilinged, paneled meeting room, with the flag of Israel draped on the wall, had none of the cold austerity of its Vatican counterpart. The familial ambience was apparently intended to put invitees at their ease rather than on edge. Almost a sea change of difference, Paolo thought. The room was, as the Germans might say, almost *gemuetlich,* comfortable. The only similarity between the two, the Vatican's and Jerusalem's, were the glasses and small bottles of mineral water on the table before each place.

Paolo and Father Angelo were formally introduced to the secret meeting's participants. Zvi Bar-Levi made a point of mentioning each man's origins.

"General Yehudah Etan, who heads *Amam,* the IDF's

military intelligence arm, was born in Zefat near the Golan. His family came from the Pale in 1887..."

Even seated, General Etan projected a swagger, a man larger than his uniform seemed able to comfortably contain. It was not for nothing that he was known popularly as "The Anvil."

Next came the chief of *Shin Bet,* Israel's internal security agency.

"Gideon Barnk, a former naval commander, was born in Tehran and arrived in Israel with his family in 1957. He's identified the Rosenberg kidnapper, the one who was doing all the talking, as a native Farsi speaker."

And so did I, Paolo said to himself.

So it went, Bar-Levi providing capsule biographies of each man, their merging areas of expertise, like disparate tesserae that fit together to create a mosaic. The team Zvi Bar-Levi had assembled formed a neat entity, organized quickly, and perfectly suited to contend with the crisis that the kidnapping and murder of Dov Rosenberg and the hijacking of the ancient objects had sparked.

After the brief introductions were completed, the scholars were escorted from the meeting room to another, cavernous room that resembled most closely the interior of a spaceship. It bristled with latest-generation technology, the functions of which Paolo and Father Angelo could only guess at. Both men were above novice level, more conversant than the average scholar when it came to technology. But what they were permitted to view in this room was far beyond their ken.

As Bar-Levi led them past a small army of technicians glued to their computer screens, babbling into headsets in an array of languages, he described a half-circle with his hands.

"Here we've the eyes and ears of the Jewish people. "Keeping an eye and lending an ear," if you'll excuse the pun. Look here, Dr. Josephus, at Monitor 20 ..."

"That's the temple, by the Tiber," Paolo exclaimed, surprised by his own excitement. "Would you care to view the footage of you two leaving Wilberg's?"

"Gentlemen," General Etan cut in, "shall we move on?" No nonsense, businesslike, a man with no patience for Bar-Levi's uncharacteristic and desultory tour of the war room's innards.

As they walked briskly past the banks of computer screens

on their way back to the conference room, Paolo remarked to Father Angelo the marked similarity between the two "war rooms." In the Vatican's, a fifteenth-century portrait of the crucified Christ dominated the room, giving every proceeding within it a certain spiritual *gravitas*. Here, in Jerusalem, in the bowels of its military control center, a photo of the nation's iconic founder, David Ben-Gurion, open-collared, sporting an Eisenhower jacket, a beret barely covering his unruly hair, was hung.

"Two fathers, Paolo, their temporal visions realized," he said. "Nicely put, Angelo."

Any comparisons between the two nation-states, however, was necessarily tenuous, a long stretch at best. The Vatican's power rested on its moral dimension, its soldiers a vast unarmed army of men and women spread to the earth's farthest corners, propagating their Lord's faith. By stark contrast, Israel's power and survival rested on maintaining its military strength, its trump card the added dimension of possessing a nuclear arsenal. No one doubted the arsenal's existence and none doubted that in the face of certain annihilation Israel would unleash its lethal weapons on the perpetrator or perpetrators. Potential aggressors knew full well that any serious effort to reverse the *alnakba,* the Arabic term used to describe the "Catastrophe of 1948," would be met with an overwhelming and destructive force not seen since the waning days of World War II. Western governments, while not stating the view publicly for fear of offending Muslim sensibilities, credited the so-called "Massada Option" with guaranteeing that the unthinkable, a full-scale attack on Israel, was kept off its enemies' agenda.

The Romans were seated at the table's head, the Israelis along one side, the long table reminiscent of the table they were seated at yesterday in Rome. Zvi Bar-Levi curiously reminded Father Angelo of Cardinal Zaccaria, a man as central to the smooth and efficient performance of a sensitive Israeli operation as was the cardinal to the Vatican's undertakings. A public yet private personage, transparent yet shadowy. Like an iceberg, only a small percentage of who Zvi Bar-Levi was— or equally Cardinal Zaccaria— and what either man did was visible to the naked eye. In fact, if the Israeli general staff officers donned scarlet robes and skullcaps, the priest thought, they could easily have passed for the pope's cardinals.

Bar-Levi brought the meeting to order, tapping a pen against his water glass. A woman entered the room and took the empty chair beside Bar-Levi.

"Let me introduce Lieutentant Lucia Vaccaro. I know Dr. Josephus needs no translator. The lieutenant's here for the father."

"That's very thoughtful," Father Angelo said, slightly miffed, fingering his crucifix as he did whenever something or someone irritated him, "but as you know I'm quite fluent in Hebrew."

General Etan laughed harshly, joined by two of the other officers.

"Zvi, with all your intelligence research, this you didn't know?" Commander Barukjibed, playfully raising an eyebrow.

Bar-Levi cleared his throat.

"Touche, Father. My oversight," he said, glancing at the priest.

"Let's hope it's your only oversight, Zvi," General Etan half-mocked his colleague, the hint of a glower in his voice.

"Can we get on with this meeting, please?" Bar-Levi said sternly, leaning forward and pouring himself a glass of water. "Yehudah?"

General Etan stood to address the table.

"First, on behalf of the government and Prime Minister Ben-Gurion, let me again welcome our guests," General Etan said gravely. "We're no strangers to international crises not of our own making and this surely is one of those. Despite what the TV people say, what you've read in *Davar, The Post, Ha "aretz,* and *Ma "aviv,* what the bloggers post - have I forgotten any of our critics?— we do know what we're doing and, yes, we knew too little to save Dr. Rosenberg. But make no mistake, whatever it takes - and I mean whatever, we will recover the stolen objects."

A universal uptick of affirming nods ensued from the officers. Elan looked first at Paolo, then at Father Angelo.

"We need your help," he continued. "You've both seen and examined the Crosspiece and the tablets as selected others have, but as the Biblical experts selected by Dr. Rosenberg..." He let the sentence linger, unfinished. "We'll get back to your roles shortly, what we're expecting of you, but I want to update everyone on the investigation's progress to date."

The general lifted his water glass and took a sip.

"Our first impression was that Fatah al-Islam learned of the objects from the Tiberias stonemason but we discarded that notion. It was unlikely, impossible that the manuscript could be deciphered by them so rapidly. We've since determined that one of the Arab watchmen at the Muslim graveyard in the Kidron witnessed what was happening, probably mentioned it to some friends in a cafe, one of whom told his son, who passed the information on, and ... well, fill in the blanks. This is still conjecture, what we figured happened - we just can't yet pin it down. What happened was from the beginning chance, a series of chance happenings— chance that Dr. Rosenberg called upon our friends here to verify the discoveries; chance that the kidnappers accidentally found out what we had; chance that Dr. Rosenberg foolishly, yes foolishly, decided to drive the objects himself to Dimona - chance, chance, chance."

Etan pounded the table angrily before taking a large swallow from his glass before continuing.

"We've learned the initial plan they'd concocted was to storm the museum in force, using weapons they'd stolen from a Lebanese army caseme near Sidon— this theft has been confirmed by Beirut—and steal the objects from the vault and maybe the Dead Sea Scrolls as well." General Elan smiled coldly, shaking his head, aware as were they all that the original scrolls were hidden away in a secure, equally secret location. "In retrospect, it would've been preferable if they'd tried. They wouldn't have gotten to the top step, the museum's door. But this is hindsight, useless. And while I'm not speaking ill of the dead, Rosenberg's misstep gave them the gift they wanted ... and cost him and Major Abramov their lives."

Etan paused to glare at Bar-Levi, whom he held partly responsible for the crisis for failing to keep Dr. Rosenberg on a tighter rein. Zvi Bar-Levi tried not to appear chastened, clearly ignoring Etan, looking down instead at his portfolio.

"Commander Baruk," Bar-Levi said with a certain formality, "where are we?" "We've made some progress in identifying some of the players but our search for the relics has hit a stone wall."

Two seats away, General Etan grunted and threw his hand up in disgust, almost upsetting his water glass.

"For all we know," Baruk continued, "they could be decorating a cave in Waziristan. NATO and the Americans are working with us but it's for them a low priority. They're not enthusiastic about losing another soldier to the Taliban, looking for holy relics stolen from ..."

Etan cut him off sharply. "This is why this situation is so different, Gideon. It's part of a war on several fronts, yes, but that's the least of it. Why do we always look to the West, the Americans, eh? These twin catastrophes could be a godsend for us. The problems created for the Islamic world with their miserable economies, the destruction of the oil pumping stations, the populations on the move, it's just the sort of chaos that benefits al-Qaeda. Are we watching the same news, reading the same papers, gentlemen? Even if you have to listen hard, you can hear the governments, even Assad's Syrians, saying almost the same thing. The chaos has to end. The chaos they're talking about isn't only the chaos caused by the flood, it's the chaos fomented by al-Qaeda, by the Muslim Brotherhood, by Hezbollah, and the other cancers - their alphabet soup allies. No matter how they couch it or play it down, their message, at least as I read it, is clear. They want some sort of order restored and they don't care who does it, only that it gets done before they're done."

"It could be a diversion, a ruse, Yehudah," Bar-Levi countered. "I'm not saying it is but they've always played that game well, the *yes* really means *no* gambit. How many times have we been close to signing agreements with them only to have them stalk out of the room?"

"They were never on the ropes before, never like this. I have to detail this for you, Zvi?" Etan's disdain was apparent. "They had leverage, stable governments, twenty-four/seven oil production, port facilities for American warships, "spy-in-the-sky" satellite stations, investments everywhere. Everything they needed to survive, to buttress their power. So the support checks from the West were always in the mail, the oil flowed, and the ships were welcomed. What do they have now? Wet sand in their shoes and Swiss bank accounts. No, my friend, they're on the ropes - one more blow and they're down for the count."

Commander Baruk interrupted General Etan.

"The prime minister's already spoken with Mubarak and Abdullah in Amman and the usual back channels to the Syrians and the Iranians are being explored. Even the Supreme Ayatollah is putting out feelers in return. Why their change of heart?"

"Don't tell me, Gideon," Zvi Bar-Levi said sharply, impatiently waiting his turn to speak. "Tehran's recognized the error of their ways and have accepted Zionism, yes?"

"Very funny, Zvi," Baruk said, unsmiling, removing his reading glasses, polishing them, one lens at a time, with a tissue. "They need help to rebuild, yes, and they're stepping on each others' necks to be the first to thank the US and the EU for taking in the refugees, and, no, they certainly don't want the Russians in their backyard again. What it is is public relations. It's okay to kill each other, to blow the shit out of this or that, but for the rulers the holy sites always remained off limits, and destroying another religion's relics is still taboo. We're excepting the Taliban and al-Qaeda lunatics, of course. Even the Americans recognized this prohibition in Iraq and Afghanistan ..."

Zvi Bar-Levi, unwilling to defer to Baruk any longer, jumped in.

"Which is why Medina and Mecca are still in one piece, one wet piece, Gideon. I've more to say. The key to the resolution of our problem lies in Tehran," Bar-Levi stated unequivocally. "The Shi'a are in the minority but they exercise power over the Sunnis. When I spoke with Cardinal Zaccaria yesterday, he assured me that we and the Vatican are on the same page in this matter. As I'm sure our guests already know."

Heads swiveled towards Paolo and Father Angelo.

"We had a private meeting with His Holiness and several cardinals but inasmuch as it was private, there's little either of us can say," Father Angelo said evenly. Paolo nodded in agreement.

"Yes, we know and respect your silence and your candor," Bar-Levi replied.

While he wasn't privy to the details of their meeting, he grasped its broad contours during his conversation with Zaccaria. He knew what he knew so the priest's and Paolo's diffidence would have no effect on decisions made in this room.

A leather-bound portfolio lay open before Bar-Levi, a folder stamped with the catchall title "Psychological Report," atop other confidential papers relating to present and future intelligence operations. The report had been prepared long before the crisis by a select cadre of psychiatrists within Israel's Anti-

Terrorist Division.

Like all governments, Israel's sought to be ahead of the curve so it sanctioned the report's preparation. But as with many relevant reports in nations the world over, it was buried out of sight for no other reason than that it dealt with a future so conditional at the time, it fit into no contemporary context.

After the first attack on the World Trade Center in 1993, portions of the report were hastily shared with the CIA. Once the Taliban drove the Russian-backed Afghani government from power and Al-Qaeda began to make serious inroads, a consensus finally emerged, spelling out the multiplying dangers. The West, Israel in particular, was facing a new, internationalized form of terrorism, a threat rapidly spreading well beyond its familiar Middle East confines, internationalizing itself. This new form was akin to the Islamic Fundamentalism that had persistently threatened Mubarak's Egyptian government and had continued to destabilize Lebanon's regimes.

Whether it was in Egypt, operating under the name of the Muslim Brotherhood, or elsewhere under other banners, outlawing fundamentalist movements was proving increasingly fruitless. They were amorphous, able to nimbly assume different forms, persistent, reemerging under other names, drawing strength from instead of weakening under the most brutal of repressive measures. Sometimes they were co-opted and supported by rival governments. Syria's backing of Hezbollah in Lebanon was a case in point, as was the financing of the Muslim Brotherhood by Saudi and other financiers to keep the wolves in Egypt and away from their own doors. The fundamentalists were canny and elusive, as difficult to capture as lightning in a bottle.

"In the minds of moderate Muslims, this is a deviant form of Islam, thoroughly misinterpreting the Koran." Bar-Levi was reading underscored parts of the report aloud.

"This interpretation mimics extermination Nazism, both sharing and promoting a virulent hatred of Jews that predates the founding of the Jewish State. It is noteworthy from an historical perspective that The Prophet Mohammed's first act after the conquest of each city in Arabia was to slaughter the Jews and seize their property." Bar-Levi cleared his throat and set the report aside, glancing around the table, then raising his index

264

finger in instruction. "But in spite of this credo of insanity the fundamentalists maintain an almost religious attachment to that which Christians call relics. Not in the sense that they represent miracles *per se* but more as a direct attachment to what they view as a glorious past."

Paolo and Father Angelo exchanged glances. The priest was a step ahead, cognizant of what was to follow as some of the others, save Paolo, appeared surprised at Bar-Levi's comment. In truth, while the adherents of the three major religions lived and worked side by side for centuries before the Jews were uprooted from the Muslim lands after 1948, very few from either faith had more than a rudimentary understanding of the other's belief systems. Under the Ottomans, there was considerable contact but it had its limitations, beginning with business and usually ending there. If the Israeli man-on-the-street was asked to define Islam, he would likely tick off The Prophet, the *muzzein's* call to prayer, the washing of the feet, endless chatter, too much noise and, of course, *jihad*. Asked to describe the difference between the Sunnis and the Shi'a, the creeds of the Syrian rulers and the House of Saud respectively, would only produce a blank stare. The Koran? It paled before the lyric beauty of the Old Testament. Fundamentalism? A revolt against civilization. Al-Queda? Fundamentalism's manifestation, the engine of destruction.

"So, Zvi, now you're telling us we'll have to deal with these butchers because they "respect" our relics?" Gideon Baruk said irritably.

"We've been dealing with these bastards for decades," General Etan put forth, defending Bar-Levi, ennui dimming his voice. Stating the obvious was always for Yehudah Etan a tiresome chore. "Zvi's right ... for once. What's the difference between this gang and Arafat's or Hezbollah or some of your old friends in Tehran, Gideon? You want to stand on ceremony now that they're all on their asses, now that we've got leverage? The prime minister wants the stolen objects back. The Vatican's standing with us. The pope wants them back and so does everyone at this table. Let's not lose sight of the goal. Without them, forget the Holy Land claim. It'll be disputed from the get-go. We could do handstands naked and sing *Hatikvah* from the top of Mount Herzl till we're blue in the face but it'll mean nothing.

What happens when the first person says "prove it" ten seconds after we make this claim? What then? What'll you say, Gideon? "Trust us?" No, we need the objects back, no question. No arguments, only proof. How we get them back and who we have to negotiate with to retrieve them is irrelevant."

"Look out the window, gentlemen," Zvi Bar-Levi rose again as General Etan bent back into his seat. "The Arabs may be in worse shape but we're only slightly better off. Our tourist business is in tatters, billions lost thanks to the damned storms and flood. I don't plan to harp on this global warming thing, but it's no joke. And the PM thinks it's no joke. Even Chief Rabbi Ya'akov issued a statement." Bar-Levi looked over at Father Angelo. "The *rebbe* said the same thing the late pope said, that we'd wasted our stewardship."

"May I say something?" A soft voice, British-accented, came from the far end of the table. Raphael Halevy had entered the room moments before, barely catching notice and unintroduced.

"Dr. Halevy's our expert on the history of Islam," Bar-Levi interjected.

"Yes, of course," Paolo said. "The father and I are quite familiar with your work. A pleasure to meet you at long last."

"The pleasure's all mine," Halevy responded graciously. His face radiated intelligence, his prominent cheekbones softened slightly by his old-fashioned horn-rimmed glasses.

Raphael Halevy was a leading Islamist, a department head at the Hebrew University in Jerusalem before his thirty-fifth birthday. His work, *The Muslim Conquest of Arabia,* was a bestseller the moment it appeared, less than a month after the nearly disastrous Yom Kippur War in 1973. His book was fair, unbiased, and immensely popular as well among Islam's intellectual elite from Lebanon to Egypt to Pakistan.

"Raphael, no lectures, please," General Etan prodded him. "Just follow today's program."

Halevy smiled at Etan.

"Some background's always necessary, Yehudah," he replied firmly in Oxonian-accented English, his eyeglasses reflecting the fluorescent lights overhead. "In any case ..." Etan said.

"Let me begin with a brief historical review so that we

have a context," Halevy began, switching back to Hebrew. "In 632 CE, or AH 2, if you will, on the Muslim calendar, Mohammad stormed from the desert and laid waste to the wealthy cities of Arabia. In the seventh century, the Jews were most numerous in Hijaz and in the cities of Yemen, working and living in relative peace with their Arab neighbors. We know from the Koran and its Old Testament roots that Mohammad was more than merely acquainted with the Jews of Arabia. As he gained in strength and power, the Jews became his main target. The path of expropriation, brutality, and wholesale slaughter is commonly known, the seeds for Muslim hatred of the Jews planted deeply as the swath of Mohammad's conquests cut far and wide."

General Etan shifted in his chair, his demand for brevity apparently ignored.

"In Islam's early history, one battle was decisive during the critical War of Fosse. This was the battle for Medina, the city from which Mohammad was expelled the year before. Defensive alliances with neighboring villages and tribes and the city's wealthy Jews were concluded in a vain effort to resist Mohammad's armies proved for naught. Medina's denizens were overwhelmed and today, as we know, it's one of Islam's three holy of holies, the last resting place of the Prophet, and host to the *Hajj*. The most powerful clan in the beleaguered city was the Koraiza. Mohammad knew that to solidify his rule the Koraiza, one and all, had to be done away with. It is recorded that in December, 623 CE, the Prophet personally dispatched the entire Koraiza clan with his own ivory and pearl-handled dagger. Heads rolled, blood poured copiously from their necks ..."

"I hope our young people understand the message, Raphael," Etan interrupted, "that these barbarians must never walk through our gates. Is there much more?"

"I'm sure they do, Yehudah, and, yes, as you know and fear, there's more," Halevy said, as Etan grunted in displeasure. "Imagine the dagger of the Prophet," he posited, looking over at Father Angelo, "as you might the True Cross or as we might the Torah. Sanctified objects, *nonpareil*. The dagger was subsequently lost but the symbolism, what it represents, has echoed over time and for some Muslim nations, it once shared space with the crescent on some of their flags."

The priest understood the parallel Halevy was drawing, but on its face, it was only conjecture. Yes, a holy relic, *their* holy relic. But it had vanished long ago and who knew where. The comparison between the two without one was moot.

"We've all been schooled in the history of modern Israel and Operation Magic Carpet when we brought the Yemeni Jews home. Well, one of them, an elder, appeared at the door of the old building where we housed the artifacts before we built the museum."

Paolo nodded knowingly. Operation Magic Carpet was foremost among his favorite tales of glory, the 1953 airlift that flew the Yemeni Jews to Israel and safety."

The guard at first refused him entry, assuming from his dress and accent that he was yet another old, slightly crazy Arab who wandered Jerusalem's streets back then.

The Yemeni persisted and, if only to rid himself of him, the guard relented and listened to his story. The guard remained dubious but said yes, okay, come back tomorrow, humoring him and figuring he'd seen the last of the old man. But the Yemeni returned at the crack of dawn, cradling a badly nicked olivewood box, and seated himself cross-legged on the sidewalk beyond the security fence, patiently awaiting the guard's appearance. When the guard emerged from the building, the old man approached, laid the box on the top step, and lifted its lid. Inside was the dagger of the Prophet Mohammad."

Paolo's eyes opened wide; Father Angelo was speechless, his mouth gone dry. The others in the room had heard the tale, hence no reaction was forthcoming. Halevy, Baruk, Etan, and Bar-Levi were among the chosen living few who had not only seen the dagger but had gingerly held it. Halevy's dramatic storytelling was solely for the benefit of Paolo Pisa and Father Angelo, to impress the only outsiders permitted into this IDF sanctum.

"Mohammad's dagger?" Paolo choked out. "You're serious? Where did he get it?"

"When the old man was asked, he only shrugged. He probably didn't know either. A family heirloom maybe, handed down through generations, its original provenance forgotten long ago. It doesn't matter from where it came. It matters only that we have it. Only a handful of people know the story. Dov Rosenberg was among them, of course, since he was the dagger's guardian. We keep it in the museum's secret vault, out of plain sight for obvious reasons. There was really no need for you or Father Angelo to view it during your museum tour with Dov," he said. "That was then ..."

General Etan stood and left the room, taking the Italian translator with him. Moments later, he returned, carrying an olivewood box, and placed it on the table before the Romans. Paolo instinctively reached out, ran a hand over the contours of the box, lifted the clasp and raised the lid. Inside the box, lined with fine green felt filigreed through with gold thread, its outside corners hammered brass, lay the dagger. Etan slipped on a pair of cotton gloves and removed it, holding it in his palms for display. On the highly polished blade was the Arabic inscription *In The Name of Allah, The Compassionate, The Merciful.* On the other side of the curved blade was etched *Mohammad A. H. 2.* When the last person returned to his seat, the general eased the dagger back into the box, closed the lid, and secured it. He lifted the box and handed it over to Lieutenant Vaccaro, instructing her to return it to the security personnel in the adjoining room.

"And be careful, don't drop it."

"I wasn't planning to," she said, under her breath. "Well, gentlemen, there you have it."

"What exactly do we have, Dr. Halevy?" Paolo asked.

"I'm getting to that, Dr. Josephus. And please, call me Raphael. Formality no longer seems necessary, does it?"

"No, quite right," Paolo chuckled.

"Yes, well, Rabbi Ya"akov, has been in contact intermittently with the Supreme Ayatollah in Tehran, the Sh'ia spiritual leader, ostensibly over his concern for the welfare of our people in Iran. As we know, there remain in Iran maybe 30,000 Jews, most too poor to leave when they could in 1979. At any rate, at the PM's behest, he sent a cable through the Swiss consulate to the Ayatollah shortly after the hijacking intimating that we had in our possession an artifact of singular importance to the world of Islam or words to that effect. The Ayatollah could only guess at what the artifact was but he knew enough to know it must be of the utmost historical importance for us to even admit we held such an object. He responded accordingly."

"Is there any sense that they know what Israel has?"

"I seriously doubt it since secrets rarely remain secret in the world of Islam. If they had even an inkling, it would've become public in no time. A billion Muslims crying out for the "liberation" of the Prophet's dagger from the hands of the "Zionist infidel?" And since the dagger resided within "the Zionist enclave" itself, you can just imagine the enormous pressure that would be brought to bear on their governments to take action. And what the end result would be can only make one shiver. No, I'm convinced they're ignorant of what we have in our hands."

Zvi Bar-Levi pulled from his portfolio a copy of the response received by Ya'akov only days later and translated by Gideon Baruk. He read a portion of it to the group.

"We share a veneration of histories marked by holy objects on our different paths to the present. These objects must be venerated and held safe and sacred. While our differences cannot be overcome and we maintain the Zionist enclave is illegitimate, we deplore the assault and the theft of relics sacred to you."

"The prime minister was elated when she read the letter since it offered the prospect of resolving this crisis quietly."

"You mean an exchange, the dagger for the Crosspiece and the tablets?" Father Angelo proffered. "It sounds far too simple." The priest had an intimate knowledge from his years as a churchman of how unexpected machinations came into play that turned the simple into the hopelessly complex in the wink of an eye.

"I can assure you, Father, that the PM and we, her advisors, are far from naive," Bar-Levi snapped. "We know that the Supreme Ayatollah wasn't alone in drafting the response. Even if they were ignorant of exactly what we possessed, you don't suppose for a moment the Iranians would chance any artifact of great import falling into the hands of, say, a bin-Laden or any of his ilk or pretenders to his throne, do you? Anyway, in his reply, Ya'akov confirmed what we had. Imagine the look on the faces of the Ayatollah's when the rabbi's last message was placed under their noses? You could almost feel a sudden urgency to resolve the crisis take hold. He who has the dagger could claim Allah in his wisdom has anointed him as the new Prophet, wave the dagger in front of the cameras as proof that a miracle has taken place, and win the support of hundreds of millions of Muslims. The incipient panic in Tehran caused by that scenario was probably so thick you could slice it with a knife. Iran seeks primacy and dominance in the Middle East, throughout the world of Islam. If they possess the dagger, it is for them their holy grail, what they need to achieve their dream. If the dagger's held by a rival nation or the head of an aggressive fundamentalist movement ...well, it's surely not something they want either to contemplate or contend with. The dagger's our trump card, our bargaining chip, our only bargaining chip."

"We hardly need another Prophet," Commander Baruk added, as General Etan stood to speak.

"We have it on good authority that Iranian intelligence working out of Iraq and Jordan have identified and located Rosenberg's killers. They haven't shared the information with us - standard operating procedure - so we don't know if the intelligence is accurate. But we expect an update fairly soon from our own sources."

"Unlike our American friends, the Iranians handle such interrogations directly and without delay. They find no need for the American practice of - what did they call it? - rendition?" Bar-Levi remarked.

Etan laughed loudly, joined by Baruk. Paolo remained stone-faced while Father Angelo reflexively tapped his fingers on his crucifix. Raphael Halevy ostentatiously cleared his throat and shuffled his feet - Bar-Levi and his colleagues' stab at humor made him as visibly uncomfortable as it did the Romans.

"The crux of the problem we're facing and why you've been invited back has to do with this. The PM was informed by the Iranians in no uncertain terms that there can and will be neither direct nor indirect dealing with Israel or any of its officials. From their point of view, any revelation that such official contact or negotiations had taken place would be politically explosive, given their strident anti-Zionism, and would be viewed as a gross betrayal of Islam. They're concerned it would rile up the so-called Arab street."

"This they're worried about now?" Elan said, with distaste. "When is this 'street' not riled up?"

"They're just covering all their bases, Yehudah. This would

be a major coup for them and they want it done secretly, with nothing and nobody screwing it up."

"Us, too, Zvi. What else?"

"We'll continue to refer to the operation as the Herod Mosaic, if only because we all lack sufficient imagination to call it otherwise," Bar-Levi quipped.

"Wonderful, Zvi, we won't have to change the letterhead," Etan remarked, annoyed. "The Iranians, what else from them?"

"They suggested - or perhaps I should say *insisted* - that the Romans who examined the relics make the exchange. Frankly, I can't think of two people more unsuited for this action but be that as it may ... This is not a criticism, gentlemen, I'm only stating the obvious. This is not your game."

"I know it's not our game," Paolo shot back. "Wilberg's dead and so's Dov. This says to me that there's also a price on our heads, and frankly, I'd like to keep mine just where it is."

"I understand but we feel it's debatable, that you're targets. Why Wilberg was hit, we don't know. The maps weren't taken, they're intact. Maybe it was just a push-in, a robbery. It happens from time to time. Anyway, we still don't know. The case's open. Dov's murder was almost incidental. They were after the relics, not Rosenberg, but once they had him, they made use of him. And when he was no longer useful, they discarded him. He was disposable. Sad end of story. You two, you're of more value to them alive than dead. You're the links, you and the priest, to this operation's running smoothly.

"And after the exchange's made? What's our "value" then?" Bar-Levi didn't answer.

"They must be aware of my background, my roots?" Paolo continued.

"Either they haven't connected Dr. Paolo Pisa with Dr. Moshe Josephus, which I doubt as far as the Iranians are concerned, or maybe they see it as a minor obstacle since you're both civilians." He looked towards the Romans, the barest hint of sympathy in his eyes.

"Let's not spend too much time trying to analyze their motives, Zvi," Elan said.

"I'm not convinced that it's not a waste of time. We're basing our response on a questionable "good will gesture" from an Ayatollah. This is the longest of long shots. I'd trust him even

272

less than I did Arafat and that bastard I didn't trust at all. They'd steal the pennies off a dead man's eyes. If it was up to me, I would've torn every goddamned Palestinian camp apart until we found the relics and got hold of the bastards who killed Rosenberg and the Russian."

"But it wasn't up to you, Yehudah," Bar-Levi reminded him. "The PM made that clear. And if you had had your way and did what you wanted to, and you found nothing, what then? We're trying to keep this well under the radar, limit the damage, and keep the body count to two."

General Etan stared hard and long at Zvi Bar-Levi.

Father Angelo felt his heartbeat increasing. He was finding the excitement of it all nearly unbearable. The Church, the alpha and omega of his being, his life's light, and now this chance ... Fate, he concluded, had favored him, and now God wanted him to retrieve the section of the Cross, to make it whole again, no matter the consequences.

God would protect him. He knew, too, that Paolo would agree to the mission, the showman within him would not allow him to act otherwise. This was his moment, not his calling, the fame achieved from the relics' rescue would outlive him as it would the priest. Father Angelo had come to realize and accept that Paolo Pisa had more in common with men like Cardinal Zaccaria than the people, Paolo's own people, seated around the table in the room. He could have remained in Israel and continued his work but he chose otherwise, to return to Rome, the city the eternal magnet, that drew him back and informed his very being. He was who he was, as Father Angelo Lorenzo was slowly learning, and the priest respected him for it.

Raphael Halevy's turn came round again. He fixed his gaze on both Paolo and Father Angelo. "Gentlemen, in for a penny, in for a pound?"

"I'm ... in," Paolo said hesitantly. "Father?"

"If it works, Father, it might put you on the path to sainthood." Bar-Levi put a large hand on the priest's shoulder, amusement dancing in his eyes. "Even if it doesn't work ..."

"Sainthood's not in the cards for me, I'm afraid," Father Angelo replied. And, yes, he would stand with his compatriot, unequivocally yes, and act as an intermediary. "For my Church and the Holy Father."

"No second thoughts?" Halevy asked. "None," each man replied.

"Good," Bar-Levi said with finality, as the meeting adjourned in silence.

CHAPTER TWENTY-SIX

Paolo Pisa and Father Angelo Lorenzo were driven to the President Park on the grounds of the Knesset, near the Israel Museum. The hotel was bomb-proofed, their rooms sound-proofed; electronic access was unavailable, the hotel grounds' perimeter heavily guarded and surrounded by a high, razor-wired fence. For good measure, unleashed German shepherds patrolled the area day and night, controlled by their handlers' voices.

Once they entered their rooms, the door to the outside world was literally and figuratively shut until the operation would commence. Its details would remain a state secret, a never-to-be-written chapter of history, bits and pieces perhaps surfacing in later years in a memoir when it no longer mattered or no one remembered enough to care. Above all, the Americans were not under any circumstances to be informed of the plan. While the Iranians remained an implacable enemy of both Jerusalem and Washington, there were always highly placed officials in Washington overly suspicious of the ease with which Israel conducted backdoor negotiations with their common enemy, a hot-button issue that could cause conflict between the allies. Better to deal with the Americans after the fact. The less they knew the better the chance for the mission's success.

For a part of the next week, Israel's Anti-Terrorism Task Force briefed the Romans on how the plan would be put into operation, trying to condition them for the expected and unexpected. At the outset, it proved difficult to transform the scholars - who instinctively questioned anything and everything - into temporary operatives who would accept as gospel whatever was conveyed to them along with the finite - detailed instructions that accompanied certain aspects of the mission. Nothing was held back by either side. By Day Two, Paolo and Father Angelo were working in reasonable concert with their patient trainers.

On Day Three of their virtual captivity, they were informed that contact had been made with the Iranians in

Amman, Jordan's sprawling capital. Two Iranian-born Israelis, one a cousin of Gideon Baruk's, had met with their Iranian counterparts at the ancient Roman amphitheatre in the city's center. Each of the emissaries was dressed as Western tourists, replete with cameras dangling from their necks, speaking with each other in Farsi as they snapped artless photos of the theatre's renovated interior.

One of the Iranians, Parviz Mussavani, assured his Israeli opposites that for safety's sake he would be accompanying the scholars when they first rendezvoused with the terrorists. The introductory meeting would take place in the iconic Church of the Nativity in Bethlehem where Constantine's mother, Helena, ordered a peg driven into the ground, marking the spot where Jesus was believed to have been born. According to the plan, Paolo and Father Angelo were then to leave the Church of the Nativity, walk north to the Franciscan Church, and descend the narrow stairway to the right of the nave. This would open onto a maze of rock-hewn rooms and chambers, allegedly part of the stable where Mary gave birth. Below these chambers was the grotto where St. Jerome was said to have translated the Bible from Hebrew into Latin, the Vulgate, the authorized version of the Scriptures. There they would be met by the Iranian who would serve as their guide.

The everyday tourist's clothing that would mark them as one of many Westerners among the now-diminished throngs that daily poured into Bethlehem was rejected in favor of costumes that would more easily blend into the religious community. Dressing the Romans in the black robes worn by the Greek priests or in the Armenian churchmen's purple and cream-colored daily wear was rejected, too, in favor of Franciscan garb. The simple, unadorned outfits of the Franciscan Order was to be the garb of choice. Brown robes with cowls that covered them from head to sandals, around their waists, cinched belts of woven rope from which hung wooden Crosses. Unobtrusive, unworthy of a second glance. Instant anonymity.

For Father Angelo, it was a perfect fit. Many believed the Franciscans or the Order of the Minorities was the model used by St. Ignatius Loyola in founding the Jesuits. Discipline, service, and absolute obedience were the order's watchwords, kindred in spirit to their brother Jesuits. While Father Angelo viewed the modern Franciscans as inadequately educated, and their involvement with liberal causes at odds with his own order's conservatism, he couldn't help but admire their unswerving, selfless devotion to the Faith and the Lord's teachings.

"It's as if we'll be in a small slice of Italy, Paolo." The priest was positively joyous, anticipating what awaited them, too far ahead of himself than reality should have permitted. And with the feast of Easter approaching, it was for him a most propitious time for such a glorious achievement as the retrieval of the holy relics.

Paolo was less comfortable and, for once, far more anxious than his colleague. Bethlehem lay beyond the wall of separation, hardly what one might call a safe zone. The security situation changed daily and political and personal violence in the streets of Bethlehem was not uncommon. When he raised the issue of safety to their instructors, one replied with a laugh: "Well, did you expect them to meet you at the Western Wall or at a mall in Tel Aviv, Professor?"

"No, but you can understand why I might have concerns, yes?"

"Yes, I do, Professor, I'm not discounting your fears. They're certainly valid ..." the trainer paused, "but I'm afraid I can't allay them."

* * *

Later in the day, Zvi Bar-Levi informed both men that the Iranians, while they had no idea exactly where the relics were held, had personally vouched for the scholars' safety.

"And you believed them?" Paolo asked, mindful of Etan's voiced distrust and regretting now that he'd agreed to participate in this mission, his doubts not assuaged by Iranian assurances.

Bar-Levi shrugged— an honest response, Paolo thought, and hardly reassuring. "Assuming this all goes off without a hitch and the exchange is made, what are we supposed to do then? Call a cab? How will we carry the Crosspiece and the tablets? They're not wafers ..."

Both men had been briefed and re-briefed and Paolo's

questions, now in their third or fourth iteration, had all been answered before. But Paolo felt a compulsion to keep asking them, like an interrogator, if only for a final time, just to make sure all the puzzle pieces were in place, that he'd missed no detail.

"Once the exchange is completed, the terrorists will have one hour's safe passage to go wherever it is they're going. At that point, we and the Iranians will activate our cell phones - the signal for us to come and collect the relics. Remember, once they take off, even if the switch is bungled, you stay put," Bar-Levi instructed them. "You'll be tracked every step of the way, positioning devices will be sewn into the robes, so we'll never be out of contact. We'll know where you are at all time."

Noting the jittery look on Paolo's face, he added, "I'm truly sorry, but this is the best we can do under the circumstances. We all know the risks involved here. We've planned it down almost to the nanosecond, every eventuality has been taken into account," Bar-Levi paused, waiting for a response. When none came, he continued.

"You'll be dropped at the wall tomorrow at five in the late afternoon. Truth be told, once the plan's triggered, you're both on your own."

BETHLEHEM
V

CHAPTER TWENTY-SEVEN

Paolo Pisa was an early riser. On this mid-March Saturday, he avoided the lure of the TV. He didn't want to be reminded of the endless tide of troubles washing in from everywhere - the Hamas shells raining in from fresh mobile launching sites in the Judean Hills, the rancorous, never-ending debate questioning the wisdom of retaining the West Bank after the Six-Day-War, particularly now after the weather catastrophe, Dov Rosenberg's sorry fate, and beyond Israel's borders, the enduring chaos the storms and floods brought in their wake. Instead, he grabbed a cup of coffee and wandered from the building, inhaling the aroma of the earth turned by the compound's gardeners, a soft breeze softening the air. Israel was having an early and warm Spring and the buds and blossoms were beginning to appear.

Saturday morning in Jerusalem, the pleasant remembrances from his Israeli childhood. Aspects of his early days in Jerusalem hadn't changed. There were still few cars on the road at this dawning hour, a rare family walking slowly together, hand-in-hand, their heads covered, on their way to morning services. Fond memories of an Israel that had virtually disappeared during the last two decades of the twentieth century and the second of the twenty-first.

He loved his parents' Jerusalem home, the former home of a Turkish merchant, its spacious rooms and high windows, not markedly different than their Roman apartment. Parents needn't have concerned themselves about their children day and night in the early years. No demand for constant entertainment, occasionally a movie imported from America, little more. Moshe Josephus had had friends in all the quarters of the divided city, secretly sharing with them the Turkish cigarettes his father's Arab workers gave him before he was of age. He spoke rudimentary but passable Arabic, some un-evolved Greek, enough Yiddish to order fresh-killed chickens for his mother in the Jewish Quarter, and proper Hebrew. Young Moshe was a novelty of sorts, a

Jewish kid in the Old City without a skullcap and ringlets, an Italian in a sea of Eastern European immigrants and native-born *sabras.*

He wasn't deluding himself. He knew he was romanticizing his youth, creating an idyllic past in retrospect. He also knew that over the nearly seventy years of its existence, Israel had by its very presence encouraged the creation of a Palestinian national identity, unifying the disparate tribes and clans whose fervent wish was to evict the Jews from the land they believed was theirs and theirs alone. With the Palestinian leaders always in competition with one another and at each other's throats, there was hardly enough unity to build a workable coalition, much less a viable state. There was, however, more than enough to foment a violent opposition to the Jewish state's existence. But back then, in the early days, there was no Hamas, no Fatah, no Hezbollah, no Fatah al-Islam and no first and second *intifadas.*

He knew, too, that the storied victory in 1967 over the Arab nations would forever remain the apex, the highpoint in modern Israel's history, a chapter demanding to be appended if the Bible was ever revised. It was even more a war of psychological redemption, a small step towards repairing the irreparable, the wound that had ripped the Jewish people apart little more than twenty years before.

As an archaeologist and an historian, Moshe Josephus was ever aware of the fate of the best-laid plans. Things never turned out how one expected them to. In all honesty, he admitted to himself, he paid less attention to the politics of the region than he did to what lay under its sands. He recollected the 1950s and the early 1960s, when he and his father would drive to the West Bank for fresh produce, occasionally picking up Arabs, and increasingly Arabs who considered themselves Palestinians, on the way back, traveling to Israel for medical care or to buy Western appliances. Like all memories, Moshe Josephus' were imperfect.

The landscape was vastly different now— this was inescapable. The hillsides surrounding Jerusalem, once lush with fruit, were today pocked with California-style housing developments, replete with swimming pools. He knew the truth of the recent past and how it merged into the present after the 1967 War. All the Arabs retained were their yellowed land deeds, a deed's value completely dependent upon the whim of a hostile government that honored necessity over a legitimate document. Such is the nature of war and its aftermath, he thought, recalling Friedrich Nietzsche's words: "A great victory can be a great danger."

In many ways, it was a truism for Moshe Josephus. If his wife hadn't been so bound to the land and had returned with him to Rome, his daughter Shana— their only child, would still be alive. Now he was himself faced with a danger both known and unknown. If the plan failed, he might lose his life to salvage a piece of the Cross that had brought unspeakable grief to his people down through recorded time. And the tablets? If they were rescued and subsequently fell into the hands of the Jewish lunatic fringe - they themselves then holding the tablets hostage to fulfill their dream of a Third Temple - what then? Internecine war, Jew against Jew, or a wider conflict, a conflagration drawing in all the Muslim nations and culminating in a world war with the West?

If his life was to come to an end this way, he hoped it would be swift, a bullet through the heart, perhaps a replay of a final scene in an American western. But he knew better. Dov Rosenberg's end was never far from his mind. In the Prophet's own words, the threat was clear: "For Allah loveth no transgressors." And what was Moshe Josephus if not a transgressor. Grim scenarios all, too horrifying to contemplate but impossible to ignore on a brightening Jerusalem morning in late March, 2012. Moshe Josephus's legs felt weak as he bent to inhale the scent of the spring roses oblivious to Father Angelo's presence.

The priest sensed his friend's disquiet.

"I'm at peace with myself, Paolo," he said, as if to encourage Paolo to do the same.

"You have your faith, Angelo. You're imbued with it. What do I have?" It sounded more a plea than a question.

"You have yourself. I long ago gave my life to Christ and through Him there is eternal life, such is the mystery of the Cross ..." Father Angelo paused, "which I suppose is what finally separates us. But tonight, we'll be as one," he continued, in an effort to comfort Paolo, "Franciscan friars. Did you know St. Francis' father was a Jew? A fact we've buried away."

Paolo forced a smile as the priest busily opened his well-worn Bible, and fingered open the pages to *Ecclesiastes,* Chapter I, Verse 14, a favorite of his. With his back to Tel-Aviv, Father Angelo looked towards the Old City, squinting away the glare of the sun as he began reading aloud:

"I have seen everything that is under the sun, and behold, all is vanity and a striving after the wind. What is crooked cannot be made straight, and what is lacking cannot be numbered."

Paolo marveled again at Father Angelo's devotion, the succor he found in his faith with its promise of a future freed from the vagaries of chance and caprice. Once, when he was walking with his father in Old Jerusalem, they passed a group of bearded Polish Jews in the their caftans and sable hats. His father smiled at them wannly but received not so much as a nod in return. "You see," he said to his son, "culture makes you that way. Deep belief, well, that's fated."

Over his lifetime, Paolo had come to learn and accept the truth in his father's observation. He was not fated nor would he ever be.

As a boy, he was his own person, a street kid exploring Jerusalem's back alleys, with their dead ends, or the Roman ruins that lined the long avenues along the Tiber, a digger with a stick searching for coins from a lost time. He saw himself as a student of another type of digger, Sigmund Freud, at certain times during his life a living affirmation of Freud's belief that a happy man was one who pursued that which gave him pleasure as a child. Digging. Unlike his priest-friend who bore the names of the famous and whose faith and Biblical beliefs propelled him into his life's work, Moshe Josephus/Paolo Pisa read the Bible from a different aspect. For him, it was a map of sorts. If he read the map correctly, he would find what remained still undiscovered under the sands and soil, artifacts that he used to populate and document his works of scholarship. Was he as contented in his life as he was in his work? As contented as Father Angelo Lorenzo appeared to be? To be honest with himself, it was a question Paolo Pisa would find difficult, even painful, to consider, much less answer.

"There are times, Angelo, that I wish I could be a little more like you, at peace with yourself."

Father Angelo smiled at Paolo.

"I appreciate that, Paolo, but don't for a moment assume that I don't suffer often from the sort of inner turmoil that afflicts us all at times. You bring to mind the letter St. Paul sent to the Jews of Rome during a difficult time when he was at the pinnacle of his ministry. It was addressed to a group living not far from us and it retains its timelessness two millennia later. We still live in a world seeking redemption. In his letter, St. Paul quoted Jesus, "He who through faith is righteous shall live," and "everyone who calls upon the name of the Lord shall be saved." Early on, I committed the letter's content to memory. I know it by heart because it's in my heart."

As the cars began arriving at the gates of the compound, Father Angelo slipped the Bible into his pocket.

"I know you don't subscribe to this, Paolo, but perhaps it may be of some comfort. I believe St. Paul was speaking for eternity and if he was here with us in this time of testing, he would repeat his words. What more's to say, my friend? We'll do our best; the rest is out of our hands."

Two helicopters hovered overhead, rustling the leaves of the trees and bending the stems of the opening tulips in the flowerbeds near the two men. One descended slowly, landing softly on the opposite side of the Knesset. When the helicopter's rotors finally shut down, Paolo, his face sober, turned to Father Angelo.

"Fate, not God, brought us to this spot, Angelo. Fate may smile on us, or perhaps frown. We'll be the first to know, I'm afraid. I do have a request of you ..."

"Yes?"

"If ... if the plan fails, if the worst comes to pass, I want you to say *Kaddish* for me."

"I'd be honored, Paolo, but I don't believe it will fail so I will pray instead that I won't be called upon to do so."

* * *

At 1 p.m. sharp, the last briefing began. It lasted two hours, an intense and final drill, complete with the now-familiar video images and computerized projections of how the plan would evolve if it was to evolve as planned.

"Only your Italian passport, Professor Josephus," he was told yet again, as if he was a distracted child who needed constant reminders.

At 3 p.m., General Yehudah Etan, Commander Gideon Baruk, and Zvi Bar-Levi entered the briefing room. Etan moved to the room's center.

"We've had our last confirmation from the Iranians and the Chief Rabbi's spoken directly with the Supreme Ayatollah this morning. According to the *rebbe,* the Ayatollah reiterated that his people want no slipups. Our eyes confirm that they're already in Bethlehem ... dressed as priests."

"You mean friars, don't you, General?" Father Angelo quietly corrected him. "Yes, Father, friars," Etan replied flatly. "Remember, the terrorists will speak only Arabic, the Iranian will not act as your translator and anything said between you and the Iranian will be in Hebrew. Any communication must be kept at a minimum since it's likely the terrorists have some Hebrew. They know you're scholars of the ancient world so speaking Hebrew won't raise any red flags but, please, no conversations, no trying to make friends, understand?" He handed each man a cell phone. "Once the trade is completed, activate the cell's power button. Simple. Do not, I repeat again, do not move from where the exchange has been made. If they insist that you accompany them, object, refuse, stall them; it's not in the plan. We'll be there in moments if anything seems amiss."

"What if they've booby-trapped the exchange point?" Zvi Bar-Levi pondered aloud.

Etan's glacial glare settled on the Minister.

"What if the moon's made of green cheese, Zvi? What's with you? You sound like a windup toy, raising the same or another goddamned question a thousand times." Etan caught himself before he said "like the Italians." "What if? We don't know, can't know, can we? We don't know where the pickup's to take place. Nothing's foolproof, this we've always accepted going into any action. This mission's based on trust. They want the dagger, the killers want safe passage and the substantial cash they're receiving in return. I'd prefer their heads instead but ..."

No one spoke as General Etan dug into his briefcase and extracted a letter bearing the embossed Iranian national crest.

"The *rebbe* received this this morning by courier. The translators left out the standard opening tirade against us, the "Zionist Enclave," the "Great Satan," and the "crimes" committed against the suffering Palestinians," Etan said derisively, and began against his normal nature to patiently read the letter's every word.

"In Isra", the Night Journey, Children of Israel, it is written "Nor take life, which Allah made sacred, except for a just cause." I have ruled that the scholars from Italy who have earned the esteem of respected authorities and have been unbiased, they are innocent and should not be harmed in any way "for Allah loveth not transgressors." We have deemed this mission so important that my brother's son will be here carrying a *fatwa* to our Sunni Brothers to execute our will. In the name of Allah, the Compassionate, the Merciful, the President of the Islamic Republic of Iran and I assure their safety on a mission forever closed and sealed in the heart of The Prophet ..."

Paolo found the Supreme Ayatollah's letter cold comfort. Promises made to the West, to Israel, to each other by Muslim leaders from the late Gamal Abdel Nasser to the late Yassir Arafat to the current Arab leaders, promises that might advance their own interests, proved more often than not ephemeral and empty. He knew in the tenets of Islam lying was approved of in the name of *jihad*. Passages drawn from *The Path* and *Hud* were unequivocally clear on the issue. Dov Rosenberg's captors, his murderers, were most probably *jihadists,* connected in some way to al-Qaeda or Hamas or Hezbollah - which it didn't matter. Paolo needed neither elaboration nor a confirmation from General Etan to tell him so.

"There you have it, trust's all we have. We know the dagger will in some way be turned on us but that's to worry about in the future. Our concern's for tonight. Best prepare yourselves."

* * *

The friars' robes were brown cotton, rough to the touch, hardly the bespoke Egyptian cotton shirts Paolo wore or the smartly tailored outfits Father Angelo ordered from the tailors that catered to the Vatican. The sandals' Birkenstocks, of course. Paolo cinched the rope belt tighter and repositioned the olivewood Cross for comfort. Father Angelo did the same. The chain on which the priest's silver Cross hung encircled his neck. The cleric considered himself doubly protected now, a fanciful thought, he had to admit to himself. With their heads hidden within the cowls, only their difference in height would distinguish one from another.

They made their way down the marble set of stairs. At the bottom, they were met by Zvi Bar-Levi, who had positioned himself before the doors of the small synagogue where Knesset members, officials and visitors came to pray and meditate.

"Well wishers await you ..."

Awaiting the scholars within the wood-paneled synagogue, standing below the Ten Commandments and the gold-leafed Star of David, was the prime minister herself, Dora ben-Gurion, wearing her trademark tailored black dress. Alongside her were Israel's Chief Rabbi in full ceremonial dress, and Cardinal Zaccaria, the Vicar of Christ's representative.

The prime minister stepped forward and offered her hand, first to Paolo, then to Father Angelo.

"I needn't emphasize how important this undertaking is," she said briskly, "for Israel, for our friends and allies." She looked pointedly at Cardinal Zaccaria. "Our prayers and wishes for success ride with you, gentlemen. I will most assuredly be here to greet you on your return."

Chief Rabbi Ya'akov was oddly diffident and deferential in her presence. A diminutive yet forceful man, he had clashed with her frequently over her unwavering insistence that the secular take precedence in all matters of state. The rabbi, supported by the nation's growing Orthodox population, consistently opposed her policies, which more often than not wobbled her coalition government. She had prevailed on a half-dozen no-confidence motions, mostly by sheer force of will, reining in her detractors with expert cajoling and threats meted out in equal measure. On the issue of recovering the artifacts, though, Prime Minister Dora ben-Gurion and Chief Rabbi Ya'acov spoke with one voice, their differences temporarily set aside for the good of the nation.

"May God's light protect you, Moshe Josephus and Father Angelo Lorenzo, and may your names be inscribed in the Book of Life."

Paolo mumbled an indistinct amen.

Cardinal Zaccaria was asked by the rabbi to offer a prayer.

His diplomatic sense intact, he omitted all references to Jesus and, following the rabbi's lead and choosing instead to speak in Hebrew, the Cardinal said: "May God bless you both and save our common heritage."

More amens.

He walked over to Father Angelo, placed a hand on his shoulder, and leaned towards him.

"Christ be with you, Angelo. His love is eternal," he whispered. "Please follow me."

The cardinal escorted Father Angelo into the small adjoining room where the rabbi robed before the service. Sitting beneath the Ark, he heard Father Angelo Lorenzo's brief confession and gave the priest an abbreviated communion. Reaching under his vestments, the cardinal picked out a small, white linen envelope, upon which was written the priest's name in Gothic script. A private note from the pope himself. Father Angelo opened it, read its heartfelt contents, his hands trembling, then replaced it in its envelope and returned it to the cardinal for safekeeping.

"Not to worry, it will be here when you get back." Zaccaria smiled, radiating his confidence as Angelo's began to falter. "The prime minister has made the Tiberias documents available to me. They're remarkable, stunning, all you've said they were. My apologies for doubting you, Angelo. The prime minister promised me that however all this turns out, she will present them to His Holiness once any shadow of doubt about their authenticity is dispelled."

But Father Angelo barely heard the cardinal's words. His mind was elsewhere, occupied by thoughts of his and Paolo Pisa's imminent departure. Cardinal Zaccaria, sensitive as most seasoned diplomats are to body language and nuance, recognized the priest's distraction, his anxiety, his anticipation of what lay before them all-embracing.

"I must take my leave now, Angelo," he said, checking his watch. "May God's light continue to shine on you, my friend." With that, he turned, walked back through the synagogue, and retreated from sight.

CHAPTER TWENTY-EIGHT

"Last check, gentlemen," General Etan said as Paolo and Father Angelo stood before him. Elan's manner was casual as if he was mustering a crack IDF unit and sending it on another mission rather than the two aging archaeologists whose nearness to danger over the years was limited to a cave-in during a dig.

Paolo Pisa's head was pounding, the aspirin he popped proving ineffective. Father Angelo tucked his shaking hands into the sleeves of his friar's robe to hide them from view.

A moment of truth lingered, unaired, always present. Paolo believed he could read what was uppermost in the prime minister's mind, what apparently plagued her, her poker player's face notwithstanding. How would Israel react and respond if the worst of all scenarios came to pass? The mission had been intricately assembled, its successful execution depended upon secrecy. If it failed, who would know but the perpetrators of the betrayal? They certainly couldn't believe that they possessed the Crosspiece and the tablets. Israel, the West, would have had no choice but to retaliate. In whose interest would that be? But what did Israel have but the word of the Ayatollah and the mercurial members of his ruling circle? And the terrorists were, despite Tehran's assurances, a wild card, the joker that could turn the mission into a bloody shambles.

Such thoughts will drive you insane, Paolo reminded himself, sure that the PM was juggling the same scenarios. A cloak of helplessness enfolded him within it. The dice had been thrown and there was no avenue of retreat, only an uncertain way forward.

"General Etan," he heard Father Angelo say, "aren't we forgetting something? The dagger?"

Etan almost smiled.

"Is there a reason you want to carry it to the car?"

"No, but ..."

"It's already in the car, Father, in the rolling suitcase,

remember? As planned. Zvi Bar-Levi's riding with you. When you exit the car, the suitcase will be locked onto Dr. Josephus's wrist. The chain will be obscured by the robe's folds. The lock's combination is this year, Twenty-Thirteen-2013. You'll both remember the year, yes?

"Not the Jewish year or the Muslim year. Twenty-thirteen CE, Father, or if you prefer, AD." Etan's barbs had no preferred target. Whoever was at hand would do nicely.

"I'm sure we will, General," Paolo replied, deflated, aware that Etan was incapable of disguising his lack of confidence in either of them.

A battered vintage 1981 Mercedes Diesel fitted with yellow Palestinian tags, its shelf life as a taxi over, grumbled curbside. Its perforated muffler competed with its engine to produce the greater racket. Father Angelo and Paolo climbed into the car's front seat, next to the driver, a Tec-9 machine pistol in his lap.

"It's not army regulation issue," the driver offered, unasked, by way of explanation, "but it's my personal weapon of choice."

Well, that makes me feel immensely more secure, Paolo thought, shaking his head, a desolate sense of foreboding beginning to take hold.

Zvi Bar-Levi slid into the back seat as the driver slipped into gear. The car jerked forward and passed through the opened gates. They soon found themselves on the Hebron Road, five miles, five long miles from their destination. Ten minutes later, within sight of Bethlehem, they passed two rickety buses filled with Arab workers wending their way south.

"They're lucky to have any work," the driver said. "It's hard to find a tourist bus these days, the goddamned floods you can thank for that. That and Hamas. Maybe some Japanese, a Korean or a clutch of Chinese every day or two. They snap their photos, smile at each other, spend forty-eight hours spinning around the country, then off they go. Too bad Moses didn't turn east and wander to Japan. It would've saved us the trip we're making tonight."

The driver's nonsensical patter quickly crawled under Paolo's skin. He needn't have pointed out that tourism had dried up faster than the floodwaters in the Negev. Even a blind man could see as much. The Arab village of Bet Jallah, for one, just outside Jerusalem where the Prophet Nathan was born, had a ghost town air about it.

Bethlehem, Jesus' birthplace, wasn't a welcoming place of late, even less than usual. The Church of the Nativity had been repaired after the damage inflicted during the Second *Intzfada* but the floods brought with them even more serious damage. Outside its massive walls, street gangs roamed, preying on whatever isolated prey they could corner and rob. The inundation's only benefit was that it made once easy pickings difficult. To steal, you had to put your back into finding likely victims these days. And only the most devout would be visiting this year, drastically reducing the victim pool. Eastertide, 2013 promised to be dismal, the choirs and tourists that the year before crowded Manger Square ancient history. The pilgrim route, the gridlocked traffic that had buses and taxis pressed together, front-to-back, was an antediluvian memory.

At a few minutes short of 5 p.m., they reached the wall of separation, the Israeli "fence," a stone and steel barrier that gradually encircled the West Bank. Bar-Levi angled himself out of the car, stretched, and surveyed the area. All was quiet at the checkpoint. He unlatched the trunk and pulled out the wheeled suitcase, attached it to Paolo's wrist, and snapped the lock closed.

The huge lights around the guard tower illuminated the area, day and night, the heat thrown from them warming and unexpectedly pleasant on this cool spring night.

As the young IDF soldier emerged from the guard booth, Bar-Levi flashed his identification.

"Old friends from Rome," he said, tilting his head in the Romans' direction, his words clipped, "visiting friars."

"Another bunch just went through," the soldier replied. "Haven't seen many lately, that's for sure."

Bar-Levi shrugged noncommittally.

"Passports."

With the suitcase in tow, the three men were waved through the opening in the wall, under the watchful eyes of the IDF sharpshooters in the tower above. Zvi Bar-Levi followed their progress from outside the fence as the Romans quickly disappeared from view.

Bethlehem, where everything had changed and nothing had changed. Elderly men still smoked and drank tea in front of shattered and steel-shuttered shops as fluttering, discarded fast food wrappers danced through the streets. A man on a donkey cart collected garbage, as children in ragged clothing kicked around a misshapen soccer ball. Bethlehem featured all the earmarks of a tawdry city in a Third World nation, a stone's throw away from a modern one where, the Sabbath ending, occasionally observant families returned on foot from temple to their homes and their Audi and Mercedes-filled garages.

From the windows of shell-pocked buildings, Palestinan, Hamas, and Fatah flags were draped; faded photos of Yassir Arafat and Hamas leaders were plastered on graffitied walls. As the three men approached Manger Square, clusters of teenagers loitered, their heads wrapped with sweatbands dyed with the Palestinians colors, ghetto-hostile looks marking their faces.

One stepped forward and spat on the ground.

"Fucking Christians, go home! You don't belong here!" he shouted, before melting back into the group. The others joined in, hurling insults in the trio's direction.

Father Angelo winced. Paolo recalled Zvi Bar-Levi's description of the hecklers they'd encounter upon entering Bethlehem.

"Gutter cowboys," he had said with reeking contempt. "Harmless for now, all talk, but in a couple of years ... future body count stats."

Paolo and Father Angelo's eyes were fixed forward as they were instructed by their trainers to do, the suitcase clattering behind on the cobbled streets, the teenagers' taunts now inaudible as they entered the square.

The Church of the Nativity overshadowed the square, its five naves divided by four rows of Corinthian columns, each bearing a faded image of one of Jesus' apostles. The gilded lamp fixtures hanging from its massive oak ceiling brightened its austere interior and its flood-dampened stone floor, through part of which the original Byzantine floor was visible.

They entered and there before them stood the Altar of the Nativity, ornately decorated in gold and silver, a splendidly massive chandelier looming above. As they approached, Father Angelo whispered to Paolo.

294

"Do as I do."

The two men eased slowly to their knees, crossed themselves, and recited the Lord's Prayer. Rising, they crossed themselves again. Moving backwards, Father Angelo inadvertently bumped into one of the four men standing unnoticed behind them. Three sported beards, the fourth was clean-shaven. All wore friars robes identical to those worn by Paolo and Father Angelo.

"Fratelli italiane?" the clean-shaven monk asked uncertainly in Italian, smiling as he did so.

"Yes, and you as well. It seems we're all a long way from home, brother. We make this pilgrimage each year," Father Angelo responded quickly, returning the smile. "And tomorrow we're off to Hebron."

The priest's voice resonated in the nave.

"What is in Hebron?" the monk asked, puzzled, as his fellow monks, equally puzzled, peered at the two Romans. "We have been warned away from it. Too dangerous, I'm told, particularly for Christians."

"An artifact, a discovery from Herod's time, a mosaic of some sort." "Yes, Herod, I believe the Jews could use a Herod these days," he said distractedly, tugging on the robe of one of his fellow monks. "Come, brothers, we must leave or we'll miss our bus." He turned back to Paolo and Father Angelo. *"Buona fortuna,* brothers, safe journey."

Paolo nodded, his head down, as Father Angelo smiled the monks off, returning the monks' good wishes.

Paolo patted his pocket, reassuring himself that the cell phone remained there. Of course it was. He rebuked himself silently. Where could it have gone? Nerves.

"What year is it, Paolo?" the priest asked.

"Still 2013. Are you joking?"

"Of course," Father Angelo chuckled, squeezing his friend's arm.

Minutes turned into quarter hours, half hours, then the first hour was gone. Closing time. A group of Japanese tourists gathered before their guide, her umbrella raised, preparing to depart. Armenian and Greek priests, and five or six Franciscans began busying themselves, locking up the consecrated objects used in the mass as two of their number swept the stone floor with large brooms. As its doors opened to permit straggling tourists to leave, the rising clamor coming from the army of ragged, shouting children, chasing each other around the steel crowd dividers, disturbed the quiet within the church.

A friar appeared next to Paolo and Father Angelo.

"Brothers, it is getting late. We are closing the doors in fifteen minutes so I'm alerting you. If you need lodging, there are some excellent hotels either on the square or on Paul VI Street," he said gently, also in Italian.

"I understand, Brother," Father Angelo replied. "We'll be on our way. I wonder if there's enough time to visit the Franciscan Church?"

"If you hurry, there should be no problem. They won't be closing the doors for another half hour or so. Are you from Rome, both of you? Your accent ..."

"Yes, we are," Paolo said.

"How is the Holy Father faring then, Brother?"

"We dined with him just last week and he seems as fine as ever." The friar laughed loudly.

"Romans. Always quick with a joke. Best be along, though, you don't want to be caught out on our streets after dark, after the curfew, not with your luggage and especially in our order's robes."

The two scholars made their way north to the Franciscan Church and, as instructed, descended the narrow stairway by the nave until they reached the grotto. Dank and cold, made danker by the dampness that had permeated its stone walls. They stood together, their eyes adjusting to the darkness, awaiting the promised guide.

Out of the corner of his eye, Paolo noticed movement and heard footsteps to their left. He pulled the suitcase closer to him. A tall man, taller than Paolo and dressed as they were in monk's clothing, walked towards them, his cowl drawn back. As he drew within an arm's length, Paolo noticed his intense pale blue eyes as they met his own. "Welcome to Palestine," Parviz Mussavani said in Farsi, quickly correcting himself in perfect Hebrew. "Please follow me."

No handshakes, no passports demanded, no coded messages, no pat-downs for weapons. Only an instruction. Paolo's heart skipped a beat and Father Angelo suddenly felt the night chill descending. They glanced at each other, a faint smile gracing their faces, both feeling foolish and uncomfortable, their outfits chafing, Paolo dragging a suitcase like an innocent tourist - a suitcase containing Mohammed's dagger, an object of such value that it could have no price. We're out of character and surely out of place, he thought, his equilibrium profoundly shaken. The world around him suddenly seemed surreal, almost a Boschian landscape.

They emerged from the church and crossed Manger Square, dodging more boys kicking airless footballs, past yet another gang of jeering teenagers, cigarettes hanging from their lips, before they turned into Paul VI Street, the Iranian leading them. They trudged past the small hotels in silence, the cobbler's shop, and an array of coffee shops that long ago replaced the stores that carried Guido Pisa's artifacts, servicing the thousands of Christian pilgrims making their first memorable journey to Bethlehem. On past the Lutheran Church on Abdul Hasser Street, emptied in the darkening hours of its more venturesome visitors, the two friars trailing the third imposter, Paolo and the treasure taking up the rear, the last in line.

The Iranian led them to a narrow-fronted, no-star hotel, its neon sign inoperable, a shabby throwback to the days of Ottoman rule. Its lobby matched its exterior seediness. The scuffed linoleum that covered the floor bubbled and curled when it met the wall. The paint on its walls was peeled away like dried, dead skin. A cracked pane of thick glass fronted the reception desk, behind which sat a teenaged boy afflicted with acne, fear freezing his face. On the wall behind the desk, its glass grimy and a third of it broken away, hung an old photo of the Hamas chieftain Kaled Mashal with an arm draped around another man, the hotel's owner perhaps. It was impossible to determine the photo's age or where it was taken. Best guess would be Damascus. The teenager inclined his head towards a lounge off to their right. The Iranian nodded, and headed in, the Romans close behind.

Sitting on the decrepit sofa, under a sagging, tacked-up green Hamas flag, were three men in Arab robes, their eyes coal black, each with a beard or a stubble start of one. Two appeared familiar to Paolo, faces from the kidnapping tape perhaps, but the poor quality of the tape made positive identification difficult. Under the lounge's low-wattage lighting, neither Paolo nor Father Angelo could be sure. The three may have all tasted blood but

Paolo noticed how each acted deferentially towards Parviz Mussavani, all accepting the Iranian's authority. Clearly they each knew a word from him would end their lives and the lives of their families and perhaps their clans as well. Mussavani was not to be trifled with. It was abundantly clear that they were not so fervent as to prefer martyrdom for their cause to the money promised them.

It dawned on Paolo that the three could just as well be messengers, pawns as much as he and Father Angelo were pawns in this exchange ballet. Perhaps this was all show, three low-level soldiers doing a master's bidding, intermediaries, a layer of protection, the true identity of the string-pullers behind the theft of the relics and murder of Dov Rosenberg still obscured. But who would entrust such a momentous exchange to underlings? And the kidnappers' spokesman had spoken Arabic with a Farsi accent ...

Paolo's head began to throb with the beginnings of a second headache.

The smallest of the three Arabs, a scrawny, truculent twenty-something with prominent ears, stood and stepped forward, pointing to the suitcase.

"Let's see what's in there."

His head was barely level with Paolo's chin. "This? Why?"

Reflexively, Paolo yanked the suitcase towards him, trading glares with the Palestinian. He's watched too many American movies, Paolo thought, his fists clenching involuntarily, snared between laughter and anger.

"What's your name?" Paolo demanded in Arabic, his own distress and fear abated momentarily, a trace of courage replacing it, sparked by the Palestinian's challenge.

"What?" the Palestinian replied, his face now in Paolo's, his voice pitched higher, enraged but clearly flustered by Paolo's question. Why is he speaking Arabic, not Hebrew? He looked at the other men, then at the Iranian. What is this?

"Your name?" Paolo insisted, his voice grown stronger, holding the Palestinian's gaze.

What are you doing, Paolo? Stop provoking him, you're not supposed to speak with them. This was not the plan. Father Angelo's face was taut with fear and worry. "Talab," the man said. An alias perhaps. Who could know? But Talab was caught off guard - the menacing look evaporated, a querulous look took its place. "Why? You want to send me a Christmas card?"

"I just might."

Paolo's defiance had unsettled Talab as much as it had relieved the Roman. The palpable hostility remained but the air of intimidation fell away. A more level playing field subtly established itself between the sides.

"It doesn't matter why!" the Iranian interrupted, clapping his hands with sudden finality, annoyed with Paolo's goading and impatient with the Palestinian's mindless bravado. "Enough! We've no time for an infantile cockfight! I apologize for neglecting the formal introductions," he said sarcastically, a baleful stare targeting both men. "No more discussions, no delays. This was agreed upon, understood! Let's get on with this. Immediately!"

Talab sullenly dropped back onto the couch.

Parviz Mussavani feared rightly that any delay would jeopardize the transaction he was assigned to shepherd through to completion. If the mission failed, there would be hell for him to pay at home, all things considered an unappetizing prospect. He was intent on concluding the exchange without snags.

The eldest of the trio, a burly, square-faced, heavily-bearded man in his forties, puffy hands in his lap, crossed one leg over the other, uncrossed them, and rose clumsily to his feet.

"My name is Qolam Hosein," he said. In the flesh, absent his *sayyid's* costume, his black turban replaced by a commonplace *keffiyeh,* his voice carried more weight. His name and his accent confirmed Paolo's suspicions. "No family name is necessary." The man's last words were delivered in rudimentary Italian.

It was him, Paolo was now sure. An Iranian, the kidnapper, Dov Rosenberg's probable murderer. Even if he didn't personally wield the knife, he had given or conveyed the execution order. Unquestionably, Qolam Hosein was the speaker on the tape. In Qolam Hosein's presence, Paolo's momentary bolt of courage began to drain from him. Glancing sideways, he saw Father Angelo's face grow pale.

"I know Italy," Qolam Hosein pronounced. "I lived there for three years, worked in Milan building houses. Nice city but not friendly. Not to us, anyway. *Troppo cattolicos.* Too many Catholics

..." he paused to laugh alone at his own joke.

Father Angelo flinched and grimaced.

Qolam Hosein spun around, facing his compatriots. He spoke directly to them, his voice lowered, his words muffled, unintelligible. An order? More probably a face-saving remark? No laughter followed. The duo nodded enthusiastically, plainly playing to their leader's seniority.

Mussavani checked his watch, excused himself, and left the hotel, returning seconds later.

"Let's go, the car's here."

"We didn't run the check for a tracking device," Qolam Hosein said to Mussavanai.

"You should've thought of that before," the Iranian said, his contempt for Qolam Hosein clouding his face. "There's no time now ..."

"Where ... where are we going?" Father Angelo was agitated.

"You'll find out when you get there," Mussavani said abrasively. "What, you thought the switch would be made in this shithole? The Israelis already turned the church, everything, upside down twice, and who says they won't give it another try? Maybe a signal was missed? They ripped through Hebron and Jenin like a whirlwind and they've probably got every public toilet in Bethlehem staked out, too. It was like your Easter egg hunt, priest. They found no eggs, no relics, only a few bombs, par for the course around here and so it wasn't a total loss for them. They cracked a few heads and hauled off and locked up a bunch of these fools."

He gestured towards the Palestinians with uncloaked distaste, unconcerned that one or the other might understand Hebrew and understand what he'd said. What after all were they going to do, file a complaint with the proper authorities?

"Search and seize" didn't work. Heavy handed, the typical Israeli approach that produced nothing," he continued forcefully. "So your good friends in Jerusalem had to swallow hard since they had no choice but to deal with us. That's why you and the other Italian are here. For no other reason. You're useful for as long as it takes to accomplish this exchange. Why are you not grasping this, priest? They're expendable and they realize it but so are you and the other Italian. Take your head out of the clouds or

300

out of your ass, wherever you're hiding it!"

Father Angelo, trembling, reached into his robe pocket for a cigarette, hopeful it would calm him. As he tried to light it, his hand shook so he dropped the matchbook. Mussavani picked it up, struck one, and held it out. Father Angelo bent towards it. The cigarette caught, the priest inhaled sharply, coughing harshly, the cigarette metallic to his taste. He ground it out in the hotel lobby's single, overflowing, ashtray, coughing again.

"You're too old to smoke, Father," Mussavani said. "It's a young man's sport. Better you stick to writing books, or reading your Bible, whatever it is you do, you might live longer ..."

Outside the hotel chuffed the ubiquitous, banged-up, extended version Mercedes, the common transport that moved Palestinians and the occasional tourist through the West Bank and East Jerusalem. Its windows were tinted, its passengers invisible. Inside, two men, shod in Nikes and wearing running pants and black sweaters, sat on the rear jump seats, their arms cuddling AK-47s. One reached out, assisting Father Angelo into the car.

The priest collapsed onto the chapped leather seat. As Paolo and the suitcase cleared the door, the one calling himself Talab slammed it shut with such force the car shook. The second man, an Arab named Hassan, shouted something at Talab. Talab sighed and opened the door again, allowing Hassan to enter, following him in and crawling over Hassan and the Romans, to squeeze in next to Father Angelo. Qolam Hosein had already situated himself up front, next to the driver, facing forward.

Mussavani, remaining outside, tapped on the window, motioning for Hassan to roll it down.

"Crude people," he said, addressing the Romans in Hebrew, shaking his head.

"Fortunately the Germans make sturdy cars."

Paolo smiled weakly, Father Angelo not at all.

Talab reached between the two gunmen and banged a fist on the glass separator. The driver nodded, punched a button and twisted a dial. The child-proofed doors locked, the air conditioner growled, and the Mercedes inched slowly away from the hotel's front.

When Paolo looked back, Mussavani had already disappeared.

CHAPTER TWENTY-NINE

"They're in a Mercedes, light blue or it once was, right fender patched with gray filler, Palestinian tag number J 21836-78 E, the sayyid's up front with Mussavani's man, our 'scholars' in the back between two of them. Another two facing, in the jump seats, weapons on their laps ... let me focus in," the IDF tech said, his voice urgent over the loudspeakers in the Knesset's basement communications center. "'Lights fading. Switching to night vision system."

As vehicular traffic crisscrossed Israel, eyes followed, eyes mounted on phone poles, on rooftops, on traffic lights, implanted in stop signs, from the Golan to the Red Sea, even within chimney nests painstakingly constructed by Baltic storks, snowbirds flocking south to winter in warmer climes. Nobody, nothing, airborne or ground-bound, was immune from electronic scrutiny.

"They were just waved through the wall. Minister Bar-Levi's car is parked parallel to the guard post. It's running, exhaust visible ..."

The prime minister's eyes were riveted to the large screen before her. General Etan stood off to her left, arms crossed, watching the Mercedes' snail-like progress.

"No time to be worrying about a speeding ticket," he said, absently checking his watch. "Time's a-wasting."

The prime minister's smile was brief and then gone.

The Mercedes turned onto the Hebron Road, in the direction of Jerusalem. The assembled in the communications center remained tense, their breaths held. The limo could still turn south or east towards Jericho and the Jordanian border. Or north beyond Jerusalem towards Hebron itself or Nablus, or, even worse, swing towards the volatile Jenin refugee camp.

King Abdullah in Amman had been notified and given the general outline of a planned action with its details withheld. The monarch nevertheless agreed to alert his security services. General Etan wondered if it might not be a blessing, a bloody blessing to be sure, if the kidnappers decided instead to cross into Jordan ... here the Hebron Road meets Remez Square, the Mercedes pulled over. "They're going to Jerusalem," General Etan declared, his relief evident. The Prime Minister and the others in the room nodded.

The Mercedes swung around an abandoned Peugeot 404 that was parked aslant on the sloping road shoulder, the decrepit car one of many unassuming IDF positions concealed along the road.

The Mercedes proceeded at its stately pace, minutes later entering the streets encircling the Old City. From the Jerusalem Brigade Road, it turned into Ha-Zanhanim Street, rolling to a stop at the entry to the Old City's Muslim Quarter: Herod's Gate. Less than four hundred yards south of the gate stood the Temple Mount, illuminated by floodlights, atop it the imposing Dome of the Rock.

"Yehudah, could they have hidden the relics inside the Dome itself?" the prime minister exclaimed, utter disbelief spreading over her face. "All this done right under our noses? How could they get them in there?"

"Who the hell knows? The Dome's the only place we didn't search."

"Maybe we should have, no?' Gideon Baruk, a silent watcher until that moment, suggested.

Dora Ben-Gurion whirled towards Baruk.

"Do you want another war, Commander? Now? Gaza wasn't enough for you?" she snapped.

Baruk instinctively stepped back, edging away from Dora Ben-Gurion, regretting his offhand remark.

The Muslim Quarter, a maze of twisted and crooked main streets, side streets, alleys, and dead-ends laid out haphazardly over centuries, is a city planner's nightmare. Unless one was birthed and raised there, the seeker of a specific address is presented with a daunting challenge. The streets are old, poorly if ever maintained, and often carpeted with trash and dog shit. Its contrast with the Jewish Quarter and its modern buildings is stark - night versus day. The old houses and small stalls, *hala* butcher shops and cafes that crowd its narrow lanes, hand-painted Arabic signs indicating their purpose, make for the occasional quaint postcard. In reality, the Muslim Quarter is a ghetto, which, like most ghettos, has an air of eternal permanence. Whatever its future disposition, the Muslim Quarter will remain the Muslim Quarter.

Below its decaying streets lay a maze of sewers and water tunnels, each bearing scarred witness to Jerusalem's many conquerors – the Romans, the Muslims, the Ottomans, before them the Byzantines, and after, until Israel's declaration of independence in 1947, the once-majestic British Empire. Each conquest left its own indelible impression on Muslim Jerusalem's cityscape, which in time faded as inexorably as did its conquerors. In 2013, as in 1913, the Muslim Quarter's trash was still collected by unwashed donkeys hauling refuse carts as men dressed in *djellabas* sat in stalls, smoking and/or drinking tea or sweetened coffee from chipped cups, passing the time of day.

"They've stopped again," Etan said, the cameras focusing on a three-story pre-Mandate home, its windows shuttered, the rim of its top floor terrace protected by a steel enclosure with a spire.

"One moment," the loudspeaker's disembodied voice said. Seconds later, he announced: "The house is off St. Elias, near Pilate's home."

"Good news," Etan said, his breathing evening out. "No Nablus, no Jenin. If it's going to happen, it'll happen here." He checked his watch again. "It's what I suspected from the get-go. We've checked every inch of film from the day Rosenberg was grabbed and the relics hijacked. How many times, I don't know. I lost count. We came up empty, nothing but the abandoned truck they used. We even dug up graves in the area, wherever we found fresh footprints. I had a kennel full of cadaver dogs sniffing around, just in case. If one of them was wounded and died, chances are they'd dig a hole and leave him in it.

"They're clever, these bastards, running us in circles, leading us on this goddamned wild goose chase," Baruk said, almost admiringly. He had found his voice again. "Rosenberg's dragged back to the West Bank, the star of their miserable little show, while the relics were always here. Jesus, I'd never have believed they had it in them, this ... this ingenuity."

"It's a lesson, Gideon, that everyone learns too late. Underestimating your enemy, what you're up against. We learn, they learn. Never underestimate. Worst case scenarios, these

305

should always be our launch point, and we go from there."

The driver cut the Mercedes engine. Qolam Hosein elbowed his door open, adjusted his *keffiyeh,* gripped the car roof and hoisted himself up, ordering everyone out. The street itself was quiet. Dinnertime. He was followed into the building by the driver, behind him the Romans, behind them Talab, Hassan, and the two armed men. The building's interior was musty, cooking odors had seeped into and remained in its walls, its porous stone ground floor, like the Church of the Nativity's, still dank from the floods.

The banister waggled as, single file, each man grabbed hold to ascend the creaking wooden stairs. At the first landing, Father Angelo stopped to catch his breath, leaning heavily against the wall.

Paolo cupped the priest's elbow. "What is it, Angelo? Are you okay?"

"The cigarettes ... and my age." The priest smiled wanly, his breath rasping.

"I'll be fine, just give me a few seconds ..."

Moments later, their climb resumed, their destination the third floor where by prearrangement they were met by the driver's wife and their three young sons. Behind them, the door to their apartment was ajar.

Qolam Hosein reached into his *djellaba* and extracted a handful of *shekels.*

"We won't be long," he said, smiling, addressing the driver's wife as he handed the driver a fistful of banknotes to pass to her. "Perhaps an hour at most. Please, buy the children and yourself something for your trouble."

The driver's wife, dressed in an indigo-dyed *thob,* a traditional robe, avoided Qolam Hosein's eyes as she took the money from her husband and continued her hurried flight down the stairs with her boys in tow.

The driver's two-room apartment was spare but for a sofa, a dining table surrounded by mismatched chairs, polyester curtains, a food-stained patterned woolen carpet, and a gray metal desk on which sat a first-generation computer. The flat's walls featured unframed photos of the latest Palestinian luminaries. Paolo could almost hear their strident voices vowing the imminent reversal of the 1948 *alnakba.* A persistent incantation parroted so often by all Arab leaders that their war cry had virtually lost its power and persuasion.

A large, flat screen TV, apparently the fruit of a recent splurge, occupied a table designed for a much smaller set and dominated the living room's far corner. But for the absence of clutter and the presence of the computer and TV, Paolo reflected on how little it differed from the apartments of the Arab friends of his youth.

"Cozy," he said under his breath, noticing a man he took to be a contemporary, seated on the sofa. The man, wiry, small in stature, his gray-silver hair close-cropped, was dressed in a business suit, tie-less and collar-less, his white shirt buttoned - the familiar uniform of the Iranian elite. He stared first at Paolo and Father Angelo, then at the chain that attached Paolo to the green, wheeled suitcase at his feet.

Nizami Khujandi. Iran's foremost expert on Islamic holy objects. A survivor, a scholar who prospered under any and all regimes. Father Angelo rarely forgot a face nor the name that accompanied it. Instant recognition. A mental gift that had always served the priest well, flattering and impressing those who considered it a compliment to be so remembered. Their paths had crossed at numerous international conferences, before and after the Islamic Revolution and the Shah's flight in 1979. 1979: the temporal fault line that separated the Westernized, often brutal rule of the Pahlevis, the Shah supplanted by the even harsher, intractable reign of the Ayatollah Khomeini and his successor ayatollahs.

Nizami Khujandi knew both Paolo Pisa and Father Angelo, the one by reputation, the other, the priest, a casual, scholarly acquaintance.

"I requested your presence here, gentlemen," he said without hesitation, in florid, barely-accented Italian. "Neither of you is political," he paused, smiling at Father Angelo. "I'm discounting the eternal politics of your Church, of course, and what requirements a reputable scholar such as yourself must fulfill to remain afloat in that troubled sea."

Father Angelo, in spite of himself, flickered a grin.

"I'm intimately familiar with your Herodian Period research, Dr. Pisa, especially your research into the siege of the Second Temple, particularly the writings of Josephus. Not history's most popular Jew, eh, Dr. Pisa? A turncoat, an ally of Titus. It's not a name that speaks well of its bearer, is it? But why don't we let that rest, eh?"

Yes, Josephus was a survivor but then Dr. Khujandi, what are you? Paolo kept his judgment to himself.

"Pure scholarship is a godly pursuit, Dr. Khujandi, don't you agree?"

"Herod, Titus, this Josephus, these parasites ..." Qolam Hosein said, his voice almost a shout. 'This is not what we're here for! Save your little chats for your next conference, Dr. Khujandi. Let's get on with this!"

Qolam Hosein's retort silenced Khujandi. He removed his steel-rimmed spectacles and pinched the bridge of his nose. Men like Qolam Hosein, children of the 1979 revolution, had no use for men like Khujandi, scholars of international repute, university people, carryovers from the Shah's era. The ruling mullahs in Tehran condemned them, their advanced Western education was termed 'polluting.' The 'polluted' lived under a cloud of suspicion, suffering for their years spent in the rarified academic atmosphere of Western universities. Cairo, Istanbul, and Rome, where Khujandi learned the art of curatorship from Western mentors, were for the mullahs and ayatollahs centers of apostasy. And the months he secretly passed digging in the Negev's sands under the watchful eyes of the IDF agent and a shadowing Iranian handler earned Khujandi another black mark next to his name.

On the one hand, his loyalty to the tenets of the 1979 Revolution under the mullahs' gimlet eyes would always be questioned. On the other hand, Khujandi was needed, tolerated by the Islamic Republic of Iran for his world-renowned scholarship. His unrivaled skill at interpreting ancient Arabic script, particularly when the script was engraved in steel or stone, was invaluable. His freedom to publish, travel, and lecture was presented to the world as a shining example of Tehran's tolerance. His ever-present attendance by unseen Iranian intelligence officers naturally passed unmentioned. The scholar accepted the rules of the devil's bargain he had made long ago and as long as he adhered to them, his survival was assured. Nizami Khujandi was not yet disposable. No, not yet.

"It's time to open the case, Dr. Pisa," Qolam Hosein said,

wafting a hand towards it.

Paolo glanced at Father Angelo. The priest nodded. Khujandi found himself nodding as well.

Khujandi switched on his laptop computer perched near the table's edge. Next he pulled a piece of white linen and two pairs of cotton gloves from his briefcase, handing one pair to Paolo, as the Roman plugged in the luggage lock's combination. As the lock clicked open, Paolo slipped the chain from his wrist, set it aside, and removed the wooden box containing the dagger from the suitcase. He lifted the lid and removed the cotton-and-bubble-wrapped dagger, momentarily hefting it in his hands before handing it to Khujandi.

The Iranian gently lay the dagger on the linen alongside the box and delicately removed its wrapping.

"No one is to touch this, is that understood?" Not waiting for a response, he added: "It is sacred to us, to Islam. Even if it has been stained by the touch of the infidels, it has the mark of the Prophet's hands upon it."

The driver, Qolam Hosein, Talab, and Hassan stood frozen in place, like bird dogs on point, as the two gunmen edged forward surreptitiously for a closer look. Paolo and Father Angelo remained where they were, stock-still, their instincts dictating discretion and silence. Khujandi produced a loupe, a miniature electronic probe, and a large, worn, leather-bound book, by the looks of it a reproduction of an ancient text. He laid the oversized book on the table beside the dagger, opening it to a page marked off by a slip of paper. He studied the etchings on the page for a moment. Then, squinting through the loupe, Khujandi inspected each of the box's golden hinges, comparing them with the book's images.

"Plug this in," he said to Talab, straightening up and handing him the long cord connected to the probe. The dagger's blade reflected the light from the naked ceiling bulb above, its yellowed ivory hilt and the inlaid pearls veined and dulled by age. Khujandi bent closer to the blade, his loupe no more than a centimeter above it. He mumbled to himself in Farsi, unintelligible even to Qolam Hosein, as he ran the loupe over the inscription. Satisfied, he turned the blade over, repeating the procedure, examining the script as closely as space would allow without touching the relic. He swiped at the beads of sweat on his brow with his sleeve. Without looking up, Khujandi fumbled to open his top button with one hand, the other holding the electronic probe. He stood back for a moment, taking a breath, leaned forward again, and ran the electronic probe along the length of one side, then the other of the dagger.

The probe transmitted an enlarged and detailed image of the blade's pittings and the depth measurement of its engravings to the screen of Khujandi's laptop. He smiled slightly, satisfied with the visual inspection. He was nothing if not thorough. More tests had to be done, more proof was required. No doubt must linger. He reached into his briefcase and extracted a small bottle. Dousing a cotton swab with the bottle's dark solution, he dabbed the dagger's jeweled hilt.

"What are you doing now?" Qolam Hosein asked, brusquely. "How much longer, professor?"

"What I'm doing does no harm to the object," Khujandi replied in Farsi, his irritation and disdain evident. "I'm merely testing the age of the pearls and ivory which I'm sure you'll agree is necessary, yes? Watch me, perhaps you'll learn something."

Qolam Hosein, tight-lipped, slowly backed away.

Khujandi's final inspection was aimed at determining the dagger's weight. The corresponding calculations provided in the book, the Egyptian method of calculating weights and measures, were in use in Arabia during Muhammad's era. If they matched, they would affirm the dagger's authenticity. Khujandi balanced the dagger in his hands, confirming and reconfirming his own estimation with the far more accurate probe, checking the figures appearing on his laptop's screen against the numbers given in the book.

"Yes, it is as they say," he proclaimed, his face glistening with sweat. "It is *halal,* pure, this is The Prophet's dagger, of this I am almost certain." And with his characteristic caution, he added a *caveat,* "Pending further tests once it's brought safely home."

"I thought you said you were sure, professor," Qolam Hosein said impatiently. "Are you or aren't you?"

"Yes, I'm sure, but ..."

"Doubly sure that this isn't a fake, a Jew counterfeit?"

"In the name of Allah, I will stake my reputation on it."

"Your reputation's worthless to us, professor. How about your life?"

"My life's always at stake," Khujandi replied firmly, waving his hand at Qolam Hosein dismissively, "you should know that, my friend."

He turned from the kidnapper and began to speak to the others in the room. "We have before us one of Islam's holiest objects, from the Battle of Bedr, the War of Fosse, the Battle for Medina, and other of our Prophet's struggles. It has at last been liberated from the infidels." Khujandi's voice practically sang with exhilaration. The significance of what lay before him was overwhelming. "And we will bring it home, to its rightful home. Allah be praised ..."

He rewrapped the dagger and returned it to its box, easing the lid closed. "Why would the Jews trade a piece of wood and two stone slabs for The Prophet's dagger?" Talab wondered aloud, scratching his chin stubble and looking around, laughing contemptuously. "They aren't as smart as everyone says." He was about to spit for emphasis when he remembered he was in a Muslim home. The driver gave him a withering look. Talab shrugged sheepishly and looked away.

It's questionable whether the driver, the kidnappers, excepting Qolam Hosein, or the bodyguards fully comprehended what was determined by the tests but upon hearing Allah's name, they dutifully responded in unison.

"Allah the Merciful, our Prophet be praised."

Paolo and Father Angelo understood the significance. The Prophet's dagger was as much a symbol for Islam as the Cross was for nascent Christianity, Khujandi's reaction the same as Father Angelo's when he first viewed the Cross. Like the Cross, the dagger was a bridge, separating the new from the old, the marker that foreshadowed a different and unpredictable course that mankind would follow.

Khujandi pointed to a hand-drawn plate in the book.

"Here you see an etching of the dagger. It was done in the month of Shawell twelve, eighty-one, in the year of the Hegira, and it's the only known picture of the holy object. Let me explain ..."

Dr. Khujandi's enthusiasm wasn't shared by Qolam Hosein, who was glancing at the wall clock.

"Save it for your classes, professor. You've done what you were brought here to do."

"Spare me one more moment," Khujandi said, halfway between a demand and a plea. "The faithful among us must understand the dagger's provenance. Let me finish, please."

Qolam Hosein's responded with a grunt, gritting his teeth. The faithful? he thought, smiling grimly to himself. These halfwits I'm saddled with?

"The dagger disappeared perhaps two hundred years ago," Khujandi said as if he was in a lecture hall "We believe it ended up in Yemen, in the hands of a Jewish family that had emigrated from Isfahan or Shiraz, that is what the legend says. How the Israelis got it, who knows?"

Hassan, previously unheard from, cried out.

"The Jews, always the Jews! They stole it, they steal everything, they stole our land ..."

"Yes, yes, Hassan, we know, we know," Qolam Hosein interrupted, holding up his hand to calm his cohort down. "Yes, we know they're all cheats and liars and demons who turned their backs on The Prophet." Then, turning to Father Angelo, he added, "And even before that they rejected your Jesus, didn't they, priest?"

Father Angelo's eyes met Qolam Hosein's briefly before breaking off, ignoring the taunt.

"Your holy robes fool no one, priest," he continued. "We all know you're in league with Satan, with the Jews. Hell's tongues of flame will consume you before long, praise Allah. You," he pointed to one of the gunmen. "Bring me the suitcase."

Qolam Hosein took a small instrument about the size of a thermometer from under his *djellaba* and, inch by inch, examined the suitcase, its every corner, inside and out, its interior lining, and clasp lock. Flipping it over, he spun the wheels, holding the instrument near them as they turned.

"Nothing. Everything reads green. No chips."

He then ran the instrument over the Roman's robes.

"Nothing here either," he said aloud, smirking. "Only the throwaway cells ... and the Crosses..."

In the operations center, the prime minister and her security cabinet's senior members stood before the large screen, the image of the three-story house and the Mercedes filling it. The speaker came alive again.

"They missed the chip," the invisible voice said. "A chip? A tracking device?" she asked.

"Yes," Baruk answered. 'The chip's in the wheel, undetectable, at least undetectable with whatever crappy sensor device they're using, something they probably bought at a discount outlet in Tel Aviv. The device in the wheel is lighter than a feather, almost weightless, a miniscule graphite strip on a finer strip of paper. You're barely able to pick it out with the naked eye. When the wheel is up, the paper's down and vice-versa. We replaced those worthless plastic American wheels that came with the suitcase with our own set. A .50 caliber shell couldn't penetrate them."

"I thought you told the Romans we'd have a tracker sewn into their robes," she said.

"Only to make them feel more secure, more comfortable. Too much unacceptable risk involved. If the bastards discovered the devices on them, they'd be killed on the spot. That is if they weren't tortured first, like Rosenberg. And if they survived, if they were still breathing, maybe they'd be ransomed off. I don't imagine you'd want to try to explain that away to the Vatican ..." Baruk paused, letting what he'd said sink in. "No, we couldn't take the chance. It's safer this way, at least for them. Anyway, the suitcase did its job. They're in our sights ..."

The prime minister nodded and looked up at the screen. "Unidentified car pulling up," the speaker voice said.

Another Mercedes, a newer model, backed into the space behind the first one.

Parviz Mussavani emerged and hurried towards the house.

"Where was he?" General Etan said, vexed. "He was supposed to be with the Romans, beginning to end ..."

"They would've had to shoehorn him in, Yehudah, no elbow room at all, no chance to maneuver if something went wrong," Baruk said. "Or he might just like to drive ... Some of us do, some of us don't need a chauffeur."

"Amusing, Gideon," Etan said, unsmiling.

"Relax. We've worked with him before," Baruk said

confidently. "Mussavani's a pro, he knows what he's doing,"

"We'd better hope so," Etan said. "Anyway, time to green light the team and move them into position."

Inside the house, beyond the camera's range, Mussavani bounded up the three flights of stairs and entered the apartment.

CHAPTER THIRTY

Inside the apartment, Parviz Mussavani relieved himself of his backpack and gathered everyone around him.

"Pay attention. I don't want to repeat myself." Nods.

"Professor Khujandi ..."

"Yes."

"You're remaining here, in this apartment. When the exchange is completed and once I call, you'll be driven to Amman. It's all been arranged."

"But I was promised I could see the relics," he objected. "That's why I agreed to be part of this."

"No," Mussavani snapped. "You're part of this because you were ordered to be part of it. Spare us all the theatrics and you're wheedling, please. This isn't one of your classrooms and it's certainly not a negotiation. You're not to move from this apartment until you have my say-so, understood?" He pointed at the driver. "Don't worry, professor. Yousef will babysit you."

"I'll report you!"

"To whom? Your friends in Tehran? See if they listen. Or care." The rising anger in Mussavani's voice startled Khujandi.

"But ..." he said shakily, feeling behind him for the couch.

"Have you gone deaf?" Mussavani snapped. "No 'buts.' Make yourself comfortable, take a nap, you look like you need one ..."

Father Angelo stepped forward.

"Why don't you let him come with us?" he asked quietly, hoping his own deference would prove persuasive. "He's a scholar, nothing more, and ..."

"He can watch it on the news," Mussavani shot back, switching to Hebrew. "It's enough I have to drag you two with us ..."

"I'm sure we can keep up," Paolo said, offended by Mussavani's slight.

"This we'll soon see." Mussavani laughed sharply. "If

you can't, you're on your own. And keep your mouths shut. Eyes open, mouths shut. Not another word."

"I'm not convinced this isn't a trap," Qolam Hosein confronted Mussavani. "This is all a little too convenient, too smooth ... you, a Persian, and the Zionists ... this whole arrangement ..." Qolam Hosein studied Mussavani's face for some sort of tic, a telltale sign, a reaction to his accusation.

"Don't be so damned stupid and paranoid! We're paying hard cash, all the money you demanded. You approached us, remember? You're the one insisting that the tradeoff take place in some hole in the ground under the Zionists' noses. We're playing by your rules ..."

Talab and Hassan lined up behind Qolam Hosein. The gunmen, off to the side and looking confused at this last-minute contretemps, glanced at each other, gripped their weapons tightly, raising the barrels slightly, awaiting some sort of signal.

"Don't be a bigger fool than you've been," Mussavani went on, his voice cold, adding, "unless you want to lose a payday ..." He nudged the backpack with his toe. "And perhaps your life in the bargain."

Qolam Hosein held Mussavani's gaze for a face-saving moment before retreating, cursing softly.

"That's better," Mussavani said flatly.

"The exchange, it was to be so simple, straightforward," Father Angelo said, disturbed by the heated exchange, concerned that everything was beginning to fall apart. "It was arranged between the ayatollah and the rabbi, the rules were clear, the dagger in trade for the relics."

"Yes, old man, we're in dire need of your pointless comments at this moment," Mussavani said in Hebrew, waving the priest away. "This isn't Rome, but perhaps you're more confused than you seem to be? You're expendable, both of you. If you're killed, who would shed a tear? A couple of old Italians ..."

"God cares for us all," Father Angelo said, anxiously fidgeting with his Cross. Exasperated, Mussavani shook his head in disbelief.

"I wouldn't bet a *rial* on it if I were you," he said, reaching down and hoisting the backpack up over his shoulder, slipping his arms through its straps. "In five minutes, I want everyone

316

changed and ready ..."

One by one the Arabs, Qolam Hosein, the gunmen, and the Romans donned variations of the same gray jumpsuit, green rubber boots, miners' protective helmets with lanterns that had earlier been stashed in the apartment's closet. Each man was issued a flashlight. When he reappeared, Talab had a thick rope coiled over a shoulder.

"We've a long way to go," Mussavani said, addressing Paolo and Father Angelo, pinching the bridge of his nose, trying to quell his misgivings. Paolo could read doubt in Mussavani's eyes, an unspoken belief that neither Roman would survive the journey.

Father Angelo tugged at his too-snug jumpsuit. An errant, absurd thought about dieting flitted through his mind, provoking a sliver of a smile.

"What's so funny?" Paolo whispered.

"I'll tell you later," the priest paused, "if there is a later."

Mussavani asked Paolo to reach into his backpack and remove a loose-leaf notebook. As he did so, it slipped from his hands and fell to the floor. Its rings snapped open and its contents, Wilberg's maps, spilled out.

"Sorry, clumsy of me," Paolo apologized. He bent down and nervously collected the scattered maps and handed them back to Mussavani.

"Where did you get those maps?" Paolo asked, laboring to sound casual, disinterested, trusting his question would be taken as an idle one. "These? Bought them in a bazaar in Amman ..."

Father Angelo pointed to the German script imprinted along one of the map's bottom edge.

Holy City: Tunnels, Cisterns, Second Temple Period (538 BC-70 AD), Aeolia Capitolina (135 AD-330 AD) Survey.

In a different script at the end of the legend, the name *Heinz Wilberg* identified the maker of the maps.

"You've lied to us again," Father Angelo blurted. "Lying is not a virtue." "Yes, priest, it isn't, is it? And? So? Wilberg, that pompous old ass. He should've taken the money instead of ..." Mussavani paused, apparently weighing whether he should go further. What does it matter, he decided, this is their last day anyway. Why not show them how ignorant they are, these foolish old men ...

"You were followed after you'd left the King David. It's as simple as that if you have a few relevant scraps of information. You can intuit and pursue your instincts. Or at least you can if you know the trade, our trade. I've been at this game for a long time ... it's not really a game, you know. It's a craft." Mussavani checked himself momentarily, wondering if he was being too incautious, too expansive. "You two, you're out of your league. This pathetic adventure of yours." A laugh caught in his throat. "As for Wilberg, hardly an ideal Zionist. Half-Jewish Nazi or whatever he was. His whole life was based on convenience, the needs of the moment, a true chameleon. It surprised me that his venality didn't get the best of him in the end. Better it worked out this way. He couldn't be trusted to keep silent anyway. We did the Israelis a favor, don't you think, Pisa?"

"There was no need to kill him," Paolo said.

"But there was, my friend. It was a necessity, sadly, a need of the moment. I'm sure Wilberg understood," Mussavani said coolly, scooping the maps back into the binder, arranging them, and snapping the rings shut.

"You," Mussavani pointed at one of the Arabs. "What was your name again? Hassan? Yes, Hassan. You carry the suitcase ..."

When they reached the first landing, Mussavani lined everyone up single file, himself at the column's head, the Romans in the middle, with the gunmen taking up the rear. The remaining flights terminated before a thick, splintered oak door that opened into the building's musty, dank cellar. Mussavani raised a hand, palm outwards, halting the group while he consulted the first of the maps.

He edged the door open. A tunnel lay behind it, damp and reeking of decay, the outline of its stone sidewalls dimly visible until they were consumed in blackness ten meters from where they all stood. Mussavani gave the order to switch on the flashlights and headlamps. Talab stepped forward and was told to play out his rope.

"Everyone maintain their positions, keep a meter's distance, and grab hold of the rope."

As they moved along the old water tunnel, Paolo strained

to recall the map's details. Under Lion's Gate, the old St. Mary's Gate? Unsure but as good a guess as any.

He shared it with Father Angelo.

"Then the Pool of Bethesda should be above," the priest replied, adding "where Jesus healed a sick man. We must be under the old Syrian Quarter, not far from the Dome.'

"I told you 'no talking,' priest," Mussavani said, turning. "Are you so old you remember nothing?"

"It was my fault," Paolo volunteered quickly, facing Mussavani, the Iranian's headlamp blinding him. "I mentioned something to him ..."

"Shut up, both of you! Do not speak unless spoken to. By me, only me!"

The jerry-built apartment building and scores like it on the neighboring streets above dated to the era of Turkish hegemony, raised upon whatever stood there before, temples, churches, markets. All that came before was plowed under, providing only the foundation for what came after. During their short post-World War I reign, the British bounced from one economic crisis to another, their exchequer helpless to bail them out, their once-mighty empire waning and another war inevitable. They occupied and then left Palestine and Jerusalem as they found it, moldering and rundown.

As they moved deeper into the tunnel, Mussavani's pace slowed, puzzlement masking his face.

"Pisa, come here a moment." He spread a second map out, his headlamp illuminating it, and pointed. "Do you see this?"

"Yes."

"Clever, wasn't it?"

"I don't know what you mean?"

Mussavani sighed, the anger in his voice displaced by disappointment.

"Maybe I'm giving you too much credit for intelligence, Pisa. You're not able to put ... what is it again - two and two together? Maybe your Arab cousins, those useful idiots back there, aren't as ignorant as they seem, at least not all of them. They didn't need Wilberg's maps. They know tunnels. Remember Gaza before the flood? A fucking network of tunnels. The Israelis couldn't plug them all up. The Palestinians use the naked eye, watchful eyes that aren't mounted on light poles. They drove to Herod's Gate, unloaded your precious relics, and dragged them into the tunnels while the Jews chased their own tails, ripping East Jerusalem apart and upending every West Bank shithole. Anyway, we're coming at the hiding place from the other end. That's why we needed the maps. Herod's Gate's crawling with IDF fuckers. We'd have to be invisible to enter the tunnel from there. They've got the whole area, all the city gates blanketed, stepping on each other's feet. We've got to go south and find the cistern under the Dome ..."

Father Angelo was just out of earshot and missed what Mussavani had said. Paolo was momentarily at a loss for words, thunderstruck at the revelation.

"What is it, Pisa? Did I lose you?"

"They knew the IDF wouldn't assault the Dome," Paolo muttered to himself, ignoring Mussavani's insult, the logic of secreting the relics under the Dome dawning upon him like a bolt. Hide the relics under their noses, if not in plain sight then just below the Israelis' sight line. "It would've sparked another *intifada* if they dared to, like the one that exploded after Sharon's visit ... At worst, this time it could've meant war."

Paolo quaked more from the realization than the penetrating dampness in the tunnel.

"Yes, Pisa, very good. It could've meant war, still could if this exchange fails."

"Where the hell are they?" General Elan shouted to no one in particular in the Knesset's operations room. "They never left the building. Where's the goddamned suitcase?"

"Somewhere underground," came the response from a rattled Baruk. "Deep in one of the tunnels, very deep. The tracking device, it's transmitting intermittently, on and off ..."

The prime minister walked over to Baruk.

"Explain to me what's happening, Commander. This seems not to be going according to plan." Dora Ben-Gurion was frowning.

"There're mazes of tunnels, cisterns, and carved-out hiding places under the Old City. We've sealed most of them up and some of the tunnels lead to dead ends, brick walls ..."

"I don't need an underground tour, Commander. Tell me

something I don't know already ..." she said.

"Bring up the old maps," Baruk said into his headset mike. Seconds later, the maps appeared on their computer monitors. Baruk picked up a cursor and ran it over his screen.

"Here's Herod's Gate and under it there's a tunnel that leads directly to the basement of the Dome. It was used by our priests in Herod's time. It's like a rabbit's warren down there, the Temple Mount's laced with interconnected passages where the priests would appear and disappear like magic ..."

The prime minister cut him off.

"What else is down there, Commander? Be brief!"

"Old water lines, phone lines from the fifties and sixties ... I understand this is how we moved into Jordan then, underground, but no one knows for sure. Some old German supposedly mapped it out for us."

Zvi Bar-Levi said nothing, leaving mention of dead Wilberg to pass. His support for the exchange mission was tepid from the get-go and remained so. He neither feared for nor cared about the two Romans' fate. People live, people die. He'd served his country for over forty years. In perpetual battle against the nation's enemies, lives were expendable. The Prime Minister's unshakeable belief that the discovery and recovery of the Cross and the tablets would somehow bind people together, work to erase the distant and recent past, and bring about an infinitesimal start to healing the wounds of two millennia struck Bar-Levi as preposterous. He had confided as much to Gideon Baruk earlier, adding, "If the Cross wasn't stolen from us, who would care, who should care? Us? It should be the Vatican's problem, not ours."

"But it was stolen from us, Zvi, so whether we like it or not, or whether it's 'fair', well. ..." Baruk had raised his eyebrows, the notion of anything in life being fair striking him as ludicrous, "it's become our problem."

Baruk's proposition was inarguable. The theft was Israel's problem and Israel's alone. And Bar-Levi knew in his gut that Baruk was right.

"Have our men secured all the city gates?" the prime minister asked.

"I ordered up additional forces this morning, Prime Minister." General Etan ticked off Jerusalem's gates on his fingers. "They're all in place. No one can get in, no one gets out. The area around the Mount is surrounded."

"Good, good work." The prime minister's smile more resembled a grimace.

"I recognize and share your concern," Baruk said to her. "There's always concern when we hook up with the Iranians on a sensitive operation but they've proven themselves moderately predictable before. The wild cards are the kidnappers, these self-style *jihadists*. If they'd managed to steal the Dead Sea Scrolls, they'd probably have already traded them for a Yankee cap. They burn down their own filling stations when they need gas and kill their own Palestinian 'brothers' if it suits an immediate whim."

"Even their own grandparents disown them. Anyway, Mussavani's got the money, *our* money I might add, and is running the show so ..." Baruk paused. "So we'll see what we shall see."

"I wish this night was last week," the prime minister allowed. "So do we all, Prime Minister."

In the tunnel, the group moved forward at a snail's pace, shuffling, uncertain, with geriatric steps. They weren't evidently the first to ply their way through the tunnel. Their flashlights illuminated the strewn-about leavings of others who came before them - broken beer bottles, used condoms, a stained mattress, even a windblown umbrella - littered their way. With each new piece of trash, the terrorists, giddy from tension, erupted in laughter, Qolam Hosein's efforts to silence them fruitless.

Even Mussavani couldn't restrain himself.

"Early Christian relics, priest?" Mussavani smirked, pointing to an abandoned sneaker, arching an eyebrow.

Father Angelo silently blessed the darkness that hid his chagrin.

As the labyrinth began to narrow, its ceiling dropped lower. The tunnel's walls glistened with condensation as drops of moisture from above pinged off the miners' helmets. The air inside the tunnel was turning fetid, an almost liquid mist enveloping the men, the smell of raw sewage everywhere. One of the bodyguards gagged; Hassan retched and the suitcase began slipping from his hands, but he caught it just before it hit the muck.

"Careful, fool, that's far more valuable than you are or

322

ever will be," Mussavani said, as he surveyed the line, counting heads again. "All still here. Excellent." He checked another map and nodded, satisfied. "It's time to crawl. Turn on your headlamps ... and put on the gloves."

Father Angelo was horrified.

"You're expecting us to crawl through ... this?"

"Do you know of another way?" Mussavani replied sarcastically. "Perhaps Pisa can play your St. Christopher and carry you on his back ..."

Ten meters ahead of them, a broken pipe hung precariously bracketed to the wall, old telephone wires protruding from where it had split apart.

"Heinz Wilberg's work," Paolo mumbled, trying gamely to distract himself from the nauseating stench that choked all of them.

What a cruel irony, Father Angelo thought, as he crept along on all fours behind Paolo and Mussavani. We're seeking the Crosspiece and the tablets, dragging The Prophet's dagger through a sea of human waste below the Dome of the Rock ...

Nine meters further, the limestone underfoot dried and the group was able to stand upright.

Mussavani held another map under his flashlight, occasionally glancing at his illuminated compass. He beckoned Qolam Hosein to approach.

"How close are we?"

"It's just up ahead."

Off to the right was a cistern piled halfway up with slatted wooden boxes bearing Russian markings, each stamped in red with CCCP.

"Russian arms," Paolo said unnecessarily as Qolam Hosein placed a hand on the corner of one of the boxes.

"Very clever, *italiano*. More clever than the Zionists. Yes, Russian arms but not necessarily from the Russians. Old perhaps but still useful and plenty more where these came from." The rope slackened as Talab joined them, his laugh competing with Qolam Hosein's. "The Zionists, they never come down here. It's reserved for us ... 'filthy' Arabs." Qolam Hosein laughed again.

"We're directly under the north of the Dome," Mussavani yelled back. "This is the opening to the tunnel leading to the Bah el-Zahira."

"Herod's Gate," Paolo said reflexively, correcting Mussavani.

"Yes, Pisa, Herod's Gate, Bab el-Zahira, call it what you wish." Mussavani shrugged.

Before them stood an old wooden door, striated with cracks, fitted with a new, sturdier lock installed above the rusted-out original, fronting a room that dated from Herod's time. Qolam Hosein drew out a key and unlocked it, shoving it open, and ordering the armed guards to enter first.

"It's clear, *sayyid*," the shorter of the two men said, sweeping his automatic weapon in a semi-circle.

The room's walls bore discernible symbols carved into the stone by the Hebrews sheltered there. In a far corner, ancient burnt and blackened timbers were scattered about, surviving remnants of the Roman siege two thousand years before when Titus' legions soaked the city above them with its inhabitants' blood before pursuing and slaughtering the unfortunates who sought shelter below.

This has all the earmarks of a killing ground, Paolo thought, his body racked with a shiver. He now regretted his decision to join the hunt for the stolen relics. Deeply. Madness, this is what this is! He remonstrated with himself as he thought the unthinkable, that the room could again be a charnel, this time with him and Father Angelo its latest victims.

Qolam Hosein pointed at the large tarp in the room's center, instructing Talab and Hassan to remove it. Hassan put the suitcase down and grabbed one corner, Talab the other, and pulled the tarp away. The Crosspiece from the Cross and the tablets, smaller than either Paolo or Father Angelo remembered them, lay exposed.

Mussavani trained his flashlight's beam on the objects. The other men followed suit.

"Scrap wood and two stones, Jew junk," Talab said, stepping on the Crosspiece with his foot.

"Which is why we're paying you all this money, for 'junk,' eh, imbecile?" Mussavani shook his head, checking his watch.

"Don't dare touch it with your filthy feet!" Father Angelo shouted suddenly, his face crimson. "Barbarians!"

The bodyguards, their ears tuned to what sounded like a threat, fiddled with their guns, flicking off the safeties and raising them to waist level.

"Take it easy, priest," Mussavani said in Hebrew, placing a soothing hand on Father Angelo's back. "Don't give yourself a heart attack over these pigs. We don't need an 'accident.' They're only shameless empty vessels, hired guns. Today, Fatah al-Islam, tomorrow Hezbollah, Hamas the day after. No loyalties, not even to their Palestinian brethren. Let's get on with it. Okay, priest, you and Pisa make a quick inspection, we're running behind schedule."

Father Angelo dropped to his knees and kissed the Crosspiece, blessed the tablets, and began reciting a prayer in Latin. Paolo squatted next to him, running the beam of his flashlight slowly along the Crosspiece, as both examined the relic closely. They repeated the procedure, then rubbed their fingers along the perimeter and the smooth marble face of the tablets.

"Why are we wasting time," Qolam Hosein shouted, increasingly agitated, his speech pressured, a sense of panic creeping up his spine. In his gut grew an indefinable feeling that something was amiss. "This is what we took from the Jews. What else could it be? Did you think by some miracle we could make copies?"

Paolo rose to a knee and looked directly at Mussavani. "It's the relics. Shall we make the call?" Paolo asked. "Give us the money. Now!" Qolam Hosein barked. Mussavani glowered at him.

"Patience, my friend. I need to make the call," he said, flipping open his phone. "Put the phone down!" Qolam Hosein ordered as his gunmen leveled their weapons at Mussavani, Paolo, and Father Angelo.

"What are you doing?" Mussavani's voice was icy calm.

"Take their cells," Qolam Hosein said, now equally calm, turning away. Paolo and Father Angelo, paralyzed with fear, guns pointed at their chests, hurriedly handed Talab their phones.

"You're double-crossing us, you imbecile? You cannot be this ignorant! You're signing your own a death warrant, 'sayyid,' or whatever you are. Why would you do this? The money's here," Mussavani said, patting his backpack. "This makes no sense what you're doing. Who do you think you'll sell the dagger to? Who'd buy it now when they learn of this?"

"It's the Jews' money, this I'd bet on. It's not yours, so why would you care? You're not losing a *rial,* my friend. And the Middle East is a very big place, you know. There's always someone with more to pay for such an invaluable piece, don't you think? They say the dagger's priceless but everything has a price... Perhaps a government other than yours would be interested, too, no? After all, the power the dagger confers beggars the imagination, yes? Even your own government might well pay dearly for it in the end, when all of today's hard feelings are soothed away? The Jews, they can keep their garbage. It's no longer of any use to us. But The Prophet's dagger, it's the true prize." Qolam Hosein's face bore a mirthless smile.

"This is insanity. It will never work."

"It will. But you'll never live to see how wrong you were, my friend. How unfortunate for you. *Inshallah."*

Qolam Hosein raised an index finger, and the bodyguard nearest brought his gun around and fired. Parviz Mussavani screamed and tumbled over, clutching his leg, the blood pumping from it fast covering his fingers.

"Fool," Qolam Hosein shouted. "You were to kill him!"
"Mary, Mother of God," Father Angelo cried out.

Almost simultaneously, the room exploded in a blinding flash of light, the sound that followed deafening, joined by an avalanche of blinding, billowing white smoke. The thundering echo from the concussion grenade obscured the sound of the ensuing gunfire. Weapons clattered to the ground as the bodyguards clapped their hands in agony over their ears. Paolo, disoriented and deafened, staggered aimlessly about, jostling the flailing, choking Qolam Hosein. He half-spun away and tripped, upended, his legs going out from under him. Talab lay on his back, groaning, rolling from side to side, one knee raised, the other shattered. Hassan, prostrate, lay unconscious atop the green suitcase. Father Angelo was curled on his side, a meter distant, trickles of blood running from his nose and his right cheek.

A second burst of gunfire was unleashed. Talab now lay still, his jaw slack, his legs splayed apart. Dead. Hassan's body jumped and twisted as the bullets penetrated it coming to rest with his arms thrown outwards. Two dead. The suitcase was kicked from him by an unseen presence who fired twice more,

326

silencing the wounded bodyguard. The other gunman was already dead, the shrapnel from the grenade having torn half his face away. Four dead. Qolam Hosein, miraculously unhurt but for punctured eardrums, cowered in a comer, assuming a fetal position. Paolo frozen in horror, watched as one of the khaki-clad rescue team strode over to the *sayyid* and fired point blank, the shot undeflected by Qolam Hosein's raised hand. Final tally: all dead but the Romans and Parviz Mussavani.

Paolo tended to Father Angelo as the priest, only fazed by a ricochet, raised himself on an elbow and began dragging himself towards the lifeless bodies.

"What are you doing, Angelo? You mustn't move ..." Paolo rasped.

The priest sloughed Paolo's hand away and kept crawling towards the bodies. Until he fell into a faint, he was heard offering up prayers for the fallen terrorists. Bewildered, two of the rescuers stared down at him, uncomprehending. Behind them, Mussavani shouted at the rescue team's leader.

"Where the hell were you?' he shrieked, writhing in pain as someone tied a tourniquet around his bleeding leg, waving another forward to tend to Mussavani's wounds as he moved towards Paolo.

"Here. Call!" he said in halting English, handing the Roman a cellphone. Paolo's trembling fingers poked in the number. No ring. It was answered instantly.

"Yes?" the voice said.

Paolo's ears were still ringing.

"Yes?" Zvi Bar-Levi repeated, raising his voice.

"We're alive," Paolo shouted, barely able to hear his own voice. "Put him on speakerphone, Zvi," Commander Gideon Baruk said. Paolo's hearing slowly began to normalize.

"We're alive but ... no one else is. There's been a bloodbath ..." His voice was raised.

Silence on the other end of the phone although Paolo thought he heard someone laugh. But he couldn't be sure. Maybe it was the transmission.

"We're glad you survived, Dr. Josephus," Baruk said flatly. "Give the phone back to Mussavani ..."

"He's wounded."

"Give him the phone," Baruk was insistent.

Paolo passed the phone back to a rescuer who handed it to Mussavani. The Iranian had been placed on a makeshift litter, a jacket pillowed under his head for comfort, the backpack at his feet. Another of the team had the suitcase tucked under an arm.

"Second sewer cover, opens up next to Herod's Gate. Understood," Paolo heard Mussavani struggle to say as he writhed in pain, the blood beginning to seep through his newly bandaged leg. "Yes, of course, Gideon. It will all be returned."

On his end, Baruk assured Mussavani that two cars awaited them at the gate; that the Iranian operative and his men would be in Amman in an hour.

"What was that about?" Paolo asked him with some trepidation as two bearers lifted Mussavani's litter and began to move forward. "Who are these men? They're not IDF."

"These are my people, Pisa. We worked it out beforehand, in Amman. Do you think I'd trust the IDF not to kill me, too? Accidentally? Or maybe not so, who would know the difference?" He grimaced in pain. "This isn't about politics, my friend, that 'strange bedfellows' and 'the enemy of my enemy is my friend' bullshit." Mussavani drew a sharp breath, pausing. "This is about faith. In the end that is all that counts. It's as it should be - the dagger is finally ours, the Sh'ia peoples' treasure is returning home.

And you have what is yours. You want more details, ask your people. And a last piece of advice, Pisa, " Mussavani said, grimacing, his face taut with agony, "Stick to your books."

As two of his men angled his litter upwards towards the manhole, the Iranian locked eyes with Paolo.

"By the way, Pisa, I lied. We didn't kill Wilberg." Mussavani forced a laugh. "When the priest wakes up, be sure to tell him. He seems to care about such minor issues.

Paolo's face betrayed his shock.

"Then who ... who did?

"Let's say there are people among you with many masks and many names," he said cryptically as he was passed though the opening above.

Moments later the room was filled with an IDF squad, two of whom carried a stretcher for the unconscious Father Angelo. The newly-appointed curator of the Israel Museum descended the ladder to personally oversee preparations for the return of the Crosspiece and the tablets. The last of the soldiers carried body bags for the remains of the terrorists that were to be loaded onto a waiting truck and promptly driven to Ramallah. By morning, the Palestinian Authority would have arranged for a proper Muslim burial and the dead would be interred.

Under the curator's watchful eye, as the smoke dissipated, the relics were carefully removed from the subterranean room and carried through a larger tunnel below the Golden Gate. As they had been two thousand years before, they were borne on their way through a timeworn opening cut into an old wall and were transported through the Kidron Valley, beyond the Tomb of Absolom— where they had lain hidden and unseen until they were unearthed by the floods of 2012. By midnight, the recovered Crosspiece from the Cross and the tablets were home again, secured in the vault beneath the Israel Museum.

PALM SUNDAY
MARCH 24, 2013
VI

CHAPTER THIRTY-ONE

Zvi Bar-Levi poked his head out the passenger's side window of the Hummer, a space shared with his dog. Around them police cars, their lights flashing, sirens wailing, formed a cordon, separating Herod's Gate from the crowd of curious onlookers peering at the IDF soldiers emerging from below ground.

"Dr. Josephus, over here," he shouted when he spotted the still-dazed Paolo leaning against a lamppost

Paolo unsteadily made his way towards the Hummer. "Where's Angelo?" he asked.

"He's being taken care of. Get in."

"Where are we going?"

"A pleasant surprise this time."

"A surprise? I've had enough surprises tonight for two lifetimes."

Inside the Hummer, Paolo leaned back, his blood-stained jumpsuit stuck to him, a reminder of the grotesque masquerade he'd been a party to. They drove along the wall past the Damascus Gate, continuing past the New Gate, turning finally in the direction of the government complex. He was still woozy but his nausea had abated. For some reason his memory of the day when David Ben-Gurion announced his resignation entered his mind. How odd the memories stress produces, he thought. Ben-Gurion's departure, not unexpected, had happened with a minimum of fanfare. Israel's first prime minister faded quietly away to his kibbutz apartment in the Negev, smaller than the grand terrace that graced Paolo's penthouse in Rome. And when Golda Meir left office after the Yom Kippur War, cigarette in hand, she too faded away, to a small Tel Aviv apartment, remarking only that, "I have done my job." No star-studded grand balls, no military parades, no cavalcade of media appearances. A few newspaper interviews, a striking absence of pomp and circumstance. That was then - informality to excess, rarely a thank you. This is now wall-to-wall media coverage. The reality of then versus the reality of now.

Paolo understood. He had lived a good part of his life here, in Israel. A Roman, yes, but a Jew, a part of the Diaspora. Many outsiders see the creative Israeli norm of what passes for civility as rude; insiders accept it as the Israeli way. As Golda Meir put it so succinctly, you do what you have to and then you go home. Paolo Pisa and Father Angelo Lorenzo did what they had to and they would soon go home. Home to Rome.

As the ornate gates to the Knesset swung open, Paolo could see the Prime Minister standing at the head of the stairs, beside her Cardinal Zaccaria, General Etan, Commander Baruk, and behind her the other planners of the rescue mission. No press, no media hordes, no Klieg lights illuminating the scene. Just those who had sent him and Father Angelo on their way earlier in the evening. The persistent media clamor that surrounded every event of any significance in Jerusalem was missing. No announcement had apparently been made yet. A media blackout prevailed. Paolo wondered how long it would last.

As he made his way from the car, followed by Bar-Levi and his driver, Dora Ben-Gurion approached him, extending her hand.

"Well done, Dr. Josephus," she said simply, and, after shaking his hand, stepped back.

Paolo could barely croak a "thank you" such was his utter exhaustion, complemented by the surreal nature of the events just past.

"Good work, Dr. Josephus," General Etan complimented. "We'll make a soldier out of you yet. It went off as close to plan as anyone could've hoped for. At least in this part of the world ..."

Cardinal Zaccaria came towards him, arms outstretched, and enclosed Paolo within, planting a kiss on both cheeks. From one Roman to another, the cardinal's eminence forgotten in the moment.

"Rome thanks you," the cardinal said predictably, speaking in Italian, "but your and Father Angelo's heroics have created a conundrum for the Church."

Paolo's face showed bewilderment. "A conundrum? What

sort of ..."

"Two Crosses."

The Cardinal, a man of subtle if often unrecognized wit, grinned, anticipating the moment the meaning of what he had just said dawned on Paolo.

"Ah ... yes. I see, yes. St. Helena's discovery. A ... a dilemma for the Church, to be sure."

"All will be resolved in good time, Dr. Pisa. As it always has been. We are, shall we say, practiced in resolving such ... contradictions?" he said confidently. "Well, I've occupied enough of your time and I'm sure the medical staff will want to give you a once-over."

After a brief physical examination at the Knesset's emergency clinic and receiving assurances that Father Angelo's wound was superficial and minor, Paolo fell into a long, if nightmare-plagued, sleep, his mind repeatedly replaying their rescue and the retrieval of the artifacts by the Iranian operatives. He dreamt of swimming against an onrushing tide of blood, his efforts to escape proving fruitless. The dream was almost palpable. Before he was swept under, he awakened with a start, for a moment confused, not knowing where he was, lost. He was drenched in cooling sweat, his nightclothes clinging to him. Ten hours had passed.

"I wondered if you were planning to sleep the rest of your life away," Zvi Bar- Levi was saying, standing bedside, his voice distant to Paolo's ears. "I was about to take your pulse."

"Where am I?"

"Still in the clinic. You passed out after the examination."

"I don't remember ..."

"Why would you? There was no point in waking you. The doctor gave you a sedative." "Angelo?"

"He's fine or as fine as he can be. No broken bones, heart's still ticking, the doctor told him to stop smoking."

"It would take a papal bull ..."

Bar-Levi smiled, picked up the remote, pressed the power button, and began to surf the stations.

CNN's commentator announced that the relics had been located and recovered, that several terrorists had died in the ensuing firefight. The details of the action were sketchy, he said, Israeli officials citing security concerns for limiting access to further information.

"So much for keeping all this under wraps," Bar-Levi muttered.

"The office of Israel's prime minister announced that the Cross will be shared with the world," the screen voice said. "She termed it 'A much-needed symbol in a perilous time. We are fortunate that it was found by two Italian scholars in our Holy Land.'"

RAJ Uno featured stock photos of Paolo Pisa and Father Angelo Lorenzo, providing a more fevered presentation, but like CNN's report, it was patchy on actual details, playing loose with the facts.

"These great men," the presenter declared, "found the Cross in the Kidron Valley after it was swept clean by the floods of last November. It is considered by most to be the greatest archaeological find since the discovery of the Dead Sea Scrolls over sixty years ago. Christians the world over are calling it a miracle ..."

Paolo and Father Angelo's photos disappeared, replaced with the familiar face of an American evangelist, his shopworn platitudes roughly dubbed into Italian.

'This is the most significant discovery of all our lifetimes," the burly pastor crowed, his Cheshire cat grin spreading from ear to ear. "It is a single victory in our ongoing struggle in the war against Satan."

Paolo groaned just as Father Angelo appeared in the doorway.

"Ah, there you are," the priest said, an unlit cigarette pressed between his fingers, a hand grasping the bedstead for support.

"Angelo, what're you doing out of bed," Paolo stammered. "You shouldn't be walking around ..."

"I'm a fast healer."

"No smoking in here, you know the rules," Bar-Levi said playfully.

"I'm aware of that, Minister," Father Angelo replied before realizing Bar-Levi was only teasing him.

On BBC, Rabbi Ya'akov was standing alongside Cardinal Murphy, both men beaming. Cardinal Murphy pronounced that, "This magnificent find reunites our two great religions. It affirms now and forever that Israel is the Holy Land ..."

"The gang's all here," Bar-Levi remarked sarcastically.

Father Angelo frowned at the Minister. Bar-Levi in turn grinned, shrugged, and walked to the room's windows, placed his hands on the sill, and looked out, for a moment watching the foot traffic below. We'll see what we shall see, won't we, gentlemen?, he thought to himself before turning back to the scholars.

"Gentlemen, you're both now immortal, your faces recognizable everywhere, your names on everyone's lips." He tapped the sill for emphasis.

Paolo couldn't know the Minister was toying with them even though his placid expression remained unchanged. Emotion, Paolo knew well enough, was plainly a stranger to Bar-Levi.

"They didn't mention the tablets," Paolo said, puzzled by its omission by the chief rabbi and the cardinal.

"Yes, the tablets," Bar-Levi repeated and matter-of-factly said: "We put them back into the vault. In a couple of days, we'll make an announcement that, yes, they're from Herod's era, but, no, they're not from the Second Temple. Just another set from a synagogue at the time of Titus' siege, something to that effect."

"But ... but why?" Father Angelo appeared baffled.

"Why? Isn't it obvious? Yes, the tablets are real and yes, they're from Herod's Temple. Imagine what would follow if word got out, Father, if the 'truth' was revealed. I'm sure Dr. Josephus can explain."

"The lunatics, the far right, our own 'true believers.' Angelo, you haven't forgotten them, have you?"

Father Angelo began to nod knowingly. Yes, of course he knew this. The painkillers, they were robbing him of his faculties.

"Don't doubt that these fanatics won't storm the Mount if they knew, demanding that the Dome be torn down, that the Temple be rebuilt, that it all be done yesterday,"

Bar-Levi continued. "The verification of the tablets is to be kept from the world. This was at the heart of the deal between the Chief Rabbi and the Supreme Ayatollah. Fifty years from now, maybe we'll 'rediscover' them but for now ..."

He shook his head, a definite no. No further explanation was necessary, none was proffered.

Iranian TV flashed on, its commentary subtitled in

Hebrew, the script predictable. The speaker, in a gray suit and contrasting buttoned-up white shirt, expertly choreographed their version of events to the Farsi-speaking world.

"The dagger wielded by The Prophet during the battle that turned the tide for our faith was found in a basement storage room in a museum in the holy city of Qom. It was long thought lost in history but it was, *inshallah,* merely misplaced. It was identified yesterday by the late Professor Nizami Khujandi ..."

"The 'late'"

"... the Islamic Republic's leading authority on the history of Islam and its artifacts. Tragically, on the drive back from a family visit to Amman, he lost control of his car which careened off the road, and struck a tree."

Bar-Levi shut off the television.

"I - I don't believe this, this was no accident," Father Angelo said heatedly. "Dr. Khujandi couldn't drive. I've never seen a tree 'roadside' on the way to Amman. Wasn't he being driven back by Mussavani's man?" He raised his hands, then let them drop to his sides.

"Believe what you want to believe, Father," Bar-Levi said, his boredom with the priest's naïveté overt. "This is the Middle East. Besides, you have what you came for, your Cross and, of course, the Tiberias manuscript. We're keeping that bit of news on the back burner for a few days, by the way. Don't want to overwhelm the world with all these riches, do we now? Too much joy is never healthy. It leads to inflated expectations, yes? Meanwhile, enjoy your celebrity, your well-deserved fame and notoriety, write your books, ponder the two Crosses, and let the world absorb what was found. In time, any problems will all work themselves out."

Bar-Levi's haughty condescension angered the priest. The look on his face said more than words would have. The Minister's response to all issues, large and small, was maddeningly consistent. A "so what" shrug. It's the Middle East. No questions, no debate. Things were as they seemed or they weren't. It didn't matter. It changed nothing. For the Minister, it was all the same. Truth or lies. For Zvi Bar-Levi, both held equal moral weight. Or no weight at all. It's the Middle East.

For Paolo, an unresolved question remained, nagging at him, demanding an answer. Who killed Heinz Wilberg? Mussavani denied complicity but Mussavani was trained to deceive. It was at the core of his life's work. What gripped Paolo in a storm of doubt was the Iranian's enigmatic remark in the tunnel before he was evacuated. There are people among you with many masks and many names.

As Zvi Bar-Levi walked to the door, Paolo's question brought him up short. "Who killed Wilberg?"

Bar-Levi turned slowly, hesitating for a split-second. Then, with feigned disinterest, he brushed the question away.

"You mean the map man?"

"You know who I mean, Minister."

"Yes, yes, Wilberg, the German Jew. Or so he claimed to be. The Iranian did him in, claimed he needed the old maps. You saw for yourself, it's a complex labyrinth down there and he didn't want to go in there blind and chance being trapped. Wilberg refused to provide him with the damned maps. Anyway, what does it matter, no one will say Kaddish for that old Nazi, not even his son." Bar-Levi waved his hand as if he was swatting away an insect, an irritation so minor that it was almost unworthy of notice.

Paolo knew in that instant that Zvi Bar-Levi was either Heinz Wilberg's executioner or he had ordered it done. He read in Father Angelo's face that he'd reached the same conclusion- Wilberg's blood was on the Minister's hands. What had Wilberg known? Had he during his days excavating the communication tunnels and running telephone lines through them uncovered something himself? Had he figured it out, wanting a piece of whatever was down there for himself? Heinz Wilberg had, for reasons that would never be shared with Paolo or Father Angelo, become expendable. And thus he'd been silenced. The Middle East. No questions, no debate. The Minister had done his job. Bar-Levi would parry whatever question Paolo or Father Angelo threw at him. It was pointless to press on. Another query died on Paolo's lips as Zvi Bar-Levi exited the room.

Later that morning, Cardinal Zaccaria appeared, carrying flowers in one hand and a letter addressed to "My Roman Sons" and bearing the papal seal in the other. In the brief, the pontiff expressed his heartfelt thanks that "God had chosen to look after you" along with His Holiness's prayer for their safe return "to the Eternal City."

Both men were released from the hospital later that day and transported to the King David. The desk in their suite was piled high with hand-delivered messages from the American Secretary of State, the EU's current president, and the various heads of state. An avalanche of invitations and requests for television interviews from the four corners of the world spilled from the desk onto the suite's floor.

The letter that caught Paolo's eye was one addressed to both men. It was from Italy's president. Elegant as was the Pope's in its brevity, it thanked both for their service to the people of their native land.

Father Angelo laughed aloud as he read one, scented, hand-written, and delivered overnight by a courier service. It was a marriage proposal from a woman in Florence.

"Apparently a non-believer," he remarked, "unfamiliar with Church doctrine." "I dread opening my e-mail," Paolo said, half-seriously.

For the next couple of hours, Paolo reveled in their growing fame. If what had come to pass through their efforts proved that Israel was unquestionably the Holy Land rather than an alien sliver, a Western creation on the fringe of a hostile Islamic landmass, then, he decided, all the sacrifices made would have been worthwhile. Time was dulling the pain.

"We have turned the wheel of history, Angelo, in this broken world, which is what, for me, counts. And from that perhaps some good will come."

But Paolo suspected Father Angelo was uncomfortable with the notion of their sudden and overblown importance in what the priest viewed as the cosmic scheme of things. He held firmly that their significance was in fact insignificant, that the sin of pride was tenacious and difficult to break free of.

"But after all, Angelo," he continued, "we did decipher the meaning of the Tiberias manuscripts ..."

Even to Paolo's own ears this proclamation sounded hollow, pompous and lame. It was as if he was rationalizing and justifying the importance that had been thrust upon them.

"Yes, we did," the priest murmured reluctantly, signaling an end to their discussion.

There was no escape from the demands that the worldwide media now visited upon them, much of it generated

340

by the ever-present Zvi Bar-Levi. The Minister arranged a savvy American-born media expert to prepare the scholars or, as Bar-Levi said, to take the Romans "under her wing." Paolo was charmed as he normally was by an attractive woman but Father Angelo objected strenuously.

"Why do we need a 'handler?'" he complained. "It's not as if we haven't any experience ..."

The priest then cited several appearances both had made in the past, particularly the one with Paolo on the *Larry King Show*.

"There's a vast difference, Father," Chana Green said, tossing her blond hair for effect, her green eyes demanding his attention. "This isn't a leisurely appearance on one show with a friendly host. You're facing a media blitz, such as the world's rarely seen. You see those satellite dishes? Each has your names on them. We've scheduled you both live on all the major American network shows, morning and prime time. And if you survive those, which I'm sure you will, there are the CBC, BBC, RAI-Uno - you'll both be wearing Italian flag pins in your lapels, of course - the German and other Euro channels, China's national network, Japan's and Korea's, too, and all the nations in between. The alphabet soup of worldwide television coverage. If you were both younger, I'd suggest you prepare by doing a hundred pushups early each morning." Paolo laughed. Father Angelo didn't. "But first, we've got to get the basic story line straight," she went on, "since you'll be repeating it till you're blue in the face ..."

By the time she'd finished her pitch, Father Angelo was, despite his doubts and discomfort, swept along, grudgingly agreeable to following Chana's dictates. As was Paolo, who always sought the limelight and seemed more than a little taken with the woman. Or so Father Angelo, with his finely honed observational skills, surmised.

"The rescue of the artifacts was less fraught," Paolo remarked, half-aloud, fatigue at the prospect of what lay before them beginning to set in.

A hint of a smile Crossed Chana's face.

"Good, Paolo, very good. Try to work that remark in during one of the interviews. And Father, make sure your Cross is always in plain sight. If you have a slightly larger one than the one you're wearing ..."

Father Angelo's sigh was ignored by Chana Green.

After two days of intense coaching, both men were deemed well-enough prepared and ready to face a world that, relegated until then with snippets, cried out anxiously for details and more details. Chana's last words before they stepped before the cameras were: "Feel free to embellish."

They opened with Larry King, reminisced desultorily about their previous visit, and visibly cringed when the host referred to Paolo as a "fellow *Landsmann,* a superstar," opining that, "When the Messiah returns to earth, I hear he'll also be staying at the King David," and ending with, "It figured that a good Jewish boy from Rome would find the True Cross with a priest from down the street. God bless the both of you."

The days began to pass more quickly, the few gaps in them filled by meetings with antiquities experts in Jerusalem, dinners with university people, and a few moments with old friends and colleagues. By Day Four both were barely able to distinguish between where they had been the day before and where they were now, to whom they were speaking and where they were due next. Chana shepherded them from interview to interview, like two wayward children who needed watching, critiquing each perfomance. For the Romans, time had been compressed, their existence blurred. As they had been in the tunnel, they were pushed along, consigned to the mercy of others, no matter how benevolent these "new" others may have been. Their lives, they were aware, were no longer their own.

* * *

Palm Sunday loomed, the day the Cross was to be exhibited to the world. The night before, as both men slumped in the easy chairs of their suite, Zvi Bar-Levi entered without knocking, as was his wont. Manners were as alien to him as was emotion.

Father Angelo comforted himself with the thought that all this would soon be over, and Zvi Bar-Levi banished to memory.

"I come in peace," he joked, handing Father Angelo a finely-crafted olivewood box with the Vatican's seal on its lid.

When the priest opened it, he saw it contained a large

silver crucifix, on it a crucified Christ rendered in gold. The note read: "A Gift From Your Pope." Father Angelo looked up, clearly overwhelmed.

"This ... this is a masterpiece." The Minister turned to Paolo.

"Dr. Josephus, Rome has not forgotten you either."

He handed Paolo the second box. In it was an oval-shaped silver medallion. On one side, the Cross and the Star of David in gold leaf. On its reverse side, the image of the pope in gold, with the date and, in the tradition of the Roman emperors, the number of years he had reigned. Paolo found himself uncharacteristically moved by the gracious papal gesture.

Palm Sunday's date had been fixed in time by the Gregorian calendar in the sixteenth century. It was immovable, conflicting with the ancient Hebrew temporal calculations. In 2013 AD, it was great good fortune that the first night of Passover fell two days later, neither too early nor too late to clash with the beginning of Easter Week.

The coincidental dates were for Israel a blessing of sorts since it had little to celebrate during the first decades of the twenty-first century. The suicide bombings; the dead-end peace talks; the Iranians' progress towards a full-fledged nuclear weapons program, severely curtailed by the storms, but soon to be revived; the 2006 invasion of Lebanon; the Gaza incursion of 2009; all of these crises then capped off with the once-in-a-millennium storms and floods that brought several nations to their knees and from which only a few were beginning to recover. The list of troubles seemed relentless and intractable. But in the month of March, the lenses of the world were not focused on burned-out buses and bombed-out homes and schools, or tanks rumbling and rockets firing, refugees scrambling to safety, or settlers claiming West Bank hilltops in the name of Yahweh. No, for this twinkle of an eye in time, the focus had changed, for a future far brighter than the recent past.

The program that the Vatican dubbed "The Presentation of the Cross" was slated for Palm Sunday, March 24th. The title was a slight variation of the Vatican's annual May 3rd "Invention of the Cross" celebration, honoring St. Helena's discovery of the *crux capitata*, the True Cross, in the fourth century. How the Holy See would reconcile the existence of both Crosses was still a mystery. Even the keen, incisive minds of the Roman scholars failed to fathom how the Church would resolve the critical conundrum.

CHAPTER THIRTY-TWO

Palm Sunday dawned crisp and sunny as the throngs began to gather for the ceremony. A gentle wind fluttered the flags of the State of Israel, the Vatican, the United States, the EU's and many of the UN's member nations that decorated the Israel Museum complex. The rising, near-blinding sun glinted off the museum's windows, auguring an unseasonably warm day. Between the rows of parallel banners leading to the grandstand, smaller flags flew, identifying the world's various Christian denominations. The blue carpet that the dignitaries would cross in ascending the grandstand featured a unique design, a global-shaped rendering of Jerusalem centered in a mosaic of the earth itself. It was a pointed recognition of Jerusalem's historic centrality before the British supplanted it by resetting the measurement of time and place for their own purposes and to their own liking.

The centerpiece designed for the event was an enormous, bulletproof glass case, over twenty-five feet in height, its width ten feet, a larger version of the box used for viewing the Dead Sea Scrolls. It had been fully assembled in anticipation of an eventual public display of the Cross in the weeks before Dov Rosenberg's kidnapping and the relics' theft. When the gruesome report of Rosenberg's murder was announced, few if any thought it would ever be put to use.

Inside the glass chamber, the reassembled Cross stood, draped in the Vatican's purple silk, desert palm fronds at its base. The Cross itself had been embedded in a piece of split limestone, a reminder of the earthquake mentioned in the Book of Matthew, on the day Jesus became The Christ. The legend etched into the glass read: *A Gift from The Nation of Israel to the World.* On an easel outside the glass casing, with candles burning next to its supports, a photo of Dov Rosenberg had been placed.

Paolo and Father Angelo were escorted up to the case by an honor guard of two bereted IDF officers, a male and a female.

In front of the display, Father Angelo crossed himself as Paolo placed a hand on the case just as he did when he visited the Western Wall in June of 1967, days after Jerusalem had been liberated from Jordan. For Paolo, it was a simple gesture, affirming his connection, the world's connection, to the past and the present. As the by now thousands of onlookers watched in respectful silence, the Romans walked slowly past the Cross, surprised - Father Angelo was startled - to see both their names, their full names in Hebrew, Latin, and English inscribed on the glass. No one had informed either scholar that this would be done. Or perhaps in the endless whirl of publicity and media appearances and handshaking, someone had whispered something and they just hadn't heard. Or understood. Executed in larger lettering above their names, in ancient Greek, was the phrase *Founders of the Kidron Cross.* Founders? Both men glanced at each other, bereft at the latest wave of relentless pomp engulfing them. Through their deeds, Paolo Pisa and Father Angelo Lorenzo realized that however unwilling they may have been, they had become helpless marionettes in this international power game.

As the IDF soldiers accompanied them up the grandstand's stairs and before they took their seats between Prime Minister Dora Ben-Gurion and Cardinal Zaccaria, the loudspeakers blared their names. The large crowd of invitees before them, the religious and secular dignitaries from every Western and most Asian and African nations fanned out on the grandstand, rose and applauded as did the pulsing crowd of onlookers separated though they were from the festivities by sawhorses fronted by a sea of mounted police officers. Later in the week, a respected American religious historian would describe the event as an ingathering of a kind, a drawing together of the representatives of Judea-Christianity, a trenchant message of unity aimed at the millions living in the lands true to The Prophet.

Paolo found what he was experiencing otherworldly. His own notoriety, the fawning of his newly-minted fans, the laudatory reviews of his works by the critics, the sweet melodies of his own fame, none of it had prepared him for the undertow that he was now caught up in. Next to him, Father Angelo sat statue-still, detached, more discombobulated than he had been when he lay wounded in the tunnel two weeks before.

"What is it?" he asked. Father Angelo didn't answer.

Dora Ben-Gurion rose and approached the podium as the crowd stood and applauded. Her words would be few and spare. There was little that she could add that would augment the weight of the occasion itself. She prefaced her brief remarks by thanking Paolo and Father Angelo for making the day possible.

"It is for all of us a day of unity in a deeply divided world," she began. 'Today on Palm Sunday in the Holy Land, in the Nation of Israel, the home of the first Hebrews and today their inheritors and descendants, home to us all from the moment Moses looked upon the Land of Milk and Honey ..." the prime minister, smiling a rare smile, was interrupted by further applause. Her rhetoric was hardly soaring but it was serving its purpose. "And now," she continued, pointing to the Cross encased within the glass, "on behalf of the people of Israel, we present this Cross to the world and at the same time remember that the Cross is but one expression of faith in a world as diverse as ours."

Again, cheering.

"It is my privilege and honor to present His Holiness who will address us from The Vatican on this Holy Day."

The two stadium-sized monitors bookending the bandstand were brought into focus. The pope appeared, bespectacled and clad in his white robes. A diminutive man in person but larger than life on the screens, he was seated behind a desk in his study. He smiled at the unseen multitudes and began reading somewhat tentatively from his handwritten speech. The speech, a mixture of Vaticanese and awkward German scholarship, was not intended to be accepted as papal doctrine nor was it in any sense a Papal Bull. It was more an unmistakably heartfelt overview blending his Church's teachings with his personal vision of the state of the world. After more than a seven years, he remained locked in the long shadow of John Paul II. He couldn't but realize that this moment with the whole world watching was his moment, the one in which he could define his papacy. He began by expressing his joy at the opportunity to attend, even at a distance, such an august gathering during the Holy Week for Christians and their Elder Brothers.

"In a few weeks," he proclaimed, speaking in Italian, the Hebrew translation appearing on the crawl at the foot of the monitors, "my office will issue a statement on the crisis the world is facing that, due to the disastrous change in the earth's climate, in part made this joyous day possible. We must remember that though it is rare, from bad sometimes comes good." He paused, as if searching for the next line, then laid his script aside, clasped his hands together, and stared directly into the cameras. "We are all aware of the climate's cyclical nature. It is part of God's plan and, in its natural course, it sustains life on our planet. It is mankind who must be responsible for maintaining our world's balance as God had intended. But mankind has lost his way. He has squandered our resources in the mindless pursuit of wealth and material goods. It is the West that has urged upon the less fortunate the greed and avarice that has spread like a plague worldwide, at the expense of human dignity. The waste of our God-given resources threatens not only all of us but our progeny, our children, our children's children."

The pope reached for a glass of water and sipped before continuing.

"We must take stock of what we are doing, the damage we have done, and where it is leading us. We must return to the more righteous path for if we fail to do so, mankind's very survival is at stake. If we pay regard to the Holy Bible, we will take from it valuable lessons. The ancient Hebrews knew to leave their land fallow every seven years so it would be spared abuse and hence turned into barren soil. All the founders of the great religions were mindful of the future and how the future was rooted in the past as well. It is a message sadly too often forgotten and buried in the relativism of today, ignoring the needy and the needs of our world in our relentless pursuit of ever increasing wealth. I beseech you to hold yourselves, each and every one of you, accountable for our future. Yes, you are your brother's keeper, and all of us are stewards of our earth. We must restore the natural order and balance of our world."

The pope paused, his gaze steady. In the audience, with the sun bearing down on them, many fidgeted with their programs. They had endured the catastrophe, each suffering loss though perhaps not in equal measure. The universality of the pope's message was already internalized and accepted by his listeners. But the majority of those who braved the hot sun hadn't done so to be lectured to about the environment. They were growing impatient because they had come today to learn how the pope would reconcile the existence of the two Crosses, the revered Latin Cross of St. Helena, and the new *crux capitata,* the so-called "Kidron Cross." Father Angelo, to his dismay, had even heard a BBC television commentator the night before refer to it as 'The Scholars' Cross."

The fussing in the audience ended when the Pope abruptly addressed the central issue, the Crosses themselves.

"Dominica in Palmis, Palm Sunday, the palm branches symbolizing the victory over the Prince of Death and the coming of the spiritual unction, is a lesson learned from Exodus XV and XVI and Matthew XXI. It is celebrated today in Rome, in St. Peter's, and churches throughout the world. It will be observed shortly in the churches of the Orthodox tradition. The first night of the Feast of Passover that marks God's sparing of the Jews will be celebrated as it was by Jesus on Tuesday, followed a week from today by Easter Sunday, the holiest day on the Christian calendar. This is, as it has always been, the Holy Week for Christians and the Elder Brothers of the Church."

"Standing before you and the world is a Latin Cross, *capitata,* that once stood on a nearby hill at the center of the Holy Land. It is at once a miracle that it was uncovered by the very forces of nature, wrought by so profound an alteration in our climate. The modern-day flood was truly of Biblical proportions, a harbinger of the future, as we know from our reading of the Twenty-Second Psalm."

"On that fateful day two millennia ago on Calvary, three Crosses stood. Three centuries later, St. Helena, the mother of the Emperor Constantine, with the assistance of an elderly Jew, found the True Cross, its components later distributed to a few selected sites where they reside today. More than sixty years ago, a young goatsherd in a cave near the Dead Sea, discovered what have become known to us as the Dead Sea Scrolls. We are still piecing together their fragments and new evidence has enabled us to understand the Word of God. The Scrolls instruct us just as the Cross instructs us today."

"The Cross that stands before us today was, as was the Cross of St. Helena, found in pieces; the parallels with St. Helena's discovery are manifest. This Cross was unearthed by an act of God, a resurrection of sorts," the pope paused again and reached for his water glass. "It was removed from the Temple of Herod during one of the most difficult times for the Jewish people. We believe that as the Roman soldiers under Titus' command sacked and burned the Second Temple, The Cross was removed and hidden away in the Kidron Valley. Now it sits in the light of God and will join St. Helena's Cross as a testament to faith with all of its mystery and powers to bring us together in a world increasingly at risk. The Church believes in the miraculous self-multiplication of the Cross, *ut detrimenta non sentreif, et quasi intacta permaneret,* a belief that many in the modern world may dismiss, but which is truly a miracle. What is before you and the world is such a miracle."

As the sun arced higher in the late morning Jerusalem sky, the rustling of programs and seat-shifting had stopped, the audience's attention remained glued to the monitors.

"At the end of Holy Week, the Holy See will arrange my second visit on May 3rd to the restored Holy Land of Israel, the day celebrated as The Invention of the Cross. And on that day the newly discovered Cross will be blessed as a true relic to be exalted in the land that gave us The Christ, Israel, the Holy Land."

As the pontiff's face slowly faded from the screen, the cameras provided a panoramic view of Vatican City and then Rome itself. The papal pronouncement electrified the air. He had deftly squared the circle, Paolo marveled, solved the dilemma, for the doubters among the faithful at least. An infinitesimal moment of silence enveloped them before the dam of restraint burst forth, a thunderous and lasting ovation greeting the pope's words and the meaning it conveyed. By his words, the pope had effectively ordered Israel's pariah status to be shed. He had unequivocally confirmed Israel as the Holy Land, fulfilling if only on paper the dream of its founder and his niece.

The impact of the pope's speech had yet to be dissected, analyzed, and measured, each word weighed and digested. Whether when all that could be said about it was said, the shroud of isolation Israel endured daily, its constant allies few, would be lifted was a question that defied a simple answer. If history was a predictable guide, the response would not be universally positive. Even before the pontiff's image had melted from the monitors, an al-Arabiya television commentator echoed what millions in the

Muslim world perceived to be the papal message.

"This is no different than what the pope said at Regensburg in 2007, his true feelings about our brothers whom he obviously still holds in contempt. It is merely a rewording of his and the Church in Rome's anti-Islamic stance."

From Cairo to Karachi multitudes poured into the streets, few having viewed the papal address but all decrying the "Christian-Zionist plot" and vowing solidarity with their Palestinian "brothers who suffer still under the yoke of the Zionist predators." Nothing had changed under the punishing sun.

On the grandstand, Prime Minister Dora Ben-Gurion escorted the pope's representative, Cardinal Zaccaria, to the podium, and handed him the small box containing the Tiberias Manuscript, the metered poem, and the map. She repeated for the audience's benefit how it was found by chance, and like the Cross itself was an invaluable gift of faith brought forth by the catastrophe that destroyed so many and so much.

"It is a Christian play rendered in the Greek traditional form. What distinguishes it from other artifacts is its dating and where it was discovered. While we cannot confirm it, we assume that the play itself was performed for the early Christians in Tiberias during the years St. Paul spread forth the gospel according to Jesus Christ. It is the poem, and the map, and the story of the accursed tree itself, the *infelix lignum,* that pointed us to the discovery which brings us here today."

Cardinal Zaccaria thanked the Prime Minister on the Vatican's behalf.

"I will personally deliver the manuscript to His Holiness. And when it is performed in Rome during Holy Week next year, we would be honored if you would join us as His Holiness's guests."

As the ceremony wound down with the politic comments coming to an end, the Israeli national anthem was sung, and the audience rose and began filing out. Father Angelo tilted his head towards Paolo and whispered.

"We must talk, Paolo," he said, his voice pitched low, out of earshot of the collective dignitaries.

"Of course, is there a problem?" "I still have my doubts ..."

"Really?" Paolo was somewhat taken aback. He had had his own doubts from the beginning - they lingered still, but unlike the priest he was hardly a true-believer.

The pope's handling of the thorny issue was adroit, putting to rest among the faithful any uncertainty. Did it really matter if there was one, two, or many Crosses? Would or could we ever know beyond a shadow of a doubt which was the True Cross— if in fact there was such— or whether the two Crosses weren't counterfeits crafted during the First Millennium? They and the attendant explanations for their existence had either to be accepted on faith or rejected. Paolo was dreading the return of the headache that had plagued him earlier in the week. "Doubt is the beginning of wisdom, my friend, and this is the Middle East ..."

"It is not so easy to explain it all away."

Paolo noticed that the priest was absently wringing his hands, struggling with his thoughts.

"We're losing sight of who we are, Angelo," Paolo said. "We're scholars, we live in a different world, a world of books and research, not politics."

"Yes, endless talk, speculation that leads nowhere. I usually follow Dr. Pangloss's advice, Paolo, but ..."

"Why a 'but?' Speculation often does lead to discovery, no? Time and again?"

However much Father Angelo may have agreed with Candide's wisdom, he remained drawn to The Cross, the pope's convoluted exposition of its authenticity confusing, doubts rattling around within, tormenting him. By his words the pontiff had spread the fuel that would soon ignite the conflagration of speculation. A veritable flood of media coverage would follow and feed it, this he knew from experience, just as he knew his friend Paolo would himself be part of it, on the circuit and likely on the arm of Chana Green. He noticed how Paolo and Chana grew closer, how the attraction between the two increased as he found himself being excluded or overlooked, shunted to the background. Well, good for Paolo, he thought kindly, and just as well. He's in dire need of someone to share his life with. What his calling is, after all, is not mine.

"Reflection will get us nowhere," Father Angelo said finally, clapping his hands on his knees as he rose, even though both men knew reflection was as much a part of themselves as were their own limbs. As both men stood, they momentarily faced each other in silence, their discussion effectively ended.

* * *

At the evening's gala farewell dinner, encomiums flew as each speaker sought to outdo the other. When it was the Minister's turn, Zvi Bar-Levi extended his hands to the Romans, his thanks fulsome and profuse, ringing patently false they were so completely out of character.

"Next year, my friends, Rome," he said, ever the conqueror setting his sights on his next conquest. "We'll sit together and watch the Passion Play. Or Herod's Mosaic, depending on how you choose to view ... things." The barest flash of a smile danced across his lips before he returned to his place on the dais.

By noon the next day, the Romans were airborne, on their way home.

For Father Angelo, his doubts of the day before had grown into a nagging, unshakeable affliction. He would harbor them quietly— his priestly duties compelled him to do so, any objections he raised sure to be squelched by his superiors. The official die had been cast. For him, the true story of the Kidron Cross remained underground. Its journey from the treasury of Herod's Temple to the Kidron Valley, through a clandestine tunnel, and from there to the impregnable steel vault that lay below the Israel Museum was a journey in time still unmapped, a mystery unsolved, all facile explanations for its odyssey credible and at the same time not. Now, the Kidron Cross had seen the light of day and been placed before the world for all to see.

In the coming year, it would personally be blessed by the pope in the restored Holy Land of Israel, amid roaring hordes waving papal flags. The Kidron Cross and the official story of its discovery and its provenance were immutable, set into stone by the Vatican and the State of Israel. The speculation surrounding it, the persistent questions would burn. Like all fires this one would blaze brightly for months. Eventually it would die down, reduced to glowing embers. In the end it would be trumped by the desires of millions across the religious spectrum, all wanting, needing to believe the authorized narrative of the Kidron Cross. In time, Paolo Pisa and Father Angelo Lorenzo, their celebrity intact, would forever be associated with the Kidron Cross. They knew, too, that they would eventually become incidental and, if they veered from their assigned path, they would, as those who had passed before them, become expendable.

AFTERMATH
VII

CHAPTER THIRTY-THREE

In the weeks following their return to Rome, Paolo Pisa and Father Angelo Lorenzo had been feted and lionized, their presence demanded at one event or show or academic gathering or church function and then another. And another. As they had expected, the first stirrings of criticism from the Muslim world over the finds became a torrent, the barrage of abuse familiar, the refrain a form of terrorist Muzak.

On a pleasant late April evening with the sun low over the Tiber, Paolo cancelled what would have been his fourteenth television appearance of the week, deciding instead to spend a quiet evening alone. Chana Green was flying into Rome to spend a few days, as pleasant a prospect as he could wish for. He missed her. And perhaps for a few hours he could empty his mind of the myriad of thoughts that had invaded it regularly since his return. He thought of phoning Father Angelo and inviting him over for an after-dinner congnac but then decided his friend probably needed respite, too.

Paolo, an aperitif in hand, eased into his chair, rested his feet on the ottoman, and turned on his TV, settling on RAI Uno's early news report. On the screen, full-faced, the Iranian president stared back at Paolo, a corona of ayatollahs arrayed behind him, and ranted over the heads of a chanting crowd of thousands. Was this a rerun of an ongoing serial? Deja vu? How many times had he viewed this scene? The hammering demonization of the West from which there was apparently no escape, no relief. No, the broadcast was live as RAI noted and had been underway for a couple of minutes.

"... the anti-Islamic pageant that took place in our city of Jerusalem," the Iranian president intoned, "'was an insult against The Prophet of such profundity that it must be avenged with the blood of martyrs ...'"

Paolo muted the sound and weighed switching channels

when the speaker clumsily bent down, his arm reaching under the podium, and reemerged with The Prophet's dagger, waving it seven times above his head.

"This dagger," he shouted triumphantly, "had the blessed hand of the The Prophet upon it. It is the dagger he used at the Battle of Bedr when he conquered the city of Medina and set about to slaughter the Jews and other infidels with its razor's edge." The Iranian president ran his fingers along and above the dagger's cutting edge, careful not to touch it and draw his own blood. "We will again slit the throats of the Jews and their Crusader allies as we have done before when we recapture their 'Holy Land'."

"Kill the Zionists and their Pope," came the roar from the crowd. "Kill them!" As the camera retreated to capture a longer and wider angle of the event, it displayed the entire panoply of Iran's rulers and military chieftains along with several of the Iranian president's aides. Standing next to the president, Paolo glimpsed the all too familiar figure of Parviz Mussavani, smiling and applauding in unison with the ayatollahs.

Paolo suppressed a knowing smile and pressed the power button, turning the screen black.

* * *

Two months later, in early June, as Rome warmed towards summer, a death notice appeared in the Italian newspaper, *La Repubblica*. In recent years, as Father Angelo grew older, he opened first to the pages devoted to memorials. It was not an unusual habit for a man of his age who watched with growing despondancy the passing of his generation. Nor was he shocked when he read the brief notice announcing the death of a Parviz Mussavani in a fiery car crash that sadly also took the lives of his wife and two of his four children. It was almost as if he expected it, as if an unseen hand was closing a circle. He wondered who would place such an obituary in an Italian newspaper and why. Mussavani was no international figure of importance, one to earn mention in an Italian newspaper. More likely a warning, directed at him and Paolo, counting on at least one of them to come across it. But what had the highly-placed Mussavani done to earn such lethal disfavor?

As he reached for the phone to call Paolo, it began to ring. It was Paolo, his voice urgent.

"Did you hear the news?"

"No ... no," Father Angelo stuttered. "What news? What's happened?" He expected that Paolo had read Mussavani's obit.

"Chana called from Jerusalem. Zvi Bar-Levi's dead."

"Zvi?" Father Angelo felt a sharp stab of terror in his gut. Mussavani. Now the Minister. "How?" He did not ask why.

"They say he fell from his balcony. Just missed a couple strolling below." Fell?

Father Angelo quickly informed Paolo of Mussavani's death in Tehran. The priest heard a sharp intake of breath at the other end of the line. "I must've missed the item ..."

Paolo quickly grasped what was happening. Two and two. It was not difficult to piece together. One by one, each of those directly involved in the recovery mission was being eliminated. Who was issuing the kill orders and why? Were they next?

"What have we done, Angelo?" Paolo whispered hoarsely. "I don't know, my friend. I don't know..."

ORIGINS

For nearly thirty-two years, Dr. Diamond and his wife have lead group tours to the former USSR, Germany, Central Europe, Israel, Jordan, France, Italy, Poland, and the UK. These trips included students from Keuka College, parents, colleagues and members of the community. Each of Dr. Diamond's fictional works have their origins in these trips including *The Herod Mosaic.*

In August 70 AD, the Jewish War against the Roman Occupation of Judea was in its third year. The military architect of the Roman Invasion of Judea was General Vespasian, who was called back to Rome and emerged as Emperor or Caesar. His son Titus took charge of the Roman re-conquest of Judea. In a well-planned assault, he took city after city and finally the heart of the Jewish world, Jerusalem, which he totally destroyed, including the Second Temple built by the Jewish King Herod in the immediate years before the Common Era.

To commemorate the victory, Titus, now Emperor after the death of his father, had erected the Arch of Titus. In a bas-relief, tourists can see the Roman centurions carrying into the Imperial City what was looted from the Second Temple.

In 2006, Dr. Diamond lead his fifth historical tour to Bella Italia. His guide at the Roman Forum where the Arch of Titus stands was Paolo Romano. After a lecture about the Arch, Dr. Diamond asked Romano if any of the treasures from the Second Temple were ever found. "We are still searching," Romano said and added, "In fact, as we speak, the Navy is using sonar to look for the seized relics under the Tiber River." Nothing was found, less some discarded military vehicles from the last war. In Dr. Diamond's mind, the wheels started to turn and in this seemingly passing encounter, the gestation of *The Herod Mosaic* is to be found.

Dr. Diamond would like to extend a special thanks to his editor at JET Literary Associates, and publisher John Locke, who worked with Dr. Diamond at Keuka College and provides design, consulting, and publishing services to new, and published authors alike, and authors who are not quite ready to consider self-publishing.

ABOUT THE AUTHOR

Sander A. Diamond is Professor of History at Keuka College, where he taught for nearly half a century. He has taught at Binghamton University and Hobart and William Smith Colleges as a Visiting Professor of German History.

His first book. *The Nazi Movement in the United States, 1924-1941* (Ithaca: Cornell University Press, 1974), re-issued in paperback in 2000, was nominated for a Pulitzer Prize in History. It is recommended by the Library of Congress as the definitive book on the German effort to cause the coalescence of the German-American community in the 1930s. In 1984, Dr. Diamond's *Herr Hitler* (Düsseldorf: Droste Verlag, 1984) was published. It examines how the American Embassy in Berlin collected information on the rise of the radical right in Germany and especially the Nazi Party, and its leader, Adolf Hitler.

Earlier, the Institute für Zeitgeschichte in Munich published two of Dr. Diamond's extended articles, "Zur Typologie der amerikadeutschen NS-Bewegung" (Heft 5/1975) and "Aus den Papieren des amerikanischen Botschafters in Berlin, 1922-1925" (Heft 3/1979). He is the author of numerous scholarly articles, which have appeared in Germany, and the UK, and in the United States, including *Germany and America: Essays* (Brooklyn College Press 1980), in the *YIVO Annual,* and "The Demographic History of the Jewish People" (London, 2000).

Dr. Diamond has co-authored two novels with a Hollywood script writer who has several movies to his credit, *Starik* (New York: E.P. Dutton, 1988), a thriller set in Moscow. A year later, it appeared in paperback under the Pinnacle Press Imprint. In 1990, E.P. Dutton published *The Red Arrow,* another thriller set in post-Soviet Leningrad and Moscow. It is in part based on Dr. Diamond's many trips on the train that connects the two cities, the Red Arrow Express.

Diamond's main interest is in German history. In 1999, *The German Table: The Education of a Nation* was published by Disc-US

Books and went through four printings. It is the history of Western Germany in the post-war period as seen through the eyes of young people, in essence, a fictional biography of an era.

Dr. Diamond has been a frequent contributor to regional, national, and European newspapers. Since 1979, over 250 articles have appeared in Gannett Papers, Gate House Publications, the LA Times, and Newsday, as well as regional papers in Germany and the Russian Federation.

Dr. Diamond lives in Keuka Park with his wife of fifty years, Susan. They have two grown children, Matthew and Meredith, and four grandchildren, Hannah, Elizabeth, Zachary, and Jake.